Backstage

Enjoy THE
Saic Tour!

E...

Want to get more FREE from Erika?

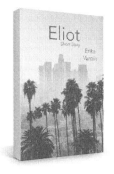

Sign up for the author's New Releases mailing list and get a free copy of the short story "Eliot." You will periodically receive free short stories and unique chapters.

Click here to get started:
https://www.erikavanzin.com/newsletter.html

To everyone who rose stronger after every fall

PRESS *Review*

News That Will Make Your Strings Vibrate

Hi Roadies!

The weekend is approaching and there are a lot of concerts happening across the country. Did you get any ideas from my last post about must-see shows? Have you already decided where to spend your evenings? I have a list of at least four bands I want to see so my Instagram will be blowing up with stories from around Manhattan.

But let's get to the headline. Word on the street is that the Jailbirds want to go big on their next tour, and they're working on a surprise that will leave fans speechless.

Will it be an early release of their new album? The sale of VIP meet-and-greet backstage tickets? New merchandise? At the moment, there's no official announcement, but sources close to the record label say the fans are going to be delirious.

Jeff Rogers of Rock Now! magazine sent out a tweet that leaves very few doubts: "There's a lot of turmoil on the scene, and even industry insiders have their ears raised, ready to be the first ones to share the news."

So, keep your eyes peeled because the Jailbirds are coming back!

Be kind and rock'n'roll,

Iris

1562 Likes 3459 Tweets 2370 Shares 957 Comments

CHAPTER 1
Damian

I get in the car, struggling through the door. I have the distinct impression it was a bad idea to leave the party the label organized and take a cab in the middle of Los Angeles. I slur the address to the man behind the wheel who has the worried look of someone afraid of having to clean up a stranger's puke from the back of his car. I lean my head against the window and watch the lights of the city flash before my eyes.

I miss New York, its tall buildings that surround you as if protecting you. Los Angeles looks so unfamiliar to me. Here, away from the heart of downtown, it's a long stretch of low-rise houses and commercial warehouses. Neighborhood after neighborhood, you feel like you're naked and exposed walking down wide streets lined with tall, narrow palm trees. In Manhattan, the buildings make you feel small and the roads are like closed in tunnels, protecting you from the world as you walk. It's an overwhelming and reassuring feeling—one of the many paradoxes of that city.

I must have fallen asleep at some point along the way because what feels like only a few seconds later the driver slips his hand through the small partition between us and shakes my leg. I give him some money from one of my pockets and, when I see his eyes gleaning with surprise, I gesture to him with my hand to keep the change as well. He doesn't make me say it twice; he puts the money in his pocket and indicates for me to get out.

At this moment I realize my first mistake: I didn't call Max, the driver. A group of fans has been lurking near our hotel for two days. Max would have had access to the underground garage; this taxi driver dropped me directly in front of the shark tank.

"Holy shit!" I mutter to myself. "The paparazzi is gonna have a field day with this one."

I've stopped counting how many times I've been in the papers this month, but it's not my fault someone's constantly putting a glass of French wine in my hand that costs more than a car at those goddamn parties.

"You wouldn't happen to be able to take me to the underground garage, would you?" I ask the cab driver, praying like a kid who wants to extend Saturday night curfew with his parents.

The man looks at me and waves me out again, more impatiently than the first time. I take a deep breath, hold on to the handle of the car, and grab onto the roof of the cab to drag myself out. I try to close the door as gracefully as possible, then I lower my head and let my long dark hair cover my face.

One, two, I can't even count to three before the girls start screaming and the paparazzi starts taking pictures over and over again. Two fucking wobbly steps and my cover's already blown. Not that I had one, since I'm the lead singer of the most famous band in the world at the moment. I'm also 6'6" with broad shoulders, but I really hoped till the last moment I could have gotten away with it. Goddamn alcohol and the shit it makes me do.

I raise my head since there's no point in hiding anymore, and I try to locate the front door. It looks blurry so I squint my eyes a couple of times but it doesn't get any better. After a few steps, I lean against a barrier which the girls are standing behind. One of them grabs me by the neck and pulls me toward her in a confused tangle of arms and hair. Their screams almost make my head explode. I lean against the cold metal of the barrier and try to get away, but a second girl grabs me, sticking her tongue in my mouth without warning. I push her away as gently as possible, trying to hold her in the "safe zone" in the upper part of the arms, but two others kiss me on the lips before one of the hotel security guards comes to help me out of the chaos I've brought on myself.

It's like this every time: I become the target to jump on, the mouth to stick a tongue into so they can tick the "I kissed the rock star" off their bucket list. Not Damian Jones, the person, but the celebrity, whoever who he is. My lips are always sticky with some lipstick I'm struggling to wash off from a kiss I got without so much as a "How are you?" or "How was your day?"

Let's face it, I've never had trouble getting the women I wanted, when I wanted and especially for what I wanted: sex without emotional complications. Always consenting adults, always healthy adult sex—just without the drama. Our fans, however, are something entirely different. They're often underage girls who dream of Prince Charming and are absolutely off-limits. Which is why this current scenario is a mess that I'm unlikely to come out of unscathed, especially with photographers who seem crazy for action.

I lean against the revolving doors of the hotel and when I

get to the other side I stumble on the carpet, falling face down, unleashing another burst of flashes. Great. The path from the floor to my bedroom is a series of confused and foggy images consisting of cream-colored walls and dark red carpet.

In the sitting room next to my bedroom door, I catch a glimpse of two confused silhouettes rising from the sofa. When they are one step away from me, I realize that they are two girls, one blonde, the other a brunette. I can hardly make out their features clearly, but I can they're barely dressed.

"Do you feel like having some fun tonight?" the brunette asks, whispering in my ear and leaning against my side, while the blonde takes me by the other arm.

It takes me a while to realize she's spoken to me, I'm too busy staggering and holding on while she grabs my shoulder. She's petite, but manages to make me lose my balance as she leans her weight against my body.

"Look, I just want to go to my room," I mumble. I'm having a hard time stringing words together.

"We'll help you, don't worry," the blonde encourages me in a soothing voice.

I'm not one to back out of sex, but I also want to enjoy the moment. Just as I don't take advantage of drunk women who can't understand what they're doing, I don't want to be just half-conscious during a fuck.

"No, I'm going alone. Go away," I say out loud. They get off me suddenly, making me sway.

"You think you're the only one in the world with a dick? Yours isn't golden, so don't be such a show-off," says the brunette, with her arms crossed.

I lean against the door, grab the magnetic card from my

pocket after looking for it everywhere, and put it against the lock until I hear the buzzing sound signaling that it's open. I stagger into the room and onto my bed, curling up as soon as I hit it. My head is spinning. I feel like vomiting. I try to keep my eyes closed and breathe deeply.

The mattress next to me lowers. I can feel my shirt rising, and with one hand, I try to lower it again, but someone takes my arm and holds it above my head. There's something wrong with this situation, but I can't get my brain to work enough to understand what's going on. I can't even open my eyes. All around me is black, muffled sounds, then silence.

A few days later, New York City

"What the hell were you thinking?" Evan, our manager, asks me, lining up three different gossip magazines in front of us on the coffee table.

I'm not gonna answer that. I'm looking down on those pictures, reading the ridiculous headlines. "Satan's Kiss," "Damian Reaches Out!" and "The Cursed Tongue of Rock." Next to me, Michael, Simon, and Thomas are sitting still, probably holding their breath. They have nothing to do with this since they stayed at the party, but Evan likes to lecture all of us, gathering us together to refresh our memories about what we can and can't do. If only I'd called Max, this whole mess wouldn't have happened, but it's too late now.

Evan goes around his desk, picks up a stack of papers, and puts it in front of my nose. "Do you know what these are?"

I look up at him. He's got a stern face, impenetrable gray eyes. I'm afraid he won't let me get away with it this time. "No." My voice comes out weak, too weak for someone who should be trying to defend himself.

"It's e-mails and letters from feminist associations railing against you. Alarmed parents who see you as Satan himself, and especially angry fans who say you have no respect for them."

He spreads them out so I can read them, and I feel more mortified than ever, especially at that last statement. If there's one thing I feel towards our fans, it's sincere and profound gratitude. Without them, we'd still be playing in the worst bars in New York City, and cleaning toilets after closing time to make a living, like we did when we were kids.

"Why don't you think before you do that shit?" he asks me, softening his tone, and I realize I got away with it, at least this once. "Sooner or later, people are gonna get tired of your rock-star attitude. There's a fine line between the fickle VIP persona and the troubled one nobody wants to work with. Don't cross it, you understand?"

"Can you fix the situation in any way?" asks Thomas, our drummer and the most reasonable of all of us. The original manager of our band, it's because of Thomas and his practical nature that we're living the dream life. Once again, his instincts kick in to help Evan. He'll never be able to set aside this part of his character, even if we pay someone to take care of our problems. He's our own personal mother hen.

Evan sits in the armchair in front of us, elbows on the armrests, hands to his mouth, and remains silent for what seems like an interminable amount of time. It's literally killing me, this waiting. I get the distinct impression he wants to tell us something that we absolutely do not want to hear. My relief at having gotten away with something is clouding with worry.

"We'll keep doing what we've been doing, interviews, public apologies, and so on, but we need to shift the focus away from Damian, and this whole thing that has blown up in the papers. We need to focus on your fans," he says seriously.

I breathe a sigh of relief. I can get out of this mess. I haven't exactly been a role model lately, but I haven't killed anyone.

"How do we do it? Make them the center of attention, right? Meet and greet? Dinner? Awards? Concert tickets? Please tell us," begs Michael, guitarist, and the craziest guy in the band. Patience is not his strong suit. Once, he decided he didn't have time to wait for our driver to move the tour bus, and he did it. I still remember Evan swearing when we called him to tell him that Michael had utterly destroyed the rooftop of a gas station because he hadn't noticed that the bus was too tall.

Evan breathes in and looks down, looking defeated.

"It's not that simple," he says, sounding almost emptied of his usual proverbial patience.

"There's sure to be some up-and-coming bands among your fans. We'll do the contest we've talked about before, but you've always refused to organize. Everyone will upload a video cover of one of your songs, then we'll select the three best entries to come play it in the studio. The winning band will open all of the dates on your next tour. Obviously, they'll have to send us a demo of their original songs; we don't want people who don't have anything to play. If they're legit, we'll sign them to the label."

The words hover over us in absolute silence for a few seconds. Nobody seems to breathe.

"But that's absurd," I explode. "The big bosses have taken advantage of this bullshit to stick us with a marketing stunt the label geniuses have been planning for months." I stand up and throw my chair back, banging it against the wall. "It wasn't even my fault! I tried to get away from the crazed fans. I apologized publicly, I did interviews. They're taking advantage of the situation to blackmail us. We're talking about our tour, our image!"

My deep voice thunders inside the office. My bandmates look at me with expressions halfway between resigned and worried. It's true, we've been through worse times together. That doesn't mean we have to accept this. A tour is a stressful event in a thousand ways, but it's also a time when the band gets even closer together. The tight spaces, the forced cohabitation, the miraculously avoided fights, the blatant outbursts, the moments of absolute loyalty to my friends, are part of a sacred rite. They can't rob us of that by making us babysit kids.

"It doesn't matter if it's your fault or not. It's what it looks like that counts, not what actually happened. You're lucky those girls were all of age—otherwise you'd be in much more trouble. The label's got the ball rolling, and they know we can't turn them down. They're clinging to the image protection clause and threatening to terminate the contract and make us pay the penalty. You made them suffer because you didn't want to do the contest, now they've found a way around it."

Evan's voice is firm and strong, the tone of someone who's doing the impossible to protect our business and our rights. I know he's done everything he can to defend us, to honor our wishes. He's been doing it since we were little more than kids who could barely change our underwear. I'm not mad at him. I'm mad at the label: they needed a new band to squeeze and a media campaign to draw attention to them.

"There's no chance of appealing this decision, is there?" asks Simon, our bassist, in a resigned voice. It hurts me to hear him so downhearted. He's always the quiet one, looking for mediation so as not to get into a fight. He sees the glass half full, and sometimes I hate him because he seems like a fucking Disney prince with that smile. But he manages to point out the positive aspects that we, in the heat of the moment, do not notice, saving us many times from getting pissed off.

"No." Our manager's tone is both harsh and apologetic.

I can see the defeated expression on the faces of my bandmates, and the anger bubbling up inside me almost makes me want to punch the wall. Without a word, I swing the door against the wall and leave the room with such fury radiating from my body everyone I encounter gets out of my way.

*

I watch Loretta get dressed after I fuck her. I called her as soon as I left our manager's office and met her, as usual, in the hotel room that I rent on an annual basis only for these kinds of situations. I don't take any women home. I don't want romantic relationships, and I want to avoid finding my apartment's address in Tribeca on every website in the world.

I like her red hair and tits that would make a porn star envious, but especially that she has no limits in bed. She's wild, and she fucks me until she drains all my energy, my anger, my fears, and insecurities. We get in touch when we need to, and we both know there's no feelings between us. She knows who I am, she's discreet and never wants money or gifts. Though a few days before Christmas she and I usually treat ourselves to dinner in a super-exclusive restaurant where I spoil her a bit. She's married, has a rewarding life, and doesn't want to turn it upside down for someone like me.

"You didn't get away with those three tongues stuck in your mouth, did you? You were an animal today." She smiles as she puts on the elegant dress she's wearing back to the office.

"So, you heard?" I ask her with a grimace as I light a cigarette.

She bursts out laughing in her delicate way. "You're on every fucking TV channel these days. It's impossible not to notice. Your face is on a whole wall of shelves at the newsstand."

"I'm not going to the newsstand," I grumble like a child, but it hit a spot. I can't even scroll through the usual sites I like without finding my wasted face everywhere.

She smiles and caresses my bare foot that is poking out of the sheets.

"You'll get over this one too," she says with a reassuring smile. She grabs her bag, fixes her hair and make-up in the mirror, then grabs the door handle and, just before leaving, turns around and says, "It's been a pleasure, as always." She winks in a sexy way.

I chuckle and wave to her. Sometimes I think she's the only friend I have besides the band.

"The pleasure is all mine." I wink at her, watch her open the door and then—surprise!—wrinkle my forehead as she moves to the side and my three bandmates walk in.

"Hello, Loretta," they greet her in chorus with a smile as she leaves.

"Jesus Christ, I still can't believe you're still fucking her after all these years. Doesn't she ever get tired of you? You're a pest," Michael says, walking to the liquor cabinet and pouring himself a whiskey.

Simon and Thomas sit on the sofa and laugh while I get out of bed without feeling the need to cover up.

"Jesus Christ! Damian, put on a pair of underwear! We don't need to see your junk," swears Simon with a disgusted face.

In response, I sit in the chair in front of him with my legs spread wide, one eyebrow raised in defiance. Thomas throws my shirt on my junk, covering it. I appreciate the drummer's aim and leave it where it is.

"I'm sorry for the mess I made," I admit with a grimace as Michael pours everyone a drink.

Simon laughs, and Thomas follows suit, leaving me surprised.

"You should have seen your face when Evan slammed the papers in front of you. Disgusted," says Simon sipping from his glass.

"I really was. I didn't want to have those girls' tongues in my mouth. Jesus, I was petrified they'd think I have a dead fish instead of a tongue. They're probably wondering how I got my reputation as the god of sex." I can already see them tweeting: *Damian kisses like my 14-year-old brother* and I'm embarrassed at the thought.

They burst out laughing. I'm here looking like an idiot and these assholes, who are supposed to be my friends, laugh out loud. I love them for it.

"It could have happened to any one of us. We were all wasted that night," admits Michael, sitting in the chair next to mine.

"I wasn't..." mumbles Simon.

"Yes, but it happened to me."

"The problem's gonna be with all those videos of our song. The contest has been open for less than two hours, and there are already 2,000 entries."

"Wow, how efficient," I say, disgusted by the speed with which the label burned us at the stake.

Thomas shrugs. "Today was just an ambush. They'd been setting everything up for days since those pictures came out or maybe even before. They wanted that contest, and they got it."

We just keep quiet and suck it up.

"What song did they choose?" I ask worriedly.

"'Jude,'" laughs Michael with his face to the ceiling.

"Holy shit, I love that song," I admit with a grin.

"Not after we've listened to the worst possible covers a thousand times, trust me. Our ears will bleed," laughs Simon. He's the one taking this almost lightly.

Now that the morning's anger has subsided, I'm happy to have my friends around. Seeing them all here together in this room helps lighten the weight I've been carrying on my chest for days. It's as if by merely being here, they said, "Man, we're here to help you out."

"So? Are we going out tonight before they lock us in a studio indefinitely? I haven't gotten laid in two nights already." Michael is clearly worried about his celebrity life having a setback.

"Stop me from drinking before knocking myself out and make sure I get in the car with Max, please."

Everyone's laughing except Simon. "I'm the one who'll be chugging gallons of soda tonight and having to babysit you idiots." He's complaining without too much conviction, as if he's already accepted his role.

"You never drink alcohol when we go out. I feel like I'm living with a cloistered nun," Michael says.

"Because you idiots don't have any functioning neurons when you have alcohol in your system. You need someone sober, so you don't make a mess. Look what happened the last time I took my eyes off Damian for five seconds. I ditched him for three fucking minutes to take a piss, and he was in a cab going who knows where."

Michael laughs out loud, me a little less, as our drummer shakes his head and grabs the phone out of his pocket.

"Give me half an hour, I'll book some clubs and make sure I have the cars ready for tonight. I can't remember if Dave and Max are on shift. Please, low profile and no paparazzi, okay? I don't want to have to deal with Evan banging newspapers all over the place again." Thomas is begging us, especially nailing me with his eyes.

The party boy, the impulsive, the wise guy, and the planner. We make a good team when we're sober. It's too bad sometimes things get out of hand and we find ourselves in Evan's office, all four of us united, as always, like the scared kids we were at the beginning who had each other's backs.

CHAPTER 2
Lilly

"No, absolutely not. No way."

I feel like I'm getting warmed up, and my stomach starts gurgling. I don't know how long I can hold it off after hearing this news.

"Please, Lilly. This is our chance," cries Martin. "How many times are we gonna get the Jailbirds to do a contest like this again? Go on tour with them and maybe sign for an album with the label?"

It's a once in a lifetime chance for us and for the thousands of bands all over the United States entering the contest. But me on a stage for a tour, with the most famous rock band in the world, never. The media attention would devour us; journalists would have a field day. It would be an avalanche of coverage from every corner of the world and, along with it, the hatred and envy of every other band who doesn't want to see us on that stage.

I feel a knot in my stomach and start to breathe without being able to expel all the air out of my lungs. My anxiety attack is about to get out of control. My bandmates look at me like I'm going to die at any moment, especially Taylor, our drummer, who seems to be trembling on the black worn and frayed leather stool. My head starts to spin. I need air, now.

I slip through the outside door, clinging to the railing of the stairs overlooking the East River side of Brooklyn's neighborhood. I start taking deep breaths, trying to inhale as much air as I can, looking around, taking in the open space and the absence of walls around me. The fear fades a bit, though the smell of garbage in the alleys isn't exactly helping.

Luke's arms wrap me in a loving grip, his chest against my back, his chin resting on my head, forcing me to follow his calm and regular breathing. The strength of his embrace makes me feel safe and allows me to focus on the positive. Luke never raises his voice. He is never abrupt or angry enough to make you feel uncomfortable. He is calm and patient. We've grown up together since the age of fourteen, and now he's the mainstay of my life, the one who manages to anchor me when my mind travels at a thousand miles per hour. He's the hand that pulls me out of the dark thoughts that sometimes envelop me.

"Anxiety attack?" he whispers in my ear.

"I managed to handle it before losing control," I admit with a little trembling in my voice.

Lucas, or Luke for us in the band, is the person who knows me best; we met at school during the Accident and since that day we've become inseparable. That same year we also met Martin, the guitarist, and Taylor, the drummer. From that day on, we spent our days between the rehearsal room and each other's houses. They were the ones who saved me when I thought there was no hope for me anymore, and, even now, Luke is here holding me so I don't fall apart.

"Come on, let's go get some coffee and talk about it."

I know the others sent him. He's usually the one who can talk some sense into me. I know this opportunity will never come again, but just the thought of getting on a stage where thousands of people can judge me and mock me makes me anxious. When those kinds of comments are thrown in my face I can't help but listen to them. I know what dark places my mind drags me to, and I also know how hard it is to get out of them.

We get to the cafe not far from the rehearsal room. It's small, intimate, and the fact that it's late summer, with the fresh air caressing your skin in an almost annoying way, feels perfect. The smell of coffee welcomes us, the colorful walls cozy and in stark contrast to the gray hues of the Brooklyn neighborhood.

When you hear people talk about New York, it's always about the glittering and impressive high-rise buildings, but that's Manhattan. Where we live, there's a mix of solid-looking, stocky buildings populated by the rich, mostly artists, with their exotic, alternative lifestyles, and a tangle of cramped, low-rise housing, too cold in winter and too hot in summer. Far from the luxurious part of the city standing tall on the other side of the East River.

We take a seat at one of the corner tables with a faux leather sofa. It's one of our favorite spots because it's slightly apart and allows us to talk for hours without anyone bothering us. In front of me, there is a steaming cup of cappuccino with cream, while Luke has just filled the cup of black coffee with sugar. I know he doesn't like coffee, but at school they always made fun of him by calling him "the British tea man", so he started drinking coffee saturated with sugar until it became sweet and disgusting. Some white grains are scattered on the dark, sticky wooden coffee table. It looks like it hasn't been cleaned recently, and he starts playing with it distractedly with his fingers, creating little circular shapes.

"Are you feeling better?" he asks me after I take a few sips.

I shrug my shoulders and nod. "The problem is, if I get a seizure just thinking about entering the contest, how can I stand there and do it for real?" My voice comes out tight, tired.

Luke looks at me, tilting his head, as he usually does when he has no idea whether I'm going to react well or badly to his words. "You're gonna take it one step at a time like you always do. You may have to take more steps, but you can't deny yourself this chance. Do you remember what our motto is? 'Fear does not control our lives'."

I lower my guilty stare at his sweet, understanding smile. "I know...but this time, the amount of stress I'll have to deal with is too much for me and your optimism. Maybe it's better if you find another bass player and enter that contest without me," I admit.

Luke puts the cup on the table and looks at me with a scary frown. I've never seen him so serious. "No way! You're the one who put this band together, and you're gonna be with us. If you're not there, we won't be there either," he says.

It's true that the idea of forming the band was mine. When Luke saved me that day, I was locked in for months and had plenty of time to learn how to play bass. One day, Luke came to my house with yet another black eye. The guys from the neighborhood he was going out with had beaten him up because he refused to deal drugs at school. That's when the idea of the band came to me. Together we learned how to play, and also got Martin and Taylor involved, who had nothing to lose since they were already the losers of the school. Without even realizing it, we were spending all our free time in the rehearsal room.

"Luke, listen to me, we're not talking about a field trip, we're talking about the opportunity of a lifetime. You could have the future you've always dreamed of; you can't give it up on a whim," I explain just as seriously. "I'm just dead weight. I'd get in the way of you achieving your dream."

Luke grabs me by the wrist and pulls me beside his toned physique, his blond hair falling over blue eyes that, at this moment, are reading deep into my soul. It is difficult to reason with him; I am an integral part of his world and it seems as though everything could crumble from one moment to the next if I am not part of it. It has always been like that with him. He makes me feel like the most important person on the face of the earth, the one for whom he would give up everything to follow to the end of the world. That's why I feel so guilty at the idea of abandoning them on the spur of the moment; if the situation were reversed, he would never do such a thing. He would find a way to overcome his problems. But I'm not Luke. I'm not as brave as he is.

"No way, Lil. If it wasn't for you, sooner or later my friends and I would've gotten tired of beating the crap out of each other and started dealing. Besides, you're a monster bass player, and we wouldn't stand a chance of getting on their radar if you weren't on bass."

I never thought I had saved them from jail, I just didn't want them to get the shit kicked out of them. We're not kids from broken homes or criminals. Our parents are decent people. Like most middle-class parents in New York who are forced to work until they break their backs to be able to support their families, ours had no time to control their children. It was easy for someone who's never seen big money to get lured into petty crime by the prospect of having a few dollars in their pocket to buy stupid but tempting things. In our case, a decent guitar or a thousand-dollar bass.

I get lost in his blue eyes, and I feel guilty. I can read it in the sincerity of his look that he really means to keep his word. These three idiots would really be willing to throw away an opportunity like this if I don't show up too, and I feel the pressure growing inside my chest about to explode.

"How am I supposed to think about being on a stage and the attention that comes with it, if I can't even control myself here with you, over coffee? You have no idea how badly my heart is trying to jump out of my chest right now. Jailbirds don't perform in shitty bars in New York City. They fill stadiums," I whimper.

Luke looks at me with a smile that warms my chest and holds me closer to him. "Meanwhile, we record the video, because it's easier to be in front of a camera in an empty room. Then, if we ever manage to beat thousands of bands, we'll think about the next step," he says with conviction, and my resistance wavers a little more.

"Do you really think there will be thousands?" I ask, almost confidently. Hope is mixed with guilt.

Luke laughs and holds me a little tighter. "I think they'll have to watch so many videos of that song that they'll hate it before they select a band," he laughs.

I look at him while moving a little away. "What song did they pick? I was so caught up in my paranoia that this information escaped me," I ask, intrigued, and less worried.

"'Jude,'" says Luke with a sly smile.

"I love that song," I say, still sipping from my cup of cappuccino and remembering what a wonderful feeling it gives me when I play it alone in my room with the acoustic guitar.

"They'll wish they never wrote it." He's amused by that idea and somehow it puts me in a good mood.

"Do you really think they'll do it? I don't think they spend their lives watching videos when they can be out with a different woman every night." I smile.

"Probably, but I guess the selection of the hundred bands that will pass the first round they will watch it too. I mean, they'll have to go on tour with whoever wins, I trust they have more say than we can imagine. I guess they don't want to ruin their image by showing up with a band that's not up to it."

I'm following his reasoning, and it's a good point. At that level of fame, they can't afford to mess up, especially when they're competing with other bands that are almost as famous as they are on the charts. We live in the age of the internet and a thousand opportunities. If they don't work continuously to stay on the crest of the wave, someone will come along and kick them off into oblivion. Years ago, it was harder to make your way in the music business, but once you got to the top, you could enjoy lasting fame. Today all you need is a YouTube channel and the right equipment to get noticed; but once you get to the top, you have to fight to make sure that the latest idol doesn't knock you down.

"So now all we have to do is make a video of 'Jude'?" I ask him after a silence that seems endless.

Luke turns to look at me with his lips arched upwards. "Are you sure? I don't want you to do this because you feel guilty."

I nod and smile at him in return. I'm not sure, but I can always try. "Like you said, there are going to be thousands of bands in it, and I can do a video with no problem...and then if they choose us...I don't know, I don't want to think about it, or I lose my nerve." I can give them a video. At least I owe them that much.

"That's my girl," he whispers in my hair before giving me a light kiss on the head.

*

If I could go back to the moment when I said, "shooting a video isn't that difficult," I'd like to slap myself on the back of the head like my grandfather used to do when I was a teenager after doing something stupid. Maybe it's because I'm nervous, knowing that our version of the song will be heard by the same people who wrote it and sang it perfectly, maybe it's because I'm afraid of the consequences of our participation.

Still, we find ourselves filming it for the seventeenth time in a row. Once, Martin is too far away and out of shot, another time Luke turns around and drops the microphone, yet another time we realize that when he dropped the mic, the cable got slightly detached, so Luke's voice was dropping out. We can't get a decent take that doesn't make us look like fools. You can't enter a competition for a tour with the most famous band in the world without showing you can stand on stage and do a little show.

"If it doesn't go well this time, I'll hang myself with the guitar strings, I'm warning you," says Martin, the drama queen of this band, sitting in front of the computer and downloading the footage from the camera.

"You're always so overdramatic. My hands are bleeding

from tapping my sticks on the fucking drum kit! Don't complain." Taylor gives him a light shove.

Martin shows him the blood coming out of his fingertips. I feel sorry for them. It's my fault that we haven't been able to make a decent recording for hours, because apart from the initial inconveniences, most of the videos we've deleted because we could only see my back. I look down at my shattered fingertips as severely as theirs and put my hands in my pockets. I have no right to complain.

Luke starts the recording and, this time, our sound isn't bad. We even manage to channel the desperation of the song how we wanted to, maybe because we really are desperate playing it for the umpteenth time.

"Look, we can see Lilly's face at least a couple of times. It's a big achievement." Martin jokes, giving me a bear hug and almost crushing me. He never does things halfway, and ever since he started going to the gym and getting in shape for the girls, when he hugs me it's become a problem.

"Moore, you're choking me," I cry out with a grimace of pain.

"Look, we're not going anywhere without a bass player," Taylor comes in and winks at me.

Martin lets me go, and, as the song comes to an end, we look at each other questioningly, ready to hear what the others think.

Luke speaks first: "We're between great and almost perfect. It was worth investing in a decent mixer and microphones that don't sound like empty cans. At least on this video we don't sound like amateurs, not like the first ones we recorded. I'd say we can upload this one to their website," he says convincingly.

A chorus of "yes, definitely" and "upload that video" and "let's not think about it anymore" fills the room, expressing all our frustration at the mere idea of reshooting it. Luke cuts the start and end piece where we turn the camera on and off and then clicks on the link that allows us to upload to the site.

"It's going to take a while before we upload it. The site is slow, probably clogged with all the files they're throwing in... beer?" he asks, turning to us.

We grab the cans from Martin's backpack, the ones his older brother gets him since we still have a year left before we can drink legally. We climb up to the roof tucked into our heavy jackets, the cold air whipping our faces as darkness descends on the New York City skyline.

We sit on the worn-out chairs we brought here years ago. The terrace is a flat expanse of concrete that covers the three-story building of the basement where we rehearse. Nobody ever comes up here. It's bare, there's not a shred of shade in the summer when the scorching sun hits this concrete slab in the early morning, and there are no walls to protect us from the icy air that scourges this weathered place in winter. The view, however, is priceless. In front of us stands the Manhattan skyline with its lights and silhouettes of skyscrapers. The fancy lifestyle we experienced only a few times, and for too little, when we went to concerts in clubs that cost us months of savings.

"I wonder where the Jailbirds are now," Martin whispers, more of a consideration than a question. His empty gaze makes me think he didn't realize he'd said it out loud.

"Fucking models," laughs Taylor.

Only a river divides us, but our lives couldn't be more different. Them with luxury apartments on top of some Manhattan skyscrapers, us still living at home with our parents in the hive-like housing projects. Them in a life of luxury and glitz, us with ninety-cent beers from the supermarket. Them, super famous with a different girl every night, us having difficulty finding someone who wants to be with losers.

"Can you imagine if we win? We could have a different model every night too."

"Don't let it go to your head, Moore. You're a loser, you'll be on the other side of the East River too. With that ugly mug you've got." Luke makes us all laugh.

"What the hell's wrong with my face?" Martin asks, pretending to be outraged.

Our guitarist is the vainest one in the band, and he has every right to be with that model face, his acne from puberty giving him a break after high school. Martin, with those big hazel eyes and square jaw, and a tuft of dark curls around his face, could model for a famous brand. Me, Luke, and Taylor, on the other hand, are definitely more anonymous. Luke has sweet, almost angelic features with big blue eyes and blond hair; Taylor has the face of a classic nerd, even if he does hide two striking green irises behind his thick-framed glasses. Me, on the other hand, I'm just your average chick: long brown hair, green eyes, and a long, slender neck. No one turns around to look at me when I walk down the street, and I'm okay with that. The only one in our group with a face for the stage and glossy magazines is Martin.

"No, Martin, your face is perfect. It's Luke who's being a dick," I say honestly.

We fall again into a comforting silence, each immersed in

our own thoughts and dreams, sipping cheap beer until it is Luke who breaks the silence. "Do you really think our lives could change if we win this contest?"

"I think so. I mean, we'd get publicity, we'd get gigs, not only concerts but also for other types of events. These things throw you into a dimension we can't even imagine," is Taylor's response. I look at him, surprised: I didn't know he had ever taken this lifestyle seriously.

"Can you imagine what we could do with all the money the Jailbirds have?" Martin's dreamy question follows.

"I'd buy an apartment for my parents, so we wouldn't have to live in that dump with the drafty windows and heating that goes out when it's cold."

Luke's words hit me like a moving train and make me feel even more guilty for hoping to lose the contest. That's what we all aspire to in the end, not so much the women and guys we could have, the good life, the cars, and the parties, but to give a decent roof to the families who raised us and supported us when we decided to become musicians. We never lacked anything. They never pressured us to get a real job. We're not on the verge of poverty, but an extra wage at home would be good for all four families.

"So let's win this contest, shall we?" The words come from my lips with a mixture of fear and hope. Two opposing and conflicting feelings that tear at my chest and make my heart jump at the thought of what might happen.

*

"Where are you going at this hour? It's ten o'clock! Do you want to go out again?" my father whispers from the couch, trying not to wake my mother, who fell asleep, like every night, after the first five minutes of TV, with her head resting on my old man's shoulder.

"I'm going for a run to clear my head. I'll be back soon, I promise," I lie.

If we win, I have to find the strength to withstand the media pressure and to do so, I can't give any reason to those who want to criticize me, physical appearance included.

"You didn't eat much at dinner. I don't have to start checking on you again, do I?" he asks me with apprehension crossing his face.

I feel guilty seeing him like this. They both aged suddenly ten years when I started to show the first consequences of the Incident; it's clear that my father is terrified that I might fall back into that dark tunnel.

"No, it's just that I ate a lot of crap with Luke and the others in the rehearsal room. I wasn't hungry when I got back." The truth is, one cappuccino and three beers is a total of 737 calories, and if I'm not careful, I risk losing the balance I've managed to create with years of patience and the help of a good therapist.

"Okay, but don't be late." He smiles at me, never taking his eyes off my face as I smile back and leave the house in my heavy sweatshirt and sneakers.

If I have to get back earlier, I'll have to run faster to cover the same route I do every day or I'll never be able to keep up with the schedule that keeps my weight under control.

CHAPTER 3
Damian

When Evan threatened to make us watch every single video for the contest, he wasn't kidding. Not the thousands of uploads filtered by some interns the record company recruited, but the hundred which made it through the selection process.

We listened to all of them, three times each, and chose ten to put on the site. The fans' reaction was very positive, actually. Now, we're still sitting in this damn office with a monitor in front of us and headphones in our ears to decide which three to bring into the studio and play live—a nightmare that has lasted for days and seems to have no end.

"If I hear the song one more time, my ears will bleed," Simon says, leaning back in his chair and faking a spasm, or at least I hope he's faking it.

We laugh desperately because we're all feeling the same way. I used to love this song, now I wish I'd never written it. It's the worst feeling a musician can have.

"Well, get ready with the bandages because we're gonna be here all night if we have to. They want to make the announcement about the top three winners tomorrow morning, and won't tolerate any delays," replies Evan, annoyed, who has also been forced into this torture for hours.

While we deal with the music part, he has to figure out if

the bands are a "commercial product" that could bring revenue to the label. However, our manager is a magician in this respect, the best in the industry. He's a few years older than us; he was still a kid when he discovered us in one of New York's infamous clubs when we were just over 18. We were his first real assignment, the first band to sign under his name as management. We grew up together, and I'll never stop thanking him for the trust he put in us when we were nobodies.

"This one, no, too much like what we do. They have good skills, but they don't seem to put much of their own into it. Since we've got nine more, I'd say we start skimming."

We all agree with Simon, and well before we expected, we're selecting the three finalist bands.

"So? Now, what's going to happen?" I ask, exhausted while sipping a fresh cup of hot coffee.

"Tomorrow, we'll make the announcement on the website and contact the bands to let them know. By the weekend, we'll have all three of them in the studio. We'll have them play 'Jude' and one of their own songs," Evan explains.

"So, we don't have plans until the weekend?" I say, amazed.

"Yeah, Damian, you can go fuck someone until your dick falls off," he says, making everyone laugh. I'm laughing, too, and I'm letting him believe it.

I smile at him with a conspiratorial glance, but I'm actually going to walk out of this room, go back to my apartment and not come out until they drag me out. All by myself with a duvet and pizza. I won't lift a finger to cook, just order takeout.

I've always been totally open with my friends, they know everything about me, and I know everything about them. Our past is inextricably linked. Still, it's sometimes easier to make them think I have a different woman in my bed every night than to explain that I prefer to be alone because I got tired of one-night stands. At first, it's fun, you feel powerful, and your young male ego benefits from that, but over time it just becomes a simple routine, exercises aimed at the pleasure that, in the long run, is not even that satisfying.

However, explaining it to my friends would prompt questions about why I don't want long-term relationships where I have to be emotionally involved. These are explanations I don't want to give, not even to them, because it would force me to look inside myself and discover my true motives. I would have to rethink my past and throw salt on wounds that never healed, ones I keep sealed under the layers I have wrapped them in for years to avoid feeling pain. If you have a stable relationship, sooner or later, that person will require your feelings in that fucking relationship and start pulling at the gauze and make those wounds bleed again. It's easier for everybody if I keep up the goddamn rockstar facade.

*

Three days after the torture by "Jude" videos, I'm back at the label building. I take the elevator and immediately regret it. According to the badge pinned on her chest, "Cindy," an intern, devours me with her eyes as soon as I set foot inside. I give her a forced smile and avoid taking off my sunglasses so as not to get involved in a conversation I don't feel like having. I turn towards the door, one step in front of her and on the opposite side of this small space, to avoid eye contact.

"You're Damian Jones, right?" she squeaks, ignoring my body language.

I nod my head with a fleeting glance.

"I'm a huge fan of yours. When I heard I got the internship here, I jumped at the chance. I was hoping to meet you." She winks as she smooths her blonde hair and moves in closer.

I'm annoyed by her disrespect for my personal space. "You were lucky," I throw in without enthusiasm, hoping the elevator will hurry to the top.

"If you want, I'll leave you my number if you'd like me to listen to something new. You know, I studied music in high school, and I'm pretty good at it." Her voice is soothing.

You're also pretty shameless, I think. On the one hand, I like decisive women; but I get irritated by those who throw themselves at my feet without restraint.

"If I happen to want to share some music, I'll definitely ask Evan for your number." I smile at her as the elevator finally gets to my floor, and the doors open to the waiting room.

"I'm counting on it!" she purrs at me, clinging to my arm before she turns and walks down one of the hallways.

"You don't miss one, do you, man?"

I glance at the amused grin on a young guy's face. Calling me man without even introducing himself makes me want to slap him to teach him manners, but I'd rather not be charged with assault. Who the hell is this guy anyway?

"The perks of doing this job," I reply with a bland smile, trying to get out of his grip.

In a few moments, I'm attacked by a group of kids who want a picture with me or an autograph. What the hell is going on? I smile and give them a few shots. Looking closer, I recognize some faces from the videos we've been watching—the bands that passed the last round. I direct a fleeting glance towards the waiting room and find four other kids on the sidelines, looking at me, but they don't approach me. Clearly, the third band is doing a great job of showing self-control. I like them better already.

"Sorry, guys, but I have to go get my coffee, or I won't be able to hear a single note you'll play in there," I chuckle as I try to get away from the iron grip.

Whoever invented this contest has absolutely no idea what it's like to live in our shoes. They enjoy the money they make off of us, but they don't really care whether we're okay with it or not. It upsets me so much that I've thought several times about quitting the record company. The problem is that every label is the same, and the alternative would be to give up making music. I would never, ever, throw this job away.

Some laugh, others apologize as I finally manage to walk down the hallway to the recording room where my coffee is waiting for me, I hope. This is the record company floor I like the most: fewer glass walls, corridors full of photos of great artists who have passed through here, fully equipped recording rooms, and few meeting rooms. I like the air here where we actually make music, unlike the other floors of this building where we get treated like puppets to be manipulated by their sales strategies. This is where I do my job, and where I like to be.

"Evan hired a new intern?" I ask, annoyed the second I step foot in the room and see my bandmates.

"I don't know. Why? Have you seen someone you haven't fucked yet?"

I respond to Thomas by giving him the finger. "No, asshole, she threw herself at me in the elevator and told me if I want to share some new tunes, she was a music freak in high school."

Everyone else is laughing but I'm not amused.

"She didn't make these proposals to me when I met her," Michael complains.

"She's such a big fan of mine, I don't think she even knows I play in a band," I shoot back at him. "You can fuck her if she gives you a boner."

"Why, isn't she good enough for His Majesty Jones?" he replies jokingly.

I shrug my shoulders in annoyance. "I don't think I've got any holes in my schedule to put her in."

They're laughing while I just want this conversation to be over as soon as possible.

"Have you been attacked by the kids, too?" Michael asks me as he hands me the steaming coffee. He's the one who supplies everyone with caffeine in the morning. At the beginning of his career, he was still drunk at meetings and knew all four of us were too, and that we had to wake up. We were unmanageable in those days. We were little more than teenagers with a mountain of money in our hands that we wasted between parties and club nights. But now we've calmed down quite a bit, the work takes up an excessive amount of energy, and we realized that to be a rock star, you also have to continually produce good music. We had two choices: to end up in oblivion after the first album or to calm down. We chose the latter, but the tradition of getting steaming coffee from Michael before each meeting remained.

"From two of the three bands, yes," I confirm, rolling my eyes and sitting on the couch next to Simon and Thomas, making them tighten up a bit.

"Those of them who sat down are already my favorites,

too," chuckles Thomas as he sips from his cup.

We burst out laughing as we wait for Evan to join us and start this long and terrifying day. The risk of a dead-end is enormous.

"Didn't one of the bands have a girl, too? Have you seen her in the waiting room?" Simon asks, raising an eyebrow.

"Yes, I think so, the one who never turns to the camera," confirms Thomas. "I don't know, the four of them who were sitting on the sidelines were all curled up in their hoodies, it could have been Miss Universe in there, and I wouldn't have recognized her."

I burst out laughing. If it's a pretty girl, none of us are backing down.

"Simon, have you set your eyes on her yet? Remember, we're potentially going on tour with her, don't fuck up your life for a lay." I tease him even though he's the only one of us who'd rather have a nice girl to walk down the aisle with than one of those one-night stands. I admire his purity of spirit.

"No, asshole, she stuck in my mind because she's great on the bass. You guys haven't heard it? She plays some licks that even I can't in that song," he laughs. "Am I the only one who's noticed it?" he asks, almost astounded.

"No, I did too. She's one of the best bass players I've ever heard," confirms Thomas, and I feel like an idiot because all that bothered me was that she stood there, showing us just her back as if we weren't worth a penny of her time. I'm ashamed of myself for not going beyond appearances.

Evan takes us away from our thoughts and slams the door behind us. "Those kids do get up your business, don't they?" The exasperated question makes us all burst into a thunderous laugh.

"Let's get started, come on. The sooner we begin the sooner we'll be done with them," I propose, and the others nod vigorously as they move around the chairs in front of the mixer.

The room is arranged like a classic recording room: on one side of a glass partition are the instruments, microphones connected by cables to the mixer, headphones for every single position, and soundproof walls. There's also a drum kit against the far wall and three racks for the electric and acoustic guitars and basses. The kids brought their own instruments, except drums, but it never hurts to have some backup instruments for any possibility.

There's a mixing board on this side of the glass with thousands of keys, levers, and indicators which, when you look at it, gives you a headache from how complicated it is. A row of monitors allows you to work on the different recording channels of the audio tracks. I have always held the technicians who manage to maneuver this spaceship in high esteem. If we were producing an album, the audio tracks would be played separately to get clean recordings of each instrument. For today we just want to hear how they sound, so they'll perform as if they were in the rehearsal room together.

Evan calls his secretary on the phone and not two minutes later, on the other side of the glass, five young kids appear. They are little more than teenagers, connecting bass and guitars to the cables and smiling as if they'd won the lottery. They're quite comfortable in a studio; it's probably not the first time they've seen one, and if that's to their advantage, their matching clothes and mass-produced hairstyles make my nose twitch. They're the exact opposite of us, who look homeless most of the time. It's like we're dealing with a boy band from some talent show.

We start them off, and in no time we're looking at each other, wondering how they got in the top three. They're definitely the ones in the video but they're overplaying so much they're slaughtering the song. Extra guitar solos, bass solos, and even drum solos just to prove they can play. The singer is attempting high notes that don't fit his vocal range or the song. "Jude" was written from the gut and sung in a voice made hoarse from generous amounts of whisky. This sounds like the soundtrack to a musical played by people on LSD. Overdoing it isn't exactly the way to get our attention, and when they're done we all agree not to let them play their original tune. The first performance is enough for us.

"Thank you very much, you can go back to the waiting room. We'll let you know when we've heard the other two bands," Evan announces with a smile phonier than a thirteen dollars bill. I admire his ability to lie so casually.

"But we haven't done our song yet!" points out the singer with such stiff hair it didn't move while jumping around like a madman for three minutes.

"You've done a unique job, we don't need to hear any more," says our manager with a hint of annoyance that only we recognize.

Unique is the definition I would have used for sure. I've rarely heard a song that ugly played live. The guys leave the room smug with their success, while we immediately delete the name from the list of winners.

"Luckily, we decided to hear them play before making a decision. Can you imagine if we took them on tour?" Simon shudders at his own words, which are followed by a chorus of "Don't even joke about it."

"It was hard to convince the label, but luckily they listened to me in the end," Evan admits, who seems to breathe a sigh of relief. "If it were up to them, we would've taken the band with more Facebook likes."

We're all shocked and speechless at that admission.

The second group goes almost unnoticed. They're good, even better than what you see in the video, but they don't stand out. A typical band that could be quite successful locally, but they wouldn't make it on the national or international charts. They lack the breakthrough factor. Musically they didn't miss a note, but they're not a band you'd remember after they got off stage. I don't think I would even remember their faces.

Confirmation that they're not ready yet for the big time is their original song. It's immature, as though they wrote it when they were teenagers and had just started playing, with only a few chords used repeatedly throughout the song. If we were to get our hands on that piece, we'd have to throw away three-quarters of it. And while we can teach them how to get on stage and perform we don't have time to mature them artistically. The creativity must already be there; we can't teach them.

"Hopefully, the next ones will be better because otherwise, we're in deep shit," says Michael, sipping his coffee with a grimace. I've rarely seen him so worried.

I nod. This stunt risks making us look like rookies. The problem is that we've exposed ourselves publicly, and we can't go back and say, "Sorry, guys, we fucked up." We'd be eaten alive. We need a winner out of this charade who doesn't make us look like assholes. The guilt grips my stomach, because if I hadn't been an idiot in L.A., we wouldn't be here risking our image with this farce.

The final band, the Red Velvet Curtains, comes in, looking like they've never seen a recording studio before. As they position themselves at the instruments, taking forever with their awkward gestures, the one I assume is the bass player stumbles over one of the cables and almost goes down. The hood of the sweatshirt slips to the side and I am amazed to see a cascade of brown hair, two green eyes that seem to light up the room—even if covered by square, thick, black-framed glasses—and a mouth that seems drawn.

She's one of the most beautiful girls I've ever seen, and only God knows what goes through my head when I stare at that mouth; he's probably covering his eyes to avoid the obscene images passing through my brain. In a fraction of a second she ducks back under the hood of her sweatshirt that is at least three sizes bigger than her body. But it's enough time to awaken parts inside my pants that I'd prefer to keep asleep while working. It's not lovely to flaunt my erection right now; I look like a maniac who can't contain himself in front of a woman, for God's sake.

They start playing, and we immediately understand who our winners are going to be. They give such an intense performance of "Jude" that I get goosebumps, and their awkward nerdiness gives them more character than I expected. They take a completely different approach to this song; we throw in all the heavy rock rhythm, almost with a wave of screaming anger in the microphone, whereas they interpret it as a melancholic ballad, making the painful lyrics almost unbearable.

When the singer closes his eyes and sings in a voice that seems broken from crying: "Jude, I watched you slip out of the sheets, and I was afraid you would never come back," I feel the hairs on my arms rise with emotion. I like the rough voice he uses, the almost calm and respectful sound others give to the musical accompaniment. The drummer manages to play with delicate touches while never failing to support the song with his rhythmic part. The guitarist accompanies the voice without ever becoming the protagonist, dragging the notes when the singer's voice becomes heartbreaking. But what strikes me the most is the bassist, because she caresses the strings with a delicacy that makes the sound of her bass sweet, discreet, like someone's heartbeat when you put your ear on their chest: a constant and vital rhythm but never overpowering.

I look at the others and see the same smile I have planted on my face. We dodged a bullet that could have killed our career with this contest.

Their original song is the one that makes Evan fall. You can tell he wants to sign them and take them under his wing. It's got mature, sometimes raw lyrics, about a woman who betrays her man. Unlike their rendition of "Jude," "Give Me Back My Heart" is a rock song in the real sense of the word, with overbearing drums that get inside your stomach and make it vibrate. The guitarist gives free rein to his fingers that look possessed by speed flying along the neck of that guitar. The sound is clean, there are no smudges despite the fast rhythm. With the corner of my eye, I notice Michael pleasantly impressed by the young guitarist and Simon holding his hair tightly, his eyes grainy with surprise, his gaze fixed on the girl.

The bass player is something portentous. During the first

song, I appreciated the sweet touch only a woman's fingers can give, but now I'm amazed at the impressive strength she brings to those strings. She's not using a pick, as you see younger bassists do more and more. She's using the index and middle fingers of her right hand to torture the strings of her bass guitar with a violence and precision that makes the sound rumble through the chest until it vibrates. Her long fingers move with agility on the neck slightly wider than usual to accommodate the six strings. Few times in my career have I seen a bassist use a fretless bass with more than four strings. Together with the drummer, she creates the frenetic rhythm that makes you want to jump up and shout the song at the top of your lungs.

In the final verse, when the young kid sings, "With one hand you ripped my heart out of my chest, while with the other you waved at me smiling. Give me back my heart. Give me back my heart," we're all standing, excited, like we're in the front row at a concert.

The few seconds of silence that follow are almost surreal. From the expression on my friends' faces, I realize that none of us expected a band of this level.

"I'll go get them and bring them to the office. You guys go break the news to the others," Evan announces.

"Why do we have to tell them the bad news?" I protest like a child throwing a tantrum.

"Because you're the one who started this mess." He raises an eyebrow in a way that doesn't allow a response.

I curl up in my chair, feeling like a schoolboy who's just been lectured. I take a look at the others who invite me to lead the way and handle the matter in an unkind manner. I get up unwillingly and approach the waiting room with a funeral step, followed by my friends at a safe distance. As soon as they see us, the boys jump up with their faces full of expectation. I feel like an asshole for destroying their dreams.

"There's no easy way to say this, so...we chose the third group," I say bluntly. How do they say? Better a tooth out than always ache, right?

"Jesus, 'tact' is your middle name," I hear Michael laughing behind my back.

I'd like to turn around and give him the stink eye, but the lead singer of the first band, the one with the lacquered toupee on his head, saves me from the embarrassment.

"You picked those losers? What kind of losers are you?" he spits, disgusted, and annoyed.

"Insulting someone who might give you a job in the future is not a great move, genius," the other singer jokes and then turns to us and smiles. A sad, disappointed smile, but still sincere. "Thank you for this opportunity, really. It's already been an honor to have reached the top three and play in front of you," he adds, extending the hand I'm happy to shake.

I smile. I like this guy.

"You know what? You may not be ready for an international tour yet, but you certainly have potential. Leave me your number, maybe there's a chance to set something up here in New York," I tell him by pulling out my phone.

The blondie seems like he might faint at any moment. Still, he handles the situation better than the singer of the other band who, indignant, marches straight to the exit, trying to slam the door behind him but failing miserably, because it's one of those automatic ones that slows down to prevent the glass from shattering in a moment of anger. I know because I've tried several times without succeeding. His bandmates are so embarrassed by what happened that they disappear in total silence.

*

On the way back, we find Evan in the hallway motioning us to one of the offices used for meetings—an anonymous room with a vast window overlooking Manhattan's spectacular view. Madison Square Park's trees extend below us, and the Flatiron building stands just beyond the park. If I approach the window, I'm sure I'll find a bustle of tourists with their noses up and cameras hanging around their necks, their eyes dreaming, and their mouths wide open. Because that's what New York does to you: fills you with wonder and amazement every time you turn the corner and discover a glimpse you don't expect.

Once inside, we find ourselves in front of the four young people who stop their conversation as soon as we open the door. They sit next to each other and are clearly embarrassed, not knowing whether to stand up like when the principal enters the classroom or sit down and be less afraid than they are in reality. We try to subdue their discomfort by sitting across from them.

I look at them carefully. They are all in their twenties and have that mixture of disbelief and hope in their eyes that makes me smile. They're lucky. I had already learned by their age that life can be a real bitch, and that it can take away so much, too much, without giving you anything, making you sweat for every single breath. Everybody's excited except the girl who, lowering her hood, looks like she's about to throw up. I watch her for a few seconds too long, and lose myself in those delicate features that look almost doll-like. It's absurd how a girl like that can handle the bass with a force that rips your insides out when you listen to it. My eyes rest on her hands, on her ta-pered fingers that are now closed in fists so tight her knuckles have turned white.

"As you may have guessed already," Evan begins with a half-smile, "our choice is you. You will be the band to open the concerts for the Jailbirds' American tour if you read the con-tract and accept the terms," he says without much preamble, leaving them speechless and dazed.

I've read that contract, and it's a great piece of paper that protects both them and us, no musician in his or her right mind would refuse such conditions. Which is why I'm completely stunned when the girl bursts into tears, jumps up and drops the chair on the floor, and runs out like we just killed someone in front of her eyes.

"Lil," the singer's whisper comes out muffled as he follows her with his eyes, undecided whether to go after her while the others look around in dismay. I look at my companions, who are as confused as I am.

What the hell just happened?

CHAPTER 4
Lilly

The recording room is empty, and it's the first place I can think of to take refuge while the tears keep rolling down my face. I hate myself for it. I'm not used to crying, especially for things that aren't exactly sad. It's the fear that takes over, and I can't control it, manage it in this foreign environment. That stresses me out so much that I run away like a little girl. I've been overwhelmed by emotions, like a wave threatening to drown me, ever since agreeing to take part in this damn contest, and our name appearing in the top hundred.

"Hey, come here," Luke says as he grabs me by the wrist and pulls me in a firm, comforting embrace. Luke, my Luke, I don't think he's gonna get me out of this mess this time.

"What do I do now?" I ask him in a whisper.

My friend breathes deeply and holds his breath for a few seconds. "Let's figure something out," he says in a tone a little lighter than mine.

"What, Luke? What?" I raise my voice and pull myself away from his grip. "You told me to do the video, and I did it because there were thousands of bands to compete against. When we entered the first hundred, you told me the chances were still slim. When we entered the top three, you told me to wear a sweatshirt and cover myself and imagine I was in the rehearsal room... Now what do I do? Brad started wearing me out as soon as he saw our name. He's not gonna stop, and you know it. I don't want to go back to being fifteen again, Luke! Now he's got hundreds of thousands of followers worshipping him like he's the god of sarcasm and witty banter." The panic is evident in my voice.

Luke looks at me with despair in his eyes, and perhaps a little pain and defeat. "For now, let's face the biggest problem—not crumbling like you did when you were fifteen," he tries to suggest.

"No way. I don't want to undermine the little bit of mental health I've managed to regain with Dr. Sue. You need to find yourself another bass player," I say spitefully.

I hate being so cranky with him. He doesn't deserve it. He's helped me my whole life, but I'm trapped, and fear makes me say things I don't want to.

"You can't spend the rest of your life hiding because you give that asshole power over you, do you understand that or not? This is the chance you've been waiting for! To take the bull by the horns, face your fears, and become the musician you've always dreamed of. It's not just a matter of exposing yourself to people like Brad. Lil, you're terrified of living!" he cries out almost desperately.

A slight knock on the already open door makes us turn, and Evan, the Jailbirds' manager, appears. Clearly, he overheard our entire conversation. His face betrays awareness and, perhaps, regret.

"Excuse me for intruding, but your friend is right," he says directly to me. "This is a chance to solve the problem that's bothering you, and we are the solution. Come to the office over there, let's talk about it together and, if we don't find a solution, you'll be free not to sign the contract. I have no interest in having you sign a piece of paper that could prove to be a failure both for you and for us, but give me this chance, give me the chance to show you that we can help each other. I don't mind saying that, hearing you play, I thought I'd just discovered a gold mine. I'll be honest with you; you're exactly what every record company is looking for right now. I'd be a fool to let you run without at least trying to find a solution. But you must be convinced enough to try."

His words hit me like a punch in the gut. I can see in Luke's eyes all the hope he's managed to reveal, and all the terror and despair of seeing an opportunity like this fade away. I can't say I'm not flattered. However, I know perfectly well that right now, he would do anything to convince me. I see no way out: mine is not stage panic. It's a mental and emotional instability that I'm afraid will lead me into a self-destructive spiral like the one that almost killed me when I was fifteen. I don't know if this time I'll have the strength to recover from it.

"I'm a hopeless case," I whisper, too weakly for my taste. I wish I was stronger.

"There are no hopeless cases, just people who need the right times and the right paths to overcome their fears. Do you really think rock stars were all born to be on stage and the center of attention? Maybe one in a thousand may love that situation, but I can guarantee you that the other nine hundred and ninety-nine had to find a way to overcome all the crap linked to success and fame. Getting on that stage exposes you to the good and the bad, but I can guarantee you that I am here to protect you and make it worth it." The knowing smile on Evan's lips is convincing. My guilt about the band doesn't help.

"Lil?" my friend's voice is so full of hope that I make a considerable effort to convince myself to go back to that room.

"Okay, let's talk about it, but I do not promise anything," I say in a much firmer tone of voice than before.

Luke's smile loosens the knot I feel in my throat, but Evan's makes me realize that he too, in his own way, cares about this meeting. Maybe he really saw something in us that's worth giving a try.

*

We go back to the office, and I go back to my chair, which has been put back on its feet. I take a quick look at the faces in front of me, which are intrigued but not incredibly angry, apart from Damian, the band leader, who has an indecipherable expression. I linger a few seconds more on him, and now I understand why women line up to get into his bed. He's the classic brooding rock star that every girl wants: handsome and breath-taking with long, dark hair flowing down his back like a mane, brown eyes topped by a pair of eyebrows that seem to challenge you, and a scar over the left one that interrupts an otherwise perfect line to mark his status as a bad guy. The long, thick beard makes him look much older than twenty-five and his dark complexion dotted with tattoos shows evidence of a hard life. And that physique...so statuesque and muscle-tight it almost makes his short-sleeved shirt explode.

I realize that I'm staring at him and my face flushes with shame. I move my gaze just enough to briefly meet that of Thomas, the drummer, who gives me a half a sympathetic smile. The fact that I've been caught staring embarrasses me: I'm not one of those fainty little girls with big eyes who fall at men's feet.

Evan breaks into my thoughts with a question, summing up what he'd heard in the rehearsal room: "If I understand correctly, your problem is with someone who makes life impossible for you, right? Are you afraid people are gonna come after you because of the media exposure you're gonna get?"

"Well, even Simon shits his pants every time he meets the paparazzi, but he solves it with two fingers of liquor every half hour in the two hours leading up to the press conferences," Michael laughs. I find myself smiling at his disarming confession.

"Thank you very much, Michael. You're making me look like an alcoholic," scolds the bass player. He turns to me. "I swear, it's just a sip an hour or so before I face the press."

I notice my bandmates next to me relaxing a little bit with their jokes, and I feel guilty for what I'm about to do. My return to this room must have restored their confidence.

"You guys really don't get it," I say by taking the phone out of my pocket and getting the attention of everyone present, including Damian, who, I must admit, intimidates me quite a bit.

"Is that really necessary, Lilly?" Martin asks me in a hesitant voice. He knows where I'm going with this.

"Should I wait until I'm on tour? They're gonna find out sooner or later anyway." I'd rather put my cards on the table right now, get my bandmates to change bass players, and let them keep playing. It's the best solution for everyone.

I look for Brad's account on Instagram and turn my phone to the others, scrolling through the pictures of me when I was fifteen. "These are from a junior high school field trip."

"You're not there," says Simon with a wrinkled forehead

and a puzzled look.

I burst out laughing, leaving them all a little lost. "Oh no, I'm here. See the fat girl in the bad clothes? Yes, that's me."

I look for another picture in his account. "These were taken during mandatory swimming hours before I jump in the water," I explain as the five faces in front of me look at me with the same pity I see in everyone who realizes how I used to be. "Here, let me read one: 'When you go to school and fear for your life. #bomb #huge #tsunami #flood.' Want me to read you some more cute captions? Because there are some really interesting hashtags describing my size. It might be instructive to learn how many ways you can say fatty without saying that word."

My heart is pounding furiously in my chest when I see myself again in a bathing suit. They wanted me to face the problem? Well, I'm doing it, proving to them that it can't be solved in any way except by removing me from the equation.

"And these started showing up when he saw the first skim of the hundred bands you chose. What do you think will happen when I get on that stage?" I ask with tears threatening to flow. Not tears of sadness, but of anger because my life sucks and I will never be normal. Or rather, I can only be a normal person because if I try to do something special, there will always be someone ready to knock me down and trample me.

"So, this asshole posts embarrassing pictures to thousands of his followers every time she does something noteworthy?" Michael asked Luke.

Luke is just nodding in his chair.

"Crap," whispers the guitarist in the world's most famous band. He, too, realizes how ridiculous the situation is. "Can't something be done?" he asks Evan.

"I can definitely call the lawyers and get them to take them down. Maybe I can stop him from publishing anything about you." Evan wrinkles his brow like he's already working out a complicated plan to put the bad guy away.

I burst into a bitter laugh that draws everyone's attention. "You really think Brad is the problem? Did you read the comments under the pictures? Sure, he's the leader of that gang of degenerates who follow him, but the cutest comments are the ones that ask how he survived the tsunami caused by my dive into the pool. Some even say I should die, or my mother should have had an abortion for the good of mankind."

Damian sighs, almost annoyed. "What the fuck do you care what people say? Don't even read them, alright?"

I look at him with resentment. His air of arrogance makes me want to slap him. "Sure, coming from a guy who calls press conferences all fucked up because he has to apologize for sticking his tongue in little girls' mouths, that's great advice. Thank you." I realize I've exaggerated only when Luke puts his hand on my knee and squeezes lightly. I don't regret saying it. I look at Thomas, and the sly smile he can't hide seems almost smug—as though he wanted to say these words himself. I like that.

"In fact, I don't give a damn what the newspapers say and, as you say, I give press conferences to give explanations to those who don't deserve them instead of working, that's what annoys me. Trust me, it's not my decision," Damian says, beaten back, and I realize I've punched him in the gut.

"Mature behavior on your part, congratulations. Wait, I'm getting out a notebook and taking notes." He has no idea how much longer I can torture him. When a person treats me like I'm stupid, I start to snap.

"Sure, because your plan of giving up a life-changing contract for you and your bandmates because you're a crybaby is really grown-up, isn't it?"

I'm so angry right now my body feels hot. "Crybaby? How old are you? Seven? Lilly's a whiner," I mimic him.

Thomas's laugh diverts my attention away from Damian, and I realize that in my eagerness to jump down his throat, I've leaned over the table, and all eyes are planted on us. The Jailbirds and Evan are amused, my bandmates are stunned. I'm ashamed of my loss of control, and look down to avoid eye contact.

Evan tries to reassure me. "It's all about image, Lilly. We can handle it, we can control who's pounding on you, and we can get them to close their accounts, they'll stop. Positive voices are stronger than negative ones."

"Sure, and can you handle my emotional breakdowns and my mental health?" I cross my arms to my chest and raise an eyebrow.

Evan looks down, saying nothing.

"Look, I got the number of the other band's lead singer; we can still stop them before they get to the airport," Damian says, getting up with the phone in his hand, ready to make that call.

They all look at him as if a he'd grown a second head. He's so snooty and confident, he doesn't even care that we're still in the room before he proposes a replacement. I'm annoyed by his pessimism, especially when I look at my friends and find them mortified. He can humiliate me as long as he has the breath, but he can't touch them. They are my family, the one I have chosen, and I will defend them to the death if necessary.

"Are you out of your mind, or are you drunk?" slams Michael. "Did you hear them?"

A half-smile crosses my face when I see the look of rage on Damian's. It feels good to be defended by someone who isn't in my close circle of friends, and I don't feel guilty for the satisfaction of seeing him scolded in front of everyone.

"She can't even deal with a few idiotic comments made by morons," he yells, getting up abruptly out of his chair and waving his arms to the sky. Up close, he looks so huge that I find myself crouching in the armchair, trying to back out despite the table diving us.

"Would you stop talking as if I'm not here?" My anger overwhelms the intimidation he's trying to pull on me.

"We're trying to find a solution to her problem, you idiot, not trying to replace them," defends Michael again, who seems to be the brazen one.

"Could we get her to file a restraining order?" Thomas questions Evan.

"Maybe! That could be possible. I don't know how his followers would react to this news." The manager seems to think about it a bit.

Michael and Simon join in to find possible solutions to my problem, losing sight of the point that, in fact, the problem is me.

"Or you can find yourself another bass player who can handle this life," I shout, attracting everyone's attention again. They look at me as if I had just slit a man's throat over the table in front of them, everyone, from Jailbirds to my bandmates. "After all, I'm the problem, not them. It's the most practical solution," I explain in a more normal voice.

Simon is the one who breaks the silence, bursting out laughing blissfully and throwing his head back. It's disconcerting. "Did you hear that?" he asks a general question to those present. "You don't realize your gift, do you? You're a monster on the bass, and I'll drag you on that stage even if it means putting a mask on your face or wrapping you in wrapping paper," he threatens with a seriousness that disarms me.

"Thank you?" I stammer. That was a compliment, wasn't it?

"He's right, we're not going on stage without you," says Taylor, speaking for the first time. I turn to my bandmates and find the same look of determination on their faces, fueled by the help they're getting from the Jailbirds. The guilt is making me sick to my stomach.

"I need to get out of here before I throw up last Christmas' lunch too," I announce by getting up from my chair and turning to the door.

"Jesus Christ." I hear Damian's exasperated whisper escape his lips and enter my skin like an annoying itch I can't get rid of.

I turn to him, and as soon as he looks up, I light him up with a look that could incinerate him on the spot. He's caught off guard, and I absolutely don't care if he is worshipped by all women, even men, in the world. For me, he is an asshole and always will be.

"You're about as pleasant as a nasal swab. You know that?" I say to him before I leave, slamming the door behind me and hiding back in the recording room. This day feels like an endless nightmare.

I inhale deeply and try to calm down, gather my ideas and find a way out of this situation. To do it quickly, I use the only working method I have to relax: I grab an acoustic guitar and start singing "Jude," which, despite everything, is one of my favorite songs.

"Is there anything you can't do in a completely brilliant way?" Thomas' voice brings me back to reality as I glance towards the open studio door. I have to learn to shut the door behind me every time, not just when I want to make a dramatic exit.

"Cooking. I'm a mess in the kitchen. I could set Brooklyn on fire all the way to Queens if you leave me alone at the stove," I answer with my heart bouncing down my throat. It's weird how knowing I'm dealing with a world-famous star completely alters my heartbeat. At the end of the day, he's just a guy a few years older than me. I should be rational enough not to have a seizure, but here I am, with my palms sweating like a teenager in her first crush.

Thomas bursts out laughing and sits on a stool in front of me. "You know you're a weird chick? You're not afraid to put Damian in his place or joke with me, but you can't get rid of this fucking fear of being judged by people," he says, smiling and tilting his head to the side, studying me openly.

"I'm immune to all this celebrity charm," I explain by waving my hand in front of his face.

He burst out laughing again. It's a harmonious laugh, almost like a melody. "No, you're not. I saw you drooling over Damian in there."

I look up at the sky, trying to hide the undeniable attraction I have for his friend. "Only a crazy woman wouldn't want to rip the clothes off all that good stuff, but I would be happy to punch him in the face when he's an asshole." I raise an eyebrow.

Thomas bursts out laughing again. It looks like I've become his favorite comedian. "Jesus Christ, I adore you already," he admits, rubbing his hand on his face and covering his two beautiful blue irises for a moment.

"Because I say your friend is an asshole?" My eyebrow rises even higher than before.

He shrugs and nails me to my stool with those two magnetic eyes of his. "He has a hard time trusting people he doesn't know, but when he melts, he becomes a little lamb," he explains with a smile.

"I doubt it...it looks like he's got a pole up his ass."

I make him laugh again, but this time he doesn't answer me. "I like the version of 'Jude' you did earlier. Would you let me hear it again?"

His request leaves me stunned, but I nod and start playing again, losing myself in the feelings this song evokes in me. Without ever taking my eyes off his, I enjoy every nuance of emotion I can tear from him. Using just my voice and an acoustic guitar allows me to give a sweet touch to a song usually sung with anger. For me, it's a beautiful love story, and the feeling I instinctively convey in my voice is tenderness.

"Okay, that's the best version I've ever heard," he admits, impressed, and my chest swells with pride. "So you have no problem playing, or even singing in front of people," he notes by wrinkling his forehead.

I shake my head. It's hard to explain what goes through my mind when I get on stage. I'm not afraid to play in front of people, but music is what saved me when I thought the only solution left was to die. I've never doubted my abilities as a musician. The problem is when I obsess on my physical appearance, which I feel insecure about. Brad never blamed me for music, but he managed to make me doubt all the other aspects of my life.

"No, I often play in front of my friends or family, or in clubs. I've never been ashamed of my voice or my music. My problem is drawing attention to myself when it's no longer music they see but a girl they can humiliate."

Thomas nods. He seems to be thinking about what I just said. "I think I have a solution to your problem," he says, standing up and holding out my hand.

I watch him for a few moments, trying to grasp his thoughts, but I can't. So I simply decide to trust him and follow him back to the meeting room and sit in my place for the third time today.

"I have an idea," he says, to everyone's intrigued expressions. "Her problem is the media exposure that comes with being selected for this contest. If we simply announce the winners' names, that asshole Brad will post all the pictures he wants of her from when she was fifteen because we don't have any way to stop him. But we can anticipate it by showing what Lilly can do—to a huge audience. When they see her talent, people will get that Brad is nothing but a jealous asshole who has nothing in his hands but old photos. Because in reality, he has no contact with this Lilly, with the one we know now. We could make a video all together, the two bands, and highlight her, so the positive noise will drown out the voice of this Brad guy."

I'm stunned by his proposal. "I thought you were the smartest of the four, but clearly, I was wrong. What the hell is it that you don't understand? I can't handle the pressure of media exposure."

"The Jailbirds will front the whole thing. They'll expose themselves for you, and their opinion counts a lot more than someone who has nothing going for him but a few followers," Evan says as if caught by a sudden flash of lightning, the brilliant idea that turns both my and Damian's head towards him.

"Are you fucking nuts?" Damian goes off, and this time I can't blame him. "We put our reputation on the line for strangers?"

"Damian, the reputation you have right now is you sticking your tongue in three girls' mouths. Do you really think it could get any worse?" Evan looks him in the eye.

Thomas chimes in: "Yeah, that would be perfect. Let's pick a song that showcases Lilly, as well as Luke's voice, and we'll add our stage presence, our fame, to the performance. She'll feel less eyeballed, sharing the attention between the three, and the audience's opinion will be what we want it to be. I've heard her do a version of 'Jude' that even we couldn't dream of doing."

Everyone smiles except me and Damian.

"For sure! We even recorded it one day in the rehearsal room," Luke adds, pulling out his phone and playing the song while I punch him in the ribs.

They all seem riveted by my voice. Even Damian seems surprised by my singing skills. Conflicting feelings are triggering inside my chest. I feel proud and also overwhelmed by the fear of the battle I'm about to lose.

"We could do the acoustic version of 'Two Hearts' in the recording studio," Evan continues. "The song is about a woman torn between two men. Damian and Luke share the verses while Lilly sings the chorus. If we start now, we can get it done before dark and upload the video with the announcement tomorrow morning as promised." He finishes as if he's just snagged the deal of the century.

Everybody seems excited. Only Damian and I sit in our chairs looking like witches about to be burned at the stake. "No one wants to hear my opinion even though you're planning something I mainly have to do?" he thunders furiously.

"You screwed up, you pay the consequences," Evan shuts him up by pointing the finger at him.

"I have no idea why he should be punished, but why do I have to get involved?" I ask, astonished.

"Please. This is gonna be fun. And we can start getting to know each other musically with no stage pressure," Luke begs me.

I can see the desperation in his eyes. He's trying to convince me to give this a chance. I think back to the conversation we had the night we submitted to the competition, on the roof of our rehearsal room. I recall his dreams being far less frivolous than just getting easy fucks, and I feel the guilt hurling at me and making me give in.

"By doing this, we can also get a feel for how the audience will react to this novelty without succumbing to the pressure of a live show," Even urges when he sees me surrender.

"Okay," I hear myself whisper.

"I'll tell Jordan to come to recording room four right now and bring one of the guys downstairs with the camera." Evan gets up and walks out of the room like a speeding bullet, maybe for fear I'll change my mind.

The others seem thrilled by what's going on, but I can't hear a single word. My brain is focusing on everything that can go wrong. I can feel Luke's arms wrapping around me from behind.

"Everything's gonna be okay," he whispers in my ear as we walk down the hall to the recording studio where Evan's already got the stools set up. On the other side, the sound engineer, Jordan, is adjusting the mixer.

I can't answer him because of the knot in my stomach when they make me sit between Damian and Luke: the devil and the holy water. I have the impression that this choice is not random. The contrast between Luke's angelic face and Damian's sinful one seems almost planned on a drawing board. Me in the middle pretending to be indecisive between the two. What could possibly go wrong? Everything. But when Michael, Martin, and Simon start to accompany us on guitar while Taylor and Thomas add percussion, everything changes.

Music is my love. While with Luke I can sing naturally and on key, given the years of practice we have behind us, I feel my legs shaking when it comes to Damian's part. He is a colossal asshole when he's off stage, but when you're in the middle of his song, everything else disappears. His eyes, like magnets, draw me. His rough and sensual voice caresses my skin, making me shiver. I forget the discussion we just had, the anger. I even forget to breathe. Singing with him is like making love without needing to touch each other. I find it extremely difficult to look away from him to Luke, who sings the next verse.

My friend's eyes are sweet, in stark contrast to the sensual charge that Damian exudes, and when the song ends, and the heroine chooses the beautiful and damned, I can understand why. My body is a river of hot lava flowing under my skin, my heart pumps into my chest, and the excitement makes my head light.

Damian is staring at me as if we were alone in this room, the coldness he's shown so far dissolved in a sensual, almost animalistic heat. I feel like the prey unable to escape the predator who wants to play with his dinner. My eyes slide down to his slightly open lips, and I struggle to shake off the desire to discover how they would feel on my skin while he kisses my neck. When I lift my eyes back to his, the lust I see almost makes me moan.

Damian is short of breath, and a slight smile curls one side of his mouth as if challenging me, inviting me to taste his lips like a forbidden fruit. Instinctively, I lick mine as if with that gesture I could taste him. His eyes follow my tongue and then up again to mine, nailing me to the spot with clear and irrepressible desire.

I'm panting. Damian didn't even touch me, and I'm short of breath as though recovering from an orgasm after a night of wild sex. All he had to do was use that hoarse voice, the one that makes you vibrate all the way down to your insides. That same sensual charge he puts out on stage has me at his feet, right here and now. I'm embarrassed by my lack of control.

"Okay, we'll do it a couple more times to make sure we have enough material to edit, but please don't let go of the energy of this first version." Evan's voice sounds metallic through the microphone on the other side of the glass, bringing us back to reality.

It takes us at least three hours to finish the recordings. Evan makes us all play together because he wants the result not to be perfect, but to look like stolen moments during our initial meeting. I'm exhausted when we finally get our jackets and leave the building that has made us the heroes of one of the most surreal days of our lives.

This morning I woke up convinced that I would never, ever accept a contract with them, now I find myself with a pile of papers to read and a series of signatures to fill out. I had planned not to be persuaded for any reason in the world, not even by the begging faces of my friends.

Precisely what went wrong?

CHAPTER 5

Damian

I walk into Evan's office, and, by the time I see them all sitting there with a thirty-two-tooth smile on their faces, I realize my day's off to a bad start. I already had my suspicions when our manager called and said I had to show up at the office to discuss the Red Velvet Curtains' tour.

"Did you see that? In less than twenty-four hours, we have over five hundred thousand views and thousands of messages." Evan looks overhyped like he's been doing coke. If I wasn't sure he's not on drugs, I'd tell him to go home and sleep it off.

"No, I'm not glued to the internet like you. I have a life." Considering I spent the evening watching a TV show on Netflix, I wouldn't consider it too exciting, but they don't need to know that. The truth is, I purposely avoided the damn video because I'm bothered by the media spectacle they're creating around us.

"Apparently, you and Lilly are the new golden couple of music," giggles Michael, making fun of me while I give him the stink eye. He loves to tease me.

I sit on the free chair and wait for our manager to explain what Michael just said. I suspect it has something to do with the comments he mentioned earlier.

"People are crazy about the video. They already love the Red Velvet Curtains, but mostly they love the chemistry between you and Lilly."

I look at him thoughtfully, with a wrinkle on my forehead. "Chemistry? There's no chemistry between her and me, how the hell did you edit the video?" Maybe I should have watched it and approved it before it got published.

"I can guarantee you there's nothing fake about it. It looked like you guys were gonna get laid any minute. She was out of breath at the end of the song, it was like she had an orgasm just looking at you." Thomas continues teasing me in that smart-ass tone that pisses me off. I can't stand it when he makes me feel like an idiot because I can't understand something he clearly sees as the absolute truth.

"We've decided to ride the wave of this contest's success and get you gigs in small clubs here in Manhattan. Like exclusive VIP parties or meet and greets, so you and Lilly can sing a few songs alone."

Everyone's smiling at this idiotic proposal. Am I the only one who doesn't see anything good in it? "What the hell are you thinking?" I blurt out angrily.

Evan comes over, puts his hand on my shoulder, and pushes me back into the chair. He points a finger in my face. "Do you have any idea how famous those kids are gonna be? I haven't felt this way since I first set eyes on the four of you. I'm not gonna pass up an opportunity like this just because you're acting out. You love being on stage with just your acoustic guitar, now you're just acting like a spoiled brat because you want to bust my balls."

How is it possible that I still feel like a rookie when dealing with him after all these years? Actually, he's right, I love my job, but what bothers me is that I have to take the girl along. I don't play with kids, even if they're good. Damn it. I hate it when I feel indebted to our manager. When it's not just work anymore, but when the whole personal sphere of feelings that's been bonding us for years comes into play. He's been like a father to us, even though he's only a few years older. He was our guide from the streets to world success, he kicked our butts when we deserved it, and rewarded us when we did well; I'm screwed.

"You guys realize we're not a boy band, right? We don't do intimate, acoustic gigs." I cling to any handhold to get out alive.

Thomas bursts out laughing, and I give him an incinerating look but he doesn't seem to care.

"You're just pissed off because she's a straight shooter even in front of us. I saw you fucking her with your eyes, and don't tell me you didn't get a hard-on when you heard her standing up to you," he says, amused amid the laughter of the other two traitors.

I didn't think my attraction to her was so obvious. It destabilized me and fucked up my proverbial coldness.

"And you want to give me an 'intimate' tour with someone I'd like to fuck? How would that be a good idea? On what planet?"

Thomas bursts out laughing, throwing his head back, and making my blood boil. "Trust me, you're gonna have to sweat it out to get between her legs. She's not gonna open them just because she's looking at Damian the rock star."

"How the hell do you know that?" The annoyance in my voice makes me angrier than before. This day started off badly, and it's getting worse.

"Because in the five minutes that I've talked to her face to face, I realized she can easily grab you by the balls and bring you to your knees if you piss her off." He raises an eyebrow, challenging me to answer back.

I have nothing to say about that. She seemed like someone who doesn't let herself be too intimidated by others, but I don't know her well enough to confirm or deny what Thomas said. I breathe deeply and try to calm myself down because I cannot escape what seems to be my death sentence. The fuckboy reputation I have contradicts the weak excuse I found to argue against the idea of concerts around the city.

"Another reason why we have to do this winter mini-tour is that they have never left the clubs in Brooklyn. We can't put them on arena or stadium stages without first preparing them, letting them get used to it. They'd be overwhelmed at the first concert," Evan admits. It's obvious he's got it all figured out from here to the end of the summer tour.

"This is a bad, bad idea, and I'm sure we'll all regret it," I say as the others look at me with a half-smile and I give up. Bastards. "Have you even told them? The girl didn't seem very keen on the tour. What if she just quits, out of the blue?"

"Of course we told them, and they're thrilled. There's a lot more positive than negative comments about Lilly, and a lot of your fans have been commenting under that asshole Brad's post. They've been slaughtering him, defending Lilly. She was relieved when I pointed it out."

"Good," I grumble since it was my last attempt to get out of it.

"By the way, you and Lilly have some songs to prepare acoustically while the rest of you come to the studio and rehearse the songs you're gonna do together."

"Awesome." A desperate sigh passes from me as I run my hand over my face. Not that I have a lot of options at this point.

*

I park under the building at the address Evan gave me and look around, taking off my helmet and putting up the hood of my sweatshirt to try and keep a low profile. If we're gonna do this thing, I want it done on my own terms, without cars with tinted windows attracting paparazzi attention in Brooklyn. I sent Max in my car a half hour earlier so I could sneak past the ones staked out at my house, and then I grabbed my bike from the garage a block away.

I look at the building in front of me, six stories high and impersonal as most buildings in this neighborhood. I approach the front door and find myself in front of twenty-four different buzzers.

"It's a rat trap," I observe. There are four apartments per floor, while I have a private elevator that goes directly into my penthouse in Tribeca. Immediately I see the difference between Manhattan and Brooklyn, the former with its manicured buildings, doorman, and security who opens doors before you even make a gesture, the renovated, clean apartments. And here, with the plasterwork coming off the outside walls, moldy stains under the cornices, and fewer people walking on the sidewalks. Paradoxically, I feel more related to this neighborhood than to the one I live in.

I ring the buzzer but get no answer. I'm almost about to do it again when the metallic noise of the door lock clicking makes me move sideways. I see Lilly coming out, tucked into a jacket bigger than her, the hood of the sweatshirt covering her head, glasses on her nose, and a classical guitar case on her shoulders. She looks at me with those big green eyes and seems almost pouty. What the hell did I do to deserve such a pain in the ass on a Monday morning?

A middle-aged woman walking on the sidewalk across from us checks me out head to toe and keeps on walking, ignoring Lilly. She smiles and winks at me. I respond with my classic conquering smile, she passes us and turns once more while I appreciate her gorgeous ass, then continues on her way. It's something that often happens. I respond to peculiar attitudes as if on autopilot. It comes naturally to me after years of having women blatantly appreciate my physical appearance. It's part of my character.

When I look at Lilly again, she rolls her eyes, pissed off. I admit that my behavior wasn't classy, but I didn't kill anyone. She doesn't have to act so disgusted.

"Let's go," I say without even saying hello since she doesn't seem too happy to see me.

I approach my bike and grab the second helmet.

"You're out of your mind if you think I'm gonna ride off with you on that hunk of junk."

I turn around, annoyed, and find her with her arms crossed over her chest, and a face halfway between pouty and disbelief. She'd be hot as hell if it weren't for the fact that she is a pain in the ass every time she opens her mouth. I had no idea a woman could get on my nerves like that.

"What is wrong with you? Are you always this sour, or is this special treatment only for me?"

"You're the one who picked me up with this infernal contraption. You could have used a car or the subway like all mortals do. Do you always have to be a diva?"

I inhale deeply to ease my anger. You can tell me anything, but not that I'm a diva. She doesn't even know me. "Have you thought about what would happen if I took the subway here? How long do you think it would be before I'd be recognized and swarmed for a selfie or an autograph?" I try to be mature instead of sarcastic.

"Put on a hat and glasses; don't you think there are other guys like you around Manhattan?" she says, raising an angry eyebrow.

I doubt many people have a picture of their face covering an entire building in Times Square, but I appreciate that she sees me as an average person who could take the subway with a cap on his head. Usually, women expect nothing less from me than a limo to drive them around.

"It's either this or nothing," I say as I come closer. Lilly is really short. She barely reaches my chest.

"Yeah, right," she looks at me sarcastically with a sneer.

"Look, don't make me be the guy who needs to remind that you signed a contract, and you have to respect it." I'm so mad I don't even know what I'm saying. She's getting deeper under my skin.

"I haven't signed anything that forces me to get on a motor-cycle," she explains as if I were a child. What does she take me for? A guy with his brain in a jar of alcohol on his nightstand?

"Look, this is what I'm picking you up with, whether you like it or not."

"Can't you give me the address so I can catch up to you?" she proposes with a little composure.

"No! I'm not giving you my home address so you can pass it on to your friends," I reply, annoyed.

She studies me for a few seconds with her mouth slightly open, as if she were shocked by my words. It wasn't my most brilliant argument, but she could avoid treating me like an idiot.

"What do you take me for? An idiot? You don't think I can just look at the road you're on or out your window to see where you've taken me? You think I don't know what New York looks like? Even someone who's never been here would recognize it," she says.

She's right, but I don't want to explain to her that on the bike I can outrun the paparazzi better if I need to. I don't want to stand here arguing about my personal life, and that's it.

"Look, I'll call Evan and tell him you're playing hard to get and that we're done." I turn around and grab my phone, know-ing my manager will kick my ass if I call him about something like this.

"Hold on, hold on. Give me that helmet. And go slow, I got a guitar on my shoulders."

Jesus Christ, if I'd known all I had to do was mention Evan, I'd have done it right away. I get on the bike, wait for her to get behind me, and only when I put the helmet on do I allow myself to part my lips and form a smile. She will pay for this, this pain in the ass, making me this nervous early in the morning.

The trip to Tribeca is a series of zigzags between the cars, accelerations in passing, driving very fast, and Lilly's fists stuck in my ribs. Her frightened screams are music to my ears. Now I'm sure she won't want to ride with me anymore, but I had a lot of fun making her pay for her impertinent tongue.

I enjoy the view of the typical red brick buildings renovated with a modern touch of my neighborhood, the trendy cafes, and high-class pastries' aroma. The sidewalks are a bustle of people walking at a fast pace, men in suits swearing in a low voice as they try to get past slow tourists with their noses in the air. Manhattan is like this, a jumble of people who have the most different stories and backgrounds, but who live on the same piece of concrete. It's a unique place in the world, and I love it for that.

"You're crazy, asshole!" she yells as she gets off the bike in the garage.

I'm giggling, amused, as I take the helmet from her hands. "You survived, didn't you? I wouldn't complain if I were you," I joke, while opening a door at the bottom of the building that allows me to cross the block through a series of corridors that allow me to move without having to go up to the street.

Lilly follows me without opening her mouth, struggling to keep up with my long strides. I don't slow down; I don't think she'd appreciate being treated differently because she's a woman. On the contrary, I think she'd bite my throat just for insinuating that she's the weaker sex. I type the personal code for the elevator, and notice she turns her head so that I can avoid the embarrassment of covering the keyboard with the other hand.

We get to my floor and the doors open onto the entrance to the living room. Her eyes and mouth are wide open in shock at the city's spectacle and the East River view through the windows covering two sides of the apartment. It's what made me fall in love with this place the first time I entered it. It wasn't so much the white marble floor or the two big sofas of the same color that fill the living room; it's what you see beyond the windows.

Like a curious child, she approaches the windows and admires the view, then looks down and struggles to hold back the surprise when she realizes where we are.

"But...we're parked under that building," she points her finger in the direction of the garage before turning towards me.

I put the helmets in the closet next to the front door and join her in front of the window. "The underground car park is there," I confirm.

"But...why is that? I mean, isn't it more practical to park down here?" Her curiosity is genuine.

I don't know if it was the fear of riding a motorbike or the novelty of the environment she's in but Lilly has put aside her resentment and I appreciate it, because I really don't have the patience to argue for the rest of the day. I shrug my shoulders and sit on the leather sofa on the other end of the window.

"The paparazzi know where I live. If I want to get in and out of the house without being seen, I have to do it from a doorway that isn't obvious. If I'd given you my address and walked in the front door, you'd be all over the nation's gossip columns. It's not normal for the girl in the band that won the contest to spend the day at the house of the singer of the band that organized it. Tomorrow morning you would have been assaulted by photographers in front of your house," I explain to her when I see the sympathy on her face. Thomas is right. She's bright, even if she's trying not to be noticed and stay out of sight in front of people.

She sits next to me, leaning her guitar on the white carpet under our feet and looking straight into my eyes. "Is this really your life? You can't even leave the house without someone trying to take pictures or follow you?" It almost sounds like there's concern in her voice.

This is the first time a woman has asked me that question. Usually, the ones I meet are drawn to the spotlight. They can't wait to make the front page of the newspaper for their fifteen minutes of fame. On the other hand, Lilly seems genuinely interested in understanding what my life is like, rather than finding out how to be a part of it.

I shrug my shoulders; I don't know what to tell her. My life sucked until I achieved fame. Anything is better than going back to living like I did before, in the crap Evan pulled me out of.

"Fame allows me to have this," I say to her, raising my hand, indicating my surroundings. "I'm willing to pay a small price for what I've earned," I tell her honestly. I just have to be grateful to this life for getting me out of poverty.

"It's not a small price if it takes away a little bit of your freedom every time." The look in her eyes makes me hold my breath. I can't lie to her, I can't get away with a joke, she doesn't fall for my bullshit like everyone else. She sees past my words. She gets right to the point, like at Evan's office the first day we met.

"It's not like they're putting me on house arrest. I just have to be a little more careful when I go out." I play it down, embarrassed.

She stares into my eyes, looking deep in thought. When she's not frightened or defensive, she's someone who gives herself time to think, to give weight to her words. "And when they won't stop at the doorstep anymore? How much will you be willing to give them? When will it be too much for you, when will it be time to say enough? Where's the limit to your fame, Damian?"

I've known her for less than a week, and her words come in like a hurricane, messing up my chest. I feel naked in the face of her honesty. For the first time in my life, a woman has totally disregarded the rockstar facade and sunk the blade into the man's chest behind it. She can't know that there will never be any feeling someone can put a leash on. But there is a limit, even for someone like me.

"When I can no longer play the music I want... That's my limit."

She stares at me with a stern look for what seems like an eternity, and I hold my breath as if I'm waiting for a verdict. Strange as it may seem to me too, I find myself wishing I'd given the right answer, the one that wouldn't disappoint her, because this was by far the most honest conversation I've ever had with a woman, and it was liberating.

She nods, holding a smile when a message on my cell phone breaks an almost electric moment of tension on this couch. "Fame must also allow you to afford a big fat heating bill. It's ridiculously hot in here," she says, erasing the seriousness of before.

I burst out laughing.

"I like to be comfortable and barefoot when I'm in the house," I explain as I get off the couch. "You make yourself comfortable, I'm going to take off these shoes. They're killing me."

I go put on a pair of tracksuit pants and a light T-shirt. When I go back to the living room, the spectacle in front of me immediately makes me regret not having worn a pair of boxer shorts, since blood directly flows in places that should be dry in such a situation. Lilly is sitting cross-legged on the carpet, barefoot, holding the guitar and playing it, down to just a pair of jeans and a white tank top that clings to her small yet well-proportioned physique. It seems almost impossible that she is the same person as in the photos she showed us. Lilly must have struggled a lot to lose all that weight, and, if I were in her place, I would show the whole world the result. Why is she hiding that body under her giant sweaters?

She's gathered her hair in a loose bun on her head, held in place by a simple pencil. The light coming in through the windows next to her underlines her slender neck covered in pale skin. With those enormous glasses that particularly suit her, she looks like something straight out of a man's naughty fantasies: the perfect mixture of intelligence and sexiness that makes my blood flow from my brain to my pelvis in less than zero seconds.

I have a hard time putting myself back together, but I move in closer, grabbing my guitar next to the sofa, and sit in the armchair next to her. I hold the instrument more to cover my semi-erection than to really play something.

"How do you want to start?" she asks with a sincere smile, losing her sarcasm in favor of something that clearly makes her feel good: playing music.

"Do you want us to try a version of 'Jude'?" I ask, since I already know what style she does the song in.

She giggles, amused, and her cheerful reaction floors me. It's the first time I've heard her laugh at something I say, at ease in my presence. "Aren't you tired of hearing it?" she asks, cheered by my proposal.

I start laughing too. "You have no idea, I swear. But the version you do has nothing to do with the original. I wish I'd written it myself." I sincerely admit it.

She tilts her head to the side, showing the details in her neck that I can't take my eyes off. She studies me for a few seconds. "But you wrote it."

The naivety that transpires from her observation makes my eyes dart towards hers and lose myself in their intense green. I need to answer, but my mouth goes suddenly dry. "The interpretation you give it, as if it were a letter you recite to someone, sweet and at the same time desperate, makes it sound like a completely different song."

She nods without speaking, as if that explanation is enough; as if I'm worthy enough for her to accept the clarification as absolute truth. Her eyes linger on mine long enough for me to realize that she sees me, for real, not the glossy rock star facade. It's a new sensation that makes me feel significant but not in the flattering way I'm used to. It makes me feel like a real person, which has never happened to me outside my close circle of friends.

Luckily, she starts playing the first chords and singing, leaving me the space to concentrate on our rehearsals, so I join her voice in harmony. It's something that goes beyond any experience I've ever had, any duet I've ever had with more or less famous singers. Her melodious and clean voice matches with mine, a hoarser and dirtier voice, but it's not so much a matter of technique, which she has mastered, it's a matter of tuning that makes the air between us almost electric. At this moment, with our voices fitting perfectly and our eyes not letting go for a moment, I realize I'm fucked.

CHAPTER 6
Lilly

If I think back to how I saw Damian's existence until two weeks ago, it was like scenes in a movie: parties, models, concerts, glossy magazines—a fairy-tale life. Playing with him every day in preparation for shows, I discovered him to be professional, meticulous, and sometimes perfectionist to the point of exhaustion. Working with him is a continuous cycle of rehearsing songs and getting the stage training our young band lacks.

It isn't enough for Damian to see me perform a song perfectly. He wants me to be able to control any unexpected stage problems without panicking. Until now, playing in small venues in Brooklyn, we never needed fancy equipment; just our instruments, sometimes amps if we didn't already have them at the venue, nothing else. We had never tried, for example, to play with earphones when the acoustics on stage are not the best. Concert venues are designed to sound great for the audience, not on the stage, so musicians have to wear earphones that allow them to hear what they are playing. It's a strange feeling to get used to, listening to yourself through earpieces rather than your surroundings, and I'm grateful to Damian for letting me try it before the show.

When Damian stops acting like a rock star and more like a professional, the days have a tight rhythm in which we try a lot and chat little. He's a guy who gives orders with an authority that often makes me flush. He's sexy as hell when he demands that you try the song again because, in the last verse, we still haven't found the right interpretation. He's a person who leaves nothing to chance.

I understand why they've reached such high rockstar status: they're not just gifted with uncommon skill and charisma, they also work without ever taking a break, without ever feeling they've arrived, always trying to improve and without taking their success for granted. It's what has kept them on top for years.

I have to admit that if I've grown more professionally in these fifteen days than in the twenty years I have been alive, I've also tripled my daily dose of coffee. Despite Damian's reproaches, I do it to stay focused when fatigue takes over. Damian, on the other hand, is a fervent supporter of supplements and physical activity. His theory is that by filling up with vitamins, combined with serotonin produced during exercise, your body can withstand greater stress loads without giving in. Being around him has made me aware of more varieties of vitamin B than a scientific documentary could cover. I was naïve to think that rock stars only preferred illegal drugs!

Honestly, when he explains the benefits of serotonin produced during physical training, my mind goes to only one exercise with him. The image my brain conjures is so naughty I blush hard and can't hide it. When he goes on to say, with that full laugh of his, that it's called the "good mood hormone,"

I'm certain that I would wake up with a smile from ear to ear after a night between the sheets with him.

Today, however, I've been waiting for Damian to pick me up like he has every day for two weeks, but in a different mood. By now, it has become customary for me to drive up to the garage a block away from his apartment and send him a message. I usually enjoy taking different routes to confuse the paparazzi or die-hard fans. I've learned that when he wants to let it be known that he's not home, he goes straight out with the driver, Max, from the underground parking lot under his apartment with the tinted windows.

I took the direct route, hiding inside my scarf pulled up to my eyes, my cap to cover me from the freezing wind and icy weather that has been blowing over New York City since the other night. It's a clear sign from the universe telling me that today I should have stayed at home, wrapped in my duvet, with a hot chocolate in my hands and a good book to read. I shouldn't have even tried to walk the streets of Manhattan. But tonight is the first concert, and I already have anxiety early in the morning.

"Where the hell did you come from? Alaska?" Damian asks when he approaches me in the garage corridor in a T-shirt, jeans, and sweatshirt.

"I don't know if you've noticed, from inside the tropical climate that is your apartment, but we common mortals have to cover ourselves so we don't die of pneumonia," I answer sharply. I make him move by placing my hand on his toned belly and I imagine my tongue going through every single inch of those well-outlined abs. I feel the heat pervading my lower abdomen at the mere thought, and curse myself for my weakness.

More than once, while rehearsing together, I peeked at that area of skin his shirt sometimes leaves uncovered. I admired the well-defined muscles you feel like touching, running your fingers lower to caress the dark hair that descends from the navel until it disappears under the belt of his pants. They call it "happy trail," and I'd be thrilled to find out where it goes, mostly because I'm sure he doesn't wear boxer shorts and, when he isn't paying attention to how he sits, the thin fabric of his sweatpants leaves little to the imagination. On more than one occasion, I had to make an effort to look away and put aside the incredibly dirty fantasies of him lying naked on that damn white sofa with me on top of him. Before I started working with Damian I restrained myself and kept a professional attitude. But hell, not even a cloistered nun could be indifferent to what I see now.

He gives me an amused look as he comes closer towards me down the hallway.

"What did you have for breakfast this morning? Sour cream?"

"I'd say yes if I could swallow anything without it making me sick," I admit honestly. He might as well know what he's getting into right now.

Damian grabs my wrist, making me turn towards him, then holds onto my shoulders and forces me to raise my eyes to his and lose myself in his intensity.

"Are you nervous about tonight?" he asks me so seriously it almost makes my legs shake.

"That's the whole point, isn't it? Me freaking out before a concert, and you babysitting me, so I don't run off to another continent," I say with some sarcasm in my voice, not enough to cover my terror. What bothers me the most is that getting on stage has always been an immense pleasure for me, a safe haven where I can be myself. I've always felt strong up there. Now Brad's taking that away from me, and all because we won this damn contest.

Damian studies me for a while, then takes me by the hand, sending a pleasant jolt through my body until it reaches the center of my stomach and almost makes me waver. I hate how he manages to turn everything upside down with the simplest physical contact between us.

"You don't need a nurse, trust me," he says with a half-smile as he drags me to the elevator.

I look at him out of the corner of my eye and try to understand what he's really thinking. Sometimes, when I think I've finally got him in my sights, he bewilders me with a sarcastic joke, or he totally clams up. "You mean I need a prince charming to come and save me?"

If there's one thing I've realized during the hours we've spent together recently, it's that we can talk about anything but his past and the fact that he's never had a woman for more than one night.

Damian laughs, filling the elevator with that big voice of his. "You don't need a prince charming, trust me. In the fairytale, you'd be the ball-busting dragon protecting the princess's tower. You spend your life giving anyone you don't think is worthy of your presence a hard time. You're a pain in the ass for any prince who would want to get anywhere near that tower. You're the one to kill, not save."

A half-smile appears on my lips. In a slightly complicated way, he managed to describe me impeccably: an independent woman who is far too proud to ask others for help.

"And who are you supposed to be? Prince Charming?" I ask him with a smile.

"There's nothing princely about me, trust me." He gives me a grim look.

"That's right, sorry, you're the bad boy who breaks hearts left and right. I forgot." I raise an amused eyebrow.

He doesn't answer me and sets his jaw, looking annoyed—like every time I prick him on a subject he doesn't like to deal with. "How touchy you are. I forgot that with you, it's only possible to talk about the weather or the job, at the most," I whisper with a little pout.

Damian looks down and eases the tension. He seems almost guilty for making the atmosphere less pleasant. "Given how much alcohol I drink, I could be a pirate," he adds after a moment of silence, with a half-grin on his lips and without looking me in the eye.

The smile reappears on my face. I appreciate the effort even though I brought up a subject Damian doesn't like to talk about. I don't have time to argue because the elevator bell announces that we have arrived at his floor, and when the doors open, it looks like a hurricane hit the living room.

"Are you changing your wardrobe?" I ask, considering an endless line of clothes is lined up in his living room.

Damian rolls his eyes and pushes me by my shoulders towards them. "They're for you, genius. Evan sent the stylist to give you a new look for tonight. You can't show up in sweat-shirts three sizes too big," he says, amused.

"Why not?" I ask, outraged. There's never been any talk of changing my wardrobe, especially not with something that looks like a miniskirt, or a belt, given the size, in leopard print, that I immediately put back where I found it.

"Because, darling, you're going to have to turn the heads of all the men in the room. They must want to take you to bed but think they can't because you're completely out of their league. You have to make them orgasm into those thousand-dollar suits." A voice I don't know makes me turn to the hallway where a tall, skinny, young man dressed in a flashy shirt comes towards me hugging me as if we've known each other forever.

His sweet perfume suffocates me, but it's his stiletto heels that grab my attention. How the hell can he walk on those stilts and look so sinuous and ethereal? He looks like he stepped off a catwalk, and I envy his gait in shoes that I can't even look at without tripping.

"I signed the contract to sing, not to prostitute myself," I point out, crossing my arms to my chest. Every second I'm getting more and more uncomfortable. I don't want to squeeze myself in a dress, I've never done it, and I get nauseous just thinking about showing off pieces of my body. Do they have any idea how much working out I'd have to do to wear a mini-skirt? What's not clear to Evan and the others? I don't want media attention on me! That's what scares me the most.

I notice Damian snickering as he turns his back on me and walks into the kitchen.

"Traitor. You're supposed to be on my side, not abandon me to the enemy," I yell as he laughs and sits at the kitchen counter with his computer, showing me his back.

"You want me to stand there and watch you undress? If those are your intentions, Lilly, just ask, and we can do it as often as you want without witnesses." He winks at me, looking over his shoulder. A gesture that makes me loosen up more than I have to.

I feel hot and I know I'm blushing violently. I open my mouth a couple of times, trying to get a sarcastic response out, but my brain can't focus on anything other than his words. Did he really just say he'd like to see me naked?

"Don't worry, we've all been through hot flashes over that one. Trust me, I'd like to do him on every surface of this apartment, too," the guy whispers in my ear as he hands me a skirt and a top.

"I can hear you, Sid," laughs Damian, amused without turning around.

"It's no mystery to anyone that I'd like to fuck you, sweetheart," he jokes, pointing to a screen I should hide behind to change. Too bad it only shields me from the people inside this apartment and not from the rest of New York that stretches behind me through the windows. Great.

"Honestly? If only I could put a gag on him. He gets on my nerves nine times out of ten," I find myself answering Sid.

"You like bondage. I thought you were a prude, but you do love extreme sex," he replies, in a conspiratorial and almost-impressed tone.

"I've actually thought about tying him up several times,

but not why you think. Sometimes it's the only way to keep him quiet. You know how annoying he is when he doesn't like something you do?" I answer from behind the screen.

This conversation is getting surreal, and fitting into the clothes Sid gave me isn't helping.

"Oh, no, honey, you've got to take that bra off," he says to me as I reappear behind the screen, trying to see in the mirror as I'm leaning against the glass next to me.

"Without a bra?" I ask incredulously. "This tank top is so see-through you can see my nipples! And this thing?" I point to the back of the thin layer of fabric that can't be called a skirt. "They can give me a colonoscopy looking up at me from under the stage." What I want to say is: *Don't you realize it doesn't even cover those damn stretch marks on my thighs that relentlessly remind me of the days when I couldn't even get into a pair of jeans or had trouble bending down to tie my shoes? Do you really want to show everyone that my inner thighs still touch when I walk, even if I kill myself running every day?*

The disappointment in my voice draws Damian over to the couch where he sits with wide eyes a few steps away from me. "No, I'm not gonna be able to keep the crazies away if you make her dress like that. I'll have to carry her off the stage," he says, searching every single inch of my body with such intensity I feel like I'm bursting into flames.

Of course, if he looks at me like that, I might think about wearing a miniskirt, maybe in private, just for him.

Sid rolls his green eyes and takes a pair of leather trousers and a bodice in the same fabric from the rack. "How puritanical you Americans are," he says in his British accent.

"It's not a matter of being puritanical. It's just the fact that that stuff doesn't even cover the minimum necessary to achieve decency," laughs Damian as he makes himself at home on that couch, making me feel embarrassed at the very idea of parading in front of him in different clothes.

I squeeze into my pants and the leather bodice that wretched Sid gave me, and I can hardly breathe. All I need is Damian's wide eyes and a quick look in the mirror to understand that tonight I won't be walking around like this. You can see my belly swelling and my stomach about to explode. I knew I shouldn't have eaten the muffin my mother gave me last night; if only I'd run those extra two miles instead of going back at the first hint of fatigue. What's a little leg burn? I would have avoided looking like a barrel today.

"Sid, honey, I can see the shape of my vagina, and my breasts are so high it looks like my tonsils are inflamed," I angrily hiss.

I do not like this stylist thing at all. Can't I just pick something comfortable out of the closet and let this charade end? Brad will have a field day if I show up in such an outlandish outfit.

"Damian, please, can you say something?" I turn to him, but I find him with his mouth half-open and a look that screams, "If you come near me, I'll bite your clothes off." Okay, apparently, I have an effect on him, too. "Damian, my face is up here," I say to him, pointing at my face, but I can't get his eyes off my breasts.

Right now, I wish the stylist wasn't in this room. Being looked at like that makes me forget to breathe, and if we were alone, I would probably give in to the desire of letting him take my clothes off.

"Look, Sid, why don't you let her choose something she's comfortable with?" he asks, looking at me, not giving the guy an ounce of attention and making me feel more naked than I did behind that screen.

"So, it's like that with you guys, always picking what you want without ever hearing my opinion?" Sid whines, falling down on the couch next to Damian in a melodramatic way.

"Lilly, try to put on something that isn't four sizes too big, okay?" Damian begs me with a half-smile.

I roll my eyes and realize that to quickly get out of this situation, all I have to do is opt for something that covers enough and doesn't make me look dressed in a burlap sack. I grab a pair of jeans and a T-shirt, and I hear Sid groaning in pain as if I've stabbed him and let him bleed to death while Damian laughs.

I come out from behind the screen and, while I look in the mirror, I hear Sid's disappointed comments. As for me, I'd prefer the jeans to fall more softly, so as not to bring too much attention to my wide hips. The shirt should be longer to cover my big butt and the top of the jeans are a bit too tight on my belly. At least the t-shirt it's wide enough not to show too much breast and arms.

"No, absolutely not. Get rid of that t-shirt now." Sid gets up and grabs the white, broad, lightweight tank top I wore at the beginning, along with a black bandeau top that should cover the rougher parts. I wear what he proposes and, when I come out, I can say I'm quite satisfied. I still feel a bit too naked for my taste, but the top covers precisely what it needs to, so as not to make me look like a prostitute. It's soft and doesn't hug my shape, and I have the perfect sweatshirt to put on over it, but Sid doesn't need to know that.

"Do I have your approval?" I finally turn to them, and I can tell by the look of relief on their faces that it passes. Sid's not smiling like Damian, but at least he's not having a nervous breakdown. I interpret it as a sign of approval.

It takes Sid almost half an hour to clear out the apartment, with the added threat of going to the concert venue that evening to do my makeup and hair. Which makes me fear the worst.

"Is it always going to be like this from now on?" I ask Damian. I'm sitting exhausted on the stool at the kitchen bar while I watch him pull the pots and pans out of the cupboard.

The kitchen mirrors the rest of the apartment I have seen: the white lacquered furniture stretches all around the wall, and opposite it, there is a massive island with a white Carrara marble top with a few grey veins, which looks like it costs as much as my entire Brooklyn apartment.

"You'll feel more comfortable when Sid figures out what you like. Imagine, from the moment I met him, he wanted to get me on stage with a pair of leather pants and a skinny mesh shirt," he laughs as he boils some water and prepares the onion and a drizzle of oil in a pan. My mother has tried countless times to teach me how to cook without ever succeeding. Food and I are not exactly on the best of terms. He's handy with knives, and I watch him cutting and slicing and doing things I don't even know the purpose of.

"Where did you learn to cook?" I ask, intrigued.

I see him letting down his guard a bit, but then he gives me a smile too big to be sincere. "Before embarking on this career, I worked in a...cafeteria," he says hesitantly. "And you're going to experience my fantastic baked pasta today." He smiles his usual smile, which I've learned to recognize as him being proud of something but doesn't want to show it.

"I don't know if it's a good idea to eat. I'll get bloated for sure!" I said, feeling insecure. I mentally calculate how many calories pasta has, and I'm sure I won't be able to get rid of it with a fifteen-mile run.

Damian stops and puts his palms on the counter, making his arms and chest muscles stand out, which makes my lower abdomen tingle. The thoughts that go through my mind for an instant are scandalous, and I find it hard to put my mind back on a Damian who is not naked.

"First rule of when you're on tour: never skip meals. You need all the energy you can muster to not be finished in the second week. The rhythms are exhausting. You are not allowed to be weak because you don't eat properly. If you don't feel like eating just before you go on stage, that's fine, but at least have a bigger meal in the morning or early afternoon," he explains.

His way of doing things is authoritative but also wise. It sounds like he cares about me and what I do when I'm on tour with them. I'm still struggling to come to grips that we, for the Jailbirds, are an investment and that it's in their best interest to make sure we learn the ropes and quickly. In those moments, when I'm with Luke, Taylor, and Martin in the rehearsal room perfecting the pieces we'll do together, we're still incredulous at the luck we've had. We feel like we're living the dream, and it's hard to think that this is really becoming a job.

"Okay, let's try this baked pasta that you claim you know how to make," I joke while watching him tinker with the stove, looking like a Greek god descended to earth to drive us mortals crazy with lust. He grabs the ingredients and puts them on the counter with such confidence it makes me want to be a tomato just to feel those strong, firm fingers on me. I can't help but get lost in the intricate weave of veins that stand out on his arms, potent and virile, imagining how it feels to be wrapped in their warmth. I would transform myself into the very fabric of the t-shirt covering his sculpted pecs if I could be in close contact with his skin.

When I squeeze my thighs to relieve the tingling sensation between my legs, I realize that the path I have to take to get my shit together is still very, very long. He's circling the island to come towards me and I pray he doesn't notice how excited I am. Coming up beside me, he turns the stool towards him and steps between my legs, grabbing a spoonful of the sauce he's cooking.

"Try it and let me know whether it's salty enough or if you prefer it tastier," he whispers, making it the most sensual sentence of the century.

I look at him inebriated as he grabs my chin with two fingers and feeds me with the other hand. At this moment, he could give me a spoonful of hamster food and I would eat it without a second thought. His eyes are full of desire while his thumb wipes a drop of sauce from my lips, which he offers to me to taste directly from his skin. I wrap my lips around his fingertip and lick the sauce off without taking my eyes off his face. Damian follows the movement without breathing, and only when I feel his erection awakening in his pants do I realize how close he is.

"It's tomato," I whisper in a hoarse voice, the breath escaping my lungs with difficulty.

Damian wrinkles his forehead. "I know it's tomato. That's how you make the sauce." He raises an eyebrow, steps away a bit, and lets me breathe. When his hand leaves my face, I almost feel like I've lost a piece of me.

"It's good...it's just salt...I mean, it's okay," I stammer, embarrassed by my inability to formulate a coherent sentence.

His lips are arched in a mischievous smile as he puts the spoon on a plate and lowers himself to look me straight in the eye. "What is it? Are you nervous?"

"No, why should I be nervous?" My thin voice betrays my words.

"I don't know, it's just an impression. I feel like your heart is working overtime." He puts two fingers on my neck to feel my pulse. His touch is so electrifying, a little moan comes out of my throat before I know it. The smile spreads over his lips, and with a slow, calculated gesture, he grazes my cheek with his nose until it reaches my ear.

"Be careful with these noises, or I'll start thinking you like it when I put my hands on you," he whispers as he gently touches the skin of my neck with his thumb.

I have stopped breathing, stopped thinking, I stopped having control over my body. I close my eyes and shamelessly enjoy his proximity. Only when I miss the heat do I open them again and focus on his face, a few steps away from me, with the smug smile and arched eyebrow of someone who has realized he has me.

I purse my lips and turn towards the stove, my cheeks on fire, short of breath. Damian chuckles as he returns to take care of the meal, and I realize that it will be a challenging tour, and not just from a business point of view.

*

I've been locked in the dressing room for at least half an hour since Sid had me change, and did my hair and makeup. I can't go out on stage like this, I can't do it, I can't handle anxiety. You can see everything from my belly to the stretch marks in my arms. You can see my nose is too big without my glasses, and my eyes look like two headlights. I look like one of those dolls with a big head and big eyes.

Not only Brad will notice that, fat or thin, I'll always have flaws, the rest of the world will have something to say about it too. All I have to do is look at how they treat the Jailbirds in the papers; how they point out what's wrong with the models who hang out with them. Models! The ones who eat an extra stalk of celery and the newspapers scream pregnancy. What will they say about me? About my chubby ass and the scars of my struggles with food on display for all to see?

"Lilly, are you in there?" Damian's voice almost makes me gasp. I told Luke I didn't want to see anyone when I kicked them out. He probably thought since I didn't listen to him, he'd give the job to someone who intimidates me.

"If I say no, will you go away?" I whimper.

"No, let me in." His voice is calm but firm. He won't leave

here until I open up.

I turn the key and lower the handle; Damian comes in and locks the door behind him. The room, already tiny, seems microscopic with his bulky size. I look up, and I can't help but see his muscles squeezed inside a simple black T-shirt and a pair of jeans of the same color. He looks good even with that worried frown on his face.

"I can't go out there. I can't...I can't." I keep saying it like a litany, unable to explain what I'm afraid of. He doesn't know how fragile I feel in front of people, my body exposed to the judgments of others.

Damian grabs my face in his enormous hands and forces me to look up at him, into his magnetic eyes. "We've practiced so many times, you don't have to be afraid. I'm with you, and you have to trust me, okay?" He says it in such a sweet way I almost forget what I was about to do. Almost.

I run to the bathroom and kneel down in front of the toilet, puking out my soul. Damian lowers himself and with a delicate gesture pulls my hair away and holds it steady. With his other hand he massages my back, leaving a warm and extremely comforting trail along my skin.

"Sorry," I tell him when I finally get up.

Damian smiles at me and from the back pocket of his pants he pulls out a bottle of water and a travel bag with a toothbrush and toothpaste. I grab it with shame for the show I've just given and use it generously while he keeps his eye on me, maybe to see if I'll go crazy again.

"I'm used to Thomas doing this before every concert," he says with a half-smile.

"Really? You've been touring for.. I don't know, years, and he still hasn't got used to it?" I ask incredulously while I rinse my mouth and brush my teeth.

Damian shrugs and smiles at me. "The stage tension doesn't magically disappear. It's what allows us to be focused every time we go out in front of the crowd. You just have to learn how it manifests itself and find a way to crush it."

I inhale deeply and try with all my might to get a sense of perspective. I'm an adult, after all, I have to at least try to take his advice. "What about you? How did you solve yours?"

A flash of lust passes across his eyes but disappears so quickly I almost feel like I dreamt it.

"I'll never tell you that, Lilly. Never." He smiles mischievously as he opens the door and drags me by the hand.

"Take it easy, I'm wearing heels," I complain.

Damian turns around, lifts me up by grabbing me from under my knees like a bride on my wedding night, and takes me to the club. As I put my arm around his neck for fear of falling, I struggle to resist the temptation to stick my fingers in his hair and savor the feeling of clenching them in my fist. The beard-covered jaw almost entices me to reach out with one hand and slide my fingers into the smooth skin of his neck. I wonder what it tastes like to put my lips on it and let my tongue tease out a kiss.

"We'll never get to the stage otherwise," he giggles amusedly as I roll my eyes. "Where are your glasses?" he asks, then studies my face.

I shrug my shoulders, resigned. "Sid made me wear my contact lenses."

"I'll have to remember to give him a little talk," he whispers.

He sets my feet on the ground just behind the curtain that separates us from the side of the stage. I hear the buzz on the other side and my stomach does a somersault that I don't like at all.

"Are you okay?" Luke asks me with one hand on my back, comforting me and easing the tension a little bit.

I look around, and I realize they're all here, my bandmates, the Jailbirds, Evan, and even some of the technicians who set up the stage. Even though they're all in conversations, I can see they're glancing my way.

"I told you I didn't want to see anyone. Traitor!" I poke him, not answering his question.

Luke laughs and hugs me.

"I've never seen you so anxious. I was afraid you'd run away, so I sent someone who might scare you. Because to be honest, Damian scares me. He's huge, always looks pissed off, and if he were to kick my ass, my parents wouldn't even be able to identify my body," he confesses in a whisper in my ear.

I burst out laughing because I totally get it. Damian can be very intimidating when you don't know him well. "Thank you. I don't know if I would have gotten out of there if he hadn't literally dragged me into it."

"Are you ready to go on stage? Evan gave us five minutes to take a deep breath and focus on the concert." He smiles at me, and I see Martin and Taylor coming up as the Jailbirds gather around them. The advantage of these little gigs is that we'll do them all together, as if we were one big band, so at least the focus will be on the Jailbirds and not entirely on us. They know how to handle things if something goes wrong.

"No, I'm not, but it's not like I can back out now, right? Have you seen how big the bodyguards are? Even if I tried to escape, I wouldn't go anywhere. They're as wide as the door."

Luke laughs, grabs me by the hand, and drags me with him up the stairs to the stage. Out of the corner of my eye, I notice a black hoodie abandoned on a chair. I grab it on the fly, and before going on stage, I put it on over my clothes. It reaches halfway down my thighs, and the sleeves are at least four inches longer than my fingers. It's perfect and makes me feel safe, considering Sid snatched the one I brought from home.

When people realize we're on stage, they start clapping and screaming. We take our seats on our stools and as soon as Damian sits next to me, I allow myself to look him in the eye. He has an amused smile on his face and shakes his head when he sees the sweatshirt. I shrug my shoulders back without saying a word. To them it's just a sweatshirt, but for me, it's the armor I need to feel safe and do what I love: play music.

We open the concert with "Two Hearts," the song we recorded in the studio as our first video because people liked it, and it's a great way to start with a bang. Until now, though, I didn't realize how huge the fans' appreciation was: the enthusiastic comments underneath a YouTube video don't give you an accurate perception of how much people expect to hear the live performance. The intense screams of the girls in the audience, when Damian and Luke alternate in the stanzas, almost make my stomach vibrate.

During my chorus, when I look at Damian, I catch him

winking at me a couple of times, as if to encourage me. A smile spreads across his face spontaneously and he grabs my hand, squeezing it gently, as a shake goes through my body. It's only a fraction of a second, an innocent gesture of support, but I feel butterflies in my stomach; when he lets go, I'm almost disappointed.

The energy radiating from the small crowd makes my chest explode in happiness as I look Damian in the eyes during the final refrain. The emotions you feel during shows are always different. You can be nervous and frustrated because the audience is cold and not responding or super excited because people are jumping and having fun, shouting, and singing. But one thing is always the same, the emotions are so amplified they make you almost dizzy. I can only compare it to drinking enough alcohol to loosen your inhibitions, but not too much to lose control. The perfect midpoint makes you light-headed and fully enjoying your emotions.

At this moment, Damian is bewildering me, approaching the stool and placing his hand on my back. My body leans into his touch, and my gaze snaps towards him. His face is just inches away from mine. What the hell is he doing?

"Relax, I just want to sing from your microphone." He smiles at me as he turns towards me and locks me between his legs.

The first words of "Jude" tremble on my lips until I get used to the idea of having him so close, with his perfume intoxicating me and his breath brushing against my sweaty skin. His eyes don't leave me for a second, and even though I know he's only doing it for the show, it doesn't lessen the almost physical pleasure I get from the intimacy of this moment. The screams from the audience are overwhelming.

I'm almost euphoric when, halfway through the concert, I notice my companions are not missing a single beat, their fingers confidently playing their instruments with ease. Thomas and Taylor are so synchronized in rhythm they seem to have merged into one. It's one of those rare times when everything is running smoothly, and you feel relaxed enough to perform even better, to think you're perfect and invincible, because at that moment, you are. Every time we get on stage, we have hours of rehearsal and sweat behind us. We've mastered those tracks to the point that they've become part of us. The only way we'd make a mistake now is if we gave in to nervousness.

The audience's response is terrific, thanks to the world's most famous band on stage. When I look at Luke, Taylor, and Martin, I see their incredulous eyes traveling over the faces of the people in the room, and I thank God I was persuaded to sign on for this tour. I would have never forgiven myself for denying my best friends this chance.

The show flies by in a succession of emotions that bring me quickly to the last song. Towards the end, I take out one of the earphones to listen to the audience singing Jailbirds' songs. For the first time since we started this adventure, I allow myself to dream that this will happen for our songs one day. At the mere thought of it I smile, and out of the corner of my eye I see Damian showing a satisfied sneer. He takes out one of his earphones too, and when he hears the girls screaming, he turns towards me and winks at me, accompanied by a sexy, confident smile. I have to look down again so as not to trip over the words of the song.

When we get off the stage, we squeeze an indescribable amount of people's hands, receive multiple pats on the shoulder and are in a daze from all the excitement around us. But one thing attracts my attention most of all: Damian's hand clutching mine in a firm grip. He promised me he wouldn't let go, and he didn't.

A gorgeous blondie approaches him and clings to his arm. He smiles at her; she devours him with her eyes. A look I've often seen in the women around him, all wishing they had a piece of this goodness. She whispers something in his ear. He laughs and responds in the same way; they talk too softly to understand their conversation, but from the way they behave, it is clear to me that there will be an after-party. I stand here, clinging to his hand like a child, the third wheel in an exchange that lasts less than a minute. He managed to get a fuck in less than sixty seconds. As much as it bothers me that I've become invisible, I have to admire him for his ability to pick up a woman.

When she leaves us after holding his arm one last time with her black lacquered nails, he turns to me, winks at me, and drags me along, making me forget everything that just happened in the last two minutes. We head to the dressing room with the others, close the door, and allow ourselves this moment alone to enjoy before going back out to feel the situation's pulse. But when my gaze rests on Evan's, my happiness wavers a little.

"What did you put on before going on stage?" he asks me, pointing to the sweatshirt.

I lower my gaze, mortified, and pull my hands up my long sleeves.

"We pay Sid to always make you look your best. You can't just do your own thing," he adds in a less severe tone, but still makes me feel guilty.

"Look, Evan, you can't force people to wear what they don't want. You know she doesn't want attention; does she necessarily have to go on stage with no clothes on?"

It's Damian who's defending me, making me turn to him, surprised he stood up against his manager.

"Okay, we'll figure something out," Evan responds, and seems incredulous at his stance as well.

When Damian turns to me, I can almost feel my legs shake. "Let's try with Sid to find something that's nice but covers you and makes you feel comfortable, okay? You really can't walk around in that sweatshirt. It's huge, it's stained with sweat from someone who's used it an entire afternoon to put the instruments on stage, and it stinks," he says, grabbing me by the shoulders and forcing me to look him in the eyes.

They all burst out laughing, including me, and when I realize he's right, I take it off immediately and throw it into a corner, making the laugh even harder. This morning I got up with my stomach in knots and the terror of starting our new life. Now I'm happy that Damian dragged me out of this room a few hours ago.

PRESS *Review*

Rock News:

The band discovered by the Jailbirds is definitely one of the best around right now. They have an already well-defined musical identity, and technically they are at a level that few bands can reach in their twenties. Too bad for the horrible singer/bass player's fashion sense. She really stood out amid the almost maniacal perfection the Jailbirds have grown accustomed us to. Compared to the others, it looked like she wore something from the trash bins behind the club. Hopefully, someone will guide her on her next shopping spree.

Mark This Name - Red Velvet Curtains!

Hi, Roadies!

As you know, last night I was lucky enough to find a ticket to the Red Velvet Curtains exclusive debut concert with the Jailbirds at 59 Club in Manhattan. I'm the luckiest woman on the face of the earth, I can guarantee you that. If I had missed their debut concert, I would have never forgiven myself. They were great! A while ago, I warned that opening the contest to all the bands without any requirements could have been a big mistake. Luckily, I was wrong! Not only are they technically at the level of the Jailbirds, but they also have enviable chemistry between them. Besides singing some of the band's most famous songs, they've also unleashed songs that would make many artists at the top of the charts envious. What a concert! What an interpretation! What about the bass player? Who would have thought? Such a full and confident voice! An unprecedented performance.

Beware, Jailbirds, you may have rivals in the house who'll knock you off your golden throne and off the top spot.

Be Kind and Rock'n'Roll,

Iris

2503 Likes 7598 Tweets 2714 shares 1536 comments

Gossip Now:
Seriously, what was that poor bass player dressed in? A garbage bag? Hopefully, they'll hire a stylist for the next gig, or she'll make our poor Damian horrified. He was perfect in his black outfit, but she resembled a stray cat in the rain. What did she think before she went on stage? Was she lucky enough to sit for an hour and a half next to the King of rock, and then dressed up like Cinderella before coming out of the attic? I doubt if Damian will ever offer her a glass slipper looking like that. Honey, if that was your goal, you've got the wrong tactic, let me tell you.

Live Music:

The Jailbirds' acoustic concert with the new opening band was a real treat for our ears. We could finally appreciate the band in a less aggressive setting, and it was really a pleasure. No smearing, no uncertainty, not even from the young band, the Red Velvet Curtains, who were able to show they could master the stage like few others. They still have to work on their stage presence, especially the bass player who hasn't shown off her physical appearance, but they are young. They have a dazzling career ahead of them and plenty of time to find the ideal outfit.

CHAPTER 7
Damian

When she gets comfortable with what she has to do, Lilly is a war machine. We're now halfway through our little tour of Manhattan clubs, and I discover I was wrong about her. She's not a kid, she's not insecure, she's not someone who doesn't know what to do on stage. On the contrary, she is an unparalleled musician, precise, professional, completely capable of handling the unexpected things that happen during a show. Her only problem is managing the stress of everything that gravitates around this environment, not so much playing with people; apart from some initial uncertainty, she does it without a problem. I would even say she's having fun.

I'll never be able to get her shining eyes out of my head when we sing "Two Hearts" at the start of every concert. She loves to play the part of a woman torn between the good guy and the bad guy, and she puts all her effort into making the blood flow from my brain to below my belt. It works every single time.

I wish I knew what happened to make her feel under so much pressure. It's true, the newspapers torment her for the way she looks on stage, wearing baggy clothes that don't flatter her physique, but she should be mature enough not to give any weight to that crap. She's started eating less. She kills herself with ab workouts and push-ups when she thinks nobody's watching and she eats that candy that makes you feel full without swallowing even a spoonful of food. She's hungry, I realize that, but she refuses to eat.

"Do you have a moment?" Evan calls me back to reality as my thoughts wander about Lilly.

"Sure." I gesture him to sit on the couch where I'm relaxing while the others get ready to go out for a bite to eat before the concert tonight.

"I've arranged an interview for you and Lilly tonight. They only want you two after the concert, but there's a problem." His jaw's twitchy, and I realize that Evan is having trouble finding a solution to a problem this time.

"If you came to talk to me about it instead of going straight to her, you're worried she'll eat you alive. She's a pain in the ass, that woman," I admit with a half-smile.

Evan puts his hand over his face and chuckles almost exasperatedly. I honestly respect him for the work he does: cleaning up other people's messes for a living is something I would never do, even if my own life depended on it.

"The interview is with Jenna from *Rock Now*. The one who called Lilly a 'wet rat covered in rags' in one of her online articles. Lilly had a hysterical breakdown, and it took Luke and me a whole day to convince her not to quit the tour."

I remember that day. We had a concert the next night, and we were all alerted to a possible press conference apologizing and explaining to stem the damage.

"Why the hell do we have to give the interview to that idiot? All she does is hide behind fake sarcasm, which is nothing but gratuitous malice." It pisses me off, women like that. She's worked her way up to the top by being evil, and she spares no one.

"They have the largest reader base and the largest distribution of any other trade magazine in the United States, and their site visits are three times as many as the runner-up. Pissing them off and having them against us is not a move we can afford. If Jenna goes to the head of the record company you work for and tells them to make you jump, you jump and thank her with a smile."

I can tell by his tone that he had a heated discussion about this with the boss in question. I'm almost sorry I asked him the question.

"Okay, I'll try to talk to Lilly, but I can't guarantee she won't leave this building before the concert."

Evan nods and manages to bring out a half tense smile. "I know, I talked to Luke about it, and he seemed so freaked out about it that he asked me to ask you because you're the only one who can handle her anxiety attacks these days."

Is it always up to me to confront her about the things she doesn't want to do? I feel like I've become her nurse when I'd really like to get into her pants instead.

At the bar of the club, I meet Luke, who shows me where to find Lilly and wishes me "good luck" with a smile that expresses all the pain he feels on my behalf.

I knock on the door of the room reserved for the Red Velvet Curtains and wait for her to tell me to come in, rather than sneaking in and finding her undressed. I'm sure that kind of view wouldn't help my semi-hard on that I have every time I have to go on stage. The irony is that when I'm nervous before a show, my blood flows to areas of my body that I'd prefer were asleep. I can often think of things bad enough to get over it, but sometimes I have to make up for it by releasing some tension. Should I screw up the serenity of the tour and hit shamelessly on her or do the right thing? Jesus Christ, sometimes it's tough to listen to Evan telling me to keep it in my pants.

"Go ahead," her voice almost chokes.

I open the door, and the spectacle in front of me is far more exciting than finding her lying naked with her legs spread open in front of me. She's kneeling on the sofa, butt in the air, jeans wrapped around her perfect curves, leaning forward to pick up something. Basically, a heavenly sight for what's in my pants—which now snaps to attention.

"What the hell are you doing?" I ask, struggling to contain my lower parts inside the jeans that have become too tight.

"Will you stop standing there and give me a hand?" she asks, looking over my shoulder, covering her backside with one hand. Busted.

"To do what, exactly?" I raise a puzzled eyebrow.

"Look for my glasses that fell down here," she says, extending an arm between the back of the couch and the wall it's resting on.

Those glasses. Sid made her take them off for concerts, perhaps because he also realized that I'd get an overbearing erection every time I have to look at them when I'm on stage. I've never seen any woman look so sexy with those big glasses on her face. They're giant and dark, but they perfectly frame her intelligent and cunning eyes.

I get closer, grab the couch on one side, and, without too much thought, I move it off the wall with her on it. I snatch the glasses on the floor, hand them to her, and return the couch to its place with the same ease. Lilly looks at me like I'm an idiot.

"Do you have to show off your muscles at every opportunity? I'm not one of your fans you fuck with. I'm not looking for two arms and pecs to spread my legs," she says, crossing her arms to her chest, pushing them under her breasts and making them stand out even more. It bothers me that she thinks I'd fuck anyone, but the reality is that everyone thinks of me like that.

However, if she continues to be provocative without even realizing it, I will slip between those legs after tearing off her pants in an instant.

"So, you noticed my muscles?" I joke. "Not bad for someone who doesn't care." I tilt my head to the side and enjoy watching her blush. "And for your information, I don't sleep with my fans." Not all of them, at least.

She shrugs her shoulders and sits cross-legged on the couch. She's more relaxed than usual, and I almost hate to break the news that's gonna ruin her day. "What are you doing here?"

"Tonight after the show, we have an interview with Jenna from *Rock Now*, the one who called you a rat in rags." I just throw it out there because there's no pleasant way to say this, and she doesn't like people sugar coating the truth.

She first turns pale as a ghost and then an unhealthy greenish color, with her big eyes and her jaw twitching, making her lower lip slightly protrude. She's having one of her attacks, I know them all too well, and I don't want her to panic. If she does we'll never end up on that stage. I grab her underneath the knees and behind her shoulders, pick her up and, in long strides, take her out of the dressing room and up the stairs to the top of the building where no one will witness her breakdown.

I gently place her on one of the sofas stacked on one side, covered with a thick nylon cloth. The grey sky makes this place look even sadder than it is. The slight stench of dust mixes with the air's humidity, giving the city its characteristic smell: lived, worn, alive. The honking of horns coming from the street, the traffic's incessant noise, is almost reassuring on this roof.

"Is it better in the fresh air?" I ask her after a few minutes when she's managed to take several deep breaths.

She nods but doesn't speak. She regains color despite the cold air and the grey sky and chance of snow today in New York City. I study her for a few minutes until her breathing becomes regular again.

"What happened to you to be so terrified of people's judgment?" I ask her directly. I'm genuinely intrigued, but the harshness in her eyes makes me realize we're not going very far.

"Nothing." A simple word, dry, pronounced with a severity that leaves no room for a reply, makes me understand that the subject is not to be touched, that not even in a hundred years will I be able to tear it out of her mouth.

I understand her, I have my secrets too, but she's not making my life easy.

"Alright. But we can't spend the night up here freezing our balls off. We're gonna go downstairs, we're gonna have a nice conversation about the questions the bitch sent us, we're gonna prepare the answers, and then we're gonna get some adrenaline flowing, okay?"

I appreciate Evan making it a rule that we are sent the interview questions before we record it. It's saved us many unwelcome surprises, and most importantly, allows us to say, "This wasn't among the agreed-upon questions," to the answers we don't want to give. Too bad it can't be done with press conferences as well.

She studies me a little, my firm air and resolute words that won't take no for an answer. I'm almost sure she'll accept, she's too professional and has a strong sense of duty. She just needs time and someone who won't give her any loopholes. Her bandmates have always indulged her without ever forcing her to face her fears. I can understand. They're kids, but I'm not, and I learned early on that when you start running away, you can't do anything else for the rest of your life. But if, by chance, reality catches up with you, it won't wait until you're ready. It's gonna run you over, knock you down and make you bleed.

Lilly nods and heads towards the door we came out of, leaving me a view of her body moving sinuously in the high heels she's wearing.

*

"You have to stick it in the hole, Jenkins, not caress it. Use the damn stick."

I get a look that makes me laugh. "You may be used to tinkering with balls and cues, Jones, but this is the third time in my life I've done this." I'm amused by her impertinence.

"You've lived in Brooklyn all your life and never played pool?" I'm shocked by her statement. I can't believe it.

Lilly gets up, letting go of the game, and comes at me with a threatening gesture, pointing the cue at my chest, tapping a couple of light, intimidating strokes. "Maybe that's normal for a guy. But a woman can't afford to be bent over a table, surrounded by the horny guys who frequents these places...unless she wants to end up with, if she's lucky, a slap on the ass and a squeeze on her tits when she gets up."

I've never seen it from this point of view. I've always enjoyed the sight of a nice ass, but I never wondered what the girl in question was thinking. Many of the girls I met in bars were really just there to play pool, and they could drink and swear right alongside the men. I've always justified it by telling myself that I would never hurt them, that I only ever looked at them, and would never go further without their consent, but I realize now how sexist this reasoning is.

"Okay, I'll show you how it's done," I say, taking the cue from her hands and bending over the green cloth myself instead of getting behind her with my bulky presence in a position that would have been embarrassing. It's the first time in my life that instead of hitting on someone I'd like to fuck, I want to protect her and make her feel safe.

Apparently, I'm an exceptional teacher because Lilly starts sticking her balls in the hole, one after the other, and, if I'm not careful, I risk my ego suffering humiliation. I have a lot of work to do to win this game and the next two.

"Are you ready to go on stage?" I ask her when Dave, the head of security, tells me it's time to start playing.

I see the smile fade but without the anxiety of a few hours ago. "Knowing that that bitch is in the audience taking notes and will tear me apart later makes me appreciate less what I love most in the world. Playing."

I can hear the annoyance in her voice, and it pisses me off. You can see that when she's on stage, she changes, that music is her whole life, and the thought of Jenna taking away the one thing that makes her feel good makes me angry. I know first-hand how music can save you from yourself.

"Don't think about it. We'll fix it later. Right now, just enjoy the moment. I'll be with you during the interview. You know I'm good at getting up and leaving if things don't go my way." I wink at her, and she laughs.

"Yes, I have a vague recollection of a dozen press conferences where you appeared for five seconds. Journalists are now terrified when they have to ask you questions."

"It's not my fault; they're shitty questions!"

Lilly bursts into a loud laugh, and I can feel the tension lifting a bit from the air around us.

Getting on stage is a piece of cake. We exchange a few jokes with each other; Luke seems to be exceptionally attentive to Lilly, which comforts me because Jenna is in the front row, right in front of us with her phone pointed at our faces. Unfortunately, it doesn't take long for Lilly to notice it and stiffen up next to me. Luckily, we decided to start off with "Jude," sung only by the two of us with the others' accompaniment.

"Look only at me," I whisper to her while I adjust the microphone.

She raises her big terrified eyes to mine and I almost melt. I know right now she just wants to run away from this stage so I grab her hand, turn her around on the stool until she is in front of me, take my microphone, and put it between us. I get closer, wedging our legs together to be close enough to share the microphone and smile at her.

She seems to hold her breath for a second, then she relaxes a bit and hints at a half-smile. I put my hand on her leg and caress her for a few moments until I see her relax that stiff posture and let go.

"Jude, I saw how you smiled when you met my look..." The words escape my lips as if Lilly were there instead of Jude. I look her straight in the eye and everything else disappears. I watch her cheeks blush, unprepared for this more intimate performance than usual. I smile to reassure her. She smiles back at me, and without thinking about it, I move a lock of hair behind her ear that falls on her cheek. The contact with her soft skin is an electric charge that reaches my chest, making my heart explode. The way she tilts her head almost imperceptibly against my hand makes it hard to swallow.

"Jude, I saw how you blushed as you kissed me..." As she utters those words, her gaze brushes against my lips for an instant and then rises again to my eyes with a disarming sweetness. God, I wish I could kiss her right now. I would love to hold her in my arms and plunge my tongue into her mouth and savor her until I am full.

"Jude, I watched you slip out of the sheets, and I was afraid you'd never come back..." My voice is hoarse, full of the excitement I'm finding hard to contain. I'd like to see her slipping out of my bed, naked, with her hair messed up after a night of tasting every inch of her skin. I wink at her and she blushes, trying to contain a smile that spreads across her face. Sooner or later, the day will come when I can admire the blush of her cheeks as she moves sinuously over me, stripped of everything except those glasses, making her look sexy and innocent at the same time.

We sing the whole first song like this, without ever taking our eyes off each other. I'd do anything to keep her from meeting Jenna's eyes again, who, in this intimate place, is very close to the stage. When the song ends, I struggle to turn towards the audience again, moving the microphone to play "Two Hearts." I deliberately avoid laying eyes on Jenna, and I see Thomas staring at me with a sly smile on his face. My lips curl upwards, unable to hold back a happiness I can't explain.

When Martin starts the song with the first guitar chord, I look at Lilly again and find her more relaxed, ready to play with winking glances at Luke and me. The guy seems amused, smiling more than usual, willing to play with her as I've often seen them do in private, with an intimacy that only two people who have known each other for years can have. A vice grips my stomach, but I try not to react to it, concentrating instead on the lips of the woman in front of me, who is singing the refrain with an innocent act, but when I meet her eyes I notice the mischievous spark in her gaze.

It's this moment when I surrender, when I can no longer contain the evident hard-on in my pants, when I'm forced to almost to hurt myself. Few times in my life have I been so excited by a fully dressed woman, and the reaction of my body puts me in trouble. I'll never make it to the end of this all-too-perfect evening, and Lilly seems to sense my discomfort because she puts her hand on my leg, just above the knee, and squeezes slightly, smiling at me. Not a wise move on her part because my heart starts pumping in my chest, the image of her hand on my naked skin imprinted in my mind and leaving me no way out. From this moment on, the concert is a series of attempts to regain my composure without success.

"We're going. Do you need us to stay until you do the interview, or will you go home with Dave?" Thomas asks while drinking his well-deserved beer at the bar.

"Go ahead, Dave already has a car ready for Lilly and me," I reassure him as I look for her among the crew to drag her to the interview. I find her talking to Luke and Martin; she still seems relaxed, thankfully. "Don't screw up," Thomas jokes.

When I turn to him, I notice he's got his eye on Lilly. "It's just an interview with Jenna. We're not going to the gallows," I reassure him.

Thomas turns to me with a half-smile on his face. "Yes, of course," he says cryptically, putting his hand on my shoulder just as Jenna approaches and makes sweet eyes at me.

"So? Are you ready?" she says in a soft voice. I've never heard her speak normally. She's always so set and controlled and sweet, it almost makes you nauseous. I wouldn't be surprised if she was a computer with no feelings, programmed with gratuitous malice and fake sarcasm.

"Yeah, I'm gonna go get Lilly. You go ahead the room Evan gave us. One thing, Jenna, the questions are as agreed, any comments out of place, and we're out of here. I don't give a shit if you have the exclusive on this interview. Do you understand?" I set the record straight and get elbowed by Thomas for doing so. He's always too diplomatic.

Jenna surprises me with a condescending smile. "Don't worry, Damian, the agreed-upon questions are fine with me. I already have everything I need already," she whispers sensually before she leaves. I see her talking to our manager, who's smiling at her like she's the only person he wants to see tonight. I really admire the nerve of that man.

"Okay, am I the only one who doesn't believe her at all?" questions Thomas, puzzled.

I don't answer because I have an unpleasant feeling, too.

However, the interview goes exactly how it should: no questions outside the pre-approved ones, and Jenna, incredibly affable, has even managed to put Lilly at ease. All professional to an unbelievable degree. Too much for my taste. What makes me most nervous is that I can't figure out where we went wrong.

*

"I did it," Lilly says to me for the hundredth time, embracing me impulsively at my waist, not even realizing what she's doing.

The interview lasted about an hour. It was intense, there were no particular exchanges other than questions, but the tension stretched me as if I had just done the New York Marathon.

"I had no doubt, but you don't trust me." I roll my eyes to make fun of her.

"You were the one who wanted to call the other band at first because you thought I'd never survive in these situations!" she says, almost outraged.

"How long did it last, ten minutes? And I didn't know you then. Don't be a pain in the ass." I grab her hand and drag her to the back door where Dave and Evan are waiting for us.

I can tell from the bodyguard's tense face that something's wrong, and I stop, getting nailed to the spot by Lilly bumping up against my back. Evan seems almost spirited, typing furiously on his phone.

"We have a problem," our manager confirms my fears.

"What's that?"

"Main and secondary entrances surrounded by the paparazzi, same with your apartment and hers," he says, nodding in

Lilly's direction.

"What the hell is going on? Why?"

Aside from the initial excitement after the contest, the paparazzi had been following us during the mini-tour. But once the excitement passed, they just took a few shots as we left the club. After all, we never did anything scandalous to attract hordes of photographers. Why are we so besieged tonight that Dave and Evan are worried about us? Nothing out of the ordinary happened.

"Jenna posted a picture on her Instagram stories of you leaning over Lilly looking like you were kissing her. Later in her stories, she exaggerated and made you two look like you were making out on stage." Our manager is direct, and anger is boiling in my stomach.

"But it's not true!" Lilly's voice is shrill.

"I know, but the paparazzi have mobilized en masse. They've been waiting months for this opportunity because they say there's chemistry between you and they want to build a story. Jenna gave them the go-ahead," Evan explains with a tight smile.

The harmony between two artists must be there to make the fans who come to see you enjoy the show. It's never pleasant to watch a concert where there is evident negative tension on stage. But Jenna has turned it all into vicious gossip.

"That bitch," I whisper, gritting my teeth. "The hotel where I have the room?"

Evan shakes his head. "There's someone there, too. And the others told me on the way home they noticed movement on the streets surrounding their homes, both here in Manhattan and Brooklyn. They know the others have gone out, so they're waiting for one or both of you. They're expecting you to take refuge with one of your bandmates."

"So, what the hell are we gonna do?" Lilly's voice is worried.

"Do you have anywhere else you can go?" asks Dave, the bodyguard who's got a really thankless job right now.

I think about it. It's not like we've got a lot of options since every place we know is being watched, so I've got no choice left but the most infamous bar in New York. "Could you take me to Joe's?"

Dave is visibly shocked at my request, and Lilly doesn't miss this, even though he nods and is already making arrangements to escort us out.

Evan seems to want to object, but he thinks about it and shakes his head slightly as if he doesn't see an alternative. "I'll go to the main entrance and try to create a diversion as you leave through the secondary one," he says resolutely, making his way down the corridor.

"Who's Joe?" Lilly worriedly asks me, shaking my hand.

"An old friend. One who gave me a place to stay and a job when I...when I moved here," I vaguely explain. There's no need for the whole story.

"You're not from New York?" she asks me incredulously.

I shake my head no. My bandmates and I have decided to inform as few people as possible about our past, and I'm certainly not going to start talking about it now. I give her a look that nips every possible question in the bud, and, luckily, she's smart enough to humor me.

CHAPTER 8
Lilly

I open my eyes and can hardly focus. The yellow walls of this place are unfamiliar, as is the big armchair at the foot of the double bed and the old and imposing wardrobe that occupies the entire wall in front of me. I move my gaze towards the window with the curtains drawn and realize I'm at Joe's, the man who, both in height and belly, is huge and balding except for a few graying clumps on the lower part of his head, and who greeted us yesterday with a baseball bat as we snuck in through the back. As soon as he recognized the man accompanying me, a smile appeared on his face, showing yellowing smoker's teeth and a heart as big as the state of New York. When he heard we were being followed by the paparazzi, he gave Damian the keys to his old room and made us go upstairs without going through the bar, which, at that hour, was full of drunks.

I look up and find Damian curled up in the chair, fast asleep in what looks like a very uncomfortable position. Last night I told him I wouldn't object if we shared the bed, both dressed and at a suitable distance, but he decided to sleep in the armchair, covered only by his leather jacket and a miserable blanket across his knees. I doubt he had a restful night.

Last night I discovered a side to him I didn't know. The Jailbirds were mysterious about their lives before they became famous, but I always believed that Damian was born and raised in New York; but I learned he had moved out on his own at an early age. His words on the subject have been few and, in getting to know him lately, I understand it's one of those topics to avoid and to which I won't receive any answer.

I need to take a shower and I need to pee, but I don't want to wander around this place alone, opening doors to rooms hiding something I'm not sure I want to know about. I stand up and stretch noisily, trying to wake Damian up. I do it once, twice, three times, but he doesn't seem to want to move an inch. How sleepy can a person be?

"Will you stop grunting like a pig?" he asks me again in the same position and with his eyes closed.

"You finally woke up. I have to pee." I sit down.

He opens one eye and looks at me harshly, making me feel like a little girl who's just been scolded.

"Couldn't you look for a bathroom? Or should I walk with you and pull your pants down?" His tone is sour.

"Of course, you're grumpy in the morning."

Damian sits up and straightens his back with a grimace. "I spent the night on this infernal trap, and I wake up thinking I'm in the room with a pig, excuse me if I'm not a flower. You know what would wake me up in a good mood this morning? A great blow—"

I throw the pillow in his face before he can finish the sentence. Even the thought of wrapping my lips around his cock gives me a twinge in my lower abdomen. "Bathroom!" I point my finger at him, standing up.

I can see his eyes lightly widening as he notices the bra coming out of my messy tank top. I settle down as best as I can, feeling my cheeks flush when I lay my eyes on his rather noticeable erection.

"Second door on the right," he says, nodding to the light layer of wood that separates us from the hallway.

I hurry out of the bedroom. After knocking and making sure there is no one there, I swoop into a small bathroom filled with sample bottles, some of them brands that went out of production before I was born.

"Does this man ever throw anything away?" I whisper as I sit on the toilet.

I look around and enjoy imagining Damian in this tiny space, struggling to take a shower, clearly too small for him. As a man, it's expected that he's the size he is, especially if he wanders around the gym every day, but I wonder what Damian was like as a kid, if he has always been so bulky. I guess that's one of the questions that will remain unanswered.

I dwell on the tiny sink in front of me, the yellow walls like the bedroom, the mirror with dark spots glued to the wall, and the light bulb attached to wires coming out of the ceiling; under the sink are two baskets with more sample bottles of shampoo and conditioner. The sight of all these plastic containers is almost disturbing. For some reason, I imagine it's a serial killer's bathroom and I move quicker, pulling up my pants and heading back to my room down the hall. Damian's tying his shoes.

"I see you didn't die going there alone!" he says, mocking

me as he gets up from his chair and moves towards me. "Come on, let's go downstairs for breakfast. Joe makes the best cheese sandwich you've ever eaten." He winks at me, and all I can do is put on my shirt and jacket and follow him downstairs, calculating how many calories I'll have to swallow so as not to upset the man who took us in for the night.

When he said the best sandwiches, he wasn't kidding. They really are mouth-watering and probably a cholesterol spike, with cheese oozing out between the slices of white bread sizzling in a pan with melted butter. But you only live once, and this is definitely an excellent way to die. Since I haven't eaten since yesterday morning, I gorge myself with little grace when Joe breaks the silence of our thoughts.

"How come you ended up sleeping around here? Not that I mind, but since you bought yourself that fancy apartment, you haven't come to reclaim your old room," he observes with curiosity.

"We were being chased by paparazzi," Damian responds between bites.

His answer makes me pull my phone out of my pocket, and I almost have a heart attack seeing my Instagram account notifications. "Holy cow," I whisper in disbelief.

Damian gives me an inquisitive look.

"Yesterday, I had about thirty thousand followers, now it's one hundred sixty thousand, and it keeps going up every time I reload the page."

He looks at me, puzzled. "And isn't that normal?" He raises an eyebrow. "I don't know, one of Evan's secretaries or interns runs my account, so..."

"No, it's not normal. It takes people months of work, eight hours a day, to achieve those results. My pictures also have hundreds of likes and comments, which never happens." I look more closely at the screen. "Some of them are really bad."

"What do they say?" He leans towards me, invading my personal space with his bulky presence and his masculine scent, making me want to rip his clothes off.

"That I'm a bitch whore, that I finally found a cock full of money to launch my career..."

The vulgarity of some of the comments leaves me speechless. Jenna's photo may have triggered the wrong assumption, but it seems like an exaggerated reaction given that everyone in the room last night can confirm there was no kiss.

I google my name. The first search result is a video clip of last night's concert; a few seconds, nothing more. In another, a TMZ headline reads: "New flame for the man who hates commitment?" and below that an article in which "witnesses," or people who followed Jenna's live Instagram during the concert, confirm we were very intimate, that the sexual tension was palpable and that someone saw us making out off stage with "tongue and hands everywhere."

"Holy cow," I whisper, as I look up at an entertained Joe and an angry Damian reading what they wrote.

He gets up and leaves his breakfast halfway through to grab his phone and start yelling at Evan.

"He cares about his privacy," Joe says, laughing as I swoop over my breakfast and try to figure out how to interpret this information from the Internet.

I try to forget the nasty comments underneath my photos,

even though once I read them, they're branded in my brain, and I feel like crying. I'll ask Luke to delete them, or I'll block them, even though I know I'll get criticized for it. I want to enjoy my music, the stage, an experience I've never had in my life. Those comments are trying to ruin what's rightfully mine to enjoy.

*

We're headed to the rehearsal studio after what feels like an endless tour of Manhattan clubs, grateful that Evan finally gave us the green light to rehearse for the arena tour. Damian is in a bad mood and doesn't say a word, but luckily, Max, the driver, is more inclined to have a decent conversation. Once in the building, a girl sent by Evan comes to pick me up; I notice Damian disappearing without opening his mouth, and I can't help but roll my eyes at his lack of patience.

"So? Have you fucked him yet?" Martin immediately asks me with a smile as soon as I set foot in the decked-out rehearsal room that makes the one we had in Brooklyn pale in comparison.

"Good morning to you too, Martin. I'm fine, thank you. And you? Have you slept well?" I'm just teasing him, given his proverbial lack of tenderness.

Everyone laughs as I sit on the couch next to Luke. The rehearsal room they've provided looks more like a relaxation corner with gear than a real studio. There are white, faux leather sofas on two walls, a small table with snacks, all kinds of drinks, a coffee machine in one corner, and on the other side of the glass the instruments; not ours, but the ones that have been made available to us. When we won this contest, I knew they would treat us with white gloves. After all, we are their investment as a band for the next few years, but I had no idea the extent of the advantages we would have. We're talking about full VIP treatment here—thousands of dollars worth of guitars, drums, and basses that we could never buy for ourselves.

Taylor was given a brand new Gretsch, and, as a massive fan of Charlie Watts of The Rolling Stones, he almost fainted at the natural shade of the maple it was made of. Martin finally got his hands on the Fender Stratocaster with its 1960s design, metallic ice blue, which he had dreamed of all his life. When he discovered it was a one-of-a-kind piece, custom made for him, with the shape of the handle asymmetrically rounded to accommodate his crooked thumb from a fall as a child, he literally jumped into Evan's arms. Luke also had his 1960s Gibson Les Paul, which he had drooled over for months in the window of Manhattan's Chelsea Guitars.

Evan, however, did a fantastic job on my instrument. Typically, it's hard to find a six-string bass with a neck small enough to accommodate a woman's hands. So, Evan went to Ibanez and had them make a custom-shaped model, completely black, opaque, with the grain of the walnut and maple wood beautifully visible. I cried when I first held it in my hands.

I'm pulled from my admiration of our new gear by Martin's insistent retort: "Don't get all holier-than-thou. You can see on the video that you're fucking him with your eyes...and he's got a hard-on. Damn it, I was too sideways to see what the hell you were doing, but the front view from Instagram is very explicit."

"No, I wasn't fucking him with my eyes or in any other

way. I was terrified, with Jenna staring at me," I say. "By the way, I managed to do the interview without throwing up on her, can you believe it?" I squeak excitedly, turning to Luke, who is laughing and hugging me. "And Damian didn't have an erection," I throw back at Martin, who keeps talking about what was in my male counterpart's pants. Everybody's laughing, and I'm lost.

"Oh, no? Then explain to me what this is," says Taylor pulling out his phone with an enlarged picture of the singer's crotch.

I look at it and admit that it might actually look like a boner from this perspective. "But it's the effect of the lights." I minimize the situation by getting up and going to put my bass over my shoulder, eager to change the subject.

"Yes, of course, the lights. I wish I had those magnifying lights when I'm in bed with a girl." Taylor makes us all burst out laughing, and I sigh with relief because I can feel my cheeks flushing. My interrogation ends when we all grab our instruments.

The rehearsal goes on until late afternoon with a lunch break in the middle where we join the Jailbirds, and everyone, no one excluded, gives Damian a hard time for his equipment. At first, I thought he would nail them to the wall with a punch, but I soon realize he has a completely different temperament than the morning. Guessing his mood swings and state of mind gives me a headache, but Evan seems to handle it better than the others, except for Thomas, who, from what I understand, is his best friend.

"Would you like to taste the life of a rock star?" Damian

asks as we enter the rehearsal room while we're putting the instruments away, completely exhausted from the busy day.

We all look confused, but it sends a spark of excitement through us. For years we've dreamed of becoming a worldwide success and we still don't realize that it's really happening.

"What is it?" I ask, since the others seem to have lost their tongues.

"An exclusive party at one of Manhattan's most fashionable rooftops," he says, expecting a delirious reaction, which there is from my bandmates, who accept immediately.

"What's up, Princess, too cheap for you to party?" He raises an eyebrow in defiance.

I roll my eyes, and gracefully show him my middle finger. "I don't know if you've noticed, but I've been wearing the same clothes since yesterday. I stink. I can't go to an exclusive party with you celebrities and scare everyone away because I look like I've come out of the barn."

Damian laughs, and so do my bandmates. Ungrateful traitors! "Sid brought something for you all to change into. It's over there." He nods his head down the hallway from where he came.

We follow him to one of the many rooms in this maze that is the record company building. I've been here regularly for months now and I still haven't learned how to navigate between the areas reserved for different purposes, from administration to marketing, to floors of rehearsal rooms of different sizes and importance. I'm sure there are still dozens of floors I have yet to discover.

"Why does Sid have to dress us even off stage? Aren't we good the way we are?" Luke whispers in my ear.

I turn to him and find him looking worried. He's not a fan of what the stylist wants him to wear on stage either; he'd much prefer the jeans and t-shirts he always wears.

"Apparently, to tour with the Gods of Rock, we have to dress appropriately. Even off stage," I giggle as my partner rolls his eyes.

"I'm here. I can hear you making sarcastic jokes about us, you know that, right?" Damian raises an eyebrow.

"Oh, I know, honey. I wasn't hiding. Did I give you that impression?" I make an innocent face that makes my bandmates burst out laughing.

"You're gonna drive me crazy," he whispers, shaking his head like he's reminding himself.

Less than half an hour later, he gets his revenge when I find myself squeezed into a pair of jeans so tight I can't even breathe. A top made of shiny black laminated fabric pushes my breasts up to my tonsils, and high heels have me walking like a T-rex. I have no alternative. It's the only thing Sid left me and, if I don't want to smell, I'm forced to wear this stuff. I swear, when I find him, I'm gonna choke him.

*

The club is located in one of Midtown's many skyscrapers. If I walk all the way around inside, which I doubt I can because of my high heels, I'd have a 360-degree view of Manhattan, and it's nothing short of gorgeous. The huge bar in the middle serves from all four sides and the otherwise open space contains sofas enclosed in small nooks. The lights are so low that someone could have sex on one of the couches and no one would notice. I almost bump into three Hollywood stars and not because this place is crowded. Apparently, this is the kind of popularity the Jailbirds attract. I don't know if I can ever get used to that.

I see them navigating with enviable ease when I squeal for a good fifteen seconds watching one of my favorite actors approach Damian and take him away. Within a few minutes, I'm left alone like a goldfish in a bowl, watching the world outside the glass, but not understanding much. Even my bandmates seem comfortable in this luxurious environment with a colorful cocktail in their hands and a couple of girls hanging around them. How the hell do they do that? We've been here exactly three minutes.

"Do you need a guide?" asks a deep voice behind me, which makes me spin around, staggering so much that the guy has to grab me by the elbow so I don't end up lying on the marble floor.

It takes me a while to recover as I find myself immersed in blue eyes and a pair of full lips arching in a mischievous smile. His light brown hair is styled to perfection and, to complete his "Armani casual" look, he's wearing a suit by the aforementioned designer, white shirt slightly unbuttoned at the collar and no tie. Just looking at this guy makes my mouth water, and it takes me a few seconds too long to realize I have to talk to him and not act like the damn goldfish.

"If you've got a map, I'll try to get my bearings."

He laughs in a quiet way that reflects his elegant, composed air. At least he's nice enough not to point out how dumb my joke is. "If you want, I can guide you through this maze. I'm familiar with these parties. My name is Archie, in case you don't talk to strangers." He holds out his hand and I shake it, intoxicated by his persuasive speech. I think I feel a little drool escaping down the corner of my mouth, but I don't have the courage or the will to control it.

"Lilly. Nice to meet you...and yes, I need someone to explain how to get to the bar without getting swallowed by quicksand," I giggle.

Quicksand? I'm really talking about quicksand? Jesus Christ, he's just a guy, handsome as a Greek god, but still a guy. I gotta calm down and try not to fall in these heels.

He snickers and offers me his arm to get to the bar. A bar we never get close to because Damian's strong hands rest on my shoulders and spin me around.

"There you are. I leave you alone for two minutes, and you have jackals circling around you," he says, incinerating Archie with his eyes.

I feel the man bristling next to me and he moves away, almost imperceptibly leaving a space between him and me that feels like the Grand Canyon. How the hell does this man have this kind of power over people?

"Damian, man, I didn't know she was with you. I wouldn't have offered to show her around otherwise." His tone is so fake, it almost creeps me out.

"Sure, right," says my supposed savior, taking my hand and entwining our fingers. "We're all over the media, and you know exactly who she is and who she came with." His voice is a low and deep whisper that makes my insides vibrate.

I have no idea how a caveman claimed a woman back in the day, but this Alpha male vibe Damian is giving off is making me want to say, "Yes, I'm yours, do what you want with me." I almost bite my tongue not to say it out loud.

Archie raises his hands in surrender and walks away at the speed of light.

I cross my arms over my chest and glare at Damian until he finally lays his eyes on me. "Do you also want to pee on me to mark your territory, or are you satisfied?"

Damian struggles to stay serious, and a corner of his mouth rises slightly in a smile. As much I hate it when men act possessive, I have to admit he's sexy as hell. "That guy would have fucked you in the bathroom before you'd even finished your cocktail."

I tilt my head to the side and raise an eyebrow. "Who says I don't want to get fucked in a bathroom before I even get to the bar?" I would never sleep with Archie, but I like catching Damian off guard.

"You're not one to get fucked like that," he says, wrinkling his forehead like he's almost asking me.

I roll my eyes and drag him to the bar. "Buy me a drink, since you've just scared my drink away," I say resolutely, hiding the fact that I have no idea how to behave in this environment and need someone to explain it to me quickly.

When the bartender hands me my frozen Cosmopolitan, Damian grabs the glass before I can bring it to my lips. I raise a puzzled eyebrow and look upset. "What the hell did I do wrong this time?"

"Never let your glass out of your sight. They'll will stick

anything into a cocktail to steal a few uninhibited or even R-rated pics."

"The bartender just gave it to me! What could he possibly have put in there?"

"Do you know him?"

I wrinkle my forehead, and look at him puzzled. "No, but he works here. I doubt he puts drugs in the customers' drinks."

"In places like this, bartenders work a few months, and then they change clubs or even cities. Usually, they're good guys, students making a living at a night job, but who's to say he doesn't just want to see you naked or make a quick buck? Always look at your glass, and, if you're not convinced, leave it on the counter."

"So, to recap, I can't trust the nice people who approach me, the bartenders, or anyone who comes near my glass. What am I supposed to do in a bar? Be the wallpaper?" I put my cocktail down on the bar, done sipping it.

Damian laughs and hands it to me again. "You can drink this one. I checked the kid, and trust me, he was too busy staring at your boobs to spike your drink." He winks at me and I flash with heat.

"Why are you here with me and not chasing your next conquest?" I look around and see a lot of beautiful girls staring at him like I look at the croissants from behind the glass at the bakery.

"Someone has to babysit you." He winks at me again, and again, I blush like a 15-year-old girl. I'll never get used to this way he flirts with women. It's exhausting, blushing every five minutes.

"And you're willing to miss a night of sex to make sure nobody drugs me and takes advantage of me?" It's a sweet idea, except it completely clashes with my image of Damian, the predator. I think Evan put him up to it, so I couldn't screw up my career before it even started.

"It's not like I'm gonna die if I don't fuck one night." He shrugs it off, amused. "And then someone will have to introduce you around here. These are the people you're going to be dealing with from now on, and you're going to have to learn to relate on their level, not just like a fan meeting the actor they have a crush on," he says, grinning at me.

I smile at his grin and shudder when he puts his hand on my lower back and pushes me towards a small group of people who greet him warmly. Ecstatic, I let myself be dragged from one side to the other of the club where, for the rest of the evening, he introduces me to celebrities in front of whom I act as though I enjoy his company.

PRESS *Review*

People:

First exclusive images of Damian Jones' new flame, Lilly Jenkins, who has no intention of leaving wide sweatshirts and comfortable jeans behind for her public outings. But the reason could be much more surprising than just bad taste in clothing: from these photos, in fact, you can see the pronounced belly of the new rising star of rock. Is she expecting a baby rock star? If the rumors are confirmed, it would be a masterstroke for her! Who wouldn't want to have that hunk of a companion at her side for the next 18 years? We are waiting for confirmation from those directly concerned, but sources close to the couple speak of sparks between them since the first days they met. I mean, if you do the math right, that would explain the large sweatshirts and the belly that's now hard to hide.

Gossip Now:

We reached out for an exclusive interview with Brad Shepherd, a famous Instagrammer and former classmate of Lilly Jenkins, the new flame of Damian Jones, front man of the Jailbirds. From the photos kindly provided by Shepherd, we see a 15-year-old Lilly much larger than we are used to seeing today. According to this former classmate and friend of the band, before stepping into the limelight Jenkins always had a passion for success and would do anything for fame. After several surgeries for drastic weight loss, she launched herself in the pursuit of fame, securing a relationship with the most famous singer of our time. According to Shepherd, who claims he was forgotten by his friends after the band's success, a possible pregnancy would not come as a surprise, given Jenkins' eagerness to secure a future. To see the full interview with Brad Shepherd and discover new spicy behind-the-scenes stories, click on the link.

Rock Now!

During the exclusive interview granted by Damian Jones and Lilly Jenkins, we'll find out more about the new collaboration with the most famous rock band on the face of the Earth. We'll talk about music, but above all, you'll be able to taste the undeniable chemistry and complicity between the two musicians who have been overflowing with loving glances and sweet smiles. During my interview, the pregnancy was not confirmed, but Damian's protective instinct towards Lilly certainly makes one think it's a much deeper relationship than just an artistic collaboration. On the other hand, you've seen my live broadcast from the concert, right? It was all looks and smiles! To see the full interview, click on the link below.

Jenna

CHAPTER 9
Damian

I walk out the front door where the paparazzi are waiting for me, which is precisely why I have to go out without Lilly around, so I can draw attention away from the made-up relationship we're supposed to be having. Pregnancy included. I mean, we're about to start a tour that will take us all over the United States. Do they have nothing else to do but focus on my sex life? That being said, as difficult as it is for me not to get hard in my boxer shorts just seeing her concentrate wearing those glasses of hers doesn't mean I have to fuck her. She doesn't strike me as the one-night-stand type, and I'm certainly not the promise-a-relationship type. Since we have to work together for months, neither of us should do anything, ever.

"Listen, will you let me through?" I'm gently pushed by a photographer who's escaped Dave and the new bodyguard I've added because of the extra attention I'm getting these days.

"Why? Are you in a hurry to run to her? Her name is Liliane Jenkins, right?" The kid's getting in my face with his camera again, as if he can capture a confession from me.

"Look straight ahead and think about something else, look straight ahead and think about something else," I keep telling myself until he throws the camera right at my cheekbone, making me lose control. "I told you to let me through! Are you deaf?" I erupt. They continue sneaking around me, blocking me from my car and making me late for the press conference.

Dave jumps in between us and shoves the reporter back a few steps. I would have gladly done it myself as I make my way through this crowd of idiots, but breaking cameras, pushing too hard, and hurting people is off-limits. I'm bigger than all of them, and the truth is I could really hurt someone. I can't afford an assault charge. That's why Dave's here. He knows when I'm about to do something stupid and stops me just in time. I have Evan to thank for this guardian angel.

"All it takes is one confirmation. We all know what it's like." Another guy in the crowd presses me.

I burst out laughing so loud it puts everyone on edge for a few seconds. "You really think you know everything? You have no idea how far 'what you know' is from reality. Really, you couldn't be more wrong, believe me," I sneer.

Every time I'm surprised at how far they go to trip you into these pitfalls, I wonder if some people are stupid enough to fall for it. I mean, if you're so famous that you have paparazzi following you, you must have the brains to understand they're taking you to the limit to break you down. Or maybe it's just me that has to be a hundred times more careful about handling my anger.

After what feels like an eternity, we get in the car, and Max gives me a look that makes me smile.

"I know it wasn't a brilliant idea, but I needed to show myself getting out of this damn building. I swear I'm gonna sell this apartment sooner or later," I explain, and this time he smiles.

I'm used to having people around who understand me and don't judge me. They don't ask too many questions, trust the instructions given to them, do their jobs well, and know to take orders only from certain people. They're the perfect employees when you need privacy and you don't want your business to end up on the streets.

We get to the record company, and this time we go around the basement parking lot. The journalists should all be sitting in the press room, set up on the tenth floor by now, and I take a deep breath to calm down. I'm always nervous before a press conference because I never know what questions they'll ask. Journalists are like loose cannons. You never know which one will go off first. Sometimes, people you've known for a long time suddenly need to earn a promotion or a new job, and they come up with the most uncomfortable and scandalous questions. Whether you answer them or not, whether you are "guilty" or not, the doubt is still there, and you have to stand there and contain the damage.

I come up from the service elevator, which employees use and gives me access to the offices, so I don't have to go through the lions' den, also known as the press area, or gossip room. Because, after all, that's what they do when they're not dealing with politics or crime news: gossip. I bet I can count on one hand the questions they'll ask about the album we're going to release or the tour we're going to do; none of them have an ounce of expertise or even a desire to find out what they're going to write about. It's a bit like me showing up on stage without learning the songs, singing whatever comes to my head.

"No bullshit, today, please," Evan begs us when we're all

sitting in his office, some in the armchairs and some on the sofa, but his eyes are fixed on me.

I raise my hands above my head as a sign of surrender. He knows I'm the hothead of the four, but it's not like he can blame me all the time.

"Look, if they ask me something personal, I'll leave. I already had to fight this morning to get out of my house. I don't want to deal with any more bullshit." I make that clear to him right away.

Evan gives me a dirty look but doesn't tell me anything because he knows I'll do it. It wouldn't be the first time I've left a press conference. The others sneer because they know that it's easy to get on my nerves today. I, too, have a tolerance limit and, while I try to keep my anger under control, sometimes I simply need to get away from the people who really make me lose it.

"This is gonna be the fastest press conference in history," Thomas giggles and I give him a dirty look. I don't need him to fuel our manager's pressure on me.

We enter the press room in a line: first Evan, then Thomas, me, Michael, and Simon. The seats have our names on them, although I hope everyone in the room can at least recognize our faces. The buzz from outside dies down when the door closes, and our manager gets everyone's attention. as we sit down. Evan explains why we're here and what we're going to answer: tours and upcoming albums. He dictates the rules at the beginning of every press conference, but I can count on one hand the number of times journalists have actually followed them. When Evan announces that the questions can start, almost all fifty journalists raise their hands. He points to one in the crowd, a blonde girl I've never seen before.

"My question is for Damian," she begins in a warm and, I must say, pleasant voice.

Strange that it's for me, that never happens, I think, but I smile and signal her to continue. The blonde pushes her chest forward and starts talking into the microphone.

"What's your relationship with Liliane Jenkins? Are you a couple?"

It takes me a few seconds to realize Lilly's name is actually Liliane, and then my smile completely fades away. She must be new, I've never seen her, and I almost hate to wreck her career like this. But to be honest, if she can't figure out the simple ground rules maybe she should change jobs now before it's too late.

I see my bandmates and Evan tense up like violin strings and I can't help but relate. "Are you really sure you want to start with this question?" I give her a second chance and a buzz of hope spreads across the room.

In the front row, Peter is shaking his head in disconsolation, knowing that he's got his work cut out for him now; I won't be as willing to answer questions as when I first arrived.

"Yes." She wants to be firm, but her voice is shaking.

I let the silence hang in the room, looking into the eyes of many of the journalists present—almost all of them I know. "Gentlemen, you can thank your colleague for making your day much harder." I see her blushing out of the corner of my eye as everyone gets more concerned, including my band-mates. "For me, the press conference is over."

I stand up, and a roar of protest explodes. The photographers' flashes in the back of the room go wild. Evan gives me an angry glare, but I know he won't get up because he'll want to try and stop the journalists' protests. He'll probably continue the press conference as if nothing happened, and after a couple of questions, they'll all leave, leaving the press there to dwell on their unproductive day.

I wait in Evan's office because I know he'll want to talk to me at the end of the conference, so there's no point in me leaving and then finding him at my doorstep. At least here I can escape when his yelling gets annoying.

*

Two hours pass before Evan enters, without a word, and I've had a chance to brood over all the possible scenarios as he's never left me alone in his office this long. When Lilly comes in too, my concern deepens; I hadn't really taken her into consideration.

"Couldn't you just say 'There's nothing going on' and answer that fucking question?" she yells when she sees me. "But no, you're too important to stoop to such a thing. And so here I am, in the middle of the day, called into an office to get lectured like a little girl." She is furious.

I guess she saw the press conference. She doesn't understand that I did it to protect her, not to be a fickle rock star. "You have no idea what you're talking about," I say without even looking at her as she sits down. I'm more focused on studying Evan.

"Oh, really? And yet it seems like a very, very simple question," she fires back at me.

"In this environment, you don't confirm or deny anything private. Do you understand that or not?" I yell at her, leaning slightly forward, caught up in my fury. I instantly regret jumping on her like this and back off, putting space between us that feels enormous.

"Leaving, though, you've made a bigger mess, don't you think?" Her voice is powerful as she turns towards me, meeting my fury.

"Who cares about the mess at the press conference! I stopped that question so it wouldn't lead to others, like why you were terrified on that stage. Should I have said you were afraid of Jenna? And when they came knocking at your door asking why, would you have answered? Because even I don't know why you're still stressed out over people's bullshit after all these months!" I scream louder than she does.

"My life and my answers are not your concern. Think about your questions. Nobody asked you to come to save me."

I let out an exasperated half-laugh. "Sure, because you could have handled the interview the same way you 'handled' Jenna's, by panicking and almost blowing a concert at the sight of her. You realize you're not ready for this yet?"

"And I never will be if you keep stepping in and messing up like you did a few hours ago!" she screams, so loudly her voice comes out broken.

"Stop it, both of you!" Evan's voice overtakes both of ours, and we snap our heads in his direction; neither of us has the guts to say a word. "Are you two fucking? I need an answer and not the pre-packaged one we give the media. I need to know if I'm going to have to deal with any photos or videos in the future. I need to know the truth."

"No!" exclaims Lilly.

"Well, could you at least not look so disgusted," I say, barely keeping a smile on my face. She gives me stern look, which is about as intimidating as a duckling running towards me. "Anyway, like she said, there's nothing. No romantic or sexual relationship."

It shouldn't be that hard to read the truth on my face. She's the only woman I've ever resisted. Though God knows I'd like to lay her on that desk and own her in every way known to man. Evan should appreciate the effort, for crying out loud!

"Okay, we'll make a joint statement where we'll clarify the purely working relationship between two very talented artists," Evan says, calming down.

"That makes no sense," whispers Lilly, getting a frosty look from Evan and me. "Why do we have to explain this? Because that bitch Jenna gained a bunch of followers? It doesn't make any sense, the whole mess they're making."

I agree with her to an extent. I don't like having to justify something that never happened, even though I wanted it to. What bothers me the most about this whole situation is that my conscience tells me that maybe, deep down, Jenna's right—I'd like to fuck Lilly, and it's freaking me out.

"Because Damian walking away from that press conference confirmed something that isn't there." Evan's voice is so calm and cold that I'm ashamed of my impulsive behavior.

"It doesn't take a genius to figure it out," Lilly says.

I glare at her. "I don't know if you understood anything I said two minutes ago, but just so you know, I did it for you! And you know what? Fuck you! Next time I'll leave you to drown in these shit situations and I won't give a fuck about the consequences you'll have to face!"

I regret my words at once; I can see they wounded her. "No one's ever asked you for anything," she whispers as she looks down her hands.

"Please stop," Evan says, trying to make us listen to reason. "We don't have time for drama between you two, okay? In the meantime, disappear for a few days and stay out of sight. Sooner or later, the rumors will die down, and they'll find someone else to torture."

Lilly's bitter laugh gets our attention. Why the hell is she so amused? "He's got a super penthouse in Tribeca he can hide in and get food for himself. I live in a 40-square-foot hole in Brooklyn with my family, who now hate me because of the paparazzi always lurking around the house. Where the hell am I supposed to go? I can't just disappear."

She's got a point. She can't even go to a coffee shop on the corner without making the front page of some media outlet. I can live in that apartment for a whole month. She can't even go to the bathroom without taking shifts. I feel responsible for her situation. At the end of the day, if it weren't for my fame, Lilly would be living it up.

"Come away with me for a few days," I find myself proposing without thinking about it.

She looks at me like I'm an idiot. "Are you out of your mind? How's that supposed to make the rumors disappear?"

"That's not a bad idea," Evan says, coming to my rescue. "Go out of state. The paparazzi won't chase you there. There are a few places we've managed to keep secret, and that would give you a chance to breathe a bit and get rid away from the pressure here."

I raise an eyebrow in a silent "I told you so" towards her, and find her staring right at me.

"No way," she stubbornly insists. I think she's the most

stubborn woman I've ever met, and she gets on my nerves like few others in my life. I almost wish I hadn't suggested it.

Evan gets down on his knees in front of her, grabs her hands between his, and softens his eyes. "Please, Lilly. Have faith in me. I'm trying to clean up the mess this hothead has made, but you need to try and disappear for a few days and make my job easier, okay?"

I look at my friend, tilting my head a bit. He could have spared me the veiled insult in order to convince her, but looking at her face, I can tell my manager's good at this.

Lilly looks up at the ceiling and makes a sound of frustration. "All right, but if I kill him during this time, it's your fault," she finally concedes, pointing the finger at Evan's knowing smile.

*

Max leaves us in front the rather imposing front door to my villa in Connecticut, and Lilly looks around like a little girl seeing the Christmas tree in Rockefeller Center for the first time: wide-eyed, open-mouthed and looking around dreamily. Luckily, she left the pissed off attitude in Manhattan

"This is yours...this...I don't even know what to call it," she says as she walks in, lingering on every detail. I have to admit that the dark, classic wood furniture, in stark contrast to the white, modern furniture in my Manhattan apartment, gives this place a rather majestic, though warm and welcoming look.

"Home?" I chuckled amusedly, remembering that I, too, at first, behaved just like her, only with less wonder and without that dreamy look on my face. She looks like a fucking Disney princess right now, the one who walks into the library and drops her pants for the Beast.

"My whole apartment could fit in half your living room. I wouldn't exactly call it home," she points out, turning to me for the first time.

I smile and put my suitcases next to the sofa. I called before I showed up here, and the maid was kind enough to light the fireplace and prepare everything. I also found a bottle of red wine and some snacks on the coffee table. I must say, she's learned my taste and knows my style. I have to remember to give her a raise for Christmas.

"Anyway, yes, it's mine. Or at least one of the companies that I own," I explain as she sits on the floor next to the table and starts pouring wine with ease. I like that straightforwardness of hers.

"You have a company?" She seems impressed, and it leaves me feeling slightly embarrassed.

"Some. You need them when you have my name, and you need to buy something the public doesn't know about."

She nods like it's the most familiar explanation in the world, and I appreciate her not sticking her nose in. I sit next to her, grab the glass of wine she poured me, and take a sip, pushing the cheeseboard over to her, hoping she'll eat some. I get the impression I'm going to spend half the weekend convincing her to eat and the other half dragging her out of the gym.

"The tour starts in a few days. Journalists will turn their attention to that, leaving us alone. We won't have to be locked in here for eternity," I promise, winking at her.

"This house is a palace. I could spend the next four years in here and not live in the same room for more than a week. I don't think I'll be bored for a while in this luxury."

I laugh out loud at her disarming honesty. "Do you think

you can handle this life?" I'm intrigued by her casual, detached attitude about certain aspects of being famous.

She smiles and puts a cracker smeared with cheese and jam in her mouth and shrugs. "I'm not famous so I don't have to worry about these things. Now, the attention is on me because you're here. After the tour, we'll go back to our lives, and they'll forget about me in a week," she says with conviction.

I smile and nod. I can partly understand her perplexity. I too, was incredulous at first in the face of such notoriety. "After the tour, this will become your life. You will no longer be a stranger who won a competition. Thousands of people will know who you are, and whether you like it or not, this will become your normal life," I try to explain.

She thinks about it for a few seconds biting into another cheese cracker and licking her fingers. A gesture that doesn't escape me, makes me sweat, and fills my mind with dirty thoughts.

"Do you really think we have enough talent to sustain this career? I've never seriously thought about what could happen next. I try not to delude myself, keep in touch with reality. At the end of the day, my fame is due to your apparent boner in a video, not exactly material to sign with a record company."

It's disarming to see how much this girl has her head on straight. Most of her peers I've met wanted to sneak into my bed and then get a selfie and post it on Instagram to gain some fame. She's the exact opposite, she doesn't give a damn about my status, let alone my money, and she certainly doesn't have much faith in her abilities.

"I know it may seem a little confusing right now because you've never done a concert by yourself, so it's hard to tell who's coming to see you. But trust me, Evan doesn't go out of his way with just anyone. I've seen a lot of bands he's launched over the years, but I've never seen him invest as much energy as he does with your band."

She shrugs her shoulders and takes a sip of wine, apparently untouched by my statement.

"When did you start playing?" I ask, changing the subject a bit.

She eats another cracker and seems to ponder the answer. "I was fifteen years old; it was a bad time, and I was home a lot. Luke brought me a guitar one day, so I wouldn't get bored, and that's when I started. First, the guitar and then the bass, I practiced until my fingers bled every day. I was not one of those who magically becomes a perfect musician. I'm extremely stubborn. What I can do is the result of methodical commitment and dedication. That's why I told you earlier that I don't know how this is going to end. As much as I can work in this environment, you also need a stroke of luck, and, until now, I've only had one that could potentially change my life: winning your competition. So no, I don't know how it will end." She smiles at me and puts the glass down, and I have to make a considerable effort not to put my lips on hers. "What about you? When did you start playing?"

The question makes my stomach tighten up, and I take a sip of wine to ease the tension a little bit. "About the same age as you. I had...nothing else to do, and when the chance came up, I jumped at it." I finish my glass and pour another one, topping up Lilly's.

She seems to study me for a few seconds, maybe to understand if I'm lying to her, or perhaps my paranoia is more noticeable than usual. "Have you always played with the same guys, or have you had changes in the band?"

I take a deep breath in and close my eyes. That's why I've never wanted a relationship with a woman: eventually, the questions end up in your past. "Always the four of us messing around! What about you, guys?"

Lilly sips and stares at me for a few moments. "We were the losers at school. No one else wanted to be around us, so yeah, always us," she says, amused. "Apart from a couple of weeks of Jessica coming to the rehearsal room to 'be a choir girl' until we found out she had her eye on Martin and wanted to use a different microphone."

I laugh, nearly spitting out my wine. "Really? And did she finally succeed?"

Lilly bursts out laughing. "Yeah. He didn't particularly like her, but when a girl offers you your first experience with oral sex at eighteen, you're not so picky. We spent a month with Martin in a state of constant oblivion," she says, laughing, as we both empty our glasses of red.

"Look, if you say blowjob, I won't yell at you," I tease her and have fun watching her blush as I get up and go to the cellar for another bottle of Zinfandel. They call it "meditation" wine, and it helps a little with forgetting my problems, especially if I break the rules and, instead of sipping it calmly, drain one glass after another.

"I know you're vulgar, and you don't get upset about things like that."

"It's not a matter of being vulgar. It's just that I like to call things by their names. When you approach a girl, you don't ask her if she'd give you fellatio. You ask her for a blowjob."

I'm pouring her glass while she's giggling, having a good time.

"When you put it like that, it makes sense. Do you have to ask that a lot?" She raises an eyebrow with a mixture of curiosity and shame. I don't think she's used to talking about stuff like this.

"Honestly, no. They're usually the ones who offer it." I hide a smile behind the glass and enjoy her big, mesmerizing eyes.

"Like what? They just come up to you and ask if they can give you a blowjob? What an incredulous question!"

I burst out laughing in the face of her embarrassment. It's all too easy to make her blush. "No, they usually get down on their knees and unzip. It's not like there are many conversations in those situations."

She covers her flaming red face with one hand and holds the glass with the other. She opens his eyes again and takes a sip. "I'll have to get used to the idea of girls doing the same thing with my bandmates, won't I?" she asks me with a mixture of resignation and fun.

I nod and settle down on the carpet in front of her, one shoulder resting on the couch. Her cheeks are red with wine, and her eyes are slightly shiny. I can tell she's tipsy, because I know her enough to know that in a normal situation she wouldn't be talking about these things with such freedom.

"Yeah. They won't turn it away, trust me." I smile at her. "Are you jealous?"

The idea that she might be jealous of one of her bandmates upsets me. I've always wondered what connection she has with Luke in particular; they're not together, I can see that, but they have such a close relationship that I wonder if there was something in the past. Just the thought of it bothers me.

"God, no, please. They're like brothers. I could never be jealous of their women."

"Has there never been anything with anyone? Not even a fuck?"

The redness of her cheeks tells me I may be pushing too hard, but I'm counting on the effect of the wine. I have an almost physical need to know.

"No. It's weird just thinking about it." She curls her nose in horror.

I feel a weight lifting from my stomach and a smile spreading across my lips.

"What about you?" she asks.

"A fuck with my bandmates? No, that's not my style. They've got too much beard for my taste." I try to laugh it off to avoid her real question.

"No, you idiot. Have you ever had a serious woman?"

I can't keep my jaw from twitching under the tension. "No, I don't have time for relationships with this career." I throw out the pre-packaged excuse that I get away with most of the time, especially with strangers.

Lilly, however, is not a stranger and stares at me for so long it seems endless. I can see in her eyes that she doesn't believe the crap I said, but I don't know why she lets me get away with it.

"It's a sin," she whispers. "Many women would give anything just to wake up next to a face like this every morning." She stretches out her hand and places her fingers just below my lower lip. Then she gently glides them in a line towards my neck, following them with her eyes.

My heart explodes in my chest, and I'm finding it hard to

swallow. If this continues, I don't know how long I can keep my promise to Evan not to get in her pants. I close my eyes as her hand keeps going down to the neck of my T-shirt, and then she puts her palms on my chest. I grab her hand and hold it over my heart, pounding furiously. I put my glass down, and do the same with hers. She looks at me with those big eyes, scared like a fawn, and holds her breath as I approach her with my lips and touch her cheek.

"Watch where you put your hands, Lilly. You might find yourself in the wolf's den without realizing it," I whisper in her ear before leaving a single kiss on her neck, savoring the delicate skin with my tongue.

I hear her moan and inhale a tiny breath. When I move away, her eyelids are lowered and her lips opened with a desire that almost makes me surrender. I don't know if she's drunk, but she's definitely tipsy. Otherwise, she never would have reached out that hand. I turn her around with a quick gesture and pull her to me until her back is against my chest. Her breathing is as shallow as mine.

I grab the glass and hand it to her. She accepts it with trembling fingers while I take mine. We remain silent and calm our hot spirits for a long time.

Evan's gonna have to give me a fucking monument in the middle of Central Park for not jumping on her tonight.

CHAPTER 10
Lilly

"Holy cow," I whisper, enchanted.

"I can't believe we're in here," echoes Luke in an equally awed tone, as if there is some reverential fear that forces us not to disturb the quiet of this sacred place, our tour bus.

It's the first day of the tour with the Jailbirds, or rather, tomorrow is their first concert, but we have our own little corner of the world to occupy before we start our gigs in three days.

"Have you seen this place?" asks Taylor, observing the modern, futuristic decor with wide eyes.

I go inside first and make room for the others. Our bus is a single story, with a modern living room complete with a bench and a coffee table with six seats, a small L-shaped sofa and a kitchen that extends on the opposite side. All the furniture is in white lacquered wood, the seats are black imitation leather. LEDs run along the ceiling and sides, lighting the room with a soft, diffused welcoming feel. I step forward and open the sliding door that divides the living area from the sleeping area. There are four cubicles for sleeping, two on each side. They look like the bunk beds on a spaceship. A little further on, immediately on the right, a bathroom is equipped with a toilet, a small sink with a mirror on top, and a cabinet for toiletries. On the left, separate from the bathroom, is a shower with a small retractable cabinet spacious enough to hang your clothes without getting them wet while showering. Finally, separated by a sliding door at the back of the bus, is the most spectacular room of all: a TV room with a flat-screen and a black imitation leather sofa covering the three sides of the small room.

"Guys, I found our paradise," I shout to get their attention. In a handful of seconds, they rush in and push me down onto the closest couch cushions.

"This place is great for bringing girls!" Martin seems to light up, and I look at him.

"Don't even think about fucking anyone in here. I don't want to sit on your bodily fluids the whole tour," I threaten him with disgust.

Taylor and Luke burst out laughing and push Martin around until he sits next to me.

Luke backs me up. "I have to agree with Lilly on this one. We have four people living together for months in these confined spaces. We need rules."

Martin rolls his eyes as if his friend's response was predictable.

"Of course, you agree with your Lilly. God forbid you disagree for once. But we're on tour, so I'm going to take advantage of the girls who throw themselves at me and give it to me good—without me having to beg," says Taylor somewhat desperate sounding.

We all burst out laughing in the face of our drummer's desperation.

"So, have you decided where you're going to fuck yet?" thunders Damian's voice from the front of the bus.

"Not in here," I say, pushing the guys in my band into the

living area. "I have no intention of finding myself with a bunch of half-naked girls in the bathroom or moaning on the other side of the wall all night," I explain to the Jailbirds, who are now sitting on the couch.

They're so big, they take up all the available space, and I'm starting to miss the air in here. They have an amused smile on their lips. I hadn't calculated that the tour bus would be the biggest problem. One thing I've carefully avoided saying and that only Luke knows is that I'm claustrophobic: I have no idea how I'm going to sleep in those narrow cubicles.

"Aren't you going to have any fun?" Thomas asks me, maliciously. "After all, what happens on tour stays on tour." He winks, uninhibited.

I watch him, pretending to be annoyed. "Wasn't it Vegas? Anyway, of course, I'm going to have fun, but not on this bus... You know, I can get a little...noisy in certain situations." I raise an eyebrow, cross my arms over my chest, and flash a big smile that makes him laugh.

I look at Damian and see a mix of feelings on his face: anger mixed with excitement.

Simon adds, "Lilly's right. They have to set some rules, or they're going to slaughter each other within two weeks of the tour. It's hard to share such tight spaces."

Michael pushes him with a friendly punch. "Just because you're the saint of the group doesn't mean others have to be like you. He soundproofed the rooms of our tour bus, poor thing," he jokes, looking around at all of us.

"I find myself staying up all night because of your shagging," Simon complains, pushing his friend in turn.

"Wait, you guys have separate rooms?" Luke asks, almost

intoxicated by the news.

The guys look at each other, frowning like we're complete idiots.

"Of course, we have separate rooms, we have a double-decker bus. We're the most famous band in the world. You want us to move like rats trapped inside those stuffy cubicles? We've been doing this for years, and we've had enough," says Damian, outraged.

"Sorry I asked," whispers Luke, almost embarrassed, and we all burst out laughing.

"If you don't get laid in here, you're gonna need the gym... And before you ask, do not to bring girls in there. I don't want to work out on your bodily fluids," Michael admonishes.

"Do we have a gym?" asks Taylor.

Thomas explains, "It's the windowless bus you saw outside. When we're on tour, we can't find a new gym in every city or spend our time taking selfies with people who recognize us. So we thought we'd fill a bus with equipment and take it with us. If you can't have fun with a woman, it's a great way to blow off some steam, and you're going to need it very soon."

"Can we see it?" asks Martin, eyes out of his head with enthusiasm.

"Not now," Damian answers. "We're about to leave, and you can't use it while we're on the move, but at the first stop, we do the full tour. Although, I'm sure you already know how to use the weights." He gesticulates toward our guitarist's sculpted physique as his chest swells with pride.

"I've always wondered why you use tour buses when clearly you can afford private jets for travel and hotel rooms," asked Martin intrigued.

In fact, we've wondered about it in recent months. Why travel long distances by bus when they can just take the plane?

"Because this young man here," Damian explains, pointing at Simon, "is terrified of flying. We're thinking of hiring an anesthesiologist to drive us around when we have to leave the United States, and can't travel on the ground. We hate it so much we're seriously considering knocking him out for the duration of the flight."

Everybody laughs, including Simon, but I totally get it. I know what it's like to be terrified of something. For me, it's the tight spaces, like the cubicles I have to sleep in.

"Okay, we're going that way, we're leaving in ten minutes, so take your seats and get settled in. This will be your home for a long time," Thomas says before he gets his friends up and out of our living room.

We sit around the table and look at each other, one part stunned and skeptical, the other part excited.

"So, we're really going, huh?" I say excitedly.

My stomach has been twitching since last night with nervousness and pleasure. I have to admit this adventure excites me, and, little by little, I realize that I like the idea of doing this life. Everything has been going well since we started with the club tour. It's true, the press is killing me, but I've learned to avoid them at all costs: I don't read it, I don't want to get caught unprepared by the comments on socials, so I've just tried to be casual about it and haven't gone into crisis mode yet. Sure, I work out a little more than usual, but it's a healthy way to relieve stress, right? Evan was right. I just need to find my own space in the end. I look at my bandmates and see their excitement, their happiness in being here.

"Yes, but we have to take turns fucking," Martin continued. I roll my eyes at him and wish for a bolt of lighting. "Is it possible that you don't have anything else to think about? Maybe you won't find anyone who will give it to you," I provoke him.

He laughs like I've made the joke of the century. "I'm sure I can find more than a few people who'd like to have this body, trust me. You have the same problem. Did you see the way Damian looked at you when you said you'd have fun on tour?" He raises an eyebrow in defiance.

I frown and stare at him like he just showed me a math theorem. "How did he look at me?"

Everyone else is laughing, and I'm more puzzled than before.

"As if he doesn't know whether to put a chastity belt on you or rip your clothes off with his teeth and fuck your brains out," Taylor explains with his usual finesse.

I look at them like they're aliens ready to suck my brain with a straw. In the meantime, I can hardly control the hot flashes spreading from the bottom of my belly to my face, making it turn red as a cherry. I have to admit, I've thought all too often about what it would be like to be fucked by Damian. Especially after three days alone in his house in Connecticut with an excessive amount of red wine and his semi-hard-on always present.

"You're completely out of your mind," I blurt out, pretending to be outraged and trying to deflect attention.

Everyone's laughing again, and it's starting to get on my nerves.

"Don't say you haven't noticed, please. He'd make you

bend over on this table and make you scream his name in fifteen or sixteen languages," continues our drummer relentlessly, moving his pelvis, simulating a not-subtle-at-all sexual act.

I'm used to their comments, but it embarrasses the hell out of me when they make them about me. "That's not true!" I scream, this time really horrified because the truth is I can imagine the physical pleasure I would feel being in that position with Damian behind me.

The bus moves and, luckily, I'm with people who have the attention span of a goldfish in an empty bowl.

"We're moving!" cries Martin.

"No shit, Sherlock," I tease him with a smile.

The bus pulls into the street, and I find myself parading, without much notice from the others, into the bathroom. Time to try the shower. Cold. As soon as I close the door behind me, the narrow environment makes me miss the air, I feel suffocated, and my hands start shaking. The feeling of nausea grips me, I begin to wheeze, and my head gets light. I open the door and throw myself out of that rat trap and into the arms of Luke, who catches me.

"Take a deep breath," he whispers and leads me to the sofa at the back of the bus while the others have their noses stuck to the window and don't notice anything.

"Breathe and look at me, Lilly." He keeps rubbing my hands and stroking my head while I try not to throw up on him.

"I can't live in here for months. I'm gonna die in here, Luke. I'm dying," I whisper with a shaky voice, closing my eyes and forcing myself to focus on Luke's warm arms that make me feel safe.

"We'll figure something out, I promise you. We'll find a

solution," he whispers in my ear as he strokes my head.

"And where the hell am I gonna sleep if I can't even close the bathroom door without getting anxiety? Have you seen that cubicle bed?"

"You don't feel suffocated in here, though, right? I mean, sitting on this couch."

I think about it for a moment, and with the ceiling well away from my head and the door open so I can see all the way to the back of the bus, it doesn't feel so suffocating.

"No, not really."

"We just found out who's going to get all the turns in this part of the bus," he giggles amusedly.

"Martin and Taylor are gonna kill me." It makes me laugh to think about telling them.

"Probably," laughs Luke as he holds me close.

I breathe deeply and almost feel like crying. And here I thought the biggest problem with this tour was going to be the media and that jerk Brad.

*

We enter through the back door with the bags of Chipotle we just picked up from the club next door. Tonight, the Jailbirds will be performing by themselves a charity concert that was planned before the tour. We'll watch them perform from our prime location at the side of the stage. In the meantime, though, we'll eat what we just bought, because we've discovered that eating on a tour bus is boring and overrated. In other words, we burned the only pan we had, forcing the driver to stop for an hour and a half to ventilate the bus. Blame Luke. He discovered the PlayStation in the back of the bus by the TV, and we all lost track of time while we waited for the eggs to cook. And maybe mine too, that I didn't set the timer, but essentially it was Luke's fault.

"What are you guys eating?" Damian asks, standing in the doorway to the room where we holed up backstage with the Jailbirds.

I notice one of the girls from the press office passing by and whispering, "Call me," to him, before snickering at one of the interns who always accompanies her. Damian answers with a discreet nod of his head and a smile that surely warms her panties. Apparently, he's already setting the stage for an unforgettable sex-and-fun tour.

"Mostly burritos and tacos. Want some?" Luke asks, showing him the bag in his hand.

Damian comes over and grabs a tinfoil cylinder containing a burrito, opens it up, and devours it in two bites, literally.

"You don't have a problem with stage fright and vomiting, apparently," notes Taylor looking at him with admiration. It's like elementary school where those who behave more like pigs get the whole class's respect, or at least the males.

Damian's bandmates burst out laughing, and he gives them a sharp look, definitively attracting our attention. He's hiding something.

"Damian has other problems before he takes the stage," says Michael, winking.

"What do you mean?" I ask, expressing the curiosity of my whole band.

"To put it in nice terms...he gets sexually excited...very excited," explains Thomas.

For a moment, we're all stunned, and then we all burst out laughing at Damian's face. It's damn true what they're saying.

"Can you not spread my business around? If this gets out, I swear I'll rip your lungs out through your mouth." His threat sounds serious. I have no doubt he can do it for real. He seems embarrassed and almost ashamed at his body's reaction to the stage adrenaline, that his blood flows to body parts he doesn't want to flaunt. If there's one thing I've learned about him, living so close to him these last few months, it's that he's never one to show off his achievements. He's so discreet that I don't even know if he slept with someone while we were out on our Manhattan mini-tour. He's certainly not the one who alerts the media when he's slept with a woman. But it would explain the smile on the press secretary's face a moment ago; maybe he just "loosened the tension" with her.

"You get a hard-on before you get on stage?" asks Luke in admiration. "What the hell do you do in those tight pants you're wearing? You can't hide it!"

Typical males comparing size, and right now, Damian is winning hands down—literally. "What do you think I do? I relieve myself." He says, raising an eyebrow at Luke like he's an idiot.

"Do you fuck before you go on stage?" Martin's found his new spiritual guide.

"Not always. I mean, it's not like I always have a girl who wants to help me with that. Sometimes I have to make do." He says it like it's the most normal thing in the world to masturbate before you perform.

Which makes me think about all the times we've been on stage in the last few months. "Holy shit, everybody, stop it. I don't even wanna know how many times I've had his...his... cum on me before a gig."

Silence falls as everyone turns to looks at me with big eyes. I didn't really say that out loud, did I? What a horrible picture I just painted! I feel my cheeks heating up when Thomas starts laughing, and everyone else follows him.

"I didn't mean it like that!" My voice comes out squeaky. "I meant, I wonder how many times he's masturbated and then touched me...in non-sexual places...not erogenous zones... nothing below the belt... Stop laughing, nothing's ever happened!" I yell at the top of my lungs, but none of them are stopping. In fact, it seems to be getting worse.

I curl up in my armchair, putting aside a taco I don't want to eat anymore.

"Honey, you'll be begging me for my cum all over you after you see me on stage tonight," Damian says, and I can't tell if he's serious or joking.

Everyone else laughs at his joke, but I'm only getting hotter. It's disarming how I can come unraveled so easily around him, but my redness this time is not embarrassment. The image of Damian fucking me is branded in my mind. I'm afraid he might be right about me.

*

Watching from the front of the stage, close to the security barricades in this privileged position, is priceless. My face lights up like with the same dreamy look as many of the fans behind me who are screaming like obsessed women. The lights are still on, and the buzz is deafening, given the twenty thousand bodies in this place. People stomping on the bleachers are getting more and more excited, exhilarated. The place is not as big as a stadium; it's more intimate which makes the atmosphere even more magical.

"Are you ready?" Luke asks me with a smile.

"Sadly, I've never seen them live. I'm afraid it's gonna be too intense for me to handle," I shout back excitedly.

The lights suddenly go down, and the roar rising from behind us makes my insides shake, or maybe they're shaking already from screaming along with everyone in here tonight. The Jailbirds come on stage with their usual confident and cocky air, looking so different from the guys we've been getting to know these days. They're sexy as hell, sex and rock gods. Now I understand why girls throw themselves at their feet: with those bad-boy looks and killer grins they manage to set you on fire and peel your panties off just by looking at you.

"You're drooling," laughs Luke, calling me back to reality.

"No, I'm not!" I scream over the roar as the music starts blasting out of the speakers.

"You're looking at Damian like you want to get on that stage and fuck him."

That is so true, I really would. "No, I'm not!" I push him with my shoulder, and he laughs. Traitor.

They start the first song, and Damian wiggles in front of that microphone pole like he's fucking the guitar in front of him. I suddenly find myself wanting to be the Gibson's neck just to feel his fingers caressing me. What the hell is going through my head? I keep my glasses from slipping down my nose because I'm sweating like a baked pig and, just now, Damian lowers his gaze on me. I'm lit by the stage lights, and he throws a sexy and mischievous smile at me that makes my hormones rage. Even my nipples snap to attention. I'm screwed.

Damian's expression is captured on camera and thrown up on the giant screens behind the stage and on both sides of it.

The crowd's roar makes my guts and heart tremble simultaneously. When they wink into that camera, it's like they're winking at every single person in this arena. Everyone here feels like the center of their world—that's their magic formula to win over audiences. At this moment, I understand perfectly why they are the most famous band in the world.

Damian sensually walks across the stage, moving his head to the rhythm when he approaches Simon and wiggling his pelvis almost obscenely towards Michael. Those two guys are an erotic charge ready to explode. Damian plays and jokes to the limit of decency, but Michael has no boundaries when he's on stage. He's always been the brazen one, but he's an animal up there. When you see them on TV, they tend to frame Damian mainly, but live it's clear that Michael contributes in a big way to the show.

They're a force of nature, there's no pause, not even between songs. The show never has a dead moment, and the delirium behind me doesn't go away for a second. I've been jumping and singing for so long without taking a decent breath, that at some point, I have to stop and take a few deep ones so I don't faint. The adrenaline circulating in my veins creates a state of constant tension that makes my stomach and soul vibrate. It is pure, vivid, and primal excitement.

When Damian sings the first notes of "Sex on the Beach", another roar surges from the crowd. The song is fast, sexy, and his hoarse voice makes you feel like you're the one having sex on the beach with him. He looks in my direction, almost as if this was a private concert between him and me. His gaze finds mine and a thrill runs through my back when the words, "lying on the sand I feed on your moans, your sighs, your pleasure," slip from his lips. I am chained to his eyes, and the sensual way he sings feels like he's moving all over my body, including inside me, to an animalistic rhythm. I push my glasses up on my nose, and his voice turns into a sexy guttural groan to die for. At the end of the song, I'm gasping with excitement, and it takes a few seconds before we both come back to reality and realize that there's an entire arena full of people around us.

"I must say that was...intense." Luke's voice makes me look away from the stage where Damian is continuing the show.

"Really?" My trembling voice betrays the will to appear detached.

Luke raises an eyebrow making me realize he doesn't believe my naive attitude. "The waves of testosterone from that stage just about pushed me to the ground."

"Oh, shut up! It was just for show."

"Lil, if sex could mark a person's possession, you'd have 'Damian' stamped on your ass right now." He laughs out loud.

I look down, blushing partly because of his comment, partially because I'm shamefully turned on.

The concert is impressive, to say the least, and for the last part we move next to the stage, where the guys will be out in less than a minute to wipe off the sweat, drink some water and head back on for the last two songs. The energy they transmit is like electricity. It flows under my skin, in my veins, like an adrenaline rush that makes me tremble excitedly. I've been to many shows, but none as exciting as this one. Maybe because we know them by now, or because we will have to open for them in a few days, but the feeling is out of this world.

The first to leave the stage is Simon, followed by Michael, Damian, and finally Thomas. The space back here is narrow and full of people who take care of their needs, handing out towels and water bottles already opened. Timing is tight and here, as on stage, it's a set of well-oiled gears that work flawlessly to keep the show flowing. I move slightly to the side, where technicians set the big crates that the equipment gets stored in. I don't want to get in the way, and from here, I still have a view of what is happening.

The excitement I feel makes me snap at any physical contact; the sexual charge that hasn't left me since "Sex on the Beach" will soon become frustration if I don't ease the tension between my legs. Damian seems to be looking for someone and, when he spots me, he slips away without too much notice, grabs my hand, and, to my surprise, throws me, almost literally, into a dark corner hidden between the cases and the wall.

Everything happens so fast that I don't register it. Damian standing in front of me with his sculpted and sweaty physique inside that torn black T-shirt takes my breath away. He puts his hands on the sides of my head, lowers himself to look me straight in the eyes, and squeezes me with a smoldering look I've never seen before. Lust permeates his gaze until it melts me. His mouth approaches slowly, very slowly until it reaches my ear.

"If you pull your glasses up again in such a sexy way during one of my concerts, I swear I'll get off the stage and fuck you in front of twenty thousand people." His hoarse, excited voice makes me wet instantly. If I weren't wholly paralyzed and oxygen-deprived, my hormones would have already taken over, laid him on the floor and stripped him naked, venting my sexual frustration that in the last few minutes has become unbearable. Instead, I stand here, unable to formulate a coherent thought.

Am I really sexy with these glasses on? That explains why I took it almost as a personal offense when Sid makes me wear contact lenses for the shows. "It'll happen again," I whisper, barely able to find my voice.

He pulls back just enough to look me straight in the eye, and the desire I read tells me he's one step away from ripping my pants off here, in the corner of the stage where anyone could peek in and see us. Jesus Christ, how I wish he would have his way and give me that orgasm that's been mounting since the beginning of this damn concert. I think back to my words in a flash of lucidity, and I can feel myself warming up.

"It won't happen...I mean, it won't happen again, sorry," I stammer confusedly.

Just him leaning his chest against my breasts almost makes me cum. His hands leave the wall behind me and sink firmly into my hips, drawing me to his erection. "That's a shame, because I can't wait for an excuse to sink between your thighs and make you scream my name in ecstasy."

Oh, baby Jesus! Why the hell are we still back here and not on a tour bus fucking like there's no tomorrow? Is it even legal to set a woman on fire with desire like this? Because in my opinion, Damian should be handcuffed...maybe to a bed. I raise my hands and cling to his shirt in a desperate gesture, drawing him even closer to me. My brain is high on hormones and that serotonin the guy holding me hostage likes so much.

Damian takes his hands off my hips, moves away just enough to look at me and smile mischievously, and then he turns around and goes back to where he came from. The roar of the crowd tells me they've gone on stage again, but I just stand there, motionless in a bundle of nerves and excitement, hormones chasing each other wildly. What the hell just happened? My legs are jelly, and I slide down the wall until I'm sitting on the floor.

How the hell do I go back to watching the last two songs and act like nothing happened? Right now, the only thing I want is to baptize every backstage surface with the imprint of our naked and sweaty bodies intoxicated by the intense pleasure of orgasm. Sex so wild we can write songs about it for the next ten years. Dirty ones that make little girls blush as they listen with their earphones on the street, heading to see their boyfriends.

Breathing deeply doesn't help me regain my cool demeanor, and I look like a shipwreck at the mercy of the waves as I stagger towards my friends.

"Where the hell have you been? I thought you got bored and went back on the bus," Martin asks me with a wrinkled forehead.

Nothing further from reality. "I was in the bathroom," I lie with a shaking voice.

"Doing what, exactly? Because it looks like you just got laid," he smiles amusedly.

I roll my eyes at him, pretending that his innuendo doesn't even deserve an answer, but I actually feel like I've just had a taste of Damian the rock star. If that's just a prelude, I have to say the reputation he's built has a rock-solid foundation.

CHAPTER 11
Damian

She just stood there staring at me, like a deer caught in the headlights. Jesus Christ, what was I thinking, saying those things? I've got to work with her, for Christ's sake. I can't sleep with her and then dump her. It'll make for a shitty rest of the tour. I roll in my bed, the bus has already stopped for a couple of hours in the parking lot near tonight's venue, but I haven't dared to set foot out of my room yet, even if I only slept a few hours last night. I look down and notice the erection pushing the sheet.

"God, it looks like a circus tent," I murmur as I pass my hand over my face and sigh.

If I keep going like this, I'll get calluses on my hand and my balls will explode. I have to find a solution soon. The little guy between my legs is pulsing and moving all over the place in excitement imagining Lilly moving like crazy over me and shouting my name.

"No, that's not an option."

I'm at the point where I'm now talking to my penis. This is ridiculous. I feel like a maniac. Right now, all it would take is Loretta and her red hair to please me and get the girl who's been invading my thoughts for days out of my head.

I open the door slightly, listening for noises. I don't hear anybody. I assume they're all at the gym.

I crawl out of bed reluctantly and get in the shower. I spend an eternity there, first with cold water, trying to calm the burning spirits without success, then under the jet of hot water, letting my fantasies run wild and relieving myself thinking about slipping between Lilly's thighs. I'm going to hell, I already know it. If I keep wanting her this way, they'll give me a fast track with my name written on it.

Yesterday we were traveling all day. We didn't get a chance to see much of each other alone, just with people around us. Today, however, I absolutely must catch her alone, ask her forgiveness, talk to her, and tell her that I behaved like an asshole. She deserves an apology.

I get dressed, my hair still wet. I put on a pair of shoes and step off the bus to go to hers, hoping to find Lilly alone. I'm freezing as soon as I put my nose out, always forgetting how hot our rooms can be. I knock on their door and pray someone will come and open it quickly.

"Come in," I hear her shout from inside. I open the door, go in, and take off my shoes before I enter.

I step inside their bus, and become paralyzed. Lilly is reaching on tiptoe towards one of the kitchen cabinets, her hand near the top shelf. That's not what's bothering me, though. It's that she's wearing a pair of tight blue boxer shorts that show half of her lower butt cheeks, and a worn-out, loose white tank top with no bra. All the blood flows below my waistband, waking up Junior, who I managed to put to sleep in the shower. Here he is, perky as ever, waiting for me to rip her shorts off and spread her legs.

"Can I help you?" I ask her in a husky voice.

Lilly turns to me and smiles. With that messy bun of hair on her head and those glasses, she's even prettier than I remember. And I swear I've recalled her many, many, many times in the last few hours.

"Would you get me the Froot Loops up there? I can't reach it. Sometimes being the dwarf of the group is torture." She has a pouty, sexy mouth.

I move behind her, grab her by the waist, and scoot her sideways, avoiding putting my boner on her ass first thing in the morning. I take the box and hand it to her.

"Have you had breakfast?"

I smile at her and shake my head. She shakes the cereal box in front of me with a questioning look.

"Okay." I don't tell her that I usually just drink black, hot, bitter coffee in the morning and that milk and cereal suck because they form a mush on the bottom of the bowl that makes me want to puke.

Lilly takes two cups, pours cereal into them, then milk, brings them to the table, and places them on one side of the table. She puts one foot under her butt while she sits down, and I sit next to her, handing her one of the two spoons I took from the kitchen drawer. I swallow the first bite, and I have to admit it's not so bad. Maybe the memory I had as a child isn't accurate enough to influence my judgment right now. Or perhaps she's fucking with my brain, making me do stupid things like eat cereal and enjoy it. I try several times to come up with an apology for the other night, but I can't find a decent one. I look at her, and she doesn't seem angry. She looks happy to be here having breakfast with me. I decide to put the excuses aside, at least for the time being. Second stupid thing I've done this morning.

"Do you have any idea how many calories this cereal contains? It's not like you have to kill yourself in the gym to eat it, is it? Although I haven't seen you work out like crazy the last few days, if I'm honest." I'm not sure it's the right thing to say. I noticed that food is always a delicate subject between her and her bandmates.

Lilly blushes slightly and looks into her bowl. "You were right. Being on tour takes my energy away, and just having all this pressure on me is tiring. I can't risk passing out on stage because I'm not eating right," she admits with a hint of reluctance in her voice.

"Hang on. Repeat what you said," I say, while taking the phone out of my pocket.

She looks at me, bewildered. "I said being on tour takes my energy away."

"No, not that part," I interrupt her. "The part where you tell me I'm right," I say with a smug smile when I see her blushing. I love it when she reacts like this to my jokes.

"You're an idiot."

"I'm not leaving here until you say so." That's a promise.

"You were right. Are you happy now?" She rolls her eyes.

I smile smugly and put the phone back in my pocket. "I'll set it as my ring tone for when you call me." I wink at her, and she punches me in the shoulder.

"So, are you ready for tonight?" I ask her.

Lilly looks up at me and smiles. "Trying not to think about it. If I start to realize that it's only a few hours away, I get anxious. This isn't small clubs in New York anymore. This is twenty thousand plus people. It's impossible to be indifferent to something like that. I'll probably go crazy with excitement during the soundcheck, but I should be more or less normal for the show," she says with a hint of conviction, but her eyes are grainy with fear.

I confess I'm a little worried about her. This is a big leap, moving from amateur to professional.

"You know you can come to me if you need to talk, right?" I ask her. I don't want to bring up that asshole Brad right now, even if he is the one that got her in this state.

She nods as a knock on the door calls our attention.

"Come in," she yells again. "Is it always busy like this?" she asks me with a smile.

I smile as I sink my spoon back into the cereal bowl and bring it to my mouth. I see Michael, Thomas, and Simon, with their hair still wet from the shower and smiling, appear at the door.

"There you are. We've been looking for you," says Michael with a little smile that I don't like at all, primarily since the other two also exchange a sly look. I'm not getting the whole story here.

"I'm having breakfast. Is that a problem?" I respond rather gruffly. I was in a great mood until two seconds ago, when I wasn't alone with Lilly anymore. The realization sends a shiver down my spine, and I'm not sure it's pleasant.

"With a bowl of cereal and milk?" Thomas asks, raising an amused eyebrow.

"Yes, why?" I accentuate my question with a tone that implies, *if you say anything, I'll break all your fingers.*

Thomas raises his hands and shakes his head. "Nothing, just curious," he says, amused.

They all sit around the table except for Simon, who starts making four cups of coffee. "Do you want some, Lilly?"

I watch her shake her head amused and look around as if the intrusion isn't so bad, and I find myself jealous of my own bandmates. The reaction pisses me off so much I want to get up and make a scene.

*

"We have a problem!" Luke runs into our dressing room, wide-eyed, looking like he's possessed. Our heads snap towards him. Simon jumps to his feet, and I sit up straight in my chair.

"Lilly's locked in the bathroom, the latch broke, and we can't get her out. She's freaking out. I need someone to help me open that door. We can't break it down," he explains when he sees the confused expression on our faces.

I jump to my feet and follow Luke back to their dressing room. It must be an emergency; if even Luke can't get her to calm down, she's in a real crisis. I've been watching those two, they're like two peas in a pod with their almost symbiotic relationship.

The chilling sound of screams coming from the bathroom, along with fists hitting wood, can be heard all the way down the hall. I run into their dressing room and find Taylor and Martin at the table, worried, as Luke points me to the door.

"Lilly, it's Damian. Move away from the door, please," I say in a tone loud enough to be heard. She mumbles something, but keeps banging her fists. "Lilly, move away from the door, please. I have to break it down, and if I hit you, I'm gonna hurt you," I say calmly, and this time at least she stops banging.

"Get me out of here!" she cries.

"To do that, I need you to move away from the door, understand? I'm gonna get you out of here."

I see the shadow from the crack under the door move and, with three well-placed forceful shoulder slams against the door, the latch breaks, and the door opens. I find her curled up in the corner, sobbing and shaking, her eyes red and swollen with tears. She's terrified. I move in and kneel down in front of her, but she's scared out of her mind.

"Lilly, it's me, Damian." I reach out my hand then draw it back when she waves me away in shock. "Lilly, listen to me: the door is open, see?"

I don't get a reaction.

"Lilly, look at the door, please," I whisper softly to her, pointing at the room on the other side. I try several times to get her attention until she finally looks up, and even then, I'm not sure she's registered the fact that she can leave this room. I reach out and hold her hand, and this time she is not scared. I get closer, and with a slow gesture, I draw her to me, holding her to my chest when I feel her give way.

My heart accelerates like a madman, running furiously inside my ribcage. It's the first time someone has depended on me like this and, on one hand, I like it, but on the other, it's damn scary. I embrace her tightly, caressing her cheek, kissing her hair, then I put my arms under her knees and pick her up, and we leave the bathroom. All heads turn in our direction, but I don't care. I sit on the sofa leaning against the wall just outside the bathroom and hold her close.

"You don't have to be afraid. I'm here," I whisper softly as if no one else is in the room with us.

She looks at me with those big green, frightened eyes of hers, and I see the exact moment she realizes she can trust me, that I pulled her out, and I won't let go of her for a moment. She nods and snuggles on my shoulder, breathing deeply into the hollow of my neck.

When I finally look up at the others, Martin and Taylor laugh, relieved, and Luke seems to breathe again. Thomas, Mike, and Simon, who apparently followed us and saw the whole thing, are smiling slyly in a way I can't decipher. I motion for them to get out and get ready. I'll stay with her until she's calmed down and go with her on stage.

Luckily, they catch on and leave us all alone. I sink my nose into her hair and inhale that apricot scent deeply, which is stronger than usual today. I smile. I've never been so interested in a girl that I recognize the smell of her hair. Lilly lowers my defenses; she melts those walls I've stubbornly built around me over the years. I've never shared so much intimacy with a woman before, only letting myself relax and be real with Loretta, but I sure wouldn't know what kind of shampoo she uses.

"I'm sorry, I didn't mean to freak out. I'm claustrophobic and not being able to open the door gave me a panic attack," she whispers in a hoarse voice.

I kiss her on the head without answering. What the hell happened to her to be so afraid of the world? She's in crisis because of people's judgment. She's almost maniacally careful not to exceed the daily calorie limit she's imposed on herself. She never leaves the stretch marks reminiscent of her childhood obesity exposed to the public. Now she has panic attacks caused by claustrophobia. It can't all be because of what Brad has been saying about her for years, or at least it can't be the only reason.

We stay like this for a long time until Thomas comes to call us.

"Can you stand up? Do you want us to go?" I whisper to her.

Lilly looks up and gives a half-smile. She's still white as a sheet, but at least she doesn't look like she's about to pass out any minute. I get her off my knees, and immediately I miss her warmth. I grab her by the hand and accompany her to the edge of the stage.

"I'm gonna stay right here, okay? If you're sick or you feel you can't handle this, look in my direction. I won't let go of you," I say to her, standing just behind the black curtain, close to the stage, in a spot that she can see with her eyes. Facing an audience of twenty thousand people for the first time in these conditions will not be easy.

Luke approaches her and puts his hand on her shoulder. "We're about to start," he tells her, and she breaks away from my grip and looks her friend right in the eye.

The lights go down, and the crowd erupts in their initial roar, the one that hits you in the gut and gives you the charge you need to start the concert with a bang. It's as though the excitement building in the audience during the hours spent waiting pours over you in the form of energy that flows through your veins. That energy lights the spark that triggers the fire you set on stage. It's an intense connection between the fans and the band that's fundamental to the show's success.

Luke is a bit awkward, but he'll recover. You can see with a bit of training that he'll become a stage animal. Taylor hides behind his drums; he's nervous, but in his stage position it doesn't show too much. Martin is... Martin's an idiot all the time, so he jumps onto the stage like he was born there. My eyes, however, fix on Lilly, who walks with her head down towards her bass, puts it on, and as soon as the song starts, looks at me and doesn't let go for a second.

This is their most crucial test: alone, they have to warm up the audience, make them dance to their music, engage the crowd even though they're here to see a more famous band. It's a thankless task, challenging in many ways—making the audience like their music when very few have listened to it and it sounds unfamiliar. They have to entertain our fans, stir up their expectations for our performance. And above all, they have to pass the most unfair test: being compared to us. They should be appreciated in their own right for what they're bringing to the stage, but our hardcore fans, here in the front rows, will be tough to convince.

I can't take my eyes off Lilly's. I'm afraid she might go down if I do, like I'm her source of security. Out of the corner of my eye, though, I can see the audience is involved; and from the screams coming from the crowd I can hear they're into the music.

They don't move around a lot on stage, but it will take several concerts before they have the confidence to use all the space available. I remember the first few times I went on a stage like this. After only playing in bars, I felt microscopic and short of breath, even just getting closer to Michael or Simon a couple of times. Thomas seemed so far away it felt like he was playing backstage.

People think the hardest thing to prepare for a tour is the

music. It's not. It's undoubtedly a key component, but not the most important one. The most work is the physical part: building up the strength and stamina to jump, run, play, and sing on stage for two and a half hours without seeming tired. People who come to see us don't want to see us out of breath after two songs. That's why I insist on Lilly and her bandmates eating and training all the time. Sure, they could do cocaine, but the effect would wear off halfway through the concert, and they'd have to power through the other half on their own.

"So, you say you're not taking her to bed." I hear the smile in Thomas' voice, but I don't look at him.

"No," I reply, focusing my gaze on Lilly.

"Then it's even worse than I thought," he laughs and pats me on the back.

I give him a puzzled look and then look back at Lilly. "What the fuck are you talking about?"

"You've been holding your breath since she went out there, and you haven't even jerked off before the show," he says, laughing.

I take a breath I didn't even know I was holding and think of my friend's words. It's true. I've been so worried about Lilly and her crisis that I haven't thought about myself.

"I wanted to make sure she didn't fuck up the first date of the tour. It would have been a mess if she couldn't get on stage," I say, to minimize his point.

The conversation ends there, but my head starts to process so many questions my brain can't contain them all. Thomas stands next to me, smiling with the awareness of someone who understands everything, and it bothers me.

*

The opening set is over, and I'm at least as excited as the guys coming offstage. They did their damn thing, didn't mess it up, and they were fantastic. After the first song, the audience started to respond, and even starting jumping around to the music towards the end. The first few rows of spectators protested them leaving, wanting to hear more.

Luke surprised me a lot. He managed to interact and make the audience laugh with jokes between songs; it's not easy to do with such a broad audience—you risk that awful, embarrassing silence if a joke doesn't land. He dared and it paid off. Joking with each other was also a winning move that you don't often see in such young and inexperienced bands. Lilly was fantastic, and from mid-concert on, she even managed to break out and have fun like she always does on stage. It's obvious that music is her whole life.

The hustle and bustle of people backstage always psyches me up for our performance. The crew has to remove their gear and set up ours, which will take at least twenty minutes. In the meantime, the Red Velvet Curtains are coming offstage amidst the audience's applause, and we all congratulate them. They've earned it, big time. Lilly runs the last few yards and, with one jump, throws her arms around my neck. It's such a sudden gesture that for a moment she's hanging like a monkey before I have a chance to throw my arms around her and hold her close. When she finally lets go, I put her down and she looks at me with a smile from ear to ear, eyes shining.

"Did you see that? We were great!" She looks like a little girl who just did something good and is looking for reassurance. It softens my heart instantly.

I hug her again and this time it's me doing it, pulling her aside to stay out of the way of the crew setting up the stage. I should be with my bandmates in the dressing room for our group ritual before every concert, but I can't get away from her. I drag her into the corner hidden behind the black boxes, push her against the wall and, without thinking twice, I kiss her, sticking my tongue in her mouth and savoring all the sweetness she can give me. At first, she's caught off guard and stiffens against my chest, but then she kisses me back as if she had been waiting for nothing else. She slips her fingers through my hair and clings to my body while I slide my hands under her shirt, the delicacy of her skin intoxicating me, pushing me almost to the touch of her bra. I can feel her shivering under my fingers and arching her back, resting her soft breasts on my chest. I move down until my hands reach her ass, squeezing firmly and pulling her into my hard-on. I make a Titanic effort not to give in to the desire to rip her pants.

She moans against my lips, and the sound is so sensual that I grab her hair, and, with a decisive gesture, I move her head back so I can have free access to her neck. I savor every inch of her skin, from her jaw to her collarbone, and when I start to suck and bite just below her ear, her fingers cling to my hair and hold me there, still, as she pants with pleasure. I repeat the gesture once, twice, and then her lips rest on my neck, returning the favor. There is nothing left of the initial indecision. She savors my skin as if it were her property, with languid and shameless tongue strokes. When she bites my earlobe, a guttural noise comes out of my mouth. I am an animal that wants to eat its prey. With a decisive gesture, I grab her wrists and push them against the wall behind her, above her head, leaving her defenseless, in need of the contact I've just deprived her of. Her excitement shines in her brightly lit eyes as her chest rises and lowers quickly, the nipples poking through her bra and shirt. The sight takes my breath away.

I'm losing my mind. I need to taste her mouth again, to feel her tongue moving sinuously against mine. I want to hear her panting, moaning, and pressing against me as if we were alone in the world. But the sound of a box being moved snaps us back to reality: we're not alone. I hate to leave her. God, how perfect she is in my arms; I rest my forehead on hers and enjoy seeing her panting. I smile slightly.

"I have to go meet the others," I whisper reluctantly.

She nods and smiles and then stands up straight and pushes me slightly, lingering for a few moments with her hands on my chest. "Come on, hurry up, before someone thinks you're the fugitive."

I laugh out loud and we return to our room, walking side by side, close but never touching. I have no idea what the hell I'm doing, but that kiss was better than any fuck I've ever had before any concert. I look at her out of the corner of my eye and find her smiling. It's not a sassy gesture, but a slight upward bend of the lips that shows she's genuinely happy. My chest feels a rush of warmth I've never experienced before. Until this moment, the only thing I ever worried about was that women thought I was fantastic in bed. With her, I just need to put a smile on her lips to feel like I've conquered heaven.

PRESS *Review*

A Beginning That Promises Fireworks...

Hi, Roadies!

Have you had the chance to attend the first concert of the Jailbirds' tour? Absolutely spectacular. I really appreciated that they didn't fill the stage with huge decorative sets but still made sure every detail of the show was seen even from the distant rows with giant screens. I swear, I've never seen such big screens, which allowed those who couldn't afford front-row tickets to enjoy the full show. The strength and energy pulsing from every single song reached everyone in the arena. Then again, I've always said the Jailbirds don't need overblown effects. Put them on stage with just their instruments, and you'll have a fantastic show.

What about the Red Velvet Curtains? Blessed be the day the Jailbirds held that contest, for I believe they have found their worthy heirs. They were born to be on that stage. Martin, the guitarist, appears to have a special relationship with the audience, who cheered him on nonstop. Luke is the mix of sweet and sexy that every woman dreams of, with that hoarse voice of his that gives you chills. Taylor doesn't miss a beat behind that drum set, but the real gem is Lilly. Have you heard what she can do with that bass? It's been a lifetime since I've listened to technique like that from a bass player, and when she gets on stage, it's like she's got music in her DNA.

I can't wait to follow the next dates of the tour (from my couch at home, unfortunately) because this will be one of the best in recent years.

Be kind and rock'n'roll,

Iris

3569 Likes 2742 Tweets 4590 Shares 1297 Comments

Rock News:
We had high expectations for the Jailbirds' tour, and we were not disappointed. The band played their old songs and included four of their latest singles from the upcoming new album. The old hits perfectly complimented the tried-and-true sound you hear in their most recent work. By now, the Jailbirds are a guarantee, and no one could knock them off Mt. Olympus at this point. They're unmatched by many of their contemporary competitors and can hold their own against past rock legends.

However, they'll have to be very careful in taking on a band that promises a lot. The Red Velvet Curtains seem to be having a real Cinderella moment: coming from nowhere, practically unknown, they have proven themselves equal to the biggest band in the industry today. We've already enjoyed their musical skills on the Manhattan clubs tour, but we're sure they're off to a brilliant career start with their first concert of the arena tour. The only drawback was the out-of-context clothing of Lilly, the bass player. She can't show up on that kind of stage with a shirt that's two sizes too big and looks stolen from her father's drawer. Let's hope she makes peace with her closet soon.

Music Live:

What a show, folks! What a show! We were in the front row at the concert that kicked off the Jailbirds' Tour, and we can assure you that if you haven't bought tickets for the next dates yet, you need to make up for it now. The energy is the same as always, plus with the new big screens they've added, even those in the last rows can enjoy the show in detail. The band played their old hits mixed with four new songs off their soon-to-be-released new album. If those songs are a taste of what's to come, get ready for even bigger hits than their previous ones. The energy is impressive and addictive, but their strength remains the front man, Damian Jones, who seems to be unleashed. I've never seen so much testosterone slammed into the faces of screaming girls—from the first to the last row—so sexily.

They won the contest with the band they decided to bring along for the concerts' opening. We'll be hearing a lot about the Red Velvet Curtains. In their first real concert in front of thousands of people, they transmit a powerful energy for such an unknown band. Too bad they didn't warn the bassist that it wasn't high school gym class. She was the only one wearing an oversized t-shirt that looked like the uniform of a school run by nuns.

People:

New photos of Damian Jones' new flame, Lilly Jenkins, working out between gigs. Seen here, Jenkins is running in her customary oversized sweatshirts and looking a little bit worn out. Hard to imagine her having a career as an Instagram fitness celebrity, given her flushed face and that sweaty hair stuck to her head.

CHAPTER *12*
Lilly

He kissed me. And it wasn't a meaningless kiss. It was one that makes your toes curl and rips the earth out from under you. When I think about it, I still get wet at the memory of being pressed against that toned body. How I wanted to tie my legs around his hips, leaning them against that marble butt, and press my whole body against his erection.

I'm lying on the sofa we've turned into a bed in the back of the tour bus, my hands on my lips, remembering his taste, and smiling. If it weren't for the fact that less than six feet away, my bandmates are sleeping, I would relieve the excitement between my legs.

However, I'm not a one-night-stand kind of person; I can't separate sex from the emotions, and the excitement I feel towards Damian is due to the undeniable chemistry between us when we play. It's like we were born to be on that stage together. I wouldn't want to sleep with him and then see him every day of the tour with a different woman. I wouldn't be able to stand it; it would fuck up my sanity during these months.

The bus stops. I look at the time on my phone and realize it's a bit early—we shouldn't be at the next location yet. We must be refueling, so I turn over and try to go back to sleep. My peace of mind doesn't last more than a few seconds before the door of our bus opens and Thomas's voice thunders through the walls of this small space.

"Are you guys really still in bed?" he asks, opening the curtains of the cubicles and looking into the small room where I sleep.

"Hey! I could have been naked!" I complain as I get out of bed and realize the other three Jailbirds are in our bus too.

"Well, I'd have had a pretty good show, wouldn't I?" he jokes.

I glance over at Damian and see him staring at Thomas furiously. If he's that upset, he could have come over and checked for himself if I was naked. I'm a bit annoyed by his reaction.

Luke, Martin, and Taylor swear audibly in their bunks. When we get back on the bus after the shows, we're so excited that even if we're dead tired we can't get to sleep before midnight, which leaves us with very few hours left to sleep.

My bandmates drag themselves out of the cubicles, still asleep. They would have told Thomas to go fuck himself if it weren't for their reverential fear of the Jailbirds.

"Why did you get us up so early?" I ask, my arms crossed over my chest, trying to cover the evident happiness of my nipples when I see Damian's muscled arms wrapped in a black T-shirt and those strong legs tucked into a comfortable pair of gray tracksuit pants. His hair is tied up in a loose bun on his head, and he looks even sexier dressed like this than when he gets on stage.

"Near the arena where we're playing tonight, there's only one place we can go to eat, and it's been stormed by fans waiting to get in. We decided to stop for a quick bite outside the city for a while, and then tonight have something brought in from the stands inside the venue," Simon explains.

"So, shower and breakfast?" Luke asks, picking up the stuff from the drawer under his bed.

"Yes, hurry up, I'm hungry," says Damian opening his mouth for the first time since he entered. Until now, he hasn't taken his eyes off me. Sleeping in a tank top and a pair of very short men's boxers makes me look practically naked. I put on a pair of cargo pants Martin left on the floor the other night. They stink.

With seven men sprawled around in our living room, there isn't much space to sit down, and so, after turning on the coffee machine, I lean over the counter following their rambling speeches. In under ten seconds, Damian's hand reaches out without looking at me, grabs me by the wrist, and makes me sit on his lap without saying a word. I'm so surprised by it that everyone notices when I get tense. The silence that falls on the bus is almost palpable. Damian, however, continues talking as if nothing abnormal happened, and, after a moment of hesitation, everyone starts talking again.

I relax a bit, sitting on his knees and leaning on his chest with one shoulder. But Damian puts his hand under my tank top, on my back, and caresses my skin in a relaxed and distracted way. I feel myself warming up, and really hope no one speaks to me because right now, I can only squeak or moan, given how excited I feel. He tortures me by poking his fingers under the elastic band of my pants and underwear from time to time, getting dangerously close to parts of my body I don't allow anyone to explore. The shivers running down my back reach the base of my neck, and I'm forced to cross my arms so the whole table doesn't see my nipples getting perky.

Damian notices and, with an almost distracted gesture, brings his hands around to the front, wandering from my navel to the curve of my breast with such a light touch it feels like he's using a feather. I hate that I can't control my breathing, which is getting more and more shallow, and I'm forced to squeeze my legs together for fear that everyone will notice I'm wet and ready to bend over on the table, letting this man own me.

How the hell can Damian be so passive? I don't even finish thinking the question before his hard-on wakes up at the speed of light and presses on my butt through the thin layer of fabric. Okay, maybe he's not as calm as he wants to pretend, although I envy his ability to keep the conversation stable when I can't seem to control my hormones.

*

Sitting at an out-of-the-way table in the little diner where we've stopped, I can see why the Jailbirds chose this place: there are mainly truck drivers, and the waitresses are too old to care about getting a selfie or even use a camera phone. We're laughing and joking at Martin's jokes, eating scrambled eggs, bacon, toast, sausages, a breakfast that'll get us through the night. In front of me, Luke is gorging himself as if he hasn't eaten in ages, and on my left, Damian is sipping a black coffee as if it were the only thing keeping him alive.

It's strange how we're all in tune with each other despite the huge differences between us. We're the rookies, excited about everything that happens on tour; they're the jaded veterans who've already seen it all and aren't amused or impressed by any of it. This mix, however, seems to work, and the balance we've created is pleasant.

"You mean you didn't bang the redhead from last night?" Damian asks Martin in disbelief, who's telling his post-show misadventures.

Martin shakes his head while Damian casually slips his hand under the table and caresses my knee. What the hell is he doing? We're in a public place, for crying out loud. I try to get out of the way, but his grip is firm, and he won't let go of me, so I stop fighting him, and stay still. He loosens his grip and keeps stroking me without even looking in my direction—the asshole.

"No, I went to get something at the bar, and when I came back, she was all wrapped up with Steve, the two-hundred-year-old man who takes care of your instruments on stage," he explains disappointedly, amid the general laughter.

Damian runs his hand along my inner thigh, lighting up parts of me that I didn't even know were erogenous zones. I think even my kneecaps are wet.

"Steve's handsy," Damian says casually. "He's been with us since the beginning of our career and, I swear to you, I've seen him fuck girls half his age. You had tough competition. When he decides he wants to sleep with someone, you can be sure he will."

How the hell can he talk when he's practically giving me an orgasm with one hand? His fingers go up my thigh, and when his little finger just grazes between my legs, I'm so sensitive I almost moan and clutch the table. I feel like screaming in pleasure. I drop my fork on the plate and, when he touches me for the second time, my right leg snaps forward and hits Luke's shin.

"What's the matter with you?" my friend asks me with big

eyes while massaging his leg.

Everyone turns to look at me, including Damian, who looks at me with a half-amused smile on his lips. Asshole. I can feel my face flushing and on fire. I get up, and my plate almost flies off the table.

"Excuse me, I just have to go to the bathroom."

I didn't realize until now that I'm sitting on the inside of the bench, the one next to the wall with the window facing the parking lot. So, without moving everyone, I have to climb over the backrest with very little grace and drag myself staggering to the bathroom.

It takes me ten minutes to get back my normal heartbeat, and when I leave the stall, all my work is shattered because Damian is waiting for me with his arms crossed over his chest, leaning against the sink.

"What the hell are you doing in the ladies' room?" I hiss between my teeth with my heart bouncing down my throat. I feel a rush of excitement at finding him here, with that sexy smile, and a rush of fear that someone will come in and find out.

"You're the only woman in this place this morning. No one will complain," he says in a deep voice that makes my legs shake.

"That's not the point!" I'm also crossing my arms to my chest, angry or nervous, I've yet to figure out which.

"I came to see if you're okay, you've been locked in here for ten minutes," he says slyly.

"I'm fine!" I shuffle towards him to wash my hands.

Damian turns around, stands behind me, hugs my waist, and pushes his pelvis against my butt; then he lowers himself just enough to whisper in my ear, looking me straight in the mirror. "You're lucky I'd never fuck you in a diner bathroom because if I did, I'd give you that orgasm right now, that one you didn't give yourself a few minutes ago under that table." He kisses my neck gently, just below my ear, and an explosion breaks loose in my chest. My heart is bouncing, pumping blood all over my body.

He disappears from the bathroom, leaving me panting, with an infinite number of questions and no ability to answer them, as my neurons are hostage to my hormones.

*

The show went better than last night. The fact that I didn't have a panic attack just before going on stage made me enjoy it more than the first one. Even the tension in my stomach was almost pleasant and gave me the right charge. The astonishing thing was that the audience sang the chorus to a couple of our songs, the ones we've got videos of on YouTube. It was incredible.

When you're a novice musician, you dream of the day when a whole stadium will be there to see you and sing what you wrote. Still, experiencing it on stage doesn't even come close to what you imagined. Every emotion is a thousand times more intense. It was just a couple of choruses in the middle of the concert, but it means that people went looking for our music and listened to it enough to learn it. I admit I've often dreamed about that happening, but dismissed it as unfulfillable. At the moment, we still are struggling to understand how much our existence is changing.

We got so pumped during tonight's show that, for a moment, just before leaving the stage, I thought Martin was going to smash his guitar like a big rock star. When I looked at Luke,

I laughed, but his eyes were opened wide and full of terror as he shook his head "no" almost imperceptibly. When our guitarist looked down and realized it was the special guitar Evan gave him, luckily, he came to his senses.

Damian was glued to the side of the stage for the whole concert, and I had a hard time keeping my gaze from wandering in that direction. If I looked at him for too long, I would remember his kiss and the meeting in the bathroom, and I didn't want my heart bursting out of my chest, thinking of those memories.

"I'm going to get some more bottles of water," I say, getting up from the couch I'm sitting on in the shared room where the Jailbirds and we are relaxing. We're waiting for Thomas and Simon to finish showering, then we'll get back on our bus and hit the road for the next stop.

"I'll come with you." Damian gets up out of his chair, and the others giggle while he gives them the finger. I don't even have the courage to look them in the face. They've realized there's sexual tension between us.

As soon as we leave, he grabs me by the hand and drags me inside the first door he finds open in this maze. These arenas have a myriad of more or less large rooms located all around the main stage area. The one Damian drags me into is a grey concrete room and completely empty, large enough not to give me a panic attack. The light on the ceiling is dim, and I imagine it is used as a storage room of some kind.

I don't have time to ask him what he's doing. He has already pushed me against the wall with his body and is kissing me, leaving me breathless.

"I've wanted to do this all day, but we've never been alone. I can't go one more night without smelling your perfume on me," he whispers with his eyes still closed. He kisses me again and makes me completely forget that we should be looking for water, not in an empty room making out like two fifteen-year-olds.

While his tongue explores my mouth with a passion that almost seems to devour him, his hands move to my hips and then around to my ass, pulling me into him; his boner more than evident. My body seems to move freely on its own, my brain on autopilot, my legs tied to his back with a little push and some help. A moan escapes his mouth and blurs into mine, making me lose control a little more. I arch my back and push my hips against his. I want to feel him on me. Damian moves, pushing me against the wall, his hips swaying to pleasure me in a way that makes me gasp.

He pulls away, to my enormous disappointment, and my lips are suddenly cold in the absence of his. We're both gasping. His hands squeeze my ass in a firm and totally pleasurable grip. I hate that my jeans separate my skin from his rock-solid, calloused hands—so manly and sexy.

"I hate it when Sid makes you wear contact lenses at concerts. You look sexy as hell with those glasses. I have a constant boner in my pants whenever I see you wearing them."

The first thing that comes to mind is that I'll always wear them when he fucks me if he likes them that much, but then I think that if I let him go on like this in this closet, there won't be a next time. It's the cold shower I need to calm my nerves.

I unhook my legs and push him away, reaching down to the floor with my feet. I can't stand very well, and luckily the wall behind me holds me up. Damian looks at me puzzled, it's clear he doesn't understand what's going on.

"We can't keep going," I say with conviction.

He wrinkles his forehead and tilts his head to the side. "Why?" he asks, trying to reach my hips with his fingers, but I put my hand on his chest and keep him at a distance.

"Because you're gonna fuck me, then you're gonna push me aside like you do every other woman, and I'm gonna have to live with the fact that I have to deal with you every day. I can't do that," I say straight up like I've always been with him.

Damian takes a step back, his eyes dark and frowning. "Is that what you think of me? That I want to fuck you and then dump you? Is that the opinion you have of me? I thought you knew me, or at least got to know me a little during these past months."

He seems almost offended by my statement, and I feel a little guilty. "Isn't that what you do with everyone?" I ask with sincere curiosity.

"The problem is that you're not 'everyone,'" he spits angrily before grabbing the door handle and walking out calmly, slamming it behind him.

I pissed him off, and I don't even know how. What the hell just happened?

CHAPTER 13
Damian

I've been avoiding her for two days, since she told me the other night that she'd never sleep with me because it would just be a fuck. It hurt. It was devastating; I thought I was more important to her. I don't know what I'd do after I slept with her, but I'd certainly still want her around. She's not like the others, and she's definitely not someone I'd ruin a relationship with, especially because we work together. This insecurity is frustrating, I've never experienced it before, and it knocks me off my game more than it should. I thought I'd learned how to control this life and my emotions. I don't know what to do when they get out of hand.

"You've been a pain in the ass for two days," Thomas says, sitting down next to me at the bar. "What the fuck is wrong with you?"

We've just finished the gig, and we're having a beer just outside town to get away for a bit. I shrug my shoulders and sip from my bottle. I can't look him in the eye because I already know there's a lecture coming. "Nothing. How should I know?" I answer grumpily.

But Thomas pays no attention to my bad attitude or my words. It's so strange that I turn and look at him after all. He usually doesn't let up on me in these situations. "Is it because of Lilly?" he asks. "Did something happen between you two? She's been acting weird too."

Thomas is the practical guy in the group, the one who cleans up our messes, and he recognizes a potential problem that needs to be addressed. "Nothing happened. I kissed her a couple of times, that's all." I'm minimizing it. It's actually a real mess. We'll never get out of it if we don't talk about it. I'm aware of that, but my stubbornness wins.

Thomas doesn't answer, making me turn to him for the second time. He's studying me like I'm a periodic table, and his gaze makes me fry on the spot. "You don't just kiss. You don't kiss at all. You fuck like an animal, and then you leave them waiting for you forever with a dumb smile," he says seriously.

He's my best friend, and he knows my modus operandi, but he also knows why I do it. He knows my past, so he should give me a break instead of breathing down my neck. "I know, that's why I didn't sleep with her. She thinks I might dump her after I fuck her," I explain.

"And you wouldn't?" his tone sounds almost surprised.

This time I face him and stand up for myself; I'm tired of him sticking his nose in my business. "Why would I ruin a relationship that would fuck up the whole tour? I'm not that dumb."

"You're pissed off because she rejected you," he says in a surprised tone I don't like. He knows me well. Why is he pushing so hard?

"I'm pissed off because she thinks I would fuck her and then dump her like all the others," I reply.

Thomas smiles, and that annoys me more than anything. "It's the first time I've ever seen you lose your head over a woman. It's fascinating, like watching a documentary about one of those rock legends," he jokes.

"I'm not losing my head over anything," I point out grumpily.

"You're angry because she thinks you're a whore, and it bothers you that she thinks that about you. You've never cared about what women thought about you. And you never gave a shit about anyone but yourself, but now you can't get your mind off of her even when you're not around her! Like I said—you're losing your head over her. "

My eyes instinctively move to the corner of the room. Lilly is sitting at the table with her band in those jeans that fit her perfectly and that buttoned-up shirt that makes her boobs stand out. She even took out her contact lenses and put on her glasses, just to make me go even crazier.

"See what I mean?" Thomas asks me with a sincere smile, not to make fun of me.

"I don't want relationships, you know that." I raise an eyebrow and point out a concept that must have been clear to him for years.

"Maybe it's time to reconsider your position," he says, getting up and taking his beer with him to go sit with the others.

I look up at Lilly and my stomach tightens. Typically, I wouldn't give a damn about her and her feelings. I'd try to get into her pants and if I couldn't I'd change course in two seconds. I've always used a new girl to forget the previous one, and it works. Like every other tour, I don't want to miss out on opportunities, but this time I don't even want to try to replace her with someone else.

It's been like that since those two big green eyes and that

mouth, those pouty lips, came into my life. I worry about her, about what she thinks of me. I want to gravitate around her all the time like a fucking satellite, and I want to smash the face of any man who goes near her.

Luke, for example. Right now, I'd like to rip his arm off because I know he's touching her, his arm resting across the bench behind her back. These feelings scare the hell out of me. I need to find a way out without my head and heart getting all tangled up together. My brain tells me fuck her and get over it; my heart tells me to wait until she's ready. My heart, that asshole, doesn't understand the concept of moving on to the next girl. It doesn't give a fuck about what my brain is screaming.

I'm gonna finish my beer, get out of this club and go hole up on the bus, killing myself with fantasies like I've been doing since this tour started.

*

This morning's wintry shower wakes me up and regenerates me for the new day. Today we'll be on the road all day, and tonight we don't have a show, but we'll have to spend the whole damn time inside this bus with the Red Velvet Curtains, setting up the schedule for the upcoming festival in North Carolina. It will be the tour's first outdoor concert, with hundreds of thousands of people, and we have to plan their debut with such a big audience flawlessly.

A festival is different from a regular show. There are a lot of bands with long careers behind them, and industry insiders who judge every move with a critical eye. It usually takes years to get on one of those stages, and they're still too inexperienced to plan such an important show. We need to help them avoid any naive mistakes that could cost them their careers.

They're experiencing huge success as our opener, and Evan has been killing us with all this extra work because he wants to sign them to our record company. To get bigger gigs and a more significant percentage of ticket sales, they have to crush it in North Carolina—a festival of hundreds of thousands of potential fans.

Coming out of the bathroom, I hear Thomas and Simon's voices and join them for coffee before heading upstairs to get dressed. Glancing around the living area with only a towel at my waist and my hair dripping, I freeze when I find myself in front of everyone, including Lilly. She's looking at me with bright eyes and her mouth slightly open. Maybe coffee can wait, even if seeing her so enthralled makes my blood flow downwards.

"Sorry, I didn't think you were all here already. I'm going to get dressed," I mumble without too much conviction as I turn around and start up the stairs.

"Lilly, shut your mouth…and your legs too," chuckles Luke, and I can't help smiling. Luckily, she can't see the satisfaction on my face at hearing her friend confirm my suspicions: she wants me as much as I want her.

I go back downstairs after putting on a pair of sweatpants and a white short-sleeved T-shirt. If I'm gonna be cooped up in here all day, I want to at least be comfortable. I realize I made the right choice when I find Lilly downstairs with a cup of coffee in her hands, her hair tied up in a messy bun, a pair of shorts that cling to her butt, and a worn-out white tank top through which you can see her black bra. She's bent over with her elbows resting on the table, reading something Simon is writing on a notepad. They're all in that position, more or less, but Lilly makes the blood in my veins rush. She turns as if she can feel my eyes on her and looks at me with that pouty mouth opened in a half-smile and those sexy glasses that short-circuit my synapses. I look away but not without seductively gazing at her lips, and licking mine, before I go to pour myself a cup of coffee.

I sit on the couch and keep an eye on what they're writing. "Are you working on the setlist yet?" I ask, intrigued.

"No, I was showing them how the festival stages will be laid out," our bassist says, wrinkling his forehead.

"Since when did you become the organizer of the event?" I ask, approaching.

"Since we have to wait for you to get a move on," he says, raising an eyebrow.

I make him move over by sitting right next to him, and in front of Lilly: wrong move, her boobs are right in my line of sight. It's going to be a very long day.

"You'll be on stage just before us," I explain to the group. "What do you say we do a couple of songs together, and then you get off stage? Other than 'Jude,' which songs of ours do you know? We rehearsed your song 'Velvet' the other night. How about we finish with that, and then we do our own?"

We've already talked to Evan about this possibility. Using our reputation to launch them would be a good publicity move for both of us. They seem to light up.

"Did you really learn 'Velvet?'" questions Luke in disbelief.

"Of course, we learned it. We've listened to all your songs..." I wrinkle my forehead and look at him like it's obvious.

"We really like the rhythm, and the lyrics are intense too.

Did you all write it together?" Thomas asks.

When listened to it, we wondered if they had help because all their songs have a finished, produced quality to them.

"Luke and Lilly wrote it...like all our songs," explains Martin.

I had no doubt Lilly had a hand in that song, especially the lyrics, but the rhythm part also has a particular flavor that says a lot about her, about her intelligence.

You leave the room, and the air goes out. You leave me here to die with my heart in a velvet box.

A jealousy grip tightens my stomach. I wish I was the one writing songs with her instead of Luke—a thought so intense and scary that I bully it out of my mind. Writing a song together requires an intimate connection with a person, a bond that goes beyond the physical relationship. It's a process that lays bare the two souls involved, and I will never be ready to show mine to a woman, not even Lilly.

"So, let's see this goddamn setlist? I'd like to relax a little today since we have a day off," I say with a forced smile.

Everyone seems to sigh with relief when I pick up the notebook. I roll my eyes. Yes, I'm picky and devote perhaps too much time to work, but I'm not a slave driver. I give the people who work with me some rest.

The morning passes quickly, and we come to a decent conclusion before stopping for lunch when everyone will get off to eat and then back on their respective buses. Lilly stays behind, and as I'm about to step out of the bus, she grabs me by the arm.

"Can we talk?"

"What about?" I answer more harshly than I intended.

"I want to apologize for the way I treated you the other night...I didn't mean to say you're shallow..." She looks guilty.

"So what? What were you implying?" I cross my arms angrily. I really don't know where this conversation is going to end.

"I can't separate sex and feelings. If you're just looking for a fuck, it will ruin the rest of the tour for me because I'm going to keep seeing you with other women, and it's going to bother me. I don't want to spend the next few months pissed off because I couldn't keep my legs closed," she says with disarming sincerity.

I didn't see it that way, I have to admit. I thought she assumed it was my fault, but it never occurred that she wasn't comfortable seeing me every day. I never worried about what a woman feels after I slept with her, and I feel guilty for not putting myself in Lilly's shoes.

"I don't think I just want to have sex with you," I said with a frown. The weird thing is that I really don't care about any other woman but her...and there are a lot of women on tour.

Lilly smiles and shakes her head. "I don't think I'm ready for you to find out what you want from our relationship," she says with a half-smile.

"What do you want from me, Lilly?" I ask her, honestly. I'm tired of guessing.

"To get to know you."

The words come out with a disarming simplicity that almost makes me light-headed, my heart pumping with fear and excitement. No one has ever expressed the desire to know me, at least not a woman. Everyone has always wanted something from me, sex, exclusive parties, fifteen minutes of fame, but getting to know me has never been on their list.

I grab her by the wrist and pull her closer, holding her in my arms. She's so tiny and perfect as she clings to my body, and when her arms wrap around my waist, I feel like I can't escape this bus anymore. Despite her slender figure, she manages to keep me anchored to this place like no other has ever managed to do before.

"It could really suck…what you find out," I confess in a moment of sincerity.

"Don't you think you should let me be the judge of that?"

Yeah, but I'm afraid she might run off to another country when she comes face to face with the truth. "I don't want you to be disappointed."

Lilly looks up and nails me with her eyes. "Damian, I'm not one of those little girls who think the rock star's life is magical and perfect. You're human; you've made your own mistakes. It's not a big deal. From what I've seen so far, you're not that bad, and I'm not afraid to find out more."

Her sincerity and dedication in trying to break down my walls, one brick at a time, frightens me.

"Okay, but I warned you. At this point, you continue at your own risk." I cut her off when I feel the pressure in my chest is too much to handle.

Lilly gives me a smile and steps away. I immediately feel her absence as if my arms have become accustomed to her warmth.

"It's enough for now. You're so stubborn that this feels like a victory," she laughs, and I feel more relieved.

"Come on, let's join the others. This afternoon Evan is pampering us for a couple of hours, so we'll show you how to live like a rock star," I push her towards the exit to prevent the conversation from diving too deep into my life again.

*

"When you told me you were going to give us a taste of the rock star life, I thought you meant wild parties with booze and drugs. I had no idea," Lilly giggles as we enter the spa pool that Evan has reserved for the next two hours.

I laugh and have her sit on one of the loungers next to Thomas, Michael, and Simon, while Martin joins Luke and Taylor in the pool, bombing and splashing water everywhere. Kids.

"Trust me, you will have enough of parties. You'll get nauseous from going to them, and you'll find they're not that much fun. In the end, you do it as part of your job with people you don't want to see sober, let alone drunk," chuckles Thomas, who followed our conversation.

"Yeah, okay, I realize it's not nice to spend time having orgies, but Simon is reading *The Great Gatsby*, and Michael is... carving wood?" I'm puzzled.

On the other hand, I can't take my eyes off her shorts and a shirt that's a little bit lower on the neckline than usual.

"Look, it's a classic. Why shouldn't I read it?" Simon asks, pretending to be offended. He's actually a man who reads an indescribable amount of books. Luckily, they've invented e-readers, or we wouldn't have room on the tour bus to move.

"Okay, but Michael is carving wood with a pocketknife. This is nothing I'd expect from a world-renowned rock star," she insists, amused and surprised.

Michael looks up and laughs. "I know, it's an unconventional pastime, but it relaxes me and, at the same time, allows me to train my concentration. Do you have any idea how hard it is to carve out a squirrel's eyes without slipping and making it one-eyed?" he asks her, drawing attention to his work of art so that she can admire it.

Lilly looks at him in awe and then turns to me. "Did he really just use the words 'squirrel' and 'one-eyed' in the same sentence? I swear, I don't recognize you guys," she whispers to me.

We all burst out laughing at the way she's watching us like we're exotic animals in a zoo cage. Actually, when most people think about the life of famous musicians, they think of excessive drugs and trashed hotel rooms. It used to be like that. You created your name and tried to live up to it: dangerous, provocative, and entirely out of control. Nowadays, if you do something like that, you're blacklisted by the media. Everyone knows that alcohol and drugs are bad for your health, and they're not as cool as they used to be. Sure, some people still do it, it's not like we've all suddenly become saints, but it's done in private, behind closed doors with no witnesses.

Lilly turns to me. "I'm almost scared to ask, but what's your hobby? If you tell me you knit, I swear I'll quit the tour!" she says, pretending to be outraged, and gets a laugh out of everyone.

"Are you crazy? Nothing that dangerous!"

She smiles at me and motions for me to sit next to her on a deckchair, and then watches Michael's craftsmanship with that branch. When she diverts her gaze back to me again, I can feel myself smiling. "I love watching TV shows on Netflix. I usually binge watch the ones I like best, but I don't have time when we're busy recording an album."

She seems pleasantly surprised by my passion, and I feel almost relieved that she approves of my choice. "What do you like in particular? What kind?"

"I like *Marvel*, *Luke Cage*, *Jessica Jones*...but also political intrigue like *Scandal*."

She turns to me with eyes and mouth wide open. "You like the shenanigans in the oval office? I didn't think you were such a bad boy," she jokes. "We should watch together sometime. I think we'd get along," she says, making Thomas laugh, who's studying us like lab rats.

I feel cornered by her proposal, which has nothing to do with me being innocent. I imagine fucking her in a hotel room with an episode of some series as background noise to our moans.

"It can be done, but in the meantime, come here, relax and enjoy this magnanimous gesture from our manager." I get comfortable on the deckchair and lure her between my legs until she rests her back on my chest. There is nothing relaxing about this gesture, with my erection pressing against her ass, but when I'm around her, I don't even try to inhale deeply and take my thoughts elsewhere. It's a losing battle, so I live in a constant state of excitement that I will devote myself to when I'm alone in the bus, like a teenager.

CHAPTER 14
Lilly

We arrive at the location of the concert in the late afternoon. After almost two months of touring, Evan decided to book a hotel, as we have two shows here before leaving for North Carolina and the festival. We need a decent bed, a shower, and some space for ourselves to keep from going hysterical.

I go to my room and take a deep breath of clean air, something we haven't had for weeks inside that bus full of four people. I put my bag at the foot of the bed and open the curtains. The view from the 12th floor of the hotel over Austin, Texas, is astonishing. From here, I can see Zilker Park with its trees, thermal pools, and botanical gardens. If I wasn't so tired and in desperate need of a day lying in bed I'd go out and enjoy the sunshine in the greenery of the park.

A visit to the Texas State Capitol would not be bad either. I've always been intrigued by the fact that it's completely covered in pink marble. It sure looks beautiful in pictures, but seeing it live must take your breath away. I look at the Frost Bank Tower covered with mirrored glass and those two angular points that stand out on top. I am almost blinded by the reflection of light, but not so much that I can't see One Congress Plaza. The palace seems to be built like a massive staircase. It is impossible not to notice its red granite standing out in the middle of downtown.

Someone knocks on my door, disrupting my scenic viewing, and I roll my eyes.

"Martin, I swear, if you forgot your underwear on the bus again, this time you'll be walking around without it," I shout as I walk across the room to open the door. It's not a vast space, but it's still a good-sized room with a king-size bed, a bathroom that looks bigger than my place in Brooklyn, and a small living area with a round table and two armchairs. Evan certainly wasn't stingy. I open the door, surprised to find a smiling Damian at the threshold.

"And I swear I won't be able to get the image of Martin on stage with no underwear out of my head. Thank you," he laughs.

"Sorry," I snicker as I step aside and let him in. He's so tall and broad that the room which seemed significant to me before now seems suffocating and small.

He looks around and nods, approving that Evan hasn't relegated us to a dump. He's wearing sweatpants, a white T-shirt, and he's barefoot. He's handsome even without the clothes Sid makes him wear on stage. In fact, I have to say I prefer him this way. I've always had a thing for men who walk around the house barefoot; I find them sexy, and Damian is no exception.

"Aren't you gonna meet the others?"

Damian smiles, shakes his head, and sits on the edge of my bed. "No, they go out clubbing, but I don't feel like going out tonight. I'd rather stay in bed and watch a movie with room service. The tour usually drains all my energy. I prefer to go out only when I have to go to some party Evan's throwing for promotions I can't miss."

"Do we have room service?" My eyes pop.

Damian laughs, throwing his head back like it's the funniest joke he's ever heard. "Yeah, take advantage of it while Evan's paying for it." He smiles at me like a kid who's done something wrong.

"Okay. Why are you here, then?"

"Would you like to come upstairs and get something to eat and watch a movie? I've got a great TV in my room. It's not as exciting as carving wood, but I promise you'll still have a good time," he says, smiling hopefully.

I feel the hot flashes rising from the bottom of my belly to my cheeks and back. I mean, I'm about to experience spontaneous combustion. Me, alone, in a room with a man who is literally messing up my hormones to the point that I feel revved up about watching a movie and having dinner on his bed. It's assisted suicide for those four neurons that have remained active after I was next to him on the bus all day.

"Okay, why not?" I hear myself say the exact opposite of what my brain suggests to me, which is to stay cooped up in my bathroom under a cold shower.

"Bring something comfortable. I can't stand seeing people lying on the bed with jeans on."

I find myself smiling when he slips me the key to his room, and a series of obscene images, including his abs and pecs, cross my mind. He doesn't have his shirt on in my head, he doesn't even have his pants on, and the show makes me blush extraordinarily.

"Top floor, presidential suite."

Of course, he's staying in the presidential suite. Where else? "Did you really give me your room key? What if I sell it to the fans waiting outside the hotel?" I raise an eyebrow in defiance.

Damian pulls out his smug, mischievous grin that always makes my legs shake. "Why? You want to do something with a lot of women? I didn't think you were so uninhibited," he mocks me.

I roll my eyes at him and push him out of the room. "Get out before I change my mind."

Damian raises his hands above his head with an innocent look and steps away. "Don't ever let me change your mind," he jokes before leaving, winking at me.

I close the door behind me, lean in, and let myself slide on the floor.

"What the hell am I doing?" I whisper to myself, holding a smile. There's nothing to smile about. This is a disaster; my hormones have taken over my reason. He's used to uninhibited girls throwing themselves at him and who know exactly how to make him enjoy it. He's the god of sex, while I'm just a girl with few awkward experiences behind me. I'm not a virgin, but how can I live up to someone like that, a real ladies' man? I'm gonna look like an idiot.

I take my phone out of my jeans pocket and send a message in our band's group chat: "Sorry, guys, but I'm gonna stay in my room tonight and relax and sleep on a decent bed."

Martin: "Use a condom."

Taylor: "Don't shout too much. Your room is next to mine."

Luke: "Use protection."

Lilly: "I said sleep, no need for protection."

After a series of laughing emojis, I find another message.

Luke: "Sure, Damian will stay in his room too."

Good job, idiot. I answer with the face emoji rolling its

eyes, but I do not add anything else. It's better not to make the hole that I have dug for myself deeper, a hole that is already big enough to bury me.

I get up and peek inside the bag I brought up with me: jeans, jeans, and more jeans. The only comfortable things are women's boxer shorts and the tank top I sleep in. Awesome. This is the dullest outfit ever. I grab them, grab my room key and Damian's, and get out before changing my mind.

The elevator ride to the top floor takes forever. I get to the landing and don't have to search much to find the room since the door marked "Presidential Suite" is right in front of me. I pass the card and go in.

The apartment, because it is not a room but a real living space, has a sitting area with modern sofas and a breathtaking view, thanks to the floor-to-ceiling windows; a dining area, a separate bedroom, and what I assume is the bathroom. There's even a small balcony that overlooks a private terrace.

"Damian? Am I in the right room, or am I about to make a fool of myself with a stranger?" I shout because I don't see him around.

I can hear him laughing from what I assume is the bedroom, and then I see him coming out with his hair in a man bun on top of his head. Could this man be any sexier with a messy bun and a smile that makes your panties melt? His light-heartedness, though, turns into a frown when he sees me.

"I said no jeans," he says, sulking like a child.

I roll my eyes and wave him away with my hand. "I couldn't come up half-naked just because of your phobia. Do you have a bathroom in this palace, or do you have to pee off the terrace?" I raise an eyebrow.

He bursts out laughing again and comes up to me, puts his hands on my shoulders, turns me around, and pushes me towards a slightly open door. When he leaves my side to open the door, I feel the cosmic void invading my shoulders. I look towards the bathroom, amazed.

"Is that a bathtub or a pool?" I wonder incredulously at the size of the tub in front of me.

Damian laughs the way he's done since I walked in here. "A hot tub for...I don't know, I think six people. You wanna try it?"

I observe his face while he talks. His expression is as sincere as a child's, there's no malice or any sexual reference in this proposal—just genuine interest in making me try something I clearly never done. "Are you coming in?" I raise an eyebrow inquisitively.

"I swear I'm keeping my boxers on. So, are you in?" His smile is hopeful.

"As long as you don't laugh at my underwear," I threaten, pointing my finger in his face.

"Why, what underwear are you wearing?" His forehead is wrinkled in a curious frown.

"Pink with cupcakes? But it's coordinated!" I quickly add when I see him burst out laughing.

"I had no doubt you could wear something like that," he says, amused.

I cross my arms to my chest, pretending to be angry. "Why? Am I no match for the women you sleep with?" I don't know why that question surfaces in my mind, but I'm almost offended by it, and it bothers me to feel so vulnerable with a man. I've worked so hard to never feel that way again, and I'm not going to start with him again.

Damian laughs again, and his reaction gets on my nerves. "No, not at all. I mean you're an independent woman, and I doubt you've ever dressed up for a man. I feel like you'd do it to please yourself, not someone else. And that's the sexiest thing a woman can pull off...other than how those glasses look on you. Those glasses will take me to hell, believe me. I have a first-class ticket already printed," he explains, and a half-smile appears on my lips.

I have no idea if he did it to save himself, to butter me up, or because he really means it, but I like his answer. "So, what? Are we gonna get this bathtub ready or not?" I ask him, starting to unzip my jeans and take my shoes off.

"You have no problem undressing in front of people. You only get stiff when it comes to the press." It's more of a statement of fact than a question.

"I don't have a problem showing myself to people I trust, I have a problem with assholes throwing my pictures online, but I don't think you're the type."

Damian studies me for a few seconds, then he smiles slyly and walks past me. "You fill the tub, I'm gonna go order some food. If we're gonna do this, we might as well enjoy it, right?" he whispers and winks at me before walking out of the bathroom.

I'm fucked.

I'm already in the tub basking in the bubbles and the heat when Damian walks in with a tray that looks huge even in his mighty arms.

"You wanna give Evan a heart attack?" I raise an amused eyebrow.

Damian places the tray on the marble next to the tub and removes the metal lids, then goes out again and comes back with a bucket of ice and a bottle of champagne inside. I take a look at what he ordered, and my mouth is already watering: strawberries covered in white chocolate, macaroons, chocolates, pastries mignon. Looks like he robbed a bakery.

"It's the honeymoon package. It was easier to order it than choosing every single thing from the menu. It was endless," he explains, taking off his pants and shirt and getting in the tub with me.

Does he want just make me come right now, on the spot? I've already seen him without a shirt, but only in boxer shorts is a divine sight. That thin fabric that wraps around his tight butt makes me bite my lip to keep from moaning. The waistband is so low that it accentuates that gorgeous V on his lower abdomen, which clearly shows the way to perdition. Christ, the wet droplets dripping down his chest could make my heart give up, already knocked down by an accelerated beat.

"Think about the fantasies some room service girl would have if she found you like this." I smile at him as I grab one of the chocolates and put it in my mouth, moaning without restraint.

Damian smiles, takes the champagne bottle, opens it, pours two glasses, hands me one, and puts a strawberry in his mouth before grabbing his drink and sitting in the tub across from me. He shrugs and smiles. "They'll think I brought someone to my room to fuck her, but I don't really care. As long as they get these ideas without investigating my real life, they're doing me a favor," he says, completely relaxed. He seems to be enjoying this moment of relaxation that I didn't even know I needed until I got into this warm and welcoming tub.

"Do you often bring girls up to your room, offering champagne and treats?" It's not an accusation or a criticism, just pure curiosity. I'm fascinated by the rock star life, and what better way to satisfy my nosiness than to ask him?

Damian shakes his head and sips the bubbly wine. "Actually, no. Usually, when I'm on tour, I avoid going out at night to get laid. And if I really want to get laid, I rent another room for the night. I don't want them to know how I live, and to be honest, I don't think they care... After all, women want to fuck the rock star, not me, Damian, the person," he explains with a candor that almost makes me swoon.

I shake my head and smile, stuffing myself with a strawberry that I swallow with wine, and then I look him straight in the eye. "I don't understand them, really. I've tried to do it too, fucking someone I don't know. I mean, it's not like I'm a saint, but I just can't have a one-night stand. I need to know the person I'm sleeping with to feel comfortable, and I usually feel embarrassed then if it doesn't happen again, but I have to see them. That's why I said no to you," I admit bluntly.

Damian shrugs and smiles. "I don't think it would be just a fuck with you." He sips again while my heart tries not to burst in my chest. "Because we're on tour together anyway, I know you, I respect you, I wouldn't want to ruin a relationship that would complicate everyone's life."

His words come out so sincere I believe them, and I'm hanging on every one of them. For a moment, I wonder why I decided not to sleep with him, and the scariest thing is that I don't know the answer. All the excuses I've made for myself are falling apart or seem absolutely ridiculous and irrelevant.

It's the wine's fault, and the fact that I'm pouring more because I've run out makes me realize how I'm not able to see reason. I should stop, not make it easy to lose control.

Damian scoots closer, hands me his empty glass, and I fill it up. He grabs a strawberry and puts it in his mouth, and this time he doesn't sit far away, but next to me. When I snatch one of the chocolates, he follows my fingers' moves as if they were the sexiest thing he has ever seen. I feel naked in front of that gaze and, when I dip my fingers in the water again, he smiles, biting his lower lip and shaking his head.

I don't have time to ask him anything because we are interrupted by someone knocking on the door.

"If you don't mind, I ordered dinner to eat in front of the TV." He smiles at me as he wraps a towel around his waist and walks out of the bathroom to open the door.

A woman's voice immediately attracts my attention; her giggles and squeals make my ears stand up. When she asks him for an autograph with a sensual and totally inappropriate voice, I feel a punch tear my stomach when Damian agrees in an equally provocative way. What the hell am I doing in this tub? It takes me forever to realize that I have to leave before I make a fool of myself, and when I get up in a rage to go, I find a perplexed Damian at the bathroom door.

"Where the hell are you going?"

"Away from here so you can get laid. The waitress is waiting for you."

Damian looks at me like I'm crazy. "I don't want to fuck the waitress." His tone is sincere and completely disorientated.

"Oh, Christ, why not? You gave her an orgasm just by saying two sexy little words, you think I didn't hear how you were flirting? I'm not an idiot. If I'm not giving you sex, you're looking for it elsewhere. I get it, but at least don't make me watch, it's humiliating." I don't think I've ever been so honest with a man.

Damian laughs and throws his head back and comes over, amused. "I love it when you get jealous."

"I'm not jealous. I'm just being realistic." Lie.

"I don't think so, but I'll pretend to believe you. I was flirting with her because I don't want her to tell people I'm being a grumpy dick of a rock star. I don't want to fuck her. I didn't even think about it."

"Why not? She was offering it to you on a silver platter." I raise an eyebrow, challenging him.

"If you haven't figured it out yet, I'll show you."

He grabs around my waist with one hand, dragging me out of the water and sitting me on the edge. Then he slips between my legs, while with the other hand, he grabs my hair and squeezes it in a fist, making me moan in his mouth as he kisses me with a passion that sets me on fire. His tongue explores me with such experience that it ignites every single cell in my body. Damian lets go of his grip on my back, holding the one in my hair firmly, then he puts his hand between my legs, making me almost jerk with pleasure. It only takes him a few moves in the right places, without even taking my panties off, to pull off one of the most powerful orgasms I have ever had. I moan without restraint in his mouth and cling to his muscular shoulders.

Damian detaches himself from me and leaves me panting on the edge of the tub, unable to move or even to breathe decently. "I want to sleep with you. I don't care about other women. But you have to ask me. This was just a taste of what you're missing." He winks at me and turns to leave.

"And you're leaving me like this?" I ask, gasping, feeling stunned.

"I'm going over there to get under the covers with my dinner. I suggest you put on those pajamas and join me. I'll wait for you before I start the pizza and Netflix." He walks out the door like it still makes sense to give me my privacy after just pleasuring me between my legs.

I get out of the bathtub and almost end up face down on the floor, legs of jelly. How is it possible that he manages to make me shake like this just by touching me? I don't want to imagine what it would be like to have sex with him because I could ask him right now. I change by leaning against the bathtub wall to support myself, then I grab the tray and wine and approach the room.

"Come here," he orders me.

The bedroom is as spectacular as the rest of the apartment: huge, with a bed that I think is custom made judging by how big it is. There is a fantastic view of the city illuminated by the evening lights and a television in front of the bed that looks like a cinema screen.

I put the tray on the bedside table, and when I get closer, Damian moves the sheet to make room for me. I sit a good foot away from him, but he looks at me, reaches out with one hand, and drags me against his muscular body. He wraps his arm around my shoulders and grabs the remote control to scroll through the list of movies on Netflix. I take the pizza box he has on his legs, and I move it between the two of us. As soon as I do it, his erection stands out overbearingly, lifting the sheet and the pants he has on. I stare in amazement at it without even feeling naughty.

"Shall we pick the movie and pretend I am not extremely horny right now?" he laughs.

As if that were possible. "Sure, what boner? What movie do you want to watch?" My voice comes out shrill as I stare at the TV screen, trying not to look down.

Damian giggles and pulls me to him.

"Take your pick, as long as it's not a cheesy, meaningless comedy or a dumb one."

It'll be a piece of cake to pick something. Yeah, a real piece of cake.

We're halfway through the movie, and I have no idea what we're watching. Damian's arms engulf me, his breathing is regular, and his heartbeat cradles me as I rest my head on his chest. My hand on his belly, tucked under his shirt, gently caressing the hair that descends to his lower abdomen. His erection is now asleep, and we are enclosed in this bubble of calm that seems almost surreal.

If someone had told me that I would spend an evening hugging Damian Jones, watching a movie, cuddling and feeling sheltered like I've never been, I would have laughed until I cried. When we won the contest, I knew my career would change dramatically, but I didn't realize that my personal life would change as well. This moment represents all the perfection I'd always dreamed of but wasn't sure I could achieve.

"Are you eating the last slice of pizza?"

"Hmm?" Damian's hoarse voice awakens me from my daydream.

"If you don't want the pizza, I'll move the box. I'm getting cramps from sitting still."

"Take it. I'm not hungry anymore." I sit up while he grabs the box and puts it on the floor next to his bed. The distance between us almost physically hurts.

This time, Damian comes back to bed, lying down and dragging me with him, covering us with the light duvet. He hugs me and holds me, breathing deeply into the hollow of my neck. I wrap my hands around his waist and then slip them under his shirt. I feel him shiver with my light touch and his fingers slip under my tank top, caressing my back. It's like he's trying to memorize my skin to the touch. A slight moan escapes him, and his lips begin to taste my neck until they move up towards my mouth, where his tongue sinks to meet mine in a slow, sensual, yet tender kiss.

There have only been a couple of kisses between us, but they were always frantic, full of passion and desire, to the point that I would have been made love to him sitting right there. Right now, though, he's taking all the time he needs, savoring me, getting to know me. It's a kiss that makes me feel safe, protected, and that, on the one hand, scares the hell out of me because this is a Damian I don't know and that I have yet to discover. He's in no hurry to get to the point, to undress me and sink between my thighs.

When he leaves me, he leaves a light kiss on my lips, one on the tip of my nose, one on my forehead, and then he squeezes me even tighter against his chest and makes me crave a routine that I had not considered but that I discover I want.

"It's hard to resist lying on a bed with you without ripping your clothes off," he chuckles amusedly.

"I don't think I'd stop you," I smile as I hold myself closer to him.

I can hear him sighing and kissing my hair gently. "To think you don't want me to stop and explicitly asking me to have sex are two completely different things. I told you, I won't get between your legs unless you ask me to."

I'm swallowing my words because no matter how ruthless my hormones are, the need to feel safe in his arms outweighs the desire to satisfy my instincts. The fact that Damian is giving me this choice makes me realize he knows it's a step I don't take lightly. I want to, sure, but I don't know if I'm ready, so I snuggle up to him and enjoy this moment that makes me feel good. The festival is approaching fast, and I'm nervous because it's a decisive event in our career. I don't think it's right to add more complications to my life right now.

CHAPTER 15
Lilly

The first time I met Luke, I don't even remember seeing his face. I had been crying for so many hours my eyelids were swollen and half-closed. When I realized he was grabbing my naked skin, I started screaming and kicking, terrified. Luke took off his shirt, made me stand up, and put it on me. That was the first moment I really saw him. He was just one of the many nameless classmates I had never spoken to before, but at that moment he became Luke, the one who saved me.

He held me close for an endless time until the sobbing stopped and I could stand on my own two feet. He held onto me until I got to his car, made me get in, accompanied me home, and stayed with me until I fell asleep in my bed. Without ever saying a word, without ever asking me what happened, without ever forcing me. From that day on, he's never left me, and I've never left him. We became one, and over time I trusted him enough to tell him about The Accident.

*

I'm sitting on the tour bus, my legs shaking. A couple of hours ago I went to see the stage where we'll be playing tonight and it was the biggest mistake of my life. Brad was there, in the front row. When he saw me, he greeted me with that smug grin of his, then mouthed, "See you later, fatso," so clearly I could read his lips. I felt fifteen again. I haven't seen him since high school, and now he's here, in the front row, ready to make fun of me.

I don't even realize anyone else is in the bus until I see Damian kneeling in front of me, with Luke right behind him.

"Breathe," he whispers to me, taking my hands and squeezing them into his.

I look into his eyes, and my heart starts pumping in my chest, furiously. "I can't go out. I can't get on that stage." I hiccup, and the tears start streaming again.

"Yes, you can. You've overcome every obstacle so far, you'll beat this too," he says in a firm but calm tone, his gaze steady.

"No, not this time...I can't do it." I shake my head and stand up and pace. I realize that my bandmates and the Jailbirds are in here, all watching my pitiful behavior. I feel helpless, like someone has sent me back to the past, to that day when the fear attacked and got a hold of me for good.

"Lilly, please listen to me." Damian gets up and tries to grab my hand, but I move away. "What the hell did they do to make you like this?" He sounds almost angry, but not at me.

"Leave me alone, Damian," I whisper.

"No, I'm not leaving you alone. You've played dozens of shows, you've made it to the top of your career, and you're acting like a little girl throwing a tantrum. I'm sorry, but I'm fed up with leaving you alone. Get off this bus and grow up!" he spits out, exasperated.

That's the straw that breaks the camel's back. Being made to look immature, added with the memory of what happened to me, amplify my emotional state to the point that I finally surrender and explode.

"Do you want to know what happened? Really?" I yell in his face, catching him off guard, while Luke stands there, wide-eyed. "Fine, I'll tell you. When I was fifteen, I liked Brad. I liked him a lot. He would ask me to do his homework, smile at me, come over to my house and get the math worksheets I did for him, and bring me doughnuts. I thought he was in love with me. Why else would he bring me doughnuts? He was the cutest guy in school, and I was the anonymous chubby girl no one looked at twice.

"So, one day I decided to make the grand gesture of writing him a letter declaring my love. Do you know how that turned out? He asked me to meet him at the gym after class, so I did, and he was with two friends when I got there. They laughed at me, teased me because I dared to think Brad might be in love with me. He made them undress me down to my underwear and bra, then they took me into the equipment room and shoved me into a half-empty wooden storage box. I was terrified and begged him to let me out, but he just laughed. Before closing the lid and putting weight on it so I couldn't escape, he wrote "FAT" across my belly with a permanent marker and left me there.

"Luke found me, five hours later, my throat burning from screaming and my nails ripped out from trying to open the fucking lid. Brad's here, front row, and you know what he said to me earlier? 'See you later, fatso.' So excuse me if I'm in no condition to go out on that stage with a fucking smile on my fucking lips!" I finish getting it all off my chest and I'm met with surreal silence in the bus. No one breathes, everyone looks at me with wide eyes. Only Luke lowers his sad expression.

I look up at Damian and find him seething with anger. "Holy shit," he barely murmurs.

"Yeah, holy shit," I say again, looking down and feeling the tears roll down my cheeks. Damian's arms wrap me in a tight, comforting embrace, and gradually my sobbing stops. I feel empty. No one reacts, no one says anything, they all stand still as if breathing could somehow break my fragile state.

Damian sits down and pulls me onto his lap. "I'm sorry. I'm really sorry. If you stop now, though, bailing out two hours before the most important festival of your fledgling career, it will be professional suicide. For the whole band," he explains to me, not beating around the bush, and I appreciate it. I don't like being pitied for what I went through. Someone has to be the adult because in this instant, I've turned off the switch that keeps the rational part of my brain alive.

"I know," I whisper as I look at the hands I'm holding together tightly in my lap like a vice. "I know that, too, but I really don't know how to do it. Seeing him out there terrifies me."

"Get on stage and show him you're not afraid of him. In fact, get on stage and show him that you've achieved something he can't even dream about. Let's go up there, sing 'Jude' together, and when he sees how great we are, give him the finger," he proposes in a whisper.

I really don't want to see Brad. I don't want him there to ruin the one thing that makes me feel really good in my life.

"Worst case scenario, you run off stage, and Damian goes on with the song." Simon finally breaks the others' silence, and they all sigh with relief.

They finally know my story and, while I feel embarrassed for exposing myself in front of everyone, I look around and realize that I am in the midst of a family that is going to protect me.

"Show that motherfucker he can go fuck himself with his criminal pranks," echoes Luke.

I look at my bandmates and see the desperation in their eyes. I'd ruin their careers and their lives too. They're the ones who stayed by my side growing up, the ones who never abandoned me. I have to behave exactly as they have with me: sticking together despite the difficult moments.

"If I throw up on him, promise me you won't leave me on that stage, okay?" I ask Damian.

His smile is worth a thousand answers and the sweetness in his eyes breaks down any barriers between us. "I won't let go of you for a second. I'll hold your hair while you give him what he deserves," he assures me.

I take some deep breaths, curl up in his arms, and try to convince myself to get off his legs. Out of the corner of my eye, I see intrigued faces observing our intimacy without saying a single word about it.

*

"Look at me."

Damian's voice rings in my ears, but I can't take my eyes off the screaming crowd in front of me, including Brad, who has a filthy grin and the phone pointed in our direction. I feel like I'm gonna throw up.

He grabs my chin with two fingers and squeezes my hand tightly, then turns my head towards him. Finally, I find his supportive eyes and some clarity.

I follow him hesitantly to the center of the stage and, when I see him grab the acoustic guitar, I do the same with mine. When the audience realizes what is happening, it explodes in a louder roar than the one that welcomed us, which rumbles in my gut. I keep my eyes on Damian and it's only when he smiles slightly and nods at me that I realize he's started playing. I take a deep breath. The crowd noise is muffled by my earphones playing back our music, and I discover it's easier to just think about singing and avoid wandering in the direction of Brad. It's like living in my own bubble, and my nausea slowly turns into familiar excitement.

Damian, as promised, won't let go of me for a moment, and it feels like I'm sitting on his lap, and he's holding me tightly. The security that he instills in me is the same. It's strange how I've always seen him as a world-renowned rock star, handsome and unreachable, almost a daydream, but now he's somehow become everything that keeps me anchored to reality. My heart pumps in my chest, not in fear, but in the emotion of losing myself in those intense eyes. I'm lying on that bed again, cuddled up to his body as scenes from the movie scroll across the screen. His hand distractingly caresses the skin on my arm. I imagine my hand resting on his belly, my head on his chest, getting lulled by his calm breath and the steady rhythm of his heart.

Next to Damian, I feel confident enough to turn my gaze towards Brad and sing my verse: "Jude, I watched you grow and become a woman. Take your fears by the hand and walk them out of your life." The feeling of power I have right now over my former classmate is almost destabilizing. I need to bring my eyes back to Damian so I don't faint from emotion, and when I do, I find him with a smile so wide it blows my mind.

As soon as we finish the song, the audience is delirious. I cast an eye in the direction of Brad, who has stopped sneering and got serious. *What's the matter? Did you think I was gonna look like shit?* I send a mocking smile in his direction and turn to my bandmates, who joined me on stage. I hurry to put the guitar down and pull the bass over my shoulder without ever looking away from Damian, who parades to the side of the stage and stops just behind the black curtains. All the Jailbirds are there, and they are smiling as if there was nothing more beautiful in the world. And maybe it is, because I realize that I just faced my worst fear and didn't die, didn't vomit, didn't faint, I just grew up. I stood in front of Brad, my biggest nightmare, and I sang, showing him that I'm not afraid of him anymore.

Luke settles into the microphone and, with a smile that goes from ear to ear, winks at me, then he directs his eyes at Brad. "This song was written by Lilly. It's a message for the assholes who tortured her when we were in school. It's called 'I Will Rise Stronger.' This one's for you, Brad."

From here, I see our former classmate frothing with rage, trying to leave, but the kids in the front row are holding him back. When Luke sings the verse, "Every time you push me down, I will rise stronger," we can hear the crowd roar even with our earphones on. I lay my eyes on Brad and almost feel sorry for him, seeing the pats of pity on the shoulder he is receiving. I look up again at Luke and find him smiling at me, my blond angel who has always looked over my shoulder, someone I couldn't live without. "Thank you," I whisper even though he can't hear me, but from the smile and the wink he gives me, I can see the message reached him.

The happiness that expands in my chest is unparalleled, and before I know it, it's time for the Jailbirds to take the stage to perform with us. I'm so excited I almost jump to the beat of the music and, next to me, Simon bursts out laughing like a little boy.

It's right now, in front of this whole delirious crowds, that I realize my biggest dream is coming true: I've become a professional musician. The crowd is out of their minds partly because the most famous band in the world is on stage with us, but also because we managed to entertain them. It's the most spectacular feeling I've ever had in my life.

We end our set with the Jailbirds introducing us, and the roar is so surreal my arm hairs stand up. We walk off then stop at the side of the stage to see them play. They are the epitome of energy, and Damian, with his guitar and his hair loose, drives everyone crazy with his voice. I've been to many concerts, but I don't think I've ever heard energy like what's on stage right now. They were born to be up there; anyone can see they were meant to bring their music and energy to their adoring fans. They're perfect, and they know it, with their heart attack physiques and tattoos making them look more like rock stars than ever. They're living the dream, and they're having a great time doing it.

"So? How are you feeling?" I turn around to find Luke, Martin, and Taylor looking at me like I'm going to shatter into a million pieces. I smile, and their faces relax a bit.

"Do you want the truth?"

They nod in unison.

"I feel more excited and alive than I've ever been in my

life. After this, nothing can stop me! I swear that was the craziest, and most frightened and excited I've ever been."

Their faces light up like children in front of birthday presents, and, without saying a word, all three of them hug me, suffocating me in a group hug. We start jumping around and laughing like twelve-year-olds.

"Do you realize they've already started talking about us? I don't know about you, but my phone is blowing up with notifications," says Luke with one arm wrapped around my shoulders.

"I have hundreds of tags to a YouTube video of 'I Will Rise Stronger' taken from the front rows. It already has tens of thousands of views. It's barely been half an hour!" Taylor's as incredulous as we are watching the numbers on his phone.

I realize now that I've been so excited that I haven't even looked at my phone. I pull it out of my pocket and try to press the power button. "Mine's dead," I giggle

"Too many notifications, even mine went to hell a few minutes ago," shrugs Martin.

"It's incredible," whispers Taylor as he scrolls through his notifications.

Evan's voice behind us makes us spin round. "Not that unbelievable, you're the best up-and-coming band around. Even Jailbirds fans are singing your songs. You've overcome the toughest obstacle of all—to win over the audience."

Standing in a shirt and jacket, but no tie, with his fancy shoes and a pair of jeans that look drawn on him, he's both casual and elegant. I don't know how he does it.

"Stop it! You'll make us blush," says Martin with a grin.

Evan bursts out laughing. "Yeah, sure. No wonder you're

blushing." He moves closer to us and puts his hand on my shoulder. "Congratulations on your performance earlier. It was perfect," he whispers in my ear, making my heart race into my throat.

I turn to him and he smiles with a conspiratorial glance. Now I'm really blushing.

"What are you doing here?" Luke asks the question we've all been wondering.

"I'm making sure no one makes you sign a contract that isn't mine. There are way too many vultures at this festival." He laughs, but he's serious.

My head is spinning. I still can't get over how we went from playing clubs in Brooklyn without ever crossing the bridge into Manhattan to attending one of the biggest festivals in the United States. "Don't worry, we have no intention of being fooled by anyone else but you," I tell Evan, and he laughs and wraps his arms around me, drawing me slightly closer.

We stand at the side of the stage, watching the Jailbirds' performance, as excited as kids until the last song. When they finish and come towards us to exit the stage, Evan puts his hand on my shoulder and guides me to the side, making room for them to get off and the next group to get on. The whole thing feels much more intense than an ordinary concert.

"Don't make me rip your arms off, Evan, please." Damian's voice comes in quiet but serious enough that I'm sure he would.

The manager raises his hands above his head in a sign of surrender. I roll my eyes while the others start laughing.

"Are we going back to the hotel? I've booked the venue on the 15th floor so you can relax," Evan announces, leading us to the rear of the stage from where we then reach the backstage exit.

"Did you just say you rented a club to make us feel comfortable?" asks Taylor.

"I did," says the manager with a grin.

"Get used to it. Sometimes you'll regret not being able to live your life with the freedom to go and have a beer with friends without being assaulted," Simon explains without too much bitterness in his voice.

"You can invite whoever you want, just don't tweet to the whole continent," Evan says. We're watching him with awe, at least my band and me are.

"Evan, the only friends we have, are here, and our relatives think we play in a little orchestra. It's not like we're popular with our peers in Brooklyn. We started playing together because we were the losers in the neighborhood," I explain to him, and the others just burst out laughing.

"Okay, I get it. It's gonna be intimate."

"Can we at least call the girls?" asks Martin with a smile from ear to ear.

Now Evan bursts out laughing. "Yeah, just don't get caught by the press, or they'll crucify you on the spot."

"So? What am I supposed to do?" he asks, worried.

"Wait until you figure out how this world works and maybe don't fuck up your career right from the start," I suggest while everyone else giggles. "How the hell did you even find girls anyway? We've been here less than six hours!"

Martin puts his arm around me and looks at me, knowingly. "Honey, two sweet little words and mentioning the Jailbirds are enough to open doors for the whole female gender."

"Martin, you need both of your hands," says Simon, worried.

I take one look at Damian and see he's looking at our guitarist like he wants to rip his arms off. I give him a sharp look: could he quit glaring at everyone who comes near me? This is getting ridiculous. I decide to torture him a bit; I pass one arm around Martin's waist and the other around Thomas', next to me.

"Have you decided to kill us both?" snickers the drummer from the Jailbirds.

"I don't seem to have 'private property' written on me, so I don't see what the problem is." I smile naively.

Everyone's laughing except Damian, who's picking up the pace and getting on the bus like a madman.

"You're gonna freak him out," Thomas whispers in my ear.

I shrug my shoulders and grimace, showing fake indifference. "It's not like he can put a chastity belt on me just because he doesn't like anyone around me."

The guy nods and smiles then pushes me towards my bus. "He's finally found someone who gives him a hard time. I've never seen him so into a woman."

I wish I was as sure as he is. I thought I made it very clear to him that I'm interested in him and that I'm not going from one bed to the next. This constant marking his territory all the time is excessive. Stopping me from touching my friends is ridiculous!

*

"I'm going to take a shower, and then I'll join you," I tell the boys and take the elevator next to theirs, alone.

I haven't even pressed the button for my floor when a male

hand stops the doors and Damian enters, passing his card on the magnetic display. He grabs my wrist and pulls me close, almost making me crash into his chest.

"I gotta go take a shower," I say.

"I have a bathroom, too."

"I need some clean clothes."

"I'll lend you mine."

I make a face and cross my arms. It's not very mature, I know, but he's messing me up.

"Don't look at me like that. You're the one who provoked me."

"What are you going to do about it? Kidnap me?" I ask, annoyed.

I don't get an answer because the elevator doors open, and Damian practically drags me into his room. By the time the door closes behind us, I'm pressed against the wall with his lips on mine. His tongue slips into my mouth without hesitation, and I'm overwhelmed by a kiss that leaves me breathless. When I raise my hands to sink them into his hair, Damian withdraws with a smirk and moves away towards the sofa.

I let out a frustrated sigh, and Damian watches me, amused as he sits on the sofa in his suite.

"And you're leaving me here like this?" I ask.

"I told you. If you want more, you're gonna have to ask me."

I move over to him and stand in front of him, my arms crossed. "What do you want?" I explode almost furiously.

"You could start by begging me, since you're being such a tease and hanging on my friends."

"No way."

"Then you know the way back to your room," he points me to the door with one hand.

"You know, you're really annoying. I'm not leaving this room."

"Is that a yes?"

I open my arms and eyes wide in disbelief. "Of course, it's a yes, you idiot!" I burst out again.

He pulls me towards him on the couch, lays his hands on my ass, and makes me spread my legs until I'm straddling him. He holds me still while he pushes himself between my thighs. The desire in his eyes is unparalleled, and all my doubts collapse under the pressure of my hormones.

I take off my glasses and pull my shirt off my head, hearing Damian grunt with guttural pleasure. "Put your glasses back on," he orders, biting his lower lip.

I look at him slightly confused.

"Put your glasses back on. You have that sexy, nerdy, little schoolteacher look that makes me want to help you enjoy the rest of the night," he says with a half-smile, then looks down and gets serious. "You know I'm proud of the way you stood up to Brad on stage today, right? You were great."

A compliment like that from him almost brings tears to my eyes, of joy this time. I don't have to hear that twice to put the glasses back on. I've been hiding behind these lenses my whole life, yet I feel more naked than I've ever felt. Damian is peering at me with such desire it makes me tremble. He grabs me firmly by the hips and presses his erection into my most sensitive area, making my head roll back in pleasure. If he goes on like this, I'll come without even taking off my clothes. When I look at him, he's smiling smugly, and it makes me want to play.

I disentangle from his grip, and stand up; Damian looks at me questioningly. With disarming slowness, I take off my shoes then start unbuttoning my jeans just as calmly, giving him a glimpse of the pink lace panties underneath. Damian can only cling to the sofa cushions with all his strength and watch as I slowly turn around and take off my pants, sliding them along my legs while bending forward. I hear him moan with pleasure, so I turn around and see him panting, eyes wide open and full of desire.

"Take off the rest too," he orders, halfway between a hiss and a begging whisper.

I see him struggling to refrain from tearing my underwear off. I undo my bra and drop it on the floor without turning around. Damian leans over, and before I can take off my panties too, he slips his fingers under the elastic and gently pulls them down. He pulls me closer until I'm standing in front of him. He kisses one butt cheek and then the other, holding my hip with one hand and with the other touching the sensitive skin between my thighs, getting closer and closer to the most sensitive part. When he touches me between my legs, the jolt of pleasure almost makes me jerk. I'm so wet that his two fingers slip right in, immediately making me moan.

That sound, and my body so ready for him, is all he needs. He sits me on the couch next to him with a decisive gesture and then stands in front of me, taking off his shirt, giving me a breath-taking view of his statuesque physique, covered in tattoos. He starts to undo his pants unceremoniously, taking off his jeans and boxer shorts, which leaves me panting; now I understand why women line up for him. His hard-on is so inviting I have no doubt it will keep me happy all night long. With a quick gesture, he takes a condom out of his wallet and puts it on without taking his eyes off me, wearing the confident grin of someone who knows exactly what he's going to give me over the next few hours.

He slips between my legs, resting his knees on the sofa and towering over me, making me feel even smaller. My heart pounds in my chest with a mixture of excitement and a little fear; it's been a while since I've had sex. He grabs me firmly under my knees, sliding me towards him and putting my legs on his shoulders, then he slips inside me with an ease that leaves me breathless.

"Oh, Jesus Christ!" I moan as I close my eyes and grab the sofa cushion behind me to support me as he pushes inside me.

He laughs and sinks into me with more eagerness until I make a guttural sound no man has ever been able to get from me before. It may be the excitement of the moment, the fact that the sexual tension has been mounting between us for months, but I have one of the most intense orgasms of my life.

I open my eyes and look at him. His smile doesn't hide the intense desire I see in his eyes. He's not finished.

"You're sexy as hell when you come," he whispers to me with a kind of reverence in his voice that takes me by surprise. It's almost as if I'm in charge of his pleasure, and the realization of it makes me dizzy.

"Then let me come again so you can enjoy the show," I challenge with a mischievous smile.

That seems to excite him even more because he pulls away from me, leaving me suddenly empty and eager for contact, and sits down on the coffee table in front of the sofa, one hand pulling me up on his lap. He puts his mouth on my boob and holds me firmly by the waist, sinking inside me again.

I will remember this night for the rest of my life.

CHAPTER 16
Damian

I open my eyes to twinkling city lights filtering through the bedroom windows, getting a boner as if the night had been just a dream, and I hadn't fulfilled my every desire with Lilly. I move my gaze and find her petite figure sleeping blissfully beside me; the sheet slipped sideways, leaving me a view of her back and ass that makes the blood flow down below my belly. I can't resist. I turn towards her and caress her butt. When I see that she is not moving, I venture a little more. I lower myself on her white skin and kiss her gently, starting from the base of her back to the upper part of her thighs.

"If you go on like this, I'll come without you even touching me," she mumbles without opening her eyes, her voice mixed with sleep.

"Is that so unpleasant? Should I stop?" I tease her a little. Considering the way she was on top of me earlier tonight, I don't think she minded sleeping with me. I have to say, I've never invested so much energy in a woman, and what bothers me the most is that I didn't even mind that she played hard to get. For the first time in my life, I want to have sex with the same woman a second time, a third time, an infinite number of times, and not just to vent my frustrations, like with Loretta. I can't get enough of Lilly. My desire for her hasn't lessened after sleeping together, quite the opposite, in fact. It seems to have ignited an uncontrollable appetite for her.

"Oh no, honey, tonight you've earned the right to do whatever you want with my body. Just don't make me move from this position because I feel like I've been hit by a truck."

I laugh out loud, kissing her inviting back. "I have this effect, I realize that," I joke casually. "Anyway, you don't have to move, I'll make you enjoy it again," I whisper in her ear as I slide myself in between her butt and press down lightly.

She smiles blissfully and breathes deeply, shivering as if she's waiting for nothing else. I move grudgingly to grab a condom from above the bedside table and put it on without waiting too long. I get close again, putting my hand between her legs, and she lets out a moan. She's already ready to welcome me, as she did last night. I stretch myself over her, holding my weight so as not to crush her. I put my hand under her belly, caressing her in the most sensitive parts between her legs. In the end, I sink in, as I did several times in the past few hours, between her warm and welcoming thighs, losing myself in this crazy sensation I feel every time my body touches hers. I sink with a fast rhythm, and it doesn't take long before we both cum with an orgasm that makes us tremble. Unlike other women, coming inside her doesn't leave me empty. On the contrary, my chest fills with a feeling I can't decipher and contain, it leaves me with the desire for more, and it's a strange, almost uncomfortable, sensation.

I move away, kissing her neck, rolling on one side, and panting for air. Lilly turns on her stomach and stretches herself, yawning, leaving me enraptured by her beauty.

"What are you smiling about?" she asks me, pulling the

sheet up to her chin, realizing I'm staring at her.

"Because this is the first time I've ever woken up next to a woman who's as beautiful as the night I took her to bed."

Actually, it's the first time in my life I've ever woken up next to a woman, period. Usually, when we satisfy our desires, her makeup smeared on her cheeks and a lipstick-stained pillow, the girl picks up her things and goes back to where she came from, opening the door for herself.

Instead, I stay here, watching her blush over the compliment I just paid her, even if it wasn't the most delicate, and wishing we could stay in this bed for the rest of the day.

Lilly's stomach rumbles noisily and her lack of shame makes me laugh. "I think I'll starve to death if I don't have breakfast right away," she giggles.

"Do you think you can hold out until they bring it to our room?" I ask before I even process the sentence in my brain. My heart pounds in my chest. I've never asked a woman to stay, let alone have breakfast together. It's so intimate, totally foreign to my usual way of doing things, and it leaves me feeling bewildered. I see her blushing and frowning.

"Okay, what did you have in mind?"

I realize that if she'd said no, I'd be disappointed, and it makes my heart sink even more deeply into my stomach. I pull myself together, grab the room service menu, and put my arm around her shoulders, pulling her to my side. I let her order what she wants, and then I devote myself a little bit to her skin, breasts, and mouth while we wait for the food. She is panting, enjoying my fingers inside her, when the knock on the door interrupts us, making us grumble, disappointed.

I get up reluctantly to open the door, putting on a pair of

sweatpants and a T-shirt to retrieve the breakfast trolley that's loaded with enough food to keep us full until the evening.

"What are you doing?" I ask when I return to the room and see her looking for her clothes.

"I'm getting dressed," she explains in a tone that seems to call me an idiot.

I raise an eyebrow and cross my arms to my chest. "Go back to bed immediately. The great thing about room service is that you can eat between the sheets without worrying about putting anything on," I explain smartly, just to make her a little irritated. She's sexy as hell when she's angry.

Lilly, in response, grimaces, annoyed. "You're fully clothed."

I challenge her with the look. "Would you rather I open the door naked?"

"No, but if you're dressed, I'll get dressed."

Without thinking twice about it, I take off my shirt and pants and drop them on the floor. I watch her eyes pan across my body. I can tell she likes what she sees.

"Shall we have breakfast?" she asks me without giving me the satisfaction of a compliment.

I get closer to the bed and place one tray on her legs, then I sit next to her and do the same with mine. She puts one of the croissants in her mouth and lets out a moan of pleasure. She'll send me to the nuthouse if she keeps this up.

"Can I eat only these from now on?" she asks, licking her fingers and making me follow the movement with more lust than I should for a question like that.

"You can if you want to."

A little bit of cream falls on her breasts, and we both look down at where it fell. When she raises her hand to remove it, I grab it and move it away. I look her straight in the eyes, lower myself down on her, and, lick it off with my tongue, lingering a little more on the delicate skin of her breasts. I can feel her holding her breath.

"See? If you had been wearing a shirt, it would have gotten dirty." I make a naive face when I meet her look full of desire.

She says nothing, stares at me with a mischievous smile. Without taking her eyes off me, she dips her finger in the croissant, pulls out some custard, and puts it in the exact spot where I just took it off. I get hard instantly. I place the tray on the floor, do the same with hers, and then I continue my breakfast, throwing myself on the custard and her breast.

*

I kiss Lilly just outside the elevator and motion for her to get in while I take the next one. If I go up with her, I may never make it to the restaurant to have coffee with my friends. All the way to the restaurant, I can't get the smile off my face—I'll remember this night for the rest of my life. I find Michael and Simon having breakfast in the restaurant but no sign of Thomas. As soon as I get my coffee and sit next to them, they stop talking. Simon looks at me with a smile from ear to ear as Michael puts his elbows on the table.

"So, is Lilly as sexy naked as she is dressed?" Michael asks with a mischievous smile.

I give him a dirty look while sipping my coffee, trying to hide my irritation. I've become hyper-protective when it comes to her. "How would I know?"

Simon bursts out laughing. "Don't deny that you slept with her. You both disappeared after yesterday afternoon's concert, and when we passed by your room, we heard loud and clear moans," he says as Thomas, who has just entered, sits next to me. "Either you were watching porn, or you were fucking."

I burst out laughing, and, luckily, I sound sincere and convincing.

"Yes, I was fucking, but not Lilly. The girl who helped me with the demagnetized key...she stayed to test if it worked," I lie with a mischievous smile, hoping it sounds convincing enough.

Simon seems to be studying me, Michael's already laughing, and the only one who appears perplexed is Thomas. I already know he'll be waiting to interrogate me later when the others leave. Unfortunately for me, that scenario materializes five seconds later when the two of them get up and leave me with only a cup of coffee as a shield against Thomas.

"What are you doing with Lilly?" he asks me when the others are far enough away not to hear us.

"Nothing, I fucked the receptionist, not Lilly."

"I saw you kissing her in front of the elevator, not five minutes ago. Try rephrasing your answer. So, what's going on with Lilly?"

I turn to him and I study him while he's sipping coffee. He doesn't seem angry but somewhat worried. He seems concerned about me. Or her.

"We just fucked." I try to downplay it, on the defensive. For the first time in my life, I don't feel like bragging about what I'm doing between the sheets to someone else.

Thomas is watching me closely. He seems almost angry. "She's a good girl; she's smart, and she has a big heart. Don't fuck her brains out like you do to the others," he says, so harshly it bothers me.

It irritates me so much that it makes my stomach go sour, and I don't even know why. Usually, these things roll right off me. I let stuff like this bounce right off me, especially when it comes to women. I don't know if it's because I don't want him poking his nose into my life, which is entirely irrational since we've shared every single thought for years, or if it's because of the exact words he used to describe Lilly and I know he's right.

"Look, I fucked her, but I didn't fuck her brains out. Don't worry." I get up and walk away and leave the coffee exactly where it is with Thomas.

"Damian, I'm not kidding!" he yells as I'm leaving, and I don't look back.

*

I arrive on Lilly's floor in a bad mood and my stomach in a knot. The conversation with Thomas upset me because he hit the nail on the head: it's different with Lilly. I knew it when I dreamt of slipping between her legs, and I knew it this morning when we had breakfast together. It was never just a fuck with her.

I knock on her door, and she opens it in her bathrobe and wet hair. I would jump on her right now if we didn't actually have to talk about what happened in my room last night.

"Sorry, I just finished showering. Did I miss any important meetings?" she asks me with a puzzled look.

I smile at her and shake my head no as she steps aside and lets me in—wrong move. The bed is so close I would only have to lift her a little bit to throw myself between her legs.

"No, we need to talk," I say as I lean against the wall and

watch her brush her hair.

"Okay...you know that's always a bad sign when a man says that to you after you've been in bed, right? Usually followed by, 'It's not you, it's me.' The worst sentences ever invented by mankind."

I can't help but laugh at her joke. She doesn't seem too serious about it. I observe her for a few moments, and for some obscure reason that clouds my brain. I feel the need to clarify with her. But I'm not sure it's the right thing to do.

"If you came here to tell me that we're not together, that we've had fun but you don't want anything serious...I know. I know you've never had a steady woman, and I certainly didn't expect to be the one to change your mind. I had a great night. I'd definitely like to repeat it because that thing you do with your tongue literally drives me crazy...but if you don't want to hear from me anymore, fine. We're both adults. We can live with that, right?"

Her words rush out all in one breath like she'd been rehearsing them for a long time—probably in the shower while she was washing away the smell of our night. While her mature reasoning makes a lot of sense, she doesn't seem particularly sure of what she just said. Almost like she's saying what I want to hear instead of what she actually wants to tell me, but I decide not to press her. Because I have no idea if I'm ready for her honesty. I don't know if I am more afraid that she wants something more from me or that she doesn't want to see me anymore. I came here to tell her precisely these things, yet I feel annoyed when she says them.

"Well, I see we're on the same page," I say seriously. "And if you don't mind, I'd be happy to repeat that thing with my tongue a few more times," I add to soften the atmosphere.

She bursts out laughing and breathes a sigh of relief that I can't decipher. "Okay, but now, if you don't mind, I have to change and go out with the other idiots...and hope they believe me when I tell them that yesterday afternoon I had a big headache and came to bed. At least it's true that I 'came'... multiple times, to be honest," she explains, grimacing, pushing me through the small corridor.

"According to my band, I fucked the receptionist," I wink at her.

Lilly smirks and pushes me out the door. I walk away from her room with the knowledge that she has said out loud the speech I was going to give her, but with the unpleasant feeling that it's not really what I want.

CHAPTER 17

Lilly

The Jailbirds' tour bus is much more luxurious than ours. Downstairs there is the living area with leather sofas and musical instruments scattered around, while upstairs the rooms are furnished with a queen-size bed and a flat-screen TV on the wall. I know this because lately, I've been sneaking out of our tour bus to get into Damian's bed. The sex with him is incredible, and after, we spend time snuggling in each other's arms, talking about everything and nothing. The only flaw in this arrangement is that we have to keep it a secret.

Damian doesn't want word to get out. Considering that we've just managed to silence the rumors circulating about him and me together, it would be annoying for everyone. I'm still shocked by the number of photographers, and the aggressiveness of some, who were lurking for the shot of the century. Until I met the Jailbirds, I thought the photos on those gossip sites were mostly the result of some lucky paparazzi. I mean, I knew they hung out where famous people go, hoping to get some shots, but I had no idea how harassing they could be.

The downside of this whole situation, though, is that I feel like a groupie fucking her favorite singer, rather than the bassist of a band that's with a musician. Because, in the end, Damian and I aren't together, we're just two people having fun. I never expected him to give me more, or even thought I could want more from him, but sometimes I wish he made me feel a little more special. Apparently, I should be over the moon because, according to Thomas, whom I've spoken to openly, he's never had anyone for more than a one-night stand, so I should be delighted. The drummer is the only one who knows about us, which makes it so much easier when I need a lookout to sneak out of this corner of paradise.

"Hey, you're awake," Damian grunts with his face in my hair while he's squeezing me. His voice is husky and sexy.

"Yeah, your little guy's been on my ass for at least half an hour. I can't ignore him much longer."

Damian takes a few seconds, then he bursts into a loud laugh and squeezes me tighter. "You could straddle me and alleviate the tension." He smiles mischievously as he turns my face towards him and kisses me lightly on the lips.

The temptation is strong, it's hard to deny myself another half hour of pleasure with him, but I have to get off the bus. We arrived in this parking lot at four o'clock this morning, and I ran out of mine like a thief. "I wish I could, trust me. But I have to get back before they find out I didn't sleep on the bus last night either. It's getting harder and harder not to be noticed," I admit with a grimace.

Damian looks at me sternly, as if about to tell me something important, but in the end, he shakes his head and smiles at me. "I'll manage on my own by thinking of you," he says with a naughty grin, massaging his boner from above the sheet.

"Jerk," I reproach him, but without any malice in my voice. I like to tease him.

"I don't think you've ever complained about what I do." He

raises an eyebrow in defiance.

"In fact, I wasn't. Actually, since you'll be all right when I walk out this door, I'll give you something to enhance your fantasies." I stand up to put on my pants and then I lift up my shirt, flashing my boobs at him.

I feel him inhale violently, and when I lower the light fabric, I can see all the desire in his stormy eyes. I hit the nail on the head, and I'm delighted. It is rewarding, in a way, to know that I can excite him so much that he loses contact with reality. I've often thought about the women he's had, but I don't know anything about them, and I imagine amazons, sex goddesses that drive him crazy. I'm just...me, anonymous and not even that experienced.

"Get out before I bite off those clothes," he whispers in a husky, longing voice.

I giggle, open the door to his room, and peek out. I hear voices downstairs and realize I can't pass without being seen and have to explain what I'm doing here. "There's someone downstairs," I whisper in Damian's direction.

He props himself up on his elbow, smiles, and then shouts out loud, "Thomas, I need you here! I need you here now."

I lock myself behind the bedroom door, and when the drummer opens it wide, he almost slams it on my nose.

"Could you help her out without people asking questions?" he points to me.

Thomas looks at me with a half-amused smile while I greet him, waving an embarrassed hand in front of my face. I'd like to sink into the ground. "The little prince wants a pizza for breakfast. What do you say? Shall we go find a pizza place that's open at this hour?" Thomas cries.

I hear "He can suck my dick" and "Asshole" from downstairs, and a lot of laughter, and I guess it's their way of letting him know they're going out for pizza. I've often heard them insult each other that way. It's a man thing I'll never fully understand.

"Thank you," I tell Damian, lowering myself to kiss his lips gently, but he holds me back for a kiss full of affection, which takes me by surprise. It's not just desire.

When I get up, I'm breathless and dazed. And it takes me a few seconds too long to make contact with reality and leave the room, taking the stairs and then leaving the bus door undisturbed. I take a deep breath, closing my eyes when I am hit by the sun's rays, and I give myself a few seconds to enjoy them. When a hand touches my shoulder, I almost jump on the spot from fright.

"That's where you were." Luke's voice is weird, and his expression too.

I watch him for a few seconds to see how I can deflect it, but I'm still leaning against the Jailbirds' bus door. It's hard to tell him I'm coming from a run in the country. "I was playing some songs with Damian," I lie with the first excuse that comes to mind. A little weak, since we don't have any more shows together, but more realistic than a vague, "I had something to tell him." Luke looks at me with his forehead wrinkled and his serious expression. He seems almost annoyed.

"Is it just me, or have you two been hanging out a lot lately... even though you don't have to rehearse together anymore?" Luke's voice is suspicious.

That's what I mean. He's my best friend: he can smell lies from miles away. I wear my prettiest mask, the one with the shy smile, and pretend I'm embarrassed.

"Yeah, well...I found out that I like to play with him. He relaxes me and makes me relieve the tension I build up during the tour. I take advantage of that because it doesn't take long to get from one bus to another." It's not a total lie. It's true that I release tension and relax.

Luke studies me for a few seconds, but then he moves a few steps away and finally turns towards me. "Are you coming?" he asks me seriously.

I nod and follow him into our empty bus.

"We never talked about what happened at the festival." He sits on the couch next to me after giving me a cup of black coffee.

"How I exploded and told everyone about the famous Accident?" I blush, thinking back to that moment.

Luke nods and watches me closely. I shrug my shoulders and inhale deeply.

"Honestly, it helped to get rid of this weight. I said it on impulse, but along with the anger, I've been carrying a lot of fear since that day. Dr. Sue would be proud of me," I smile, trying to make him understand that it was an admirable thing.

"What about seeing Brad again?"

I was expecting that question. When he heard Brad was in the audience, he wanted to go smash his face in. It took Martin and Taylor together to hold him down.

"The truth? When I started hearing people screaming enthusiastically as I sang, I realized how much power I had given to Brad's words. I always saw him as someone not to be angry with, or else he'd make my life impossible. But up there on that stage, Brad was just one person among a hundred thousand other people cheering me on. There, I finally realized he's just a voice in the middle of the crowd and it's easy to tune it out. I was the one who had the power. He couldn't do anything from his front-row seat. Thanks for dedicating the song to him. Ever since it went viral, I've been getting messages of encouragement. This never would have happened if you hadn't called him out so directly."

Luke smiles at me and kisses my head, tightening his arms around me. "I'm glad. You have no idea how happy I am that that asshole is finally out of our lives," he whispers without moving from the hug.

"So am I." A peaceful smile curls my lips.

*

We leave the stage sweaty and excited like every night. By now, the clumsy and awkward girl I was at the beginning has vanished. Or rather, she's still there, but I've learned to turn my embarrassment into positive energy, into concentration, determined to use the tension that invades me for something useful. I must say, I'm succeeding well. After I got rid of the nightmare that is Brad and his judgment, I even started dressing without the huge sweatshirts. Not that I'm a hottie, but at least the media aren't slaughtering me for it anymore. Usually, my bandmates congratulate me for doing well, which is why tonight I feel a bit bad when they get off the stage without looking at me and hide in the backstage room in silence.

I go in after them and watch them for a few seconds before I get my bag. "I'm gonna go change in the bathroom, do you mind? Does anyone else want to go first?" Lousy way to break the ice in a tense situation that I can't get a handle on.

They all shrug their shoulders and give me a little less than an annoyed look, so I hole up in the bathroom, staying there longer than I have to, trying to get over feeling guilty and not having the slightest idea why I feel this way. When I finally find the courage to come out, I'm staring into an empty room.

"Where the hell have they gone?" I whisper to myself. Usually, we wait till the Jailbirds have finished their show and then we go out for a bite to eat. I send a message in the group chat: *Where the hell are you guys? I don't know where to reach you.* Seen and unanswered. I swear whoever invented this blue double checkmark thing should burn for eternity in the fires of hell. I just sit here, like an idiot, waiting as usual for the Jailbirds to finish.

"Are you alone?" Thomas asks, the first one coming in after the show. He looks surprised, since we're usually never separated; it's always the four of us like we were at school.

"The others went out while I was changing, and now they're ignoring me," I admit with a grimace of disappointment.

The rest of the band has come in, and they watch me frowning. Simon also seems a bit worried. Damian picks up the phone and writes something.

"They're already on the bus, they've got a pizza, and they're eating it there," he lets me know in a tone that seems almost irritated.

"Thank you," I say, lowering my head and grabbing my things before I left.

Damian tries to stop me by grabbing me by the wrist, but I'm too ashamed to stay. How did he manage to get an answer to his first text, and my forty were ignored for the last hour? It's humiliating, and I don't even understand what I did wrong.

I open the door of the bus, and the voices I heard talking

outside immediately drop. I find them there, eating pizza, and when I stop with my arms crossed and my eyes raging, no one says a word. You can cut the tension in here with a knife. "Why the hell are you guys mad at me?"

Nobody answers, they just keep eating their pizza. I hope they choke on it, at least a little bit.

"Did I do something to you? Cause I don't really remember doing anything to make you act like this." I'm furious.

They finally drop the damn pizza, turning to look at me with expressions that are halfway between bored and angry that I'd like to slap away.

"Are you sure? Because I can think of one thing that really pisses me off," Martin says in a very irritating tone.

"Yes, I'm sure." I'm not moving from my position.

"Seriously? Or are you getting ready to launch your solo career or maybe partner up with Damian? Otherwise, why would you keep going to rehearse with him?" says Taylor, while Luke looks down desperately towards his pizza.

The question hits me like an icy cold shower. Is that really their concern? I almost laugh at the idea, and I can't hold back an amused smile that irritates them even more. "I'm not planning any solo career, trust me. You are my band, and you always will be," I say with my heart in my hands.

"We don't believe you, Lilly. You keep lying to us and sneaking into Damian's tour bus. It's not just a fling here and there. You're there every night. If you're not composing music with him, what the hell are you doing? You think we're stupid enough not to notice? Really, Lilly?" Luke's voice is filled with resentment and disappointment, and it makes me sick.

They're my friends, Luke's my best friend, I can't stand

them feeling betrayed by me, my behavior, and my lies.

"We fuck!" I blurt out in the middle of their silence, my face burning with shame. I watch them look at me like I'm insane.

"Damian and I are having sex," I explain when clearly they seem too dazed by my statement to put the pieces together.

"You mean intercourse?" Taylor asks me, weird and amused at the same time.

I look at him sideways and relax a little bit by putting my hands in my back pockets. "We fuck, we screw, we shag, we fuck like rabbits...I mean, we have sex..." I keep explaining in the incredulous silence of the bus.

Martin starts laughing and reaches out to Luke. "I knew this would happen. You owe me fifty bucks." He snickers as Luke grabs his wallet and reluctantly drops the money.

"Would you stop betting on my sex life?" I give them a dirty look as I fetch a plate from the cupboard and approach the table.

"Absolutely not. I was sure I'd win. You eye-fuck each other every time you're in the same room together. I knew you'd get down to business. Easiest fifty bucks of my life," laughs our guitarist.

Luke looks at me wrong. "I was counting on you. Traitor. I thought you, at least, were immune to the allure of the sex machine," he whispers slowly.

I burst out laughing at Damian's nickname and fill my plate with a slice from every carton of the three pizzas in front of me, slapping Taylor's hand trying to stop me when I reach his. It's punishment for getting mad at me for stupid reasons.

"I'm sorry, honey, but he deserves all the praise he gets

from that point of view. I can guarantee you I'd never stop giving it to him. The man makes you reach Nirvana and then takes you further," I joke back to Luke.

Taylor and Martin burst out laughing while Luke looks disgusted. I know he doesn't want to hear about my sex life, but that's the punishment for betting on it.

"So, that's why you go on their bus every night?" Taylor asks me in disbelief.

"Yes, and this has to stay between us. If the media found out about this, they'd slaughter us, and we don't want that kind of publicity." I point my finger at each one of them and look at them threateningly.

They all nod seriously, understanding exactly why I don't want them to make such insinuations about Damian and me, after everything that happened before the tour. I eat my pizza without talking, and they resume eating as well. They're my family, of course they're gonna be pissed off if I even think about leaving. My heart fills with a calming warmth that makes me feel loved, and I smile.

We are twenty years old, with a career that is taking off at the speed of light. I spend my nights between the sheets with the god of sex and evenings playing music with my dearest friends... and we're paid to do it! In a few months, we've raised enough money to afford an apartment in Manhattan, and people sing our songs when they come to our shows. I feel intoxicated, invincible, like nothing bad can touch me.

CHAPTER *18*
Damian

We stop on the way for lunch and, since there's no show tonight, decide to spend some time in the desolate countryside we are going through. Living all year round in an apartment in the middle of skyscrapers, sometimes I forget how huge the distances between one city and another are. Around us, the expanse of sunburnt land and low bushes stretches for miles.

Except for this gas station with the diner, there are no houses or anything to remind you that people live in this place. Every now and then, a car pulling a trailer with a boat headed for the Great Salt Lake, near Salt Lake City, speeds along the highway. A yellow sign warns us not to stray in the middle of the brushwood to avoid being bitten by the rattlesnakes that populate this area. It makes me smile: I guess they've never seen the rats roaming around New York. Those are creatures you have to fear.

The diner isn't very big, but it's two o'clock in the afternoon, so it's empty, and it can safely contain our whole crew. What I like the most about touring is the family atmosphere it creates, not only among the band but with all those who live around us: sound engineers, musicians, stage crew. There are dozens of people who live elbow to elbow with us, some of them for years, others are new, but all share the same passion for music. They are the roadies, and they are the soul of every tour.

I sit next to Luke and Martin, across from me is Thomas, next to him, Lilly and next to me, on the other side, Simon.

"Do I have time to fuck the waitress?" Martin asks after the girl leaves after bringing us beers.

We all burst out laughing.

"She set her eyes on Damian first, then on Simon and then on me. You have to beat the competition before you can get between her legs," says Thomas, amused, and I can only laugh.

"How come you get first choice of every girl?" Martin asks in a tone somewhere between annoyed and good-natured envy.

"Because we worked our asses off for years to become Gods of Sex. It takes hard and meticulous work, leaving women satisfied so they can go and tell their friends about the mystical experience. And who are we to deny women healthy pleasure?" I answer.

Thomas smiles behind his beer, Simon rolls his eyes, Luke snickers, and Martin makes a funny face. "Yes, Lilly told us you're more than living up to your reputation. How did she put it? Ummm, oh, you bring her to Nirvana and further? So, our bass player confirmed you're a sex god. Go ahead, give yourself a pat on the shoulder. She's usually very selective in the choice of men she sleeps with." Martin's words slam everyone at the table, and tense silence follows. "Oops. Did I just say that out loud?" He throws a worried look at Lilly.

I look at Lilly, who keeps eating as though she doesn't hear our conversation, but her utterly red-as-a-traffic-light face tells me she absolutely heard Martin's comment. Thomas looks up at me, worried.

Simon rescues us from our embarrassment with a joke aimed at Martin. "So how do you plan to approach the waitress? Have you tried begging on your knees yet, or is that your next move?" Everyone laughs except the person concerned and me.

Lunch goes by as if nothing happened, but I notice the looks coming from the tables next to ours. It seems quite the opposite; everyone heard it. I might just be paranoid, but the kid's statement just about made me choke on my lunch.

*

"Why the hell did you go and tell Martin?" I hiss, blocking Lilly before she can get on her bus.

We're stuck between our tour bus and theirs, and no one can see us unless they have to get on this bus. Still, arguing with her out in the open makes me feel uncomfortable, and the fear of someone seeing us becomes more real.

Lilly shrugs, slightly distraught. "They suspected that I wanted to leave the band and start a solo career because I kept disappearing to your bus. So I was forced to tell them," she explains with a sorrowful grimace.

The anger is working its way into my stomach. Does she have to be so honest with those guys all the time? They clearly can't keep a secret. "Couldn't you lie? Do you realize what a mess you've made?"

I immediately regret the words once they're out of my mouth when I see the pain in her eyes turning to rage—hard fury that nails me to the spot.

"You're the one who wants to keep me a secret like I'm a whore you're ashamed of. I have no problem telling my friends who I'm sleeping with because they're friends and care about me. Get over yourself, Damian. So what if people know we're sleeping together? It's not a big deal. I never ask you to go out to dinner, watch a movie, nothing. I know I'm nothing but a fuck to you, and I decided to swallow my pride and let it be what it is. But don't blame me for your guilty conscience. And now, if you'll excuse me, I'm getting on the bus. I don't know if you've noticed, we're outside. Someone might see us together." Her words are so cold that I feel the air in my lungs freezing.

I watch her falter when she sees Thomas a few steps away watching us, but she immediately recovers and gets on the bus with her head held high and her proud look, slamming the door behind her. I realize I've been an asshole, the biggest jerk ever, and the anger rises in my stomach, clutching me like it hasn't happened in a long time.

"We're leaving," announces my best friend with a stern expression. I know he thinks I've fucked up everything beyond repair, and I walk towards him with a tearing sense of guilt and a sinking heartache.

I get on the bus and find Michael and Simon already waiting for me. Behind me, Thomas puts his hand on my back, inviting me to sit down. Their faces are gloomy, and I know I'm going to get an earful from them too.

"We asked you, and you specifically told us you weren't fucking her," Simon scolds.

"I didn't want it to get out," I say without much conviction. It sounds ridiculous, even to my ears.

"Don't be a dick," slams Michael in anger. "You could have counted on our discretion, but now the whole crew knows. How long do you think it'll take the media to find out? There's practically a bounty on your head for any information about you, and that's the queen of bullshit for the fucking front pages!"

For a moment, the room fills with a tense silence that doesn't allow me to breathe. I put my head down, ashamed as an idiot for the mess I made. And I even blamed Lilly. I deserve the "Asshole of the Year" award for this one.

"You told me you were just having fun, that she was cool with it, too," Thomas snaps with spite. "From the conversation I just witnessed out there, it sounds like a one-way street to me. You're having fun. She just accepts what you give her because she knows; otherwise, she'd have nothing else. I have no idea if she's in love with you, but it's more than obvious she's invested feelings in it. Meanwhile, you're still the piece of shit who uses women, and that's it!" And that's the straw that breaks the camel's back.

I get up on my feet and head for the stairs, stopping only when I hear Simon intervene. Usually, he is the quietest of the group. "Yeah, that's right, run away, you prick," his tone a mixture of annoyance and anger.

"Why the hell aren't you guys on my side? I made a mistake. I don't need you to insult me and make me feel like an idiot. I expected at least some support from you," I snarl angrily.

Simon turns and looks at me with an expression of pity that almost hurts. "You've ruined everything with the only decent girl that's ever come into your life. If you'll excuse me, I'm not on your side on this one. Now go call Evan and tell him the truth, he's gonna have a lot of damage control to do."

Just hearing our manager's name makes my stomach clench miserably. He's gonna crucify me worse than these three put together. And even though I know I deserve it, I'm not happy about getting into more shit. I clench my fists and stomp up the stairs. It's gonna be a long, painful phone call.

*

Thomas gets on the bus after we stop for breakfast. I didn't get off, partly because I've been in a bad mood since yesterday and partly because I don't want to see Lilly. We haven't spoken since our conversation outside her bus; seeing her right now wouldn't do any good. My friend throws six gossip magazines at the table in front of me in sequence: all showing pictures of Lilly and me together, taken during concerts. I read a couple of them and almost throw up.

People:

Sources close to the couple say the relationship has been going on for months now, and in front of everyone. While there are still no photos that testify to the couple's official status, it seems that Damian and Lilly now live under the same roof, or rather inside the tour bus. The same sources say official confirmation of the two's involvement will be soon, maybe during a romantic dinner or a date. We just have to be patient enough to get some photos to confirm the new golden couple.

Gossip Now:

Apparently, the Jailbirds' contest wasn't so random. Sources tell us that Damian Jones and Lilly Jenkins have been having an affair since long before the Red Velvet Curtains won the competition that took them on tour, sharing the stage with the biggest band in the world. Those who didn't think Jenkins was worthy of a stage of that magnitude were right, and some rumors are circulating that the talents that got her there are not musical. The "no comment" issued by the band representative seems to confirm a lack of explanation for these accusations.

"Your famous 'fuck them all' expression was translated by Evan into a more appropriate 'no comment', which the press interpreted as an admission," Thomas states coldly. Though his statement sounds completely indifferent, his eyes hold nothing but anger towards me.

"Lilly could have made a statement, denying everything..." I know my suggestion is the dumbest I could give.

"You realize she's the most vulnerable one in all of this, don't you? She's the one who's gonna get slaughtered by fans, chased by paparazzi, slammed across the front page like another girl trying to make a name for herself at your expense, right? They're not gonna go easy on her, and you're lucky she's not already on this bus kicking your ass."

I'm still sipping my coffee but the lump in my throat keeps me from swallowing. I know she's gonna come out of this with broken bones and, as much as it bothers me to get involved, I feel compelled to protect her. I just don't know how. I have no idea how to fix a situation that got out of control because I couldn't keep it in my pants long enough to finish the tour. I don't regret sleeping with her, and it's not just the sex; I miss everything about Lilly right now, including holding her close when she falls asleep on my shoulder.

"How's she doing?" I ask.

"Why don't you go ask her yourself, and maybe even apologize?"

I've been up all night thinking about what I want to say to

her, but I couldn't find anything sensible that would make up for my behavior yesterday. How do you apologize for being a jerk? Sure, I could just go up to her and say, "I'm sorry I was a jerk," but I couldn't bear seeing all that anger, disappointment, and sadness in her eyes. I grab my cup of coffee and slip back into my room.

PRESS *Review*

Twitter @damian4ever:
We all knew that they won the contest just because she spread her legs. Now you're surprised?

Twitter @JailbirdsTrueFan:
I didn't think Damian had such bad taste. Why did he choose that slob?

Twitter @damianIsMyBae:
Are we going to send that bitch home? She can't even hold a guitar in her hand, but she can open her legs without any problem!

What About Your Brain and Your Ears? Are They Connected?

Hi, Roadies!

Many of you asked me what I think about the Damian-Lilly story, and I decided to clarify once and for all my position. IT'S NONE OF MY BUSINESS! Yes, I wrote that all in caps, and I'm not sorry. In this blog, I've never written gossip of any kind;

I've always talked about music, not about the private lives of the bands I follow. This will be the only post where I will talk about this topic because you are clogging me with private messages.

I keep saying that the Red Velvet Curtains are the best-emerging band out there right now, without a doubt. Lilly deserves to be on that stage with her whole band because they're terrific musicians, with a musical maturity that you rarely meet in such young bands. So if you expect me to get on the bandwagon of those who say it's all a farce, you'll be disappointed because, for me, that place on stage is well deserved. The private life of their members is indeed private and should remain that way for everyone.

Be kind and Rock'n'Roll,

Iris

16762 Likes 15320 Tweets 12593 Shares 3498 Comments

CHAPTER 19
Lilly

In the beginning, when they announced the contest, I was in a bad mood because I didn't want to participate; when we won, I was in a bad mood because I didn't want to face fame. I never thought my mood would turn black again—after overcoming my worst fears—as a result of getting fooled by that asshole Damian.

What he said to me yesterday, the blame he laid on me, opened my eyes to what I really mean to him: nothing. What angers me the most is that I fell for it. He told me straight to my face that we're just fucking. I even agreed that I was okay with it, ignoring my heart screaming at the top of its lungs that I just can't do it, I can't do sex without the feelings. That's what pisses me off: that I was stupid.

"Will you come out for coffee with us?" Luke asks me.

Since yesterday afternoon Martin's been apologizing about what happened, saying he didn't want to get me in trouble, and I believe him. He didn't do it on purpose but because Damian provoked him, and I can't blame the guy. That doesn't change the fact that the damage is done, and I thank God for my friends who are helping me filter the waves of hate coming from the social networks, where apparently the Jailbirds' fans think I'm a prostitute. Someone even made a comic strip that shows me in skimpy clothes escaping down a street and Damian, getting treated by a loving nurse for the STD I gave him. Even I laughed at that damn comic because I have to say that, despite everything, even though it hurts like hell, it's well-drawn. They got my boobs too big, but I guess they fit the stereotype.

"We're in the middle of nowhere," reassures Martin when he sees me peeking out the window of the bus.

I get up the courage to get off with my friends and approach the small shop entrance next to the cafeteria, surrounded by two angels that protect me: Martin on one side, Luke on the other, and Taylor leading the way. I look around to see if I can find the one person I absolutely don't want to meet right now.

"He didn't come down." Thomas' voice almost scares the hell out of me. When I turn around, I find him smiling at me with his mouth but not his eyes. I nod and look down as I keep walking, but he grips my elbow gently so that I turn around.

"I'm sorry for what you're going through. If it helps, we all have your back. We're not gonna let you down right now... Damian too. He acted like an asshole, but I think realizes the shit he did."

"It's my fault. He always made it clear that he didn't want anything else...and as for what they're saying about me online, whatever, they'll calm down," I say with a smile that I hope doesn't look too fake.

Thomas seems to weigh my words. "You do know there will be dozens of paparazzi waiting for us on the next few dates, right? This is news they're going to celebrate," he notes without sugar coating the news. I like this guy.

I shrug my shoulders. "What can I do? Lock myself on the

bus? I'll find a way not to be too noticeable," I say with a grimace. I'll stay out of the way, try not to be around too much, try not to do anything stupid. That's the best I can do.

Thomas wraps his arm around me and smiles at me. "You're a wise woman. Come and let me buy you coffee."

"With all this fuss, I want a muffin too," I sneer honestly.

Thomas bursts out laughing. "And you're also someone who gets what she wants. I like you," he says, dragging me into the little cafe.

*

"Max said there are more paparazzi and fans in front of the arena door. Let's get inside quickly, okay? Let's not stop and sign autographs like we usually do," Thomas explains to us in the bus before grabbing the door handle and disappearing as swiftly as he arrived.

"Let's let them go ahead and follow them at a distance. That way, we'll share the attention," Luke suggests, and we agree that might be a good idea.

I let Luke step out of the bus first, peeking out. "The parking lot is deserted. It's closed off by a gate, apparently. But the entrance isn't," he explains.

I decide to follow them anyway, but my sweatshirt gets caught on the hook of the lock. It rips, leaving a slash of about four inches on the side. Too big to go unnoticed. "Fuck it," I say through gritted teeth. "Go ahead, I'll change and catch up to you."

"Are you sure?" Luke asks me, puzzled.

"Yeah, don't worry. I won't be long."

I don't want them to feel compelled to protect me every single step of the way. It's only a few yards; I can make a run for the door. I return to the bus and look for a new hoodie, cursing myself for not wanting to do laundry. Turning the drawer upside down without much success, the only clean thing I find is a red plaid flannel shirt. I don't even remember packing it. I quickly take off my sweatshirt and put the flannel on. Since I'm here, I go to the bathroom to pee, and then I get off the bus, being careful with the hook and closing the door behind me.

When I get to the gate, I see what Thomas meant by "a bit of movement," and I don't like it at all. There must be at least a hundred people, including about twenty paparazzi. They are photographing the Jailbirds, who have not yet gone inside, and my band that has joined them in the meantime.

"What the hell are they waiting for?" I whisper, annoyed.

The noisy commotion is getting on my nerves; I can see that security is struggling to contain them, and I'm surprised there are no barriers to divide us. Maybe they weren't expecting all this activity. I inhale deeply and reach for my hood, cursing myself when I remember I just changed, and then lower my head and try to be as inconspicuous as possible. I decide to walk slowly; after all, they're all focused on the band so nobody is looking at me.

My discreet approach lasts exactly four steps before someone notices me and shouts at the top of their lungs. In a few seconds, they are all over me. In the pandemonium, someone pulls me, everyone pushes me, someone insults me. Mostly the paparazzi ask me to turn around so they can point their camera lenses in my face. But the fans are the worst; they're all over me, tugging at my shirt, making me trip and, with so many people around, I lose my balance and fall to the ground like a sack of potatoes.

Before I even have time to think about how to get up, I feel two firm hands grabbing my arms, pulling me up, holding onto me, and leading me undisturbed through the screaming crowds and the shooting cameras. I'm crouching in Damian's arms, holding and shielding me from what's happening around us. In a handful of seconds, I find myself in the silence of a corridor, barely standing, and groping for Luke to support me after what felt like a roller coaster ride. What the hell just happened?

Damian's the last one in the room and slams the door hard. Dave, the head of security, is as tense as I've ever seen him before. "Why the fuck wasn't anybody with her?" Damian yells. "And you, why the hell didn't you come with the group? You wanted to make the diva entrance?" He's out of his mind, mad as hell.

"And you're an asshole," yells Thomas like I've never heard him before. He's at least as angry as Damian, but not with everyone, just his friend. "What the fuck were you thinking, running into the crowd and shoving those photographers? You wanna bring on a lawsuit?"

I didn't realize in the commotion of the moment that Damian was shoving people.

"If she wasn't alone, I wouldn't have gotten in the way! But she wants to do it her own way, and I had to do it my own way," Damian yells like a madman.

Simon approaches the two of them, worried they might get their hands on each other, but my anger is blinding me.

"Enough!" I shout loudly, banging a notebook that I find on the table in front of me. "Enough!" I scream, banging it again. "Enough!" I scream even louder for the third time. This time everybody is looking at me, shocked. I turn to Damian. "Stop blaming me when you're the one who created this mess in the first place! Stop blaming me for everything. Stop getting pissed off at everyone but yourself. And you," I turn to Thomas. "Stop throwing gasoline on the fire. After all, he didn't do anything illegal. No judge is going to blame him for coming to save my ass."

An exchange of glances I don't understand between Thomas and Damian makes me shudder to the bone. All the anger turns to pure terror for a second, and then confusion. I don't understand the look, only that it wasn't good, which makes me think this conversation isn't getting any better.

"Unless you're hiding something from us," I whisper. Damian's downward glance and tense expression tells me I guessed right. "Either you tell us what, or I swear I'm leaving this tour. We need to be able to trust each other. I've told you all about me, you know my story, I demand the same honesty," I whisper, making the threat seem much more severe than I intended.

"Yeah, I'm leaving too if you don't talk." Luke, to my surprise, has my back.

I'm so angry that, for a moment, I forgot how many people are in this room. The band in front of us glances at each other, worried, then Damian finally emits a resigned sigh. "If we're gonna have this conversation, you're gonna have to sign a confidentiality agreement. You, Dave, are a witness that they consented to the signing, okay?"

The man nods his head, a gesture that seems almost solemn in the silence of this room.

"We'll sign the fucking agreement, but now speak," I hiss through my teeth.

Damian looks me right in the eyes for a few seconds, and, for a moment, I see the fear in his. "Do you know what real jailbirds are?" he asks us seriously. "In slang terms, they're people who are stupid enough to go to jail as soon as they get out. People who are always in jail, who can't do anything else with their lives."

A vice grips my stomach, especially seeing the shameful faces of Thomas, Simon, and Michael. Right now, I want to tell Damian to stop. I've heard all I need to know: I'm not going to like this story.

"We chose it because that's what we heard every day from the guards at the juvenile detention facility where we were locked up," Damian adds, looking straight into my eyes with a painful expression that makes my heart ache. Now I understand the fear in his eyes before he says it.

"Holy shit," whispers Taylor with his mouth wide open like Luke and Martin.

"Yeah. The band was formed because we were part of an at-risk child recovery program. We didn't go to jail for anything too serious. They gave us a chance to get out so we grabbed it as soon as we could and escaped the shit we were in. We all met in there."

Getting to know them these past few months, the kindness they showed us, the respect they gave, the generosity with which they welcomed us, and the help they offered, it seems almost impossible that they could have done anything to end up in prison.

"What do you mean by not so serious?" questions Martin, hesitant, and the Jailbirds smile.

"I can't speak for the others," Damian says, "but I can tell you that when I was eight years old, I was in my uncle's care, not exactly a decent person. At twelve I was already stealing cars. At fifteen, I stole an SUV from a woman who was loading her shopping bags into the trunk of the supermarket parking lot. I didn't realize that there was a baby seat in the back seat until a couple of miles later. When he started crying, I panicked, and not knowing what to do, I left him in front of the first hospital I found. Nothing happened to the baby, but they grabbed me and put me in jail. The aggravating circumstance was pretty serious."

My head is spinning. Too much information that I can't process, never mind understand. "How the hell have you kept it a secret all these years? You're the most famous band on the planet!" I ask.

"You get a lot by paying big money and circulating false rumors, quite believable stories, stories that people love to hear. In short, we throw women, parties, and scandals in front of the prying eyes, and hope they don't look any further," confesses Thomas with a shy smile.

Give people something to hold against you so they won't focus on what you want to hide. Simple and effective, I must admit.

"And a complaint from a photographer could get your record exposed," Luke says out loud.

"That's right."

"Couldn't you have told us this before?" Martin asks, saying out loud what everyone here is thinking.

"It's not like people always react well if they know you've been in jail..."

Martin shrugs, and Taylor echoes him. "It's not a problem

for us."

I can see the four guys' faces relax a bit, and look younger than they are. Now I understand their bodies covered in tattoos, their muscles, and the fact that they seem to protect each other with an unspoken agreement. It's probably what they did as kids when they were forced to grow up fast.

"So doesn't that freak you guys out?" Damian is a little bit suspicious.

"Why should it?" The words come out of my lips honestly. "You fucked up when you were young, you paid for it, now you're respectable adults. I don't see why we should have a problem with you. It's not up to us to judge you or make you feel bad about it."

Damian can't hold back the smile on his face. "Good."

"Hey, hold it right there, bad boy. I said it's okay if you've been in jail, but I haven't forgiven you for treating me like shit. You've still got a lot of work to do before I decide not to rip your balls off with my bare hands." I point my finger at him before I move to the door.

Damian rolls his eyes and steps aside when I pass him without having the courage to look me in the eye.

"Shit, Damian, between her pissed off and prison, I'm pretty sure prison's better," whispers Michael as I grab the door handle, pull it open, and slam it, hearing the others laugh at his joke.

CHAPTER 20
Damian

I watch her from afar as she prepares for a photoshoot that Evan has organized for the official launch of the Red Velvet Curtains with the record company. It's a big commitment, and I can see she's stressed and embarrassed in a skirt that's too short and a very deep neckline. That's not her; Lilly is a sweatshirt and jeans, tank top and running shorts kind of girl; or tracksuit pants with the Captain America t-shirt. Yet, she's accepted the rules of this environment, which require her to look as sexy and glossy as possible.

It's been four days since I left her, four days of agony where my mind regularly returns to her skin under my hands, my lips, my tongue. She's not the only woman on earth I could fuck. I wish I was in New York, calling Loretta and fucking all night long, so I could forget Lilly.

"If you keep staring at her like that, you'll set her on fire," Thomas' voice brings me back to reality.

"At least it warms her up, she's practically naked." I can't stop looking at her from afar like a pervert.

My best friend snorts. "I never thought I'd meet a girl who could keep you on your toes like that," he says, laughing.

I give him a stern look. "I'm just trying to see where she goes so I can avoid her. Sooner or later, voices will calm down if they don't see us together." The words come out of my mouth like a child trying to convince his parents he's learned his lesson.

"Do you really believe that shit you're saying, or are you trying to show me a good time? Because if it's the latter, you're doing just fine." He raises an eyebrow, smiling.

"Look, I haven't touched her, I haven't been near her, I've been avoiding her, and she's okay with that," I admit with a twinge of anger in my stomach. I've never been one to worry about whether or not a girl misses me. In fact, if I'm honest, the idea never even crossed my mind, but the fact that she stays away from me too, and she's okay with it, it bothers me. The worst thing is that I can't understand if it's because of my wounded pride or because I really care what she thinks about me.

"And that's exactly what you shouldn't do," Thomas mumbles amusedly.

I turn to him and look at him, exasperated. "What the hell is wrong with you? First, you tell me not to touch her. Now that I'm away, you tell me not to. You're about as consistent as a politician during an election," I grumble angrily.

Thomas bursts out laughing, and it makes me even more irritated. "I'm just saying, you finally found a woman you care about besides yourself and our band. We are your brothers, and we will always be your brothers, you know, but you have to find a way to live your life and enjoy it a little bit...and not only in the physical way."

His tone is too loving, too full of feelings, and I don't want to listen. Weren't drummers once all about sex and rock and roll? Why does he have to have a conscience? Luckily, Michael approaches, pulling us away from this conversation that's getting too personal.

"She looks sexy in that outfit, doesn't she? She's always been a hottie, but now they're getting her to the next level," he says with an almost dreamy air as he undresses Lilly with his eyes.

Michael's comment is so irritating that if it weren't for the rest of the tour, I would have already ripped his limbs off with my bare hands. Thomas looks at us and giggles while Michael whitens when he looks at my angry face. Literally.

"I'm sorry. I didn't mean to. I was just thinking out loud. I swear I'll never do it again...not even in my head. I'll have the part of my brain that has dirty thoughts about Lilly removed, I swear...I'm not making it better, am I?" Michael says, stammering, embarrassed, and seriously concerned for his physical safety.

"No, I don't think so. Shut up, Michael," Thomas suggests laughing.

"Okay. Anyway, I just came by to see if you guys wanted to hang out tonight. It's been ages since we've been out clubbing, and even longer since I got laid, so I need booze and women. Simon's obviously a monk locked up in a convent. What about you?" he asks hopefully.

Why not? I need distraction after all, and maybe this is just the thing. Evening out with my friends and easy women, since Loretta isn't around. With the right amount of alcohol to relax me, sounds like a great plan. "If Thomas doesn't start lecturing me about who and how I should fuck, that's fine by me," I threaten him with my eyes.

My friend raises his hands in surrender and shakes his head.

"Do what you want. It's your life. Just don't come crying to me," he says, shrugging his shoulders and leaving with Michael.

I don't know why, but this statement leaves a bitter aftertaste in my mouth that annoys me. I swallow it down and follow them out of the studio, but not before I take one last look at Lilly, who seems to be on the edge of tolerance. A smile appears on my lips when I imagine this scene when she can't stand that idiot photographer anymore. I wish I was here just to see his horrified reaction when she goes out of her mind and marches out of the room.

*

The club is typical of many here in Boston: dark, loud music and a bunch of tipsy people dancing, oblivious to what's happening around them. It's the perfect place for us to discreetly sneak in through the back door and up to the private area upstairs, escorted by a couple of huge bouncers. They're bigger than me, which is saying a lot.

"Jesus Christ, I thought my head was gonna be crushed against the wall when I accidentally bumped into his back," sighs Michael as the two guys return to staking out the private entrance.

Thomas and I burst out laughing, genuinely frightened. It's no coincidence they're guarding the private area entrance, keeping out those who try to sneak upstairs without reservations. Which would be very difficult tonight as Michael has booked half the room. Actually, it's not really a room, but a circular terrace that overlooks the downstairs club dance floor. The music pumps from the speakers in front of us, and the leather sofas line the outside walls so the people downstairs can't see who's up here. On the other side of the club, the tables are busy in front of us; some girls are dancing, but apparently, they're not particularly interested in us. After all, if you have the kind of money to book a corner of this place, seeing a famous person is not news.

The waitress brings us a bucket with ice and a bottle of champagne. It's not my favorite drink, but it's what you get when you book these places, and I'm not complaining. She notices us, widens her eyes for a few seconds when she recognizes us, but then composes herself and discreetly walks away, as is required by her job.

"Have you decided when you're going to fuck her yet?" Thomas laughs.

I watch her go away in that little black dress that hugs her toned body, her blond hair falling in perfect waves on her back, her butt swaying under the thrust of high heels, and those fake breasts that, unfortunately, I can recognize before I even put my hands on them.

"I need to relax for now," I say, picking up the bottle and pouring three glasses.

Thomas looks at me thoughtfully but has the foresight not to say anything. Michael, meanwhile, beckons the waitress again and orders a bottle of whisky.

"I have a feeling you'll need something stronger than champagne to get her. You didn't seem too impressed when you looked at her," he grinned.

Too bad. I have no idea what's happening to me since I had no reaction below the belt. Usually, when a beautiful girl shows up in front of me, even if she's not exactly my type, it affects me, at least physically, but tonight seems to be a dry spell between my legs. No sign of life, nothing, not even a drop of blood that would accidentally take that road. Maybe if I go over there and touch what she has to give me, it'll change.

I get up, catch up with the waitress, and approach her with a smile. She does the same, and I realize up close she's not that beautiful. I concentrate on her body, because that's what I need for a good fuck, right? "Is there a place where we can be alone for a while...you know, to talk?" I've noticed that being shy often gets you more than acting determined. Women love a vulnerable man, especially when accompanied by a rude look. It's like saying, "Look, I'm dropping the bad boy mask just for you," and they open doors you didn't even know existed.

She beckons me to follow her and pulls me into the staff room that locks when we enter. It's a mostly bare room with a row of lockers, two chairs, and a worn-out sofa on which the girl pushes me without even saying a word. That's fine with me, especially when I'm sitting astride her and the dress reveals a pair of black lace panties that...tell me absolutely nothing. She sticks her tongue in my mouth and it tastes like cigarettes and chewing gum, not exactly the best flavor I've ever had. Not like Lilly after she's had a cup of milk and cereal in the morning. That awakens all my senses. Down there, though, it doesn't seem to have any effect. I almost suspect that my penis was stolen from me tonight, and I didn't notice it.

I put my hands on her ass, too skinny for me, then on her fake breasts. I gently push her away. "No, it's not working, I'm sorry," I tell her by sliding her next to me on the couch.

"Did I do something wrong?" There's fear in her tone.

Even her whiny voice annoys me. "No, really, it's not my night." I try to be as honest as I can. After all, it's not her fault

I can't get laid here in this bare, smelly place.

I open the door and take long steps towards the sofa, with a feeling of disbelief, irritation, and even humiliation that twists my insides and leaves me breathless.

"Well, that was quick!" Michael raises an eyebrow while Thomas watches me, perplexed.

They're not joking around, maybe because my face is dark, and you can tell from a mile away that I wouldn't take it well. They look worried, but I say nothing. I pour myself some whisky and take a sip without appreciating the taste.

"It didn't even get up, did it?" Thomas asks me when he realizes what really happened in that room. I don't say anything, just strike him down with a glance. "Why don't you just admit that you've fallen in love with her? For Christ's sake, can't you see you can't stay away from her?" he scolds, sipping from his glass.

"Don't even go down that road. You know I don't even want to argue about it," I hiss in my teeth.

"You're not your father, Damian. You never were," his tone is calm, serious, like he actually believes what he's saying.

I don't believe him. I know what I might be capable of, and I don't even want to go down that road. I want to avoid it for the rest of my life. I've been doing it for twenty-five years, and I'm gonna keep doing it. "It's not true. I'm his son, he's a part of me. I can't help it."

"You stay away from her to protect her. That already proves you're not like your father," Michael says, pouring himself a glass of whisky.

I remain silent, brooding over their words.

*

I enter the hotel from the garage, taking the stairs not the elevator, which is occupied. I left Thomas and Michael at the club to have fun and brought my bad mood back here before it ruined the evening for them too. I walk into the hall and find her there, squeezed into a pair of jeans that cling to her shape and a white silk tank top that falls softly to enhance her perfect breasts. The mere sight of her glasses awakens in me an unprecedented erection.

"Traitor," I whisper between my teeth as I look at my crotch.

Without even realizing what I'm doing, I run to take the elevator she has just entered. With one hand, I stop the doors from closing and notice her surprised face when she sees me enter and press the button. She hides in a corner and looks down. Without thinking about it, I move towards her and crush my pelvis against her belly to make her feel how much I want her right now, sinking my tongue into her mouth. She is surprised at first, but then she kisses me back as if her life depended on it. I lose myself in her, in her touch, in her fingers clinging to my shirt to draw me even closer. I release her reluctantly to catch my breath and find her panting in front of me.

"What the hell are you doing to me? Less than two hours ago, I had a girl rubbing up against me, and it didn't turn me on at all. Now just seeing you in an elevator makes me explode in my pants." The words come out whispered, like a confession.

It's the wrong thing to say. I realize this when an expression—first disappointed, then furious— crosses her face as she angrily pushes me away. I admit my communication skills are pretty rough, but it hurts me to see her so angry.

"Are you telling me that you tried to fuck someone else before kissing me? Do you really think I'd like that in any way?" It's angry, sexy, and it's short-circuiting my brain. "News flash, honey, a line like that works only in the movies. In real life, you get kicked in the balls and punched in the face!" she yells at me.

I instinctively move my hands to cover my privates. She is so angry she might do it. I love this fire that burns inside her, this blatant way she doesn't let anyone get the better of her. I watch her furiously press the number to her floor and march out with such force it practically opens the doors wider. I say nothing and, when the doors close behind her, I lean against the wall and slide down to the floor.

"I'm an asshole," I whisper under my breath, putting my hands on my face and letting the realization of what I've just done overwhelm me.

CHAPTER 21
Lilly

Furious. I'm still utterly irate from the episode with Damian in the elevator last night. I haven't slept, I've been tossing and turning like I'm possessed, thinking back on his words and trying to find even the tiniest little reason not to feel completely humiliated and angry with him. Did he have to tell me he tried to fuck someone else but couldn't?

"Come in," I growl when I hear a knock on the door.

Luke, Martin, and Taylor tiptoe in like they're walking through a minefield. I can tell by the way they look at me that I'm the bomb.

"Why are you packing those clothes as if you're trying to make them disappear and then reappear in another dimension?" Martin asks me in a shaky voice.

"Because I was looking for something to put on, and I don't have anything," I yell furiously as I go to pick up some clothes off the chair.

"Are you on your period or something? Because if you are, we'll leave you alone and come back in three days," asks Taylor, concerned.

I look at them and realize I must really look like a lunatic, and it takes some of the anger out of me. I sit on the chair and inhale deeply, closing my eyes.

"No, I ran into Damian in the elevator last night, and after he kissed me, he said he'd just tried to fuck someone else, but he couldn't get it up. On what planet is that something to say to a girl after you kissed her? Really, I cannot get into a man's head and understand how his only neuron works."

The great thing about having three male friends is that they often help you understand specific male dynamics. Damian seemed miserable that he made me angry, and I can't understand how he could not have foreseen such a thing. Do I really look like someone who wanted to hear that?

Luke crosses his arms like a teacher, studying me carefully. "What exactly did he say to you?"

"Exactly, the way he told you is crucial to understanding the issue," echoes Martin.

I look at them strangely, not realizing what the hell it means, since, either way, he said something terrible to me. I tell them, doubtful. "He said, 'What the hell are you doing to me? I can't believe two hours ago, someone was rubbing up on me, and I wasn't excited, but just watching you take an elevator made me explode in my pants.'"

"Ah!" Taylor bursts out, clapping his hands while Martin and Luke look at each other with a smug smile on their faces.

"The explanation is easy," Luke says. "He's so into you that even if another girl spreads her legs in front of him, he just can't do it. That's the gist of it. You're basically holding him by the balls, and you don't even know it."

I stare at them with my mouth open like they're penguins that just escaped from the zoo. "Are you serious? But he's the one who told me I'm nothing but a fuck. You guys are as delusional as Damian!" I'm in disbelief.

"He probably doesn't even realize it, but last night he must have realized that you work like a cockblocker," explains Martin.

I raise an angry eyebrow waiting for an explanation.

"Yeah, it's like you're his chastity belt...sort of. In the sense that only you get him excited and no girl can give him a boner anymore," Taylor explains, as if this were a scientific experiment.

I put on my shoes and get up. "Please, let's get out before I rip your heads off with my bare hands," I say as I push them out of my room, and they chuckle.

I must admit, though, that in all the absurdity of that explanation, I find my heart doing a few too many somersaults. I can feel it: my naive organ that pumps blood is deluding itself that this could mean something. But my brain is stronger this time and forces me to leave my feelings inside this room, because I cannot afford to delude myself and then be crushed by yet another, inevitable, disappointment.

*

We've been sunbathing for at least an hour in Lederman Park, enjoying the day off. It's been a long time since we've done something alone as a band. All the hustle and bustle of the tour has limited the time we have to relax. It's not like Central Park, it's microscopic by comparison, but there are baseball fields and grass. Plus, from this location, we can enjoy the Charles River's view of the city on the other side.

"Do you realize that six months ago we were nobodies and now we have people paying to come and see us in concert?" Luke asks with his eyes still closed and his face reddened by the sun.

"Technically, they pay to see the Jailbirds, not us," I say, the others snickering.

"Details," says Luke with a frown.

"Luke is right. Everything has changed, and you know how I know? Girls on the other side of the world, who have never met me in person, message privately on Instagram to confess their strangest secrets," says Martin.

We all burst out laughing. It's evident that girls are into him.

"Don't laugh, I'm serious. If you think about it, there's someone on the other side of the ocean who knows we exist. Do you realize how massive this thing is?"

We all get quiet and think. This may sound stupid and shallow, but he's right. I've been forced to block comments and messages because of the hatred I get from the Jailbirds' fans. Girls are calling my bandmate's names outside the arenas we play in; since we've been added to the Jailbirds tour, our follower numbers have grown by several digits. Sometimes we still find it hard to believe it's real.

"Do you think at the end of this tour people will still remember us?" I ask curiously.

"I think so...," Taylor says. "I mean, we have to work on a debut album, but with the record company behind us, it shouldn't be so hard, right? I mean, that label is huge. We're not kids recording an album in the basement and then putting it up on iTunes. They'll promote us, we'll do interviews, we'll tour." He sounds convinced.

We stay quiet a little longer. Our life is really changing, and I realize why Damian gets so angry when it comes to maintaining his privacy. Maybe I'm starting to understand what it's like to make my life accessible to everyone, even people on the other side of the ocean who don't know me, and it scares me. I feel like everyone wants a piece of my soul.

*

Martin and I watch in the park as Luke and Taylor play baseball with some guys who approached us a bit ago, asking if we wanted to join them in a game.

"They're really hopeless, aren't they? Good thing they chose to be musicians for a living or they would have starved to death," Martin comments when Luke misses a ball a six-year-old could have caught.

I laugh out loud because it's true, I've never seen anyone play worse than them, including myself. "Seriously, it's like they've got...I don't know...two left hands or something."

Martin laughs his head off and then gets up, giving me a slight shove. "Look, I'm sick and tired of watching them make a fool of themselves. Do you want to go get a milkshake?"

Martin and his milkshakes. I don't think I've ever seen anyone more obsessed; he's almost got an exclusive relationship with vanilla ones, and thinking about it makes me laugh. He really is a kid in some ways. "Gladly." I grab his hand and stand up.

It takes us an hour and a half to find a place where they make milkshakes because, according to Martin, what's so great about walking around a new city if you have to watch a screen? I agree with him, but I would have gladly used Google maps to find the place after forty-five minutes. We crossed the river, walked through Cambridge with its red brick houses, passed by the MIT Museum, and climbed a bit further until Martin decided that there was nothing on this side that interested him.

We went back, crossed the river again using a different bridge, and ended up at Shake Shak, a place near the park where we were lying down. I'm thinking about killing him.

The guy behind the counter hands us our two drinks, and when I go to get my wallet out, Martin stops me. "It's on me." He smiles at me while he's paying, and we leave the cafe looking for a bench with a view of the water.

"Thank you, but you didn't have to."

"I want to make it up to you for the mess I made," he confesses, looking down guiltily.

"What mess? You didn't do anything."

"When I told the whole dinner you two were fucking?" He gives me a half smile.

I burst out laughing and point to a bench. "It's not your fault, we'd get caught sooner or later, it's not something you can keep secret for long." I hug him and give him a light kiss on the cheek.

Martin smiles and ruffles my hair like he usually does when he doesn't know what to say and feels embarrassed.

"Did you know we were almost caught doing it in a hall bathroom before a concert one time? We stood motionless and didn't breathe with him between my legs until we heard the voices going away. Needless to say, we didn't finish," I confess, amused, to make him feel a little less guilty.

If he hadn't brought it up, maybe we could have kept it more discreet, but now the damage is done and I don't want Martin to feel any more guilty than he already does. Those were hard days for me, who was attacked on several fronts, and for the band, who were asked questions they couldn't answer. In short, we had to learn quickly how to move into this environment and what to do to survive.

"I don't even want to know where you two had sex," he admits with a disgusting and, at the same time, amused grimace. I burst out laughing and he adds, "Remember, at the beginning of the tour, you were worried we might have sex in the TV room on the bus? Now it turns out you're the only one using it for that."

We both laugh at that.

"That's not true. You have girls around you too!" I joke and push him a little bit.

"Don't think it's that easy. They're either too young, and we can't trust them to make any moves because we don't know if they're underage or not, or they're older and much more experienced than us. Do you know how terrifying it can be for a guy when an older woman wants to take you to bed, and you suddenly feel like a high school kid, insecure and full of pimples?" he asks with a smile, but a seriousness in his voice.

I'd never seen it like that, I thought guys had a lot less trouble, but I realize now that they too have a lot of insecurities and, like us girls, they're afraid of not being up to it.

"You'll find one that doesn't terrify you. And then, you might not believe me, but even the Jailbirds don't seem too keen on having a different one every night. After all, Damian hasn't slept with anyone but me. I thought he had a different one every night, but I was wrong. Things are often not what they seem. Maybe it's the atmosphere of the tour that's so frenetic that, in the end, it prevents us from living it up all the way." I try to reassure him while he's sipping his milkshake, enjoying it as if it were his last meal before a death sentence.

"And here I thought it was all sex, drugs and rock and roll.

The next thing you know, I'm knitting, living the same life as my grandmother on the couch in Brooklyn. Michael carves wood! Have you ever seen anything less rock and roll than that?"

We both burst out laughing. Finally, after all the stress we've been through since we first sent that blessed competition video, I linger a bit to breathe in the air that caresses my face. I appreciate the sun that warms my skin and allow myself to enjoy an afternoon like we did when we were nobodies, and our biggest worry was finding a club to play in the evening. After months of frenzy, I finally feel grounded, my head is not spinning, and I have some peace.

PRESS *Review*

People:

Looks like we'll have to wait to see the wedding photos of Damian Jones and Lilly Jenkins. As you can see from these pictures taken yesterday, it seems that Jenkins' heart doesn't beat for one man. In fact, she was seen on a very intimate date with Martin Moore, guitarist of the band she's been playing with for years. According to witnesses, he paid the bill like a true gentleman. We are waiting for reactions from Damian Jones, although we can anticipate that they will not be flattering.

Gossip Now:

Trouble in paradise? Looks like the relationship between Damian Jones and Lilly Jenkins is over. However, Jenkins already seems to have put an end to it, going out on a romantic date with Martin Moore, guitarist of her band. The two have known each other for many years, and, according to sources close to the couple, they've already had an affair in the past, and it seems that the tour has triggered a comeback. How did the dark rocker guy take it when he was replaced so quickly?

Twitter @damian4ever:

But isn't she even a little bit ashamed to go from one bed to another as if she were a professional? She's ugly too #LillyYouAreRidiculous

Twitter @JailbirdsTrueFan:

Finally! Damian deserves better than such an ugly and sloppy one. What's it been since the breakup, two days? #LillyYouAreRidiculous

Twitter @damianIsMyBae:

Now that you've achieved the success you wanted, you don't need Damian anymore, right? #LillyYouAreRidiculous

CHAPTER 22
Damian

I've been awake for a while now, lying with my arms under my head, staring at the ceiling of my room without any particular thoughts in my mind and a lack of someone at my side. At this point, it has become a physical ache that I can hardly cope with. I've never been one to lose sleep over a woman. Yet, here I am, waiting for a decent hour to have breakfast without ordering room service.

The sound of someone knocking on my door makes me sit upright. It's not a violent knocking, but it's so firm that if I were asleep, it would have woken me up. I get up, go to open the door, and find Evan in front of me with papers in his hand.

"What the hell are you doing here?"

"I came on the first flight because you obviously can't handle the press, and, at this point, a statement is required." He slams it on the table, a fresh printout of the headlines of several gossip sites portraying Martin and Lilly in intimate positions.

"Trouble in Paradise?" "Lilly Dumped Damian for a New Flame?" An endless list of click-bait titles that make my blood boil. I stare at them for I don't know how long—an hour, a few seconds—the anger mounting inside me to the point of insanity. I don't believe in gossip magazines, but it still hurts to see them together. And I feel like an idiot: dumped, replaced, and being laughed at behind my back. When the hell did we get to this point? When did things get so out of hand?

"Why was she out there alone? Couldn't you have sent someone after her? I swear I'm gonna fire that tour manager." His questions awaken me from my dazed state.

"They're grown adults; they certainly don't need someone to take care of them. They're not so famous that they need someone to look after them. From these photos, they didn't even realize they were being followed by the paparazzi." I find myself defending them against my will.

Evan seems to be taking my words into consideration and eventually sits down. "I've already got everyone out of bed. They're on their way here for a meeting to deal with this."

"Why the hell don't we go somewhere else besides my room?" I ask.

"Because I need privacy to handle this!" Evan calls out right as someone knocks on the door.

It's Martin, still drowsy with sleep lines from the pillow on his face. Then Lilly, Thomas, Simon, and everybody else. The two full bands are in my room. Just great.

"Can you tell me what these are?" questions an angry Evan, handing the papers to Martin and Lilly, who are looking at them with wide eyes.

"I swear we just had milkshakes, like we used to in New York." The guy decides to explain it to me first, then to Evan. "Nothing happened."

If he weren't so lovey-dovey in his own clumsy way, I'd punch him. I don't know what makes me angrier, the fact that he makes me look like an idiot or that he gets to hang out casually with Lilly during daylight.

"You got me out of bed for this? Do I also have to account for where I've been and what I've done with all of my free time?" Lilly's voice is full of rage.

"Yes, princess, you have to give us an answer because you make me look like an asshole!" I blurt out without even thinking about it, and I shudder when she looks at me with rage. I take one step back. It's terrifying to see her so angry.

"What do you want from me? First you fuck me, but you don't tell anyone. Then you get pissed off about the gossip and blame me, but you answer them with a 'no comment'. Then you avoid me like a bad smell, but you kiss me in the elevator and then you tell me you can't fuck anyone but me. What the hell do you want from me, Damian? What do you take me for? Your very own, personal escort?"

The silence that follows her rant seems eternal. Only now do I remember that there are nine of us in this room, even though she's the only one I see.

"Okay, let's calm down. We need to make a statement," Evan tries to mediate, giving me the stink eye and a sweeter gaze to Lilly.

Lilly bursts into sarcastic laughter as she throws her head back and crosses her arms. "A statement? What are you gonna say this time? 'No comment,' again?" she asks Evan, but I know it's directed at me.

She snatches the phone out of her pocket, grabs a dazed Martin, and pulls him towards her. "I'll give you a statement," she snaps angrily and, before we know what's going on, the notification that she's going live on Instagram snaps us back to reality. "Hi, guys!" She's smiling from ear to ear and looking calm, as if five seconds ago she wasn't screaming her lungs out like a lunatic.

"I know it's early, and not a normal Red Velvet Curtains Instagram live, but Martin and I were woken up this morning because apparently, your imagination has been running wild tonight. Right, Martin?" Martin says hello with a forced smile and a hand wave like he's the Queen of England, while Lilly laughs. "So, let's get one thing straight: Martin and I? No! Never! Not for any reason in the world! We've known each other since high school, so it would be like dating my brother."

Her words make me exhale with a relief I didn't know I was holding. Martin sticks two fingers in his mouth and pretends to vomit, a little too dramatic if you ask me. Evan's sweating bullets, his eyes are wide, and his hand is running nervously over his tie knot.

"It's like kissing my little sister," says the guitar player, supporting her.

"Exactly. Having said that, I see you're asking me if I'm with Damian, and the answer is no. We're not friends, we're not lovers, we're not a couple. We're nothing, and everything that's been said about us was made up by the media. He's a great musician, he's someone I'm great with artistically, but that's all, there's no romantic relationship between us."

We're nothing. The words rumble in my chest, crushing my heart so tightly it hurts to breathe. That's what I've always wanted from women: no feelings. So why is it so heart breaking to hear it like that in front of everyone? I look up and see Thomas looking at me with sadness in his eyes, and that sight gives me a lump in my throat that makes it almost impossible to breathe.

Lilly bursts out laughing, amused at some comment she

reads. "I know you've already chosen the ship name, but I'm sorry to disappoint you. I'm happily single, and I don't need to find a man. I'm on tour with my band. I'm having the time of my life. Why should I ruin it with sentimental drama?"

Yeah, why?

"I'm gonna say goodbye now and leave you to your day... and sorry we woke you up so early."

They both wave with one hand and a smile, and when this agony finally ends, Lilly's face turns dark and angry again.

"There's your statement. I'll even put it in the stories and you know what? Even in the highlights, like this, so everyone will be able to see how things really are, forever," she says as she slips the phone into her pocket and walks out the door, slamming it behind her and leaving us all in silence.

"Well, that's one way to make a statement, too, isn't it?" Michael's voice calls us back to reality, and we all turn to him.

Evan gives me a look of disappointment I've never seen from him before, shakes his head and, without saying a word, leaves the room. I've never felt so humiliated for disappointing someone. Evan is the one who trusted us from the beginning, encouraged us, saw the good in us even though we had just gotten out of prison. My respect for him goes beyond our working relationship. We're friends, we've always supported each other in carrying the weight of our past on our shoulders, and it makes me sick to see that he's lost respect for me. His opinion is important to me and knowing that I've behaved in a way that he disapproves of and blames me for makes me feel inadequate. I have to make it up to him.

*

I knock on the door of Lilly's room and wait for her to open it. I know she's in there. If I know her even a little bit, she's shut herself up alone, trying to let her anger out. And after a few seconds, she opens the door.

"What the hell do you want?" She's not accusing me, it's more like exasperation in her voice, and I can't help but wonder if that's what I'm doing to her.

"We need to talk," I say as I enter the room from the little gap she leaves open before closing the door completely.

"What do you want to talk about? I think we've already told each other everything."

"You've talked. I haven't said anything." I feel the irritation in my voice, and I regret it. I don't want her to think I'm here guided by my wounded pride.

"You've already said what you needed to, Damian. I was just a fuck, and you're over it, period. I can't see anything to add to that." She crosses her arms, resentful.

"I want to know if you're okay," I blurt out.

She looks at me, puzzled for a second, then she laughs. "Now you want to know if I'm okay? Really? Couldn't you have thought of that before taking me to bed? Honestly, Damian, what do you want from me? What do you want me to do? Dematerialize off the face of the earth? Because you tell me you don't want any part of this, but then you act like a jealous boyfriend. You push me away, but then you kiss me. I don't understand you, Damian, I really don't." It sounds like desperation in her voice, like she's looking for an explanation from me so she can get some peace of mind... and maybe I owe her one.

I sit on the bed and inhale deeply, passing my hands over my face as if I could find the courage and strength for a conversation for which there will never be enough courage and strength. "I've already told you that when I was little, I was entrusted to my uncles." I look down but can see she's turned the armchair towards me and sits down in silence.

"What I haven't told you is why I was entrusted to them. We lived on the outskirts of Detroit at the time. My father was a very grumpy guy and...strict, let's say. We weren't doing well, my mother was a hotel maid, my father worked in a factory. With the crisis, my father lost his job and couldn't find any work. The whole family was on my mother's shoulders. The fights became more and more frequent, and often my father laid his hands on my mother. I tried to intervene, but I was too young to stop him, and I got a few slaps that sent me straight back to my room."

I inhale deeply and try to swallow, even though my mouth is parched. I can hear her holding her breath, but I don't have the courage to look at her.

"One night, the fight was particularly violent...the police intervened, and, from that moment on, I was entrusted to my aunt and uncle." I'm trying to explain without going into too much detail. I never want to relive that night again. It's not the whole truth, but it's enough. My last words come out in a whisper, and it takes me a few seconds to recover.

"Oh, Damian," Lilly's broken voice makes my heart ache.

"That's why I don't want any relationship, anyone in my life. I don't wanna be like my father."

"Damian, look at me," she says, taking my face in her hands and turning it towards her. Her eyes are full of tears and sadness. "You're not like your father, you're a generous, protective person who cares about others. You only have to see how you act with your friends to understand that you will never hurt anyone, let alone the people you love. You've helped me overcome my greatest fears. How could you think you could hurt anyone?"

I disentangle from her grip and get up, putting some distance between us. "I went to prison, Lilly. Did you miss that? I was there because I took a baby away from his mother. I'm just like my father, I'm exactly like him." My voice comes out trembling with anger and pain.

"It was a mistake. You didn't know there was a baby in the car, don't you understand? When you realized what you did, you left him in front of a hospital, you did the right thing... that's why you're not like your father," Lilly tries to reason, but my heart won't listen to it.

"You don't go to jail by mistake," I whisper before I grab the door handle and walk out of the room, so I don't implode and choke.

CHAPTER 23
Lilly

"Damian, wait," I call him. I know he hears me, but he doesn't answer.

He's been avoiding me for days. We haven't spoken since he left my room after telling me about his father. I can't even imagine what it's like to grow up in a violent family, but that doesn't mean he has to become like him. We're not our parents. We're not their blood. We can learn from them, sure, but we can learn from their mistakes, even when they're as hard to deal with as Damian's father.

"Give him some time." Thomas' voice behind me makes me turn. I show him a forced smile.

Time. I've been trying to give him time for days, but I don't think that's what he needs at this point. "I just wanted to give him back the sweatshirt he forgot. Do you mind giving it to him?" I hand him the sweatshirt with a grimace that's supposed to be a smile.

"Would you like some coffee?" he asks.

I watch him for a few seconds. I know he's Damian's best friend, so I assume he wants to talk to me about him. My cheeks are starting to burn from humiliation. I already know he's gonna tell me I'm making a fool of myself with these clumsy, ill-concealed attempts to approach him. He's going to tell me how it works in this environment, that it's normal to fuck with someone, and there is no talking after it's happened. He will tell me that I'm no different from the others he's taken to bed, to grow up, not to be a little girl, and forget what happened. I was just a pastime for his friend. But when Thomas Simons from Jailbirds asks you to go for coffee, you say yes, and you don't refuse just because you don't want to hear the things that are obvious to everyone.

"Yeah, why not? We have time before the show."

He signals me to follow him, and we walk into the parking lot. Max is leaning against an Escalade, reading a book while sipping a cup of coffee. The sight of this big guy, six feet tall with broad shoulders, reading a book with yellowed pages and a bookmark between his fingers makes me smile. I have the impression that I'll have to get to know him better. Maybe he's someone I can exchange book suggestions with. When he sees us, he straightens up and puts the bookmark between the pages.

"You are the man of my life. You bookmarked instead of bending the corner of the page." I put my hand on my heart in a theatrical way, making Thomas giggle.

Max seems surprised by my comment, but then his face opens with a smile. "Only the children of Satan fold the pages of a book to mark their place," he says, grinning.

We all burst out laughing as we get in the car and the tension I was carrying slips away, exchanging jokes that lighten the weight I've been carrying for days.

*

The elevator goes up to the building's top floor, where the view opens onto the city from the three glass walls that enclose the room we enter. The city's skyscrapers that surround us open up to a few glimpses of the neighborhoods of two-story houses arranged neatly in rows along the streets. The greenery of their gardens contrasts with the glass and mirrors of the buildings from which they emerge. It is an exclusive place that occupies the top floor of a luxury hotel, with well-separated tables and only few people who seem intent on conversations that no one should eavesdrop on. No one gives us a glance, perhaps because, in here, we are the most ordinary people who sit at one of the corner tables that look directly onto the glass wall. I believe that, not far away from us, there is an Arab sheik intent on haggling, leather briefcase in hand, with a man in a suit and tie who, with a straight face, could easily have a gun hidden under his blue suit jacket and white shirt with diamond cufflinks. Everything about the conversation at that table oozes importance and secrecy.

I feel underdressed in my tank top, shorts, and Vans. Then I look at Thomas in jeans and a T-shirt, and I feel a little reassured.

Max moves over to the counter to submit our orders.

"You want to tell me to stay away from Damian? That he's just having a good time, and I don't have to press him?" I ask without beating around the bush.

Thomas smiles, amused. "Right to the point. I like it."

"More than anything else, I want the humiliation to end as soon as possible. I know Damian doesn't want anything from me. He made me realize that in a thousand different ways. When the tour's over, I'll disappear, I swear."

Thomas laughs, this time more openly, leaving me a little surprised. "It's the exact opposite of what I wanted to ask you," he says, looking straight into my eyes, sipping the coffee Max just brought before walking away and sitting at a table a short distance away.

"Really?" I ask, surprised. "I thought..." I'm not even able to finish the sentence since his words caught me off guard.

"Give him time. Damian's not easy, but honestly, I've never seen him worry about a woman as much as he does about you. He needs to understand that what he's feeling is right... that he's not gonna hurt you. He just needs your time and patience."

"He told me about his father, why he was put into foster care."

This time, it's me who surprises Thomas. He seems pleasantly impressed with my statement, and stunned. "Really? He told you about that night?"

"Not in detail, he told me the fight escalated, the police intervened and they put him in foster care. I'm assuming the social workers imagined he used to beat his mother some time ago."

Thomas seems to weigh my words very carefully. Then he takes a deep breath and continues seriously. "It took him over a year and a half to confess to us. He kept pushing us away at first because he was afraid of hurting us. When we were in jail, he would often end up in fights, throwing scary fists. He had a temper he couldn't control, and, in my opinion, it was his way of 'proving' that he was like his father. Then he met the prison psychologist, he met us, and that anger went away a little bit... but I think he's afraid that it might come back out of the blue, like with his father, and he might hurt somebody."

The words hit me so hard that I start putting together pieces

I missed, and the more I think about it, the more convinced I am that he's not like that. "Damian's not bad. He's not like his father, no matter how little I know him, he's not a person who could physically assault someone," I say with conviction.

Thomas smiles and nods. "I know. I'm convinced of it, too. But even if he is not a bad guy, it takes him a lifetime to trust the people around him and realize that he could never hurt them. That's why I'm asking you to be patient. Are you willing to wait for him? You really have no problem with him being in prison?" His question is as simple as a punch in the stomach.

In the last few days, I've been thinking a lot about Damian, how I feel about him. He's not just some asshole who doesn't give a shit about other people. I knew that before his confession, and then I got confirmation. And I got proof that I'm not capable of separating sex from emotions. He got under my skin and went straight to my heart. I feel tied to him, to his presence, to his person. I thought about prison, of course. Beyond my initial reaction, where it almost felt like he was talking about someone else, when the news settled in my head, I thought about the possible repercussions.

"I'd be telling you a lie if I said I didn't think about juvie. I mean, it's a fact serious enough to have consequences, even in relationships. But you managed to get out of it, make a career out of it. I've come to find that you are good people and decided that it's not important to me. Or rather, it is important how you treat me right now, not how much you have done wrong in the past. You were given a second chance, and you used it to do the right thing and straighten your life out. You are to be admired, not condemned. To be fair, Brad has never been in prison, but he is still a disgusting person, which puts things into perspective. As for Damian...right now, I'd be willing to agree to sleep with him without any emotional complications just to be near him somehow...does that sound so desperate?" I ask with an embarrassed grimace.

Thomas smiles and shakes his head. "It sounds more like a person in love to me," he whispers before looking up at Damian, who is approaching with a rugged look on his strained face.

My heart skips a beat when I see him, but when I lay eyes on Thomas, he smiles at me. He arranged this meeting, and I don't know whether to thank him or punch him in the face.

"You wanted to talk to me?" Damian asks him without looking at me.

"I think she should give you your sweatshirt back," Thomas says, getting up and then whispers in my ear, "I'll wait for you at the bar with Max and Dave," he puts his hand on my shoulder and squeezes it lightly in a reassuring gesture.

Damian sits down and doesn't say a word. We look at each other for a while in silence, him with a frown, me feeling my mouth parched, and the fear that if I start to talk, he might make a scene and leave.

"I don't know what to tell you. I don't even know why you and Thomas are here. Are you plotting behind my back?" His tone is gruff, clearly troubled and feeling ambushed.

I smile and nod my head. I sip my cappuccino and inhale deeply to sort out the overlapping ideas in my head. "No, no conspiracy, I was lured here under the guise of coffee too." I smile at him and see that he relaxes a bit. "Damian, I know you're avoiding me. Let me just say a few things, and then I promise I'll give you your space."

Damian nods, not saying a word, but at least he's not leaving.

"I haven't known you long. I never knew you before, when you were in prison, but one thing I've learned about you: you're the kindest, most generous person I've ever met. You took our band under your wing, and you helped us. You grabbed me by the hand and accompanied me when I was terrified of my surroundings. You held my hair when I threw up in the bathroom because of the anxiety I felt. You even brought me a toothbrush and travel toothpaste so I could feel less embarrassed after I threw up." I smile at the memory.

"You risked bringing on a lawsuit and going back to prison to save me from getting trampled by a crowd. You picked me up and carried me safely to the arena. You protect me from gossip, you protect me from paparazzi... I don't know you, Damian, but I'm pretty sure that's the behavior of a good person. It's not the attitude of someone who would hurt a human being. We're not our parents, Damian. We can learn from them, from their mistakes, even if they're big, but we're not them. We're people who can separate good from evil, and you've proven you know how to do good every single day that you've stood by me. I don't know you, Damian, but one thing I do know about you. You wouldn't hurt a fly."

I finish in one breath, looking into his eyes and observing the waves of feelings that agitate him, though he remains motionless, with his elbow resting on the armchair and his hand over his mouth. I watch him as he contracts his jaw, while his breath becomes as thick and heavy as his emotions. I put my hand on his knee and squeeze lightly, feeling him stretching under my touch. I stand up feeling lighter, approach the bar, and join Thomas, who is studying me with some concern.

"Are you okay?" he asks me with one hand on my arm.

"Yes, will you walk me back to the bus, please?" I ask him, smiling, this time, more calmly than before. "I've given Damian enough to think about."

CHAPTER 24
Damian

"Are you coming with us to the gym?" Simon asks, dressed in his workout clothes, a towel, and a water bottle.

Ever since I started avoiding Lilly, I've been getting a lot of workouts in. I've practically been living inside the truck with the equipment. I've been consumed with the muscles under my skin and the constant thought of her tormenting me when I'm asleep and even when I'm awake. But yesterday, after what she told me over coffee, the honesty with which she spoke to me, my legs take me everywhere but the gym.

I don't want to forget Lilly. I need, instead, to remember those words that somehow made me feel better. It doesn't matter whether I believe the words, I'm always convinced that a part of me carries with it the rottenness that my father passed on to me. But the way she said them, the sincerity with which they came out of her lips have partly soothed those wounds that I've been carrying since that night.

"No, I think I'll go for a walk." I smile at him.

Simon looks at me for a few seconds, then shrugs and walks away with a smile. I know Thomas told Michael and Simon about what happened. We always worry about each other, and I know they understand that it's a difficult time for me. I'm not as upbeat on this tour as I usually am, and I have to admit that

Lilly makes a difference this time.

Without me realizing it, my legs have taken me to the Red Velvet Curtains' bus, and I find myself knocking on the door without even knowing why. It's Luke who opens up to me with a sleepy face and a surprised look.

"Can I help you?" he asks me when he sees I'm not saying a word.

What am I doing here? What the hell do I tell him? "Is Lilly here?" I ask finally, though I have no idea what to say to her.

I'm supposed to avoid her, not knock on her door to talk to her. I don't even know about what...but maybe that's the point, I just need to see her. I need to look at her like a junkie needs his fix. I'm beyond saving.

"Uh... no, she went out with Martin for a run."

"For a run? How many times a day does she go running? I saw her go out last night at ten with her tracksuit on. It's been how many hours since she got back? Seven?" I burst out, stunned.

Sure, for a simple friendship, like siblings, they spend a lot of time together. The jealousy grip on my stomach is an unpleasant sensation that bothers me. I'm not the jealous type, never.

Luke snickers, amused. "I don't know, don't ask me, man. I've known her all my life, and I'll never fully understand what's going on in her head. Every time I think I've got her figured out, one of her quirks leads me back to square one. Anyway, I think this whole media thing is making her a little insecure about her body. More than usual, at least. But I'm keeping an eye on her. I won't let her go back to not eating for fear of getting fat."

I smile, glad she has someone who cares about her and who can recognize any signs of relapse on her part. "Okay, thank you."

"I'll tell her you came by if you want," he suggests with a hopeful smile as if he wants to let her know I've tried a reconnection.

I can't figure this guy out. Clearly, he's very close to her. I think he wanted to smash my face in several times when I hurt Lilly. He's not gay because I've seen him drooling over girls, but he seems immune to her charms. I should learn from him how to stand next to her without having a constant erection in my trousers.

"No, it's okay. It was just some insignificant bullshit." I minimize it and wave my hand like an idiot. I look like a kid making up excuses to see the little girl he likes. I walk away with Luke staring perplexedly at me from the open bus door.

"What the hell are you doing around there?" Thomas asks me. He is on his way back to our bus with a breakfast bag and a tray of four coffees in his hand.

"I went to look for Lilly, but Luke told me she went for a run with Martin," I explain, although I am aware that this conversation will lead to more questions.

Thomas raises both eyebrows, puzzled. "I have no idea if I'm more shocked that you went looking for Lilly of your own free will or that she went running again. That girl runs more than a marathon runner in training."

I burst out laughing and open the door and then give him room to come up and follow him inside for breakfast.

"What are you going to do about her?"

I shrug my shoulders and inhale deeply. "I don't know,

maybe I'll start by apologizing to her, and then I'll see what I can do from there. I've never been in a situation like this before, and I'm messing it up."

Thomas laughs with gusto, but then he looks at me with the understanding frown of a brother.

"I've never had meaningful experiences with relationships, and I can't tell you how to behave, but have a little faith in her. She's a smart girl with a good head on her shoulders."

That's true, but in this story, I'm the real mess to clean up.

*

When Lilly told me she was gonna leave me alone, I didn't think she'd literally disappear from my life. After the incursion on her bus this morning I didn't see her, not at soundcheck, not even during lunch break or in the Red Velvet Curtains dressing room. The only time I laid eyes on her was when she came on stage, and there I was, in the wings behind the black curtains, like a fucking peeping tom spying on her. What hurts me the most, though, is that I only started breathing again when I laid eyes on her. At that moment, I realized how dependent I've become on that woman.

I'm so down at the thought of another twenty-four hours without seeing her again that I'm surprised, almost stunned, when I see her at the bar after the show. Tomorrow's show is closer, so we don't have to leave immediately like we usually do. We can relax for a bit with a beer and a chat without changing and being holed up on the bus heading to the next destination.

I smile when I lay my eyes on her and the Vans she's wearing. She took off her heels the second after getting off the stage. She also took out her contact lenses and put on her glasses, which makes her look sexier than I remembered. Could she have gotten any prettier? Is it possible she's laughing at Martin's jokes and putting her hand on his arm so confidently? My anger starts to boil over.

"Come have a beer before you break the kid's neck with your thoughts!" Michael's voice calls me back to reality, and I walk the last steps to the bar without looking in their direction. I'm so stubborn and focused I don't even notice the stool I knock over, which makes everyone turn around.

Grabbing the bottle Simon hands me, I whisper with exasperation, "I should be drinking bleach to forget rather than a beer."

They both burst out laughing, and I can see they're having a great time at my expense. Idiots.

"You're the one who pushed her away. You can't complain if she's directed her attention elsewhere." Michael challenges me with a raised eyebrow.

Does he really have to remind me of that every time the conversation turns to Lilly? "Big deal. If she likes a guy like Martin, it's her problem. She's laughing at his jokes, you know. Martin wouldn't be funny if you painted his face like a clown," I say sarcastically, and I realize I'm being ridiculous.

"Am I sensing some jealousy in your voice?" Simon stings me as we walk away from the bar and stand against the wall across from Lilly and Martin.

She looks so peaceful when she's with him. She's laughing, joking, she's even resting her forehead on his chest now.

"I'm not jealous," I say, even though I'm seething with anger.

Martin puts his hand on her hip, dangerously close to her

butt, and I can't take it anymore. With two long strides, I reach the two of them and grab his hand, shaking it so violently that the guy loses his balance and falls to the ground. I immediately regret it because as soon as I turn to leave with my tail between my legs, I find myself in front of a very angry Lilly, who punches me in the eye. I'm completely stunned, not because of the fist itself, she has the strength of a bird with those hands, but because of the gesture. I didn't see it coming. Throwing a glance around the room, I discover everyone's looking at me, shocked. No one's ever seen me like this, and I'm deeply ashamed of myself.

I help Martin get up then go out to look for her. When I reach her, she is already near our buses, and I have to grab her wrist and turn her around to make her look at me.

"Forgive me," are the only words that come out of my mouth.

"Forgive you? You knocked Martin down!"

"Because he was putting his hands on you!" My justification is so stupid I feel like an idiot.

"Hands on me? He put his hand on my hip!" she yells as she turns around and tries to open the bus door, not realizing that in her fury, she has confused ours with theirs.

"I know, and I'm apologizing. I saw you flirting with him, and I couldn't take it anymore," I confess.

She turns in amazement and watches me, wrinkling her forehead. "He asked me to make the bartender jealous for turning him down." She's annoyed, and her explanation makes me feel like even more of a complete asshole. "And you were jealous?" There's hope in her voice.

I can see in her eyes that she's hoping to detect some real

interest from me. I don't know when it happened, or if my confession had any effect, but it's disarming to see a woman trust me so blindly. She's not afraid I might hurt her. The question is simple and damned difficult at the same time.

"I don't know...maybe." I sound like a fifteen-year-old boy in a hormonal crisis. I look down.

"Really?" she asks incredulously.

"Do you want a written confession?"

I don't get an answer, but suddenly her arms are around my neck and her lips are glued to mine. She's giving me the trust I don't deserve. My body reacts instinctively, before my brain has time to process it. I push her against the side of the bus and stick my tongue into her mouth, savoring that taste that I missed like air. I detach myself from her only when I feel her push slightly, and immediately a twinge in my chest makes my legs shake. Does she regret that kiss? The very thought terrifies me, but I immediately see she's just trying to open the door. I smile as I take her hand off the lock, grab my keys out of my pocket, and open it.

"How the hell..." she swears softly.

"This is my bus, not yours," I whisper in her ear as I open the door and push her up the stairs.

She looks up, puzzled. "Oh," she admits, embarrassed.

I laugh as I let her up and close the door behind me. When she turns around, I see her waiting for me to make the first move, leaning against the kitchen cabinet with a shy, damn sexy look.

"Are you sure?" I don't want her to regret our night together.

She nods and puts her hands on my chest. I'm sure she can

feel my heart pounding in my ribcage against her fingers. I grab her butt and lift her off the ground, taking her upstairs to my room, while she sinks her face into my neck and covers my skin with kisses and small bites that literally make my head spin. I kick open the door of my room and throw her onto my bed.

She giggles amusedly until she meets my yearning gaze, and then she starts to tease me, unfastening the button of my pants. I bend down to take off her shoes, then I grab her jeans and panties and slip them off quickly. I grab a condom from the bedside table and tear the packaging open with my teeth, dropping my pants and boxers down to my ankles. I slip my cock between her legs, sinking in, enjoying her sighs and moans. There's no foreplay, there's no game, we don't need it; we've stayed so far away for so long that our bodies and hearts attract each other in an almost primal and animalistic way, relieving that tension that has grown between us these past weeks.

I hear her moan and sink her nails into my butt, pulling me towards her. Seeking such closeness with our skin we almost fuse together. I don't think my heart has ever exploded with so much happiness as it does right now.

CHAPTER 25
Lilly

"Lilly, are you in here?"

Luke's voice makes me jump. I take one look at Damian struggling to hold his breath and laugh. "Yeah, I'll be right out." My voice is shrill, panting, and completely unnatural.

"Oh, for God's sake, don't tell me you're still locked in the bathroom with Damian," my friend blurts out, exasperated.

" Hi, Luke, can you leave the room, please?" asks Damian, about to burst out laughing.

Luke mumbles something we can't hear, but eventually, he closes the dressing room door, and we both sigh with relief. Damian laughs while I'm not amused at all. Having secret sex in the most unthinkable and indecent places has become a constant that's making me nervous. At least this time our bandmates know about it and help keep things under control. I push him away and see his smile turn into disappointment.

"You're leaving me like this? Without finishing?" he asks, pleading.

"Honestly? Luke's intrusion ruined the moment for me." I raise an eyebrow as I fix my pants and the tank top that half slipped off my shoulder.

His expression is indecipherable. He looks repentant, a little disappointed, but not irritated. "Next time I'll close the dressing room door," he mumbles as he fixes his pants.

"Or maybe we don't fuck in a bathroom behind the stage and do it in a bed like normal people," I blurt out angrily. "I feel like a prostitute doing it like this, in these places, afraid someone might open the door and catch us at any moment."

Damian grabs me by the arm before I can leave, studying me for a few seconds, and I struggle to keep a calm and smiling face. I'm not serene at all.

"You told me you were okay with how it is between us, without commitment," he says thoughtfully, almost worried. "If you didn't want to sleep with me, you could have just told me, it's not like I'm forcing you or anything...I mean, you're free to say no whenever you want. I hope that's clear."

His voice sounds worried, or guilty, like he thinks he's forcing me to do something that hurts me, that I feel like I have to say yes. It couldn't be further from the truth. I'm so into him that right now, I'm okay with whatever Damian wants to give me. I don't want to force him into a relationship that embarrasses him because he can't handle it. I get why he's acting like this with me. I know it's not me, but he is. As much as that's a cliché, it's a simple truth: Damian can't handle a relationship with another person because of what he went through when he was a kid. I can understand it, I can accept it, but that doesn't mean that I don't feel bad about what I want but can't have. Because, despite everything, Damian is someone you love effortlessly. It's impossible not to get lost in his grumpy but protective attitude. The problem is that you fall in love with him, but he doesn't let himself be loved, and what hurts me most is that he thinks he doesn't deserve to be loved by anyone.

"Damian, stop. I know. You don't have to ask me that again.

I said yes, I'm fine with it, and I was honest. But I don't like doing it in a dirty, smelly bathroom. I just like it better when we're in your room, where no one can bother us, and we can take our time," I explain with a smile that this time, luckily, doesn't come out forced.

He studies me for a few moments and scrutinizes me with his intelligent eyes that often make me feel like he's reading me and I'm afraid of what he sees. He nods, then comes closer and holds me in an embrace that lasts longer than any other he has ever given me. He kisses me on the head, profoundly inhaling my perfume as if wanting to imprint me into his memory. It's such a tender gesture, one he's never done before, that it almost makes my legs quiver. It feels like the action of someone who really cares about me—a feeling that doesn't last, and when he detaches from me it slips away.

"Damian, can you come to the dressing room, please?" Thomas' voice brings us back to reality, and his tone makes my blood run cold in my veins.

"Is there a problem?" Damian is worried and confirms my fears when he opens the door and we see Thomas' face.

He looks embarrassed and uncomfortable. Like he doesn't want to say anything in front of me. "Evan came here to talk to you." He tries to make Damian understand without me prying.

"I'm going to the bus; the others are waiting for me," I say quickly, trying to save them the awkwardness, even though I'm worried sick. If Evan's here, it means it's something urgent, something that can't be said over the phone. We have a tour manager to clean up all the messes related to our life on the road; Evan being here means it's about him, personally, and my heart is pounding in my chest.

"No, come with me." Damian's voice is calm, but I can tell by his face that he's not relaxed at all.

I don't know what to do; on the one hand, I'd like to be near him, on the other hand, it scares the hell out of me to see him so afraid.

"Damian, Evan would like to talk to us alone. I think it's important." Thomas tries to be as gentle as he can, but his voice almost shakes.

"No, if this is something that required Evan getting on a plane on a Friday night and showing up here after a show, I need her with me." He's crushing my hand like he's afraid I'm gonna go somewhere.

Thomas seems to think about it, studies me carefully, then nods and signals us to follow him out the door. The few steps that separate us from the next room seem miles long, and my heart almost explodes in my chest.

When we enter the room, I notice that only Simon, Michael, Evan, and Dave are present and they're wearing funeral faces. My stomach twitches in a death grip that almost hurts. When the door closes behind me, Evan becomes aware of my presence and looks at me with a kind of desperation.

"Lilly, this is a delicate matter. Could you wait for us on the bus?" he asks gently but with a grave expression.

"I'm the one who asked her to stay because if you came all this way tonight, it means I'm gonna need all the support I can get." This is the first time I've ever heard Damian's voice shaking, and it scares me.

Evan nods and signals us to the two empty chairs around the table. "You better sit down, then."

I don't even register the automatic gesture of bending my

knees and putting my rear on the cold plastic. All I can do is try to breathe, which is getting harder and harder.

"Do you know someone named Eva Bail?" Evan asks Damian in a somber tone.

"Should I?"

Evan pulls out an eight-by-ten photo. It shows Damian asleep on a bed with his shirt up almost around his neck and a blonde girl naked from the waist up, smiling, her head resting on his chest. Her hair is a mess, and her cheeks are red, like someone who's just had sex. I feel like gagging, and I can hardly hold it in. Damian's forehead wrinkles as he looks closely at the picture. He doesn't seem to understand what's going on.

"No, I have no idea who this is or when she took it. I can't remember." He's sincerely surprised about it.

"Are you sure she's not one of the girls you slept with, but you were too drunk to remember?" Evan urges.

"No, I remember the girls I sleep with, even if I'm drunk," Damian insists, getting more and more worked up. "You gonna tell me what the hell is going on? Why are you asking me these questions?"

Evan pulls out another picture of the same size; this one shows just the girl against a white background, her face swollen with purple bruises. I'm holding my breath, and I'm sure Damian is doing the same thing.

"This girl has accused you of rape. She said that when she refused to sleep with you, you beat her and raped her." Evan's blunt words are like a knife stabbing my chest. Tears start streaming down my cheeks. I can't hold them back.

Damian's looking at him like he's gone crazy. No one

breathes, no one says anything. We're all just looking at that picture and don't know what the hell to say.

"No, that's not true, that's not possible," whispers Damian in disbelief.

"I know you would never do something like that, but these are the photos I managed to get through our lawyer. Apparently, it happened in L.A. before the contest. Are you sure you don't remember it?"

Damian shakes his head but says nothing. He looks terrified. "Do you remember seeing her?" he asks the others.

"No, maybe she caught up with him that night when he came home drunk in a cab," Thomas dares to suggest, and it seems to be the only thing that makes any sense.

"It wasn't me. I didn't even touch her." He looks up at his friend, and only now do I see tears streaming down his eyes. In all the time I've known him, I've never seen him so vulnerable

"I know, man, but there are pictures of her lying naked on top of you, so somehow you had contact, and we need to figure out what happened," Thomas says.

I can see that Damian is desperate, destroyed, completely lost and vulnerable here. The Damian I know is sweet and protective, the one who tries to keep me safe in dangerous situations and could never do something like this. And yet, these pictures of Damian lying on a bed with a naked woman who, in the next photo, has a face swollen with bruises, a torn lip, and makeup running with tears, tell a different story. I'm reminded of how he pushed aside the photographers to save me, how he shoved Martin down when he put his hands on me, how he's afraid to become like his father, and how he did time in prison. Nausea invades my stomach and throat and is almost unbearable.

"Did she go to the police? Did she report it? Why didn't the hospital report the rape right away?" Simon fires out the questions with apprehension.

"She didn't report it to the hospital," Evan sighs. "The photos were taken by her friend, who she sought refuge with when she got home. She only went to the lawyer recently. The lawyer has contacted us for compensation, but she will file a complaint tomorrow, and these photos will probably come out in the press as soon as tomorrow night."

"So? Is he being charged or not?" Michael interrupts.

"Not yet. Since there's no medical report and no police report when it happened, they'll have to investigate. It's her word against Damian's."

"I didn't do anything," whispers Damian.

"I know, but you'll have to prove it. Right now, we need to figure out how to deal with what's about to blow up in a few hours. Tomorrow night is the last show. Do you feel like going on stage? We can always cancel it, say you got sick, and refund the ticket money."

"But if this story comes out in tomorrow's paper, won't that be like an admission of guilt? Like he knew about it and covered his ass?" says Michael, who seems to ask what's on all of our minds. Evan thinks about it and shakes his head but Michael persists, almost angrily. "Listen, you said she went to our lawyer asking for compensation, can't we just pay her?"

"Her face is swollen with bruises, and you want to pay her to keep her mouth shut?" I growl. And for the first time, they seem to remember that I'm in the room, too. Damian turns to me; the look on his face full of disbelief and pain.

"Do you really think I would do something like that?" he asks me like he's seeing me for the first time.

I can't speak. I can't even open my mouth. No, the Damian I know couldn't have done such a thing. He's generous, protective, good. To *me*. But the Damian I don't know stole cars and got into fights in prison. What if he really did hurt that girl when he was drunk? What if he doesn't remember? There are pictures of him lying on a fucking bed with her naked. I didn't dream it, I see them with my own eyes, just like I see the bruises. But he says he never met her. Either he's lying, or he doesn't remember—because the evidence is here on this table in front of me.

Either way, I'm scared to death because I don't know who I'm looking at anymore. How can he say he's never met her? Even though the fucking pictures of them are on that table?

"Lilly, maybe you should leave the room." Evan's voice is quiet but firm.

No one tries to stop me this time when I get up from my chair and walk to the door. No one wants me in this room anymore. Just outside, I lean against the wall by the door and let myself slide to the floor, unable to hold in my sobbing. I desperately need someone to tell me that Damian is innocent, that this is just a nightmare from which I will wake up, but the reality is that I'm not sure of anything anymore. Even if my heart is telling me that Damian couldn't do something like this, that the person I know is noble and generous. Still, those pictures are branded in my mind, and I don't have a logical reason to believe Damian isn't involved.

"Lilly, come on, let's get on the bus." Luke's voice wakes me up to reality, and when I look up, I find Martin and Taylor looking at me worriedly.

The sobs still rattle me as we get on the bus and seat ourselves quietly around the table. None of them have asked me anything, even though I see the worry on their faces.

"You know you just have to say the word, and we'll go smash his face, don't you?" Martin asks me when the bus finally gets moving.

"He may be big, but there's three of us, and we're gonna kick his ass," Taylor joins in.

I nod but say nothing, a slight smile appearing on my lips, but not reaching my heart. Luke holds me close, and the journey to our last stop becomes a silent approach to a hell I don't want to face.

CHAPTER 26
Damian

I open my eyes when the bus parks and see the early morning light coming through the window. The sun has just come up, it's early; I like waking up at this hour and having the whole day ahead of me to do a thousand things. It feels full of potential and expectation. Not today. I spent the night thinking and rethinking about that woman's face, about the fact that I don't know her, but we were photographed in the same bed. Then I recall Lilly's face, the terror printed in her eyes, and the certainty of having lost her. All I can do is hope she forgives me for all the crap I've done, but the suspicion of what I may have done is something I can never erase from her heart.

It's a strange feeling—one of those moments when I wish time could have stopped two days ago and left me on tour for the rest of my life. When a tour ends, I always feel a mixture of emotions. I want to go home, get my life back, relax, have decent meals, start a routine I know I'll enjoy again after a few months, but one I only seem to appreciate by going on tour. This time, however, it's a suffocating feeling. Going home means facing an accusation that is driving me crazy. I never touched that woman, but I can't even explain those bruises. I even wondered if I really drank so much that I don't remember doing it. After all, I have my father's blood running through my veins, right?

"Are you awake?" Evan peeps his head in after a light knock on the door.

"Yeah."

"Did you get any sleep?"

"I more or less collapsed from exhaustion by morning." I get up and put on my sweatpants and a short-sleeved shirt.

"I checked the newspapers and major gossip sites. They haven't fed the news to the press yet. I think they're trying to figure out how best to play their cards right now." He's trying to reassure me, but it's not working.

"You know it wasn't me, right? I know my father..."

"Damian, stop." He turns me around, and I see an almost paternal smile on his face. "You're not your father. I have no doubt it wasn't you, don't even think that. We all know it's a false accusation. Nobody's insinuating otherwise."

"Lilly...Lilly's not convinced that..." I can't even form that sentence it hurts so much.

Evan breathes in and holds his breath as he looks up to the sky. "Lilly is twenty years old, and she doesn't know you. She met the rock star, the handsome man everyone knows, but not the Damian of the old days. Those pictures shook her up because she knows your past, but not all of it. Tell her what happened that night, she'll understand it wasn't your fault. Nor was it your fault with that girl. Don't take responsibility for something you don't have to, don't hold the weight of the world on your shoulders, let someone help you carry this cross."

His words hit me like a tornado. Telling her about that night won't be easy, telling her about how I saw my life shattered into thousands of little pieces, the difficulty of putting them back together into a shape that doesn't even resemble the child I was.

"If you don't feel like getting on that stage tonight, I can understand that. You can still cancel the concert," he says kindly.

"Give me a few hours to figure out how I feel."

Evan barely nods and leaves me to think, closing the door behind him.

*

It's late in the morning when I go to see Lilly on her tour bus. I manage to convince Luke to leave me alone with her, even though he's reluctant at first. I don't think she told him about what happened last night, but he knows I hurt her again, and he won't let me near her. When I reach her in the sleeping area, she's curled up on the sofa, a light blanket over her, eyes swollen with tears.

"May I?" I whisper. She nods and sits down to make room for me. "I don't even know where to start." My voice is uncertain, totally unprepared for this conversation. "I prepared a speech before I came here, but now I feel like it doesn't make sense."

"Maybe you should start by telling me you didn't pay that woman to shut up."

"I didn't. Evan's here in L.A. with our lawyer. They're talking to the other lawyer right now."

"Did you really do what she's accusing you of?"

I can feel all her pain in avoiding using the word "rape." I'm afraid she's disgusted by me, my past, and the weight it carries in this context.

"Do you remember I told you I was entrusted to my uncles

when I was a kid because the police intervened during a fight between my mother and father?"

She nods.

"That's not the whole truth. My dad had been drinking a lot that night, and my mom came home late because she had to work later than usual. When he got up from the couch and didn't find his dinner ready, he started yelling, pulling at her, raising his hands. I ran to her and tried to separate them, but my father was furious. He slapped me so hard I fell to the ground. He was coming at me when my mother started hitting him to draw attention to herself. When he turned to hit her, she shouted at me to run, and I did. I ran to the back of the room and locked myself inside the cupboard, sitting on a pile of dishes that were creaking from my shaking.

"The cabinet door stayed cracked open enough for me to see what was happening. He hit her until she fell to the floor. He sat on her chest and started slapping and punching her in the face. My mother raised her arms, trying to defend herself, but he was stronger...my father was always strong, I got my size from him. When he grabbed her by the hair and started banging her head against the floor, her arms weren't moving anymore. She couldn't fight him anymore; she just lay still in a pool of blood. When the police arrived, he was still there with bloody hands and knees. Sitting still and peaceful on the floor as if he hadn't just killed my mother with his bare hands."

The silence that follows is suffocating, and when I look at her, I see tears, fear, and horror. I don't know if it's the story or the realization that she's looking at the son of a murderer, who's also done time in prison. Either way, I can't stand how she's looking at me.

"Oh, Damian..." Her voice is a whisper.

"If you're asking me if I hit that woman, I don't know. I don't even remember her, but I'm in those pictures, and you saw her face full of bruises." I wince, remembering Lilly's face last night when Michael proposed to pay her.

"Damian, I know you. You couldn't have done something like that." Her voice is uncertain. She needs reassurance from me, something I can't give her.

"Really?" I get up off the couch, my voice harsh. "I've been to prison, Lilly. Do you realize that?"

"But not for beating a woman," she says in a soft voice. I see her struggling.

"How do you explain those pictures? How? I'm the son of a murderer, Lilly, and as much as I want to convince myself I didn't do anything to that woman, there's a picture of me naked in my bed with her that I don't remember taking."

"There has to be an explanation..." But even she's not convinced.

"What is it? Give me one reason why that woman is lying!" I'm screaming now, in desperation.

"I don't know, but I refuse to believe you did it. I refuse to believe that I've fallen in love with a violent person." She looks down.

The words hit me like a moving train. I was terrified this would happen, and now that she's confessed it to me, my heart doesn't want to stay behind my ribcage. The feeling of happiness I get from those words scares me; I can never give her the future she deserves.

I don't even acknowledge that she says them, and say coldly, "Exactly, you don't know, because you're trying to convince yourself that I'm a good person. But the reality is that I'm like my father. You're a naive little girl if you think I'm not. The one you fucked was the rock star, the handsome singer who took you on a rollercoaster ride. The best ride of your life, probably, but like all rides, you gotta get off at some point. Get a life, Lilly."

Tears roll down her cheeks as the hiccups shake her chest. My heart tightens until it hurts.

"What do you want from me, Damian?"

"You've been a mediocre fuck, and when we get home the day after tomorrow, you better stay away from me. I got bigger problems than babysitting a girl who spends her life counting calories because her boyfriend called her fat." My tone is beyond harsh.

I see on her face the exact moment Lilly's heart breaks. And though I want to go to her and say I don't really think those things, I turn around and try to get out of here fast. I find Luke in the living room. His eyes are full of anger when he pulls his fist back and punches me in the jaw. I don't even react. I don't defend myself; I simply walk out.

When I got onto that bus, I wanted to convince Lilly I hadn't done anything, but the more I went on with my speech, the more I realized I couldn't drag her into the shit that is my life. My past isn't ever gonna leave me alone, and the future isn't as rosy as I thought. As much as my heart tells me I would never have the courage to do that to a woman, my father did the same things to my mother. Those pictures prove that my blood is as rotten as his. Lilly deserves a life, a career, not to stand next to someone who's accused of rape. I can't drag her down with me while I'm sinking.

I get on our bus and find Thomas, Michael, and Simon looking like someone just died.

"It's in the papers." Thomas' voice is thick with emotion. "Outside the stadium, the photographers and crowds waiting in line for the show have gone crazy."

The first hiccups seize me before I even notice, then the tears start flowing. I collapse on my knees in the middle of our bus, my hands over my face, my friends' arms holding me tight, so I don't fall apart. I haven't cried this much—two days straight—since my mother died.

PRESS *Review*

People:

Damian Jones, front man for the Jailbirds, is accused of rape by a Los Angeles woman. The singer denies all accusations, but the photos of Eva Bail's swollen face have now gone viral. The woman's husband claims that after refusing to have sex with the singer, Jones beat her and sexually assaulted her. If this is confirmed by the investigation, it could mean a prison sentence and the end of the singer's career.

Gossip Now:

Apparently, the famous singer Damian Jones isn't as good as everyone thinks he is. Eva Bail, a bartender at a Los Angeles club, accused the singer of battery and sexual assault. Photos of the woman's swollen face have gone viral, leaving the Jailbirds in an uncomfortable position. The singer denies any involvement, but the evidence against him appears to be strong.

CHAPTER 27
Lilly

Luke's arms hold me tight as I wipe away the tears. I'm still sitting where Damian left me less than twenty minutes ago. Martin and Taylor are in the living room, checking every existing news site in an almost frenetic way, and between one "holy shit" and another, I understand that things are not going well for Damian. They tell me the story is going viral, and everyone is lashing out at him.

"You knew about this? Is that why you were crying last night?" Luke whispers to me.

I nod. "That's why Evan rushed to Los Angeles. Her lawyer contacted them."

"Damian came to tell you he didn't do it?"

"He told me he doesn't remember ever meeting that woman. But there are pictures..."

"Do you believe him? Do you think he might have done something like this?" he asks hesitantly.

We're all surprised and overwhelmed by the news. I know he's sincere when he says he has no memory of that night, but I wonder how a person's brain could have short-circuited to the point that there's no trace of such a violent event in his memory. Maybe because of the trauma of seeing his mother die the way she did? I'm so overwhelmed with emotion I can't think coherently enough to find a logical explanation for it.

"You know Damian. He's gruff and tough, but in the end, he's a good person," I reply to Luke. "On the other hand, there are the photos, tangible proof that he met that woman, and I don't know how to piece the puzzle together. I believe him when he tells me he doesn't remember, but..."

"But that woman couldn't have made it all up. There must be something real," my friend finishes the sentence that I couldn't bring myself to say.

I nod and look down. "It won't be our problem anymore, will it? The day after tomorrow, we go home, continue with our career, and we won't have to deal with them anymore." I smile bitterly as I look into his eyes.

"Lil...about what he said to you... I think he was just angry about this situation." His tone is hesitant.

"No, Luke, I told him I loved him and he said I was a mediocre fuck. There's nothing to misunderstand, no double meaning, not even a little hidden meaning. Don't get my hopes up. I'm already sick as it is."

Luke seems to want to answer me, but Taylor peeks in my bedroom door. "Evan wants us all on the Jailbirds' tour bus right away for an emergency meeting." He puts on a half-painted smile of pity when he looks into my puffy eyes.

Luke and I get up and go join the others. We figured there would be a meeting since we're supposed to be in full sound-check now, but haven't even gone near the Staples Center's doors. As soon as we step outside, we hear the noise of the crowd that's here for the concert. It's far away from us, but we can hear the buzzing.

"Do you think they'll go ahead with the concert or move it

to another day?" Taylor asks what we've all been wondering the last few hours.

"I'd be more worried whether or not they'll arrest him, given his record." Martin quips, and gets a nasty look from Luke and me. "Excuse me, but have you read the papers? It's pretty serious. Did you take a look at her face?"

I look down and say nothing.

"The papers also said you were fucking Lilly. I don't think that's true," Luke remarks.

We keep quiet until we get to the bus, then we knock, and Simon lets us on. He has a tight smile, and when I walk past him, he puts his hand on my shoulder and squeezes lightly. The comforting gesture almost makes me burst into tears again. We stand, leaning against the small kitchen shelf, while the Jailbirds sit on the sofas, their faces tense. Thomas tries to smile at me, but I look down, not wanting to meet Damian's eyes. I glance at him out of the corner of my eye. His gaze is fixed on his fingers crossed tightly in front of him, his eyes red... I've never seen him so vulnerable. Last night he was shocked, almost stunned by the news, incredulous and unable to find the words. Now he seems resigned to a fate that has already condemned him as guilty.

All four of them seem to have aged ten years, and my heart breaks for them. This story will bring to light all of their secrets. I have no idea why they kept it hidden that they were in prison, but no one deserves to be exposed in this way without telling their side. The press will condemn them for something they've already paid for. In these past months, I've come to understand that you cannot escape the media taunting, and now more than ever, I comprehend Damian's obsession with privacy.

Evan's voice from upstairs almost scares the hell out of us. He's screaming on the phone with someone, we hear him kick something, then silence and the sound of his shoes coming down the stairs. When he appears on the threshold, his face is haunted, and for a split second, he seems surprised to see us standing here.

"I've been waiting for you," he announces in a tired voice. "I've just spoken to the record company. They won't cancel tonight's concert unless it's strictly necessary."

"What more do they want to happen before they decide to pull the plug? How can we go out on stage and do a show with all this stuff coming down on Damian?" slams Thomas, angry, while his best friend doesn't move an inch.

I shouldn't be so worried about him, given how he treated me earlier, but it's impossible not to feel pain at his suffering.

"I know," Evan says, trying calm Thomas down, "but they say that until there's a complaint from the girl, it's just her word against Damian's. Before you freak out, I know they're assholes. Right now, we're trying to contain the press out there. We'll have a press conference, the five of us, where we'll strongly deny the charges. Damian, do you feel like talking? You don't have to answer the questions, I can handle that, but if you make a statement to the press, it'll be more credible."

Damian just nods. Evan waits a few seconds for an answer, but then he lowers his head. He's done all he can, and the pain in his eyes is not just that of a manager who has to get his client out of a huge mess: it's that of a genuinely concerned friend.

"You stay away from socials, don't respond to comments, don't delete the bad ones, absolutely zero," he says to us, who are just nodding. "Pretend your accounts don't exist. If we're really going on stage tonight, you won't be there. It's going to be a tense evening. You're too inexperienced to handle a situation like this. Don't take it so hard. You'll have your share of scandals to worry about." He smiles melancholily, trying to lighten the situation.

"Is there anything we can do to help?" My voice comes out faint but seems to be the only sound that brings Damian back to reality. He says nothing but looks up at me, a grimace of pain on his face. His eyes are veiled with tears, then he looks down again.

"Be quiet on your bus, don't let anyone see you around, and don't respond to the provocations of the journalists. They will try to reach you in any way they can."

"Evan, there's someone here." Dave's quiet voice makes us all jittery.

"Dave, you're gonna have to wait. I can't handle any more problems right now."

"It's the girl who accused Damian. She's outside."

His words snap us to attention. My heart bounces inside my chest with rage, my head spins, and I have to lean on Luke to keep from going down. He grabs my hand as Dave lets the woman pass through us once their manager has agreed to let her in. Her face is still covered in bruises like in the picture. How the hell is that possible? Wasn't this supposed to have happened months ago? Damian's been with me the whole time. My mind starts to retrace every single moment of the last week, and I don't remember ever seeing her near Damian.

"Breathe," Luke whispers in my ear. I didn't even realize I was holding my breath.

Damian looks paralyzed, his eyes wide open, staring at the woman like he's seeing a ghost. Evan moves a chair for her, then hands her a cup of coffee that she holds with trembling hands. She's dressed in a long-sleeved jumpsuit, even though it's a hundred degrees outside. He smiles at her, but he's tense and alert to her every move. No one in the room dares to move, only Simon's eyes bounce between his bandmates and the woman. Michael is studying her as if he's trying to remember if he's seen her before.

"Eva, I looked for you this morning, but all I could find were your husband and your lawyer," says Evan.

The girl lowers her eyes, seems ashamed. "That's not my lawyer. It's my husband's. They put this story together."

My heart explodes in my chest, I take a breath, my legs shake, and my grip on Luke gets stronger.

"Okay. So the bruises aren't from Damian."

She shakes her head no. A general sigh of relief rises up in the room. Only Damian keeps staring at her as if he still cannot believe she's in front of him.

"Can you explain to me, please, how this whole thing came about?" Evan asks her calmly, but I can see his desperation to know the truth.

"I met Damian months ago when you guys came to L.A. My friend and I managed to break into the hotel, and we waited for him."

"Was that the night he was photographed kissing the three girls outside?"

The woman nods.

"But you're not one of them, are you?"

"No, we waited for him in the lounge outside his room.

He came up drunk, we tried to pick him up, but he turned us down. We were a little offended because he's got a reputation for fucking every girl, but he sent us away, so when we saw the room key fall to the floor, we grabbed it and went in right after him."

Anger takes over my stomach. I wish I could protect Damian from this whole absurd situation, but I'm as silent as everyone else.

"He collapsed in bed, so we undressed and took some pictures together. It was supposed to be between her and me. It wasn't to become public knowledge."

"What part does your husband play in all this?"

"Three days ago we bought two new phones. He set them up and asked me if he could back them up online. I said yes, thinking he was just going to copy the data, but a few hours later, he came into the kitchen furious and told me I was a whore. He saw my pictures with Damian and started beating me up and made me look, well, like this. When he left, I left the house and went to my friend's. I didn't want to go to the hospital, but she convinced me to take pictures if I wanted to report him later. I only found out today, when I saw the photos in the newspaper, that he didn't really do a backup but just got access to the contents in my phone, including the pictures of the bruises."

Son of a bitch. I look around, and I see we're all finally breathing again.

"So, he took the photos and tried to blackmail Damian behind your back."

"Yeah, Damian never touched me. Forgive me." The hint of a smile on her lips makes me angry on the one hand because she risked ruining an innocent man's life. On the other hand, it's the confirmation we all needed and took a weight off my chest.

We're all waiting for a reaction, but Damian doesn't open his mouth for what seems like an eternity. "I never laid hands on you, ever? Not even that night?"

The question takes the woman by surprise, but I know why he asks it. He's afraid he's done something and doesn't remember it. He's terrified his subconscious will turn him into his father. Damian has taught his rational side not to hurt anyone. He's lived for years imposing himself not to hurt others, physically or emotionally, but a part of his brain is terrified of having a blackout and bringing out the beast that was his father. That's why his words from before hurt even more. He *wanted* to hurt me.

"No, although you were completely wasted and couldn't understand anything, you were a gentleman. You didn't even touch me with a finger, not even to move me when I clutched at your arm. You're not a monster, Damian."

This time he smiles tenderly, and I see the tension leave the body of the man I love. He got the confirmation he was looking for. He was able to find that little piece he was missing.

"Would you like to come with us to the press conference and deny the accusations your husband made against him?" Evan's question comes out almost in a whisper like he's afraid to scare her.

"Don't make me repeat the whole story in front of the reporters," she begs him.

"I'll tell it myself and leave out the private details. You can answer the questions if you want. Only the ones you feel like.

It would help us dismantle the accusation. Otherwise, it would be Damian's word against your husband's, and the photos he released are...hard to explain."

"Can I refuse to answer if I don't want to?"

"Of course."

"Okay." The relief on everyone's faces is liberating.

Evan tinkers with his phone and sends a text message, but no one else makes a sound yet. We're all focused on her, on her slim figure inside that big suit. We're not staring at her openly, but out of the corner of our eye, we're studying her. It takes courage to do something like that, coming here, knowing that journalists have laid siege to this place.

"The reporters are already in the room for the press conference. Let's go." Evan stands up, and we all follow him in a straight line.

We decide not to hole up in the bus. None of us can stay locked in there waiting for the outcome of this walk to the gallows. We don't go into the press conference room, but we sit outside in the corridor, on the concrete floor, silent. No one even dares to move. From inside the room come muffled noises, some a little stronger than others. It lasts an hour and a half. No press conference has ever been this long, but Evan probably wants to be sure the message is loud and clear: Damian is innocent, the woman's husband is to be locked up.

When they finally come out the door we're sitting next to, Dave and two other goons escort the band to another room. Damian looks at me in passing, but he doesn't stay long enough to sustain my gaze, let alone a conversation. I just wish I knew how it went in there. Martin tried to watch the press conference live, but the reception in this bunker sucks, and we finally gave up. Thomas turns to me, winking at me with a smile that gives me serenity.

Evan catches up with us and explains. "Tonight's concert is still on. If you want, you can stay on the side of the stage and watch from there. I'm sorry you can't finish the tour, but these two days have been heavy for everyone. We still have to figure out how the fans out there are reacting, and I'd rather not let you face a potentially difficult situation."

"No problem, really," Luke reassures him. "We'd love to watch the show."

"How's he doing?" My voice is weak. I'm almost afraid of the answer.

"He'll get over it. Damian's got broad shoulders, and he'll get over it. Why don't you join him and go ask him yourself? He'll be happy to see you." He smiles tenderly, like a father.

I lower my embarrassed gaze before I look up into his eyes again. "I don't think it's a good idea, but I'll enjoy watching the concert. Tell him I'm glad it worked out for the best."

Evan looks at me, puzzled, but says nothing. He just nods and then follows the Jailbirds into the room.

"Can we punch him in the face another day?" I look at Martin, puzzled. "Damian just got let off a rape charge. I'd rather not punch him for hurting you right at this moment. Let's give him a couple of days off," he says, trying to lighten the moment.

"That's not necessary, really. At the end of the day, I knew what I was getting into when I slept with him. I never thought I was the miracle girl who would turn him into a one-woman man." My heart hoped for it, but after this morning's conversation, I know he stopped deluding himself.

The three of them smother me in a hug and then drag me backstage to the Staples Center.

"It's a shame. I've always dreamed of playing in here," Luke says, peeking on stage where the musicians are rushing to finish tuning the instruments, since the soundcheck blew up completely today. Usually, musicians deal with these things when the band can't physically get on stage to do it themselves. Today, though, things have been so surreal that until an hour and a half ago, they didn't know if Evan would allow Jailbirds to play; regardless of what the record company wants, his manager would never let Damian on stage just for the money.

"We'll make it up to Madison Square Garden. That's our home. We'll be invincible there." I turn to Taylor. The dreamy look on his face makes me smile for the first time since last night. It's been nine months since the contest, and we've reached the end of this tour. It's been challenging. There have been times when I thought I wouldn't make it, I fell in love, and I'm heartbroken, but the look on my friend's face erases all the tears shed.

CHAPTER 28
Damian

"Damian, I'm really sorry for everything my husband put you through."

I asked Evan to let me talk to her alone. I need to clear this up personally as well as in the media. I don't know how I feel. Her swollen face brings back memories I'd rather keep buried in the back of my mind and away from my heart.

"Eva, it wasn't your fault. You mustn't feel in any way responsible for what happened." I get close to her and sit on a chair in front of the sofa where she's sitting.

"If we hadn't come into the room and taken those pictures, my husband wouldn't have been angry."

I grab the hand she's been torturing by biting her cuticles, and I squeeze it lightly.

"Eva, no man has the right to hit you, or even insult you, for the way you act. You can fuck the whole state if you want, but there's no justification for what he did to you."

She nods but doesn't answer. She looks down in shame. It's a look I saw too many times as a kid, the one my mother had when she hid her bruises with makeup.

"You have to promise me that you'll leave him." My words catch her attention, and she looks me straight in the eye. "No matter how many times he apologizes to you, how many times he comes back regretting it with his tail between his legs, he'll keep hitting you, he won't stop until one day you wake up in a hospital bed, if you're lucky."

Tears fill her eyes. "I don't know where to go. What if he finds me?"

"I asked Evan to find you a place for tonight. Tomorrow I'll send someone I know who handles cases like yours. Her name is Loretta, she's from New York, and before she met the husband she's with now, she went through what you're going through. We'll find a divorce attorney and put the bastard away."

"Damian, I'm a waitress. I can't afford a lawyer. I can't even pay rent without my husband's help."

"You don't have to worry about money. I'll take care of it. You just have to get away and get a new life."

She looks at me like she's trying to figure out if I'm lying to her. "Why are you doing all this? Until last night you didn't even know my name, and now you're planning a full-scale rescue mission."

"Years ago, I couldn't save someone close to me. I don't want to make the same mistake again."

"Did she have a husband who beat her?"

I look down searching for a way to survive the twinge that tears at my chest. "She had a husband who was a murderer." When I look back at her, I find her with tears streaming down her cheeks. A slight knock on the door makes us both turn around. "Come in."

Evan's head peeps in. "I found an out-of-town shelter that has security. I've already spoken to them, and they'd be willing to take you in right away. There are other women there in the same situation as you. They have a doctor who can check your bruises and prescribe you something for the pain."

Eva seems hesitant. I told her about a hotel, now Evan proposes a shelter. I don't know if she'll accept this solution.

"Please have faith in us. I know it can be scary at first, but there are people there who can help you. Loretta, the woman I told you about, is a volunteer at a center like this in New York." In fact, I met her there after a generous donation; they invited me to see the wing of the center they were able to build with the money I donated.

She breathes in deeply, and her gaze shifts from my face to Evan's. "Okay, if you give me an address, I'll call a cab," she whispers.

"No way. I already have Max out here ready. He's good at dodging the paparazzi, and chances are they're gonna try to follow you. They will try to get some exclusive interviews from you. If you trust us, we can make sure they don't get to you, and your husband can't find you."

At Evan's suggestion, she gives in entirely and gets up to follow him, turning to face me one last time. "Thanks, Damian."

I smile at her and let my manager take care of her. As they leave, Thomas, Simon, and Michael enter the room and sit on the couch.

"Can we just skip this day and wake up in New York in a couple of days?" asks Simon, putting his hand over his face.

"They want us to go on stage." Thomas is not yet feeling the pressure of the record company.

"Have you seen the Red Velvet Curtains, by any chance?" I ask out of the blue.

They study me for a few seconds in silence.

"I think they're around. Evan decided not to let them play tonight. They're probably enjoying the end of the tour."

I'd like to talk to Lilly, apologize for what I said to her this morning. I acted like a jerk, and if she doesn't forgive me, I can't blame her. I've always known I wasn't capable of having a fling. I've never had one in my life, and I've never questioned myself about that. I ended up slamming into a wall, and I didn't even try to slow down. Whether I want to admit it or not, what I have with Lilly is a monogamous relationship I can't give up. It's not just about sex anymore because I care about her. I put her happiness first, and pushing her out of my life this morning was the hardest thing I've ever done in my entire existence.

"What the hell have you done this time?" Thomas asks me in a stern tone.

"A mess."

"Tell me you didn't make her cry again." Simon looks at me wrong.

I say nothing, and I shrug my shoulders.

"So those puffy eyes were your fault, not the rape charge. For a moment there, I thought she believed the whole story," Michael ventures.

"No, she tried to convince me that it wasn't possible," I admit with shame.

"And what did you say to her?"

"That she couldn't explain those pictures to me because she's just a little girl. I may have even told her she was just a mediocre fuck and to get out of the way at the end of the tour."

My friends stare at me, wide eyed and open mouthed.

"Jesus Christ, what's wrong with you?"

"I know, I fucked up."

Simon laughs his head off. "You fucked up? You've completely fucked up any chance of forgiveness. How many times has she let you make a mistake and always taken you back? Two? Three? You can't possibly believe she'll come back to you after this."

"Actually, I hope so."

Michael's laughing his head off. "God, how ridiculous you are when you're in love. You're a lost cause, you know that, don't you? Even I couldn't make a worse mess than you."

"You're not helping," I complain.

"How the hell are we supposed to help you? You treated her like shit while she stood by you despite a rape charge. We can't work miracles," chuckles Thomas.

"Anyway, you'll have to think about that after the show because we have to get on stage." Simon checks the time on his wristwatch.

I can hardly breathe, let alone swallow. I don't want to go on that stage. The day has been exhausting, to say the least. I just want to talk to Lilly, make up, get on the bus and hold her in my arms. I know it's an impossible dream, at least for the moment, because if I ever get close, I'm sure she'll rip my hair out of my head.

I get up with the others and we head down the hallway backstage like we're going to the gallows. Typically, we would be concentrating on the setlist, our entrance, and the last details for the show tonight. We haven't even changed our clothes since this morning.

When we get near the stage I see her there, looking at the

audience that has already filled the arena. She's as beautiful as ever, in her glasses and comfortable, loose clothes. I get up the nerve to move closer. Luke sees me first, and the anger emanating from his eyes tightens my stomach. I must say, he's got balls, that kid, always defending her like a tiger. I like that.

"Lilly, can I talk to you?" I'm hoping she says yes and we can walk a few steps away from her friends, who clearly want to rip my skin off with their bare hands.

"Damian, you have a gig in a few minutes. I don't think it's a good idea to talk right now. I'll see you later, okay? I promise, I won't run away. I'll be here when you get off the stage. I'm glad the story with that woman went well." Her tone is steady, her smile almost formal, like she's trying to sell me life insurance, eyes cold as ice.

If she had punched me in the stomach, it would have hurt less. Lilly's a hothead when it comes to dealing with my shit. She screams, she gets pissed off, she gesticulates furiously. Not this time. She's a piece of ice drifting away from me. The feeling of losing her is devastating, especially since I've just realized that life is meaningless without her. Thomas puts his hand on my shoulder and drags me towards the stage.

"Let's finish this and then talk to her," he whispers in my ear while one of the assistants helps me put the earphones on, running the wires under my shirt.

Thomas' words are just what I need to get my feet moving towards a stage that terrifies me tonight. We go up without warning, the lighting technicians are not ready for our entrance, and it takes the audience a few seconds before they realize it's us. Only when my bandmates grab their instruments do they start screaming.

I reach for the electric guitar, knowing I should put it around my neck and start the concert with the setlist we used for the last show, but I can't. I feel almost dazed, and the audience notices it because they aren't shouting anymore. It's just the buzz of people talking, not the usual excitement. I approach the microphone and stop for a few seconds to look at the perplexed faces in the front rows. I can see them well because the lights are still high above us.

"You know what?" I say into the microphone, and it's almost entirely silent. I take my earphones off, and the feeling is surreal. "Until not even half an hour ago, I was in a back room with a woman who was beaten by her husband, the same husband who tried to blackmail me by accusing me of raping her. I have spent the last 24 hours in a state of total apathy, trying to convince myself in every way that something like this couldn't happen to me... that I could never do this to another human being."

The silence inside the arena is absolute, almost surreal.

"Fortunately, as you've seen from the press conference, things have been resolved, the accusation proved unfounded, but I can't get on this stage and pretend that nothing happened. I'd be fucking with you."

A few cheers, a few whistles of encouragement come out of the audience, but they don't last long. Silence falls again.

"I don't feel like singing and jumping and having fun and winking at a camera because there's nothing funny about what happened. There's nothing funny about the violence that woman suffered."

The audience bursts into a warm applause, and I turn to my companions, who smile and encourage me. They're just waiting for a nod from me to see what they have to do. I look for Lilly and spot her. I realize that she has her hands over her mouth and her eyes are shiny. Luke's arm is around her waist, holding her, and for the first time, I'm not jealous of him but grateful that he's protecting her.

"I know you guys came here for a rock concert, and you're gonna get it, but not tonight. Keep your ticket, we'll repeat tonight's show when we're ready, so you can use it for the next concert. Tonight, though, I'd like to offer you the acoustic show we did around the clubs in New York." I turn to my mates, who nod and take off their instruments and then help the technicians scrambling around looking for acoustic guitars and stools for everyone.

The audience applauds, shouts, happy with the choice, and they seem to have understood it.

"There's something else I'd like to say." A few laughs come from the audience. "I know this speech is getting long and boring, but just give me a couple of minutes, so the engineers have time to change all the equipment. I've made life difficult for them tonight." A few more laughs and my heart starts pounding in my chest so furious it's liable to explode. "For the last twenty-four hours, one good thing has happened."

The quiet returns to total silence, and I'm almost panicking. I turn to Lilly and set my eyes on hers. I'm immediately overwhelmed by a feeling of warmth.

"I found someone who, despite such a serious accusation, stood by me...and I, like the perfect asshole I am, pushed her away." Whistling and giggling go up from the audience again.

Thomas brings me an acoustic guitar and a stool with a grin from ear to ear, and I want to choke him. I'm terrified, I've never made a statement like this before, and he laughs. I sit down, adjusting the guitar and microphone, and then I look back out at the audience.

"These days I've been writing a song. I didn't know who it was for until I reread it this morning and realized there's only one person I think about when I sing those words. It's only a few verses, it's not complete yet, but I need to play it for her."

The girls' cries are deafening as I play the first notes on the guitar. I look at Lilly and find her white as a sheet with watery eyes and Luke, Martin, and Taylor struggling to hold back a laugh. I don't even want to turn around and look at Michael's face, he'll be fucking with me for the rest of my life.

"You found me on top of the cliff
And you grabbed me before I could fall
You guided me when I couldn't see the light
You were my eyes on the road
You lit the fire
When there was no more heat in me
You found my heart empty
And you put it in your pocket.
You poured all the love you had in it
And you brought him back to life."

When I finish the few verses of the song, there is a moment of absolute silence, then a roar rises from the crowd. I look towards Lilly, and I find her blushing, embarrassed, but smiling happily.

"Tonight the Red Velvet Curtains didn't have time to perform, given what happened, but it doesn't seem right to steal the warmth and excitement of the Staples Center from them. I say we let them play with us. What do you say?"

The audience explodes in a second roar, and I wave to the guys to join us as they pick up instruments, stools, and microphones. I stand up, and when Lilly catches up with me, I step forward. She looks me in the eye with a love I've never seen in anyone before. I grab her face in my hands and caress it. She squints, and I lean over to her ear. "I wanted to apologize for what I said to you this morning and let you know I don't think those things. I wanted to push you away so you wouldn't have that nightmare," I whisper to her.

Lilly nods, tears of joy veiling her eyes.

"I'm not good at making statements, I know, but I hope you know that I'm in love with you," I add, embarrassed.

Lilly bursts into a half laugh that catches me off guard. "Are you serious? You set the bar for making a romantic statement so high, anyone else will have to work hard to get there."

"Did you find that romantic?" I joke with her.

"It was so sweet it almost gave me diabetes," she smiles as she looks me in the eye.

I can't resist. I lean down, and I kiss her with all the sweetness I can give her while she's holding on to my shirt. The audience is delirious and won't stop screaming.

"Get a room, you two!" Michael screams into the microphone, calling us back to reality.

Screams, whistles, and laughter rise up from the crowd, and when I turn around, I realize that every phone is pointed at us. We'll be on all their Instagram lives but I don't care. I take her by the hand and sit her down next to me. This concert started under the worst possible conditions, but it's enough for me to have her with me in the storm.

PRESS *Review*

People:

Soft-hearted rock star, Damian Jones, has decided to declare his love for Lilly Jenkins on stage. After the rape charges were retracted after only a few hours by the woman who accused him, it seems that the Jailbirds' front man has finally found happiness. It appears that the two have come to a conclusion, although we are still waiting for a statement from their press officers. Should we expect a pop breakthrough from the band? Let's hope not.

Gossip Now:

If you thought a rock star wasn't capable of making sweet, romantic gestures after seeing Damian Jones bowing at Lilly Jenkins' feet, you'd have to think again. The singer made a statement last night onstage in front of a Staples Center crowd, full to the brim. What could have possibly provoked him to do such an extreme gesture? Everyone's wondering, but no one seems to have an answer, mainly because after the rape charge was dropped, immediately retracted by the victim, everyone thought the singer's career and love life were at an end. Apparently, however, the two seem like they're still cultivating their passion. Sure, we're not used to seeing the dark and beautiful

Damian as the lost puppy, but hopefully, it's just a passing phase.

CHAPTER 29
Lilly

I reach out my arm and find half the bed empty. Opening my eyes, I feel lost when I see Damian isn't next to me. Last night, after the concert, we went back to the hotel together and talked for hours. About how he felt after the accusations made against him, how I feel after what he said to me, how we'll move forward from here, since telling the whole world he loves me. We don't have all the answers, but one thing we are sure of, we want to build something together.

I know he's not used to this kind of relationship; he's said several times that he's going to screw up for sure, but I've decided it's worth a try. We made peace—or rather, we made love—three times to reassure me that he was lying when he told me I was a mediocre fuck. I believe him. Waking up without him in bed, though, it upsets me, and I'm a little afraid he's had second thoughts.

I turn my back, ready to get up, and find him sitting in the armchair next to the bed, looking at me with a smile. He almost gives me a heart attack. "Has anyone ever told you you're creepy when you sit there watching people sleep?"

Damian laughs, then gets up and comes over with a breakfast tray. "You're beautiful when you sleep."

"Just so I know, are you gonna be sweet and cheesy like this all the time, or can I have the gruff bear I fell in love with back in the beginning?"

He laughs and kisses me on the forehead before he sits down next to me to eat the cinnamon rolls and coffee he ordered. "I'm still the same, except I'm happy."

I raise an eyebrow. "You're talking like a fortune cookie."

"Will you stop making fun of me?" He kisses me and bites my neck, making me shudder.

"Never," I laugh.

He gives me a light kiss on the lips, then grabs the coffee cup and sips it. "What time's your press conference?"

I look at my cell phone and grimace because I'm late. "In an hour, I have to hurry up and do my makeup."

"Are you nervous?"

"Evan just wants to introduce us to the world as his newest signing. Why would I be nervous? It's not like there's any pressure from the label." I roll my eyes.

Damian smiles, and then he hugs me. "It's gonna be okay. Evan will intercept the most difficult questions. He's particularly good at this. He saved our ass several times at the beginning of our career. And you know the first question they're gonna ask you is gonna be about me, right?" He smiles.

I look at him, outraged. "No, it won't be about you. You declared your love last night on a stage. And you ruined the gossip in the media by doing it so blatantly."

Damian laughs but doesn't press it while I get up and change into the clothes Sid left us.

*

The hotel room set up for the press conference is already packed with photographers. I turn to Luke, Taylor, and Martin, and I realize they're just as nervous as I am. This is our first press conference as a band, our first encounter with journalists.

"Your faces are terrified." Evan approaches with a compassionate smile on his face. Who knows how many times he's calmed bands down as rookies? I can't imagine the Jailbirds were as lost as we feel at first.

"It's because we *are* terrified," says Martin.

Evan puts his hand on his shoulder and smiles at him in that fatherly way he has. "They won't eat you, don't worry. Remember, I'm here to intercept any questions that might prove critical. I've tried to extend the invitation only to journalists I've known for a while, and they won't go too far."

He doesn't give us time to answer before opening the door wide and pushing us in. The flashes start as soon as we make our appearance, and the nervousness sets in. However, the fascination of sitting on this side of the table with all the microphones in front of us is exhilarating. The audience of about thirty journalists is not as scary as I expected. Most of them are middle-aged men with harmless faces.

"Luckily, our names are on the back of the nameplates on the table because I've already forgotten where to sit," Martin whispers in my ear, and I burst out laughing. I, too, forgot about the arrangement Evan suggested.

Our manager starts the press conference as he always does with the Jailbirds, introduces us as his new group, then opens it up for questions.

"The first question is for Lilly." A relatively young guy smiles from the third row, drawing my attention. My stomach's in a vice grip. "What would you call your relationship with Damian Jones?"

I look at him for a few seconds with eyes wide open, then I look over at Evan, and he seems irritated.

"No personal questions," our manager says.

I think back to Damian's words, and I burst out laughing so loudly that all eyes are on me, including those of my bandmates. Nervousness really plays tricks on me. "Sorry. I didn't mean to...but just out of curiosity..." Evan's looking at me all wide-eyed, and the reporter seems surprised that I've turned the question back on him. "There are twenty thousand videos of Damian sticking his tongue in my mouth on stage at the Staples Center. Isn't it clear?"

The reporters all start laughing and Martin can't hold back either, while Luke, on the other side, has a hand in front of his mouth, trying not to laugh. Evan's rubbing his temple with his fingers while a smile spreads across his face. The guy who asked the question laughs and sits down again.

"Are you getting married?" thunders someone from the back of the room that I can't quite see.

The room is in turmoil after the question.

"To go from tongue in the mouth to ring on the finger in one night seems excessive even by Hollywood's fast standards," I reply as the reporters laugh, and I'm peering to find out who asked it.

I catch a glimpse of Damian, leaning against the back wall, and when he steps forward, the journalists notice him and start snapping in his direction. Evan's already got his hand in front of his face. I don't think he planned this for the press conference.

"Was that a marriage proposal?" one of the reporters asks him.

"No, but that was the direction you were going in, wasn't it? I saved you the trouble." He winks at me, and I find myself smiling like an idiot.

"Why are you here?" asks another.

"I came to see how my girlfriend's doing, but I see she's standing up to you. I don't have to worry about her." One more wink from him and I'll melt on the chair. How can he be this sexy even when he's sneaking in to harass the press?

Damian's diversion works, because the questions come back to the music.

"The next question is for Luke. Do you have a debut album ready yet?"

Why do they ask him questions about his career while they ask me questions about my personal life? I hate this sexist attitude, but at the moment, I can hardly concentrate on the answers my friend is giving because I can't look away from the back of the room where my boyfriend, as he defined himself earlier, keeps staring at me with a smug smile on his face.

*

"You know that tomorrow all the papers will give the wedding date for sure, right? My mother's gonna have a heart attack." I'm kissing him on the lips, leaning over the armrest of the seat in this private jet taking us to New York.

"I wanted to make fun of them the way they make fun of us all the time. They can write whatever they want in those newspapers. Only you and I know what's true."

I snuggle with him, and sip from the glass of orange juice the flight attendant has brought us.

"Then don't complain if they chase us all over Manhattan. Where's the 'no comment' man I once knew?"

"I'm tired of hiding. You're not something I have to be ashamed of, and I finally realized it's liberating to live your life in the open. I never thought I'd ever feel like this."

"Does this mean you're taking me out to dinner?"

"Tomorrow night at the Chef's Table at Brooklyn Fare?"

I turn bewilderedly to him. "How the hell are you gonna get a reservation for tomorrow night? There's a waiting list a month long."

He laughs, amused. "The advantages of being a rock star. I have to teach you a couple of tricks now that you're famous."

His words make me blush, but it's true. We had our first press conference today, and we really are famous. The reporters were there just for us.

"But I have all the time in the world because I'm not going to let you get away. Today I made a joke about marriage...I wasn't asking you to get serious so soon, but I'm going to try to go in that direction. I may not be good at relationships, but I'm good at figuring out who I want in my life or not. The people I choose to be around are few, but they're with me for life."

His words make my heart explode with joy. In these months, I have learned that Damian can be a very intense person, for better or worse, but when he lets you into his life, you become part of his world. It's like an on/off switch. You're either in or you're out. There's no middle ground. I just realized how happy it feels to be in.

EPILOGUE
Damian

"Do you think we got enough wine?"

"Yes." Lilly looks at me, smiling as she opens a bag of chips and pours them into a bowl.

"And beer? We didn't get enough meat! Maybe we should have had a full dinner...even with the appetizers."

"Damian, stop." She turns to me and puts her arms around my neck. "We have enough food for an army, and if they drink all this alcohol, we'll have to take them to the hospital for alcohol poisoning. Are you nervous or something?"

I lift my shoulders and look down. Yes, I am nervous, and I hate to admit it. I mean, I've been through so much in my life I shouldn't be anxious about dinner. I've been to more parties than I can count, so I have plenty of ideas to steal from, and yet this time it's different.

"I don't know how to christen a house. I've never done it..."

Lilly looks at me with her big, sweet eyes and smiles before giving me a light kiss on the lips. "It's just a dinner party like we used to have in your old apartment. How many did we have in two months? Ten? It's the same thing."

I lift her up by the hips and sit her on the kitchen island, then I slip in between her legs.

"It's not the usual dinner. It's the christening of our apartment, the house we live in. There's nothing common about it."

She caresses my face gently and smiles at me. "Do you have any doubts about moving in together? Is it too soon?" she whispers, but there's no uncertainty in her tone, just sympathy for a step that's important to me.

"Absolutely not. No doubt about it."

I emphasize the concept by grabbing her face and drawing her to me for a passionate kiss. My tongue plays with hers in sinuous rhythm, and her hands slip into my hair. I let out a slight groan.

"Excuse me, you know we're in the room too, right? You're not gonna rip your clothes off and have sex up there, are you?" Thomas' voice snaps us back to reality.

Lilly pulls away from me and giggles as I give him the middle finger.

They're all there: my bandmates, Evan, the Red Velvet Curtains. We invited them to christen the house where Lilly and I decided to live. When we came back from the tour, she practically moved in with me. She was spending more time in my penthouse than in Brooklyn, so we decided to just make it official. She liked the apartment I lived in, but I wanted her to have her own place, one that she helped choose, and I was right: this apartment has nothing to do with the one in Tribeca. It's all exposed red brick, wooden floors, darker furniture; it's warm, cozy, especially with the orange curtains on the windows. When the light comes in, it feels like a sunset by the sea. This house is Lilly, and I am happy to have made this choice.

"It's not like we live naked" Lilly grabs the bowl of chips and brings it to the table where everyone is already seated, waiting for me to take dinner out of the oven.

"By the way you two were all wrapped up, you wouldn't know it," Luke jokes.

"That's the advantage of living with a woman," I tease as I bring the bread and cheese, recently brought back from France, to the table.

"Christ, how low you've sunk," Michael mocks me, shaking his head almost as if to scold me.

Everyone laughs, including Evan, who studies me like I'm a rare animal. It must be weird for them to see me so caught up in something I've always denied wanting. They think I'm going crazy or overboard and sooner or later, I'm going to get tired. I can't explain to them that I'm not. When I realized I was in love with Lilly, it was like turning on a switch and seeing the light. I used to fly by the seat of my pants, day by day, but now I make plans for the future, and I'm not afraid. Life with her doesn't terrify me, and it's such a pleasant feeling that I'm almost overwhelmed by it.

"When you can fuck any time of the day or night, on any surface of your house, trust me, that you will change your mind," I reply with a smile that goes from ear to ear.

"Freeze! Stop it," Martin interrupts. "Too much information, Damian, way too much information. We have to work with her every day. We don't want inappropriate images in our heads when we look at her."

"Also, because you need your head on your neck if you want to finish your debut album." Evan points his finger at him when he sees I give the kid the stink eye.

"No, it's not like we're having those kinds of thoughts... I mean, I didn't mean we're picturing her naked or anything…" he stammers. "Jesus Christ, you're scaring the shit out of me," he whispers under his breath, and everybody laughs.

I like to tease them and be tough. They have such devotion to us they almost worship us like saints. I take advantage of it until they realize that we're actually dicks.

"How's your album going?" Simon asks, saving the kid from embarrassment.

Luke starts answering, and everyone focuses on him. I see they're all happy as they pass food, exchange jokes, laugh, and take an interest in each other's lives. It's one big extended family that has chosen to be with me, by my side despite everything. Before there was only Thomas, Michael, and Simon, meeting in a situation that forced us to get to know each other. Our relationship is much deeper than friendship. We saved each other's lives when the only alternative was to succumb and die, either in prison or on the street. Evan joined later. He saw in us an opportunity to earn money and make a career, then his selfless soul protected us as friends and an older brother.

The Red Velvet Curtains, however, are the greatest miracle, the one I never expected. They don't have to be around us to be friends. It's true, they won the contest, but now they have an independent career, they're standing on their own two feet, they don't need us. On the contrary, we obscure their light with our fame. It's their time to shine in the spotlight. Yet here they are sharing this moment as if we were family.

Family. It's a term that has been foreign to me all my life. When my mother died, I no longer had a real home, apart from my friends. When I look at Lilly, though, I'm sure I've found one, a companion to share life with. From this moment on, it's her and me along a road that we decide to walk together, uphill or down, we'll decide how to move forward like a real...family. I wrap my arm around her shoulders and pull her close to me, inhaling the scent of her hair, breathing deeply into what seems to be true happiness.

Want to get more FREE from Erika?

Sign up for the author's New Releases mailing list and get a free copy of the short story "Eliot." You will periodically receive free short stories and unique chapters.

Click here to get started:
https://www.erikavanzin.com/newsletter.html

Acknowledgements

The first person I would like to thank in this book is the one who "lent" me the name for the protagonist: my nephew, Damian. I'm sure he will become a rock star, whatever he decides to do in life.

My family, all of them at our extended family lunches and dinners, I can never thank them enough for the support they always give me, whatever my life choice.

My husband Dario, sometimes my big and scary decisions have turned into our best adventures.

Stefania, the woman who, with her critical eye, helped me transform this novel, supporting me even when fatigue took over. Alessandro, who helped me get the word out about it.

I would also like to thank all the bloggers who, with each new novel, are ready to support me; they are the ones who give us writers a voice, helping us to reach our readers.

Finally, I would like to thank you, those reading these lines. Thanks to you, Lilly and Damian have found a new home and have started a new life. Thank you for your support.

About the author

At the age of eight, Erika asked Santa for a typewriter. That was when her parents, quite surprised, realized that she was not like all the other children. However, when she received her first heavy, professional and brand new "Olivetti Letter 35" that Christmas, it was love at first sight. She immediately started writing the words that soon became her first short story. Over time she bought a much more efficient computer, but that typewriter will always have a special place in her heart: it was her first love.

Erika was born on December 6, 1979 in Valdobbiadene in the province of Treviso, a small village at the foot of the Pre-alps. Both her parents were born and raised in the same town where they still live today. Erika moved to Padua at 18 to attended university, and after graduation, she did not return to Valdobbiadene but followed her heart and traveled worldwide, living in Los Angeles, Vancouver, and London and visiting North America and Europe.

It was at Nicolò Bocassino primary school where she met the teacher who made her fall in love with books, writing, and studies in general, encouraging her creativity and eventually starting her on the path toward being a writer.

Made in the USA
Middletown, DE
08 June 2021